RAVISHED

Bloody hell. Thea wasn't like any other Englishwoman he'd ever met. He stalked toward her bed and leaned over her with one thought on his mind, to put a stop to her nonsensical notion.

Her lips parted, but she didn't argue as he had expected.

Instead, her brilliant blue gaze became fixed on his lips. Her eyes glazed over with desire, and all thought of the argument fled his mind. He wanted her lips and he took them, the desire that had been building in him since he first met her exploding in a sudden conflagration of need.

More praise for Lucy Monroe . . .

"Monroe pens a sizzling romance with a well-developed plot."
                                                    —*Romantic Times*

"A fresh new voice in romance . . . Lucy Monroe captures the very heart of the genre."   —Debbie Macomber

"If you enjoy Linda Howard, Diana Palmer, and Elizabeth Lowell, then I think you'd really love Lucy's work."
                                                    —Lori Foster

Touch Me

LUCY MONROE

BERKLEY SENSATION, NEW YORK

THE BERKLEY PUBLISHING GROUP
Published by the Penguin Group
Penguin Group (USA) Inc.
375 Hudson Street, New York, New York 10014, USA
Penguin Group (Canada), 90 Eglinton Avenue East, Suite 700, Toronto, Ontario M4P 2Y3, Canada
(a division of Pearson Penguin Canada Inc.)
Penguin Books Ltd., 80 Strand, London WC2R 0RL, England
Penguin Group Ireland, 25 St. Stephen's Green, Dublin 2, Ireland (a division of Penguin Books Ltd.)
Penguin Group (Australia), 250 Camberwell Road, Camberwell, Victoria 3124, Australia
(a division of Pearson Australia Group Pty. Ltd.)
Penguin Books India Pvt. Ltd., 11 Community Centre, Panchsheel Park, New Delhi—110 017, India
Penguin Group (NZ), Cnr. Airborne and Rosedale Roads, Albany, Auckland 1310, New Zealand
(a division of Pearson New Zealand Ltd.)
Penguin Books (South Africa) (Pty.) Ltd., 24 Sturdee Avenue, Rosebank, Johannesburg 2196,
South Africa

Penguin Books Ltd., Registered Offices: 80 Strand, London WC2R 0RL, England

This is a work of fiction. Names, characters, places, and incidents either are the product of the author's imagination or are used fictitiously, and any resemblance to actual persons, living or dead, business establishments, events, or locales is entirely coincidental.

TOUCH ME

A Berkley Sensation Book / published by arrangement with the author

PRINTING HISTORY
Berkley Sensation edition / September 2005

Copyright © 2005 by Lucy Monroe.
Excerpt from *Tempt Me* copyright © 2005 by Lucy Monroe.
Cover art by Franco Accornero.
Cover design by George Long.
Interior text design by Kristin del Rosario.

ISBN: 0-425-20531-2

BERKLEY® SENSATION
Berkley Sensation Books are published by The Berkley Publishing Group,
a division of Penguin Group (USA) Inc.,
375 Hudson Street, New York, New York 10014.
BERKLEY SENSATION and the "B" design are trademarks belonging to Penguin Group (USA) Inc.

PRINTED IN THE UNITED STATES OF AMERICA

10 9 8 7 6 5 4 3 2

For my sister, KT.
Your support and encouragement means more to me
than I could ever say.
You are an incredible, special woman,
and I love you.

And with special thanks to Michael Mooney,
for his help in researching sailing vessels.

You both have my deepest gratitude.

Prologue

THE BABY CRIED.

Her son. The beauty of the squirming infant hurt in a way she wanted never to end. She had given birth to life. Wonderful, innocent life.

She pushed herself up in the huge four-poster bed, ignoring the admonishments of both her maid and the midwife to rest. Pain stabbed through her lower body. She could not give in to it. She had to see her son. Each moment with him was a gift. Fear sent tension through her, intensifying the pain in her body. Langley would be here soon to tear the babe from her arms.

No.

Surely not.

Even her coldhearted husband could not take away the child they had created together.

The heavy door of the master chamber slammed against the wall. Her gaze flew to the sight of the towering masculine frame outlined in its opening. He had come. His face wore the same chill expression it had every moment since he had accused her of infidelity. He met her eyes, and in that brief glance she knew nothing had changed. He hated her. He would take her son.

Even as he turned to the midwife, Anna cried, *"No. Please. No."*

"Give me the babe."

"It is a son. *Our* son." Desperation clawed at her. "Do not do this." She reached out her hands, begging for something he did not have. Mercy. "Do not take him from me. I am his mother." She did not bother to protest her innocence again. Months of pleading for understanding, for trust, had proven futile.

He would not believe her.

"Geoffrey, please."

He turned to her, his eyes filled with mocking contempt, and an aching sob wracked her body.

"I must congratulate you, madam, on having the good sense to give me a son. I need an heir, but I do not know if even that necessity could have forced me back to your bed."

His words lanced through her, cutting the final vestige of hope in her heart. But even that pain became overshadowed as her belly tightened with another contraction. She gasped, then bit her lip. She had shown enough weakness to this man she had loved. She would show him no more.

But the pain. It was intense. Did not the pains stop when the birth was over? She longed to ask the midwife, but Geoffrey had not yet left. She would remain strong.

Finally, he turned, her son bundled in his arms, and left the room. Tears burned a path down her cheeks. She bit her lip on another contraction and tasted blood. She watched the door through which her husband had taken her son until the pain in her lower body became unbearable.

Turning to the midwife, she forced words out of her throat, tight from holding in a scream. "Help me."

Melly, her maid, rushed to her side. "What is it, milady?"

"The pains. They have returned." Anna met the eyes of the midwife. "I thought the pain was supposed to stop . . ." The words trailed off into a scream as the contractions grew stronger.

The luxurious surroundings of her bedchamber receded as terror overshadowed Anna's mind. *Why had the pain not stopped? What was happening to her?* She fell back against the bed, panting.

The midwife touched her stomach and Anna screamed again.

"Hush, milady. Do not carry on so. You gave birth to your son without all this screaming. Will you do less for this babe?"

As the words penetrated her haze of pain, Anna's eyes flew open. "This one? There is another babe?"

Twins. As another contraction tightened Anna's body almost beyond bearing, she felt a hysterical desire to laugh. Two babies. Geoffrey Selwyn, Earl of Langley, had planted two babes in her womb. Would he take this one, too?

She felt an overwhelming need to push and bore down desperately. Vowing that Langley would have to tear this baby from her lifeless hands, she gave birth to her second child.

Melly cried, "It's a girl!"

Anna put her arms out. "Give her to me."

The midwife wrapped soft white linens around the crying baby. "She's a healthy one, she is." She handed the squalling infant to Anna.

She looked up from the beautiful face of her daughter at the emotion she heard in the midwife's voice. "Will you help me?"

The midwife's wizened face shuttered. "What do you mean?"

"If we don't do something"—her voice broke and she took a deep breath to control it—"my husband will take this baby from me as well. I have already lost a son. I cannot bear to lose my daughter."

She waited, knowing that if she had miscalculated, Langley's contempt for her would only be made worse when the midwife told him her tale.

The older woman stared at Anna for what felt like an eternity. Her heart beat faster and she tightened the grip she had on her daughter. The baby cried. She immediately loosened her hold and leaned down to whisper soft assurances to her baby. The crying stopped. Anna smiled.

"I'll help you, milady. A man, even a nobleman, doesn't have the right to tear an infant from his mother's arms."

Joy burst through Anna like flowers blooming in the spring. She met Melly's eyes. "You will help me?"

Melly wiped at the moisture on her cheeks. "Yes, milady."

Anna smiled for the second time in the five months since Langley had discovered that blackguard Estcot trying to force himself on her. She gazed into the eyes of her daughter. "I will call you Althea Johanna because you are God's gift to me in my innocence."

One

What would I have done had God not seen fit to grant me the gift of Thea? Her sweet innocence keeps my heart beating when it would have shattered from Langley's harsh treatment. I pray that Thea never gives her heart to a hard man like her father. How my love for him mocks me now. My own weakness torments me. I will teach her to be both wiser and stronger than her mother.

November 10, 1797
Journal of Anna Selwyn, Countess of Langley

British West Indies
Twenty-three years later

THE SKIRTS OF THEA'S HIGH-WAISTED GOWN swished around her ankles, allowing welcome air to cool her legs as she strode through the warehouse. The tall ceilings and dark interior of the building did little to mute the oppressive Caribbean heat. Beads of sweat trickled between her shoulder blades. She itched to press the

muslin of her gown against the moisture, but years of train-
ing by her proper English mother prevented her.

Mama, if you were here, you'd be tempted as well.

But Anna Selwyn was not there, nor would she ever be.
Thea's heart constricted. Ten years and she still mourned
the loss of the strong, determined woman who had given
her birth.

"Afternoon, Miss Thea."

She stopped at the sound of Whiskey Jim's voice. She
smiled into the old man's weather-wizened face. "Good afternoon, Captain."

His one good eye twinkled merrily at her while the
patch that covered his other eye shifted as his face creased
into a grin. "See you're moving with the main sail at full
mast like always."

She waved the air in front of her face. "Perhaps I should
let down some sail and move more slowly. It's so hot today."

"That it is. That it is." He pulled a large bandanna from
his pocket and wiped his forehead. "This old man should
know better than to try to load his ship on a day like today."

Thea smiled. Old man indeed. He looked about a hundred, but he was still one of the fastest captains employed
by Merewether Shipping. "When are you sailing?"

"She looks to be loaded by the day after tomorrow."

Satisfaction spread through her. The timing could not
be better. She needed to take action before Uncle Ashby
became aware of the pilfering going on in the London office. He would insist on making the trip to England to investigate, and his health would suffer for it.

She owed him more than she could ever repay. When
her mother had died of the fever that killed so many Europeans in the West Indies, the Merewethers had insisted on
caring for Thea, treating her like their own daughter.

"When do you expect to arrive in Liverpool?"

"Don't."

Thea stopped fanning herself. "What do you mean?"

"I'm up to Charleston and then on to New York this trip."

"But I thought you were going to England."

He scratched the side of his head. "Nope."

They weren't expecting another ship for weeks. *"Sacré bleu."*

The old man's eye twinkled. "What did you say?"

Although the seamen and even Uncle Ashby could turn the air blue with their curses, she would have a peal rung over her for letting the French phrase slip from her lips. "Nothing."

There was no hope for it. She would have to sail on someone else's ship.

The captain bid farewell and ambled toward the far end of the warehouse where his crew moved without regard to the heat, loading the heavy barrels of sugar and rum onto wagons for transport to his ship.

She turned and walked toward Uncle Ashby's office, the problem of finding berth on a ship to England weighing heavily on her mind.

A droplet of perspiration trickled down her neck, and the relative privacy afforded by the opening between two stacks of wooden crates became too strong a temptation to resist.

Slipping between them, she cast a furtive glance around her. No one was in sight. Reaching behind her back, she awkwardly patted the fabric against her damp skin. *Oh, heavenly.* She lifted the skirts of her gown just a few inches and flapped the edge to force more air against her legs. She closed her eyes in bliss. Wouldn't it be lovely to go swimming right now? She could almost feel the refreshing water against her skin.

"Mademoiselle Thea. *Mademoiselle Thea.*"

Her eyes flew open. The sight of Philippe, the warehouse

manager, staring at her as if she'd been caught dancing
naked on top of the crates rather than fanning herself behind
one of them, momentarily froze her wits. The dark contours
of his face were set in lines of rigid disapproval. Well, drat.
If she had to get caught, couldn't it have been by someone
like Whiskey Jim, not her self-proclaimed duenna?

Thea straightened, tossing her skirts back to decorously
cover her ankles. "Philippe. I didn't see you."

"That would have been difficult, yes? With your eyes
closed and while cavorting in such a fashion?"

How could a mountain-size black man sound so prissy?
"I was not cavorting. I was fanning. There's a difference."

Philippe frowned. "Not for a lady."

Everyone took for granted that she wanted to be a lady.
Thea was not convinced. It certainly hadn't done her
mother any good, and the title carried more restrictions
than benefits as far as Thea could see.

She much preferred the persona of plain Miss Althea
Selwyn, raised in the West Indies with a freedom no London debutante would ever know. Oh, she *knew* the important strictures of life as a lady—Aunt Ruth and her mother
had seen to that. But she was rarely forced to adhere to
them.

Which did not mean she wasn't taken to task for her
behavior.

She was. Frequently. And she found it most annoying
indeed.

How could she behave as if she'd been raised to grace a
drawing room when in fact she'd spent her entire life around
sailors, plantation workers, and freed slaves? Despite Mama
and Aunt Ruth's efforts, she'd spent more time learning the
shipping business and how to keep an accurate ledger than
she had how to be a lady. And she certainly hadn't learned
life's basic skills from a tutor or a proper English nanny.

Philippe had taught her French. Whiskey Jim had taught

her to tie knots, and she'd learned to swim the same way as all the other children on the island, naked in the lagoon. Her mother had nearly swooned when she'd found out, but the truth was, Thea was better suited to life in the islands than she ever would have been to life in England.

Deciding that ignoring Phillippe's outrage was the best way of dealing with it, she asked, "Was there something you needed?"

"Mr. Drake is looking for Mr. Merewether."

Philippe stepped aside, revealing another man standing behind him. A man every bit as tall as the warehouse manager, but there the similarity ended. *Drake, like the famous privateer.* The name fit. This man could very easily be a pirate. He did not look like a man who balked at danger.

Although he matched Philippe for height, he was built quite differently. Thea's gaze snagged on the muscles that pressed against the gentleman's long pants. Uncle Ashby and the other men of Thea's acquaintance still wore the breeches popular in the last decade. She had never actually seen a gentleman wearing long pants. They should have hidden his well-developed legs, but they didn't. His obviously well-made clothes were worn in the understated fashion of the English.

She forced her gaze higher, only to be sidetracked again by the fact that the gentleman's upper torso was every bit as muscled as his legs. When her eyes finally reached his face, she sucked in her breath. He had noticed her perusal. *How could he not?* His mouth tipped in sardonic humor, and brown eyes, the color of dark molasses, mocked her.

Realizing that her mouth had dropped open, Thea shut it with a snap. Her cheeks felt hotter than the tropical sun. "May I help you?"

"I'm looking for Mr. Merewether." His voice held all the authority that his posture implied.

"He's not here." Wonderful. Not only had she gawked like a desperate spinster, but now she sounded like a bacon-brained idiot. Obviously Uncle Ashby wasn't with her. "I mean to say, I don't know where he is. Perhaps I can help you."

There, that sounded better, much more appropriate.

"My business is with Mr. Merewether."

Thea stifled a retort. Many gentlemen had aversions to doing business with a lady. Evidently Drake was one of them. "Then I will not keep you."

"I am sorry to disturb you, Mademoiselle Thea. We will search for Mr. Merewether elsewhere." Philippe nodded his head in formal dismissal and turned to leave.

The Englishman did not follow. "First, we will escort the young lady to her destination."

Thea stiffened at his peremptory tone. "That will not be necessary."

He reached out to take her arm, his dark hair and even darker expression making him appear almost menacing, despite his excessive masculine appeal. "I insist."

She stepped back toward the high stack of barrels to elude his grasp. "Thank you, but I will be fine."

His expression hardened. "Nevertheless, *I* would feel better if I saw you safely to your destination." His brown eyes narrowed in obvious censure. "A warehouse is no place for a lady." His tone of voice implied she might be anything but.

She wanted to give him a proper set-down, but business must always come first. Uncle Ashby would not thank her for offending Drake. She pressed her lips together and imagined loading an entire wagon with storage barrels in her mind before she felt calm enough to speak.

By the time she imagined the wagon leaving for the dock, she was able to summon a formal smile. "I am quite at home in this warehouse, but as we are looking for the same person, perhaps it would not hurt to find him together. I was on my way to Mr. Merewether's office."

She stepped forward, but apparently not quickly enough because the Englishman's hands shot out and grabbed her waist.

She gasped. "Really there is no need—"

He yanked her against his chest, backing up as he did so. She had barely registered the strange phenomenon of being held by a man when she heard an unholy crash behind her. She started, her hands going around the neck of her captor involuntarily.

Drake continued to move with agile grace, carrying her several feet from the crash. She craned her neck, turning her head to see what had happened. Her hands convulsed on Drake's neck and she shuddered against him at what she saw. Several small storage barrels rolled across the floor and a large storage crate had broken into splinters on the spot where she had stood. The broken contents looked like porcelain, although it was difficult to tell from the hundreds of tiny shards mixed with packing hay.

She turned back to face the snowy cravat of her rescuer. Taking a deep, shuddery breath, she inhaled his uniquely masculine fragrance. Shattered cargo, her near miss, even Philippe's presence receded in her consciousness as she became wholly occupied with the sensation of her breasts flattened against his waistcoat and her lower body pressed against the hardness of his thighs. She could not seem to lift her gaze from the patch of white cloth in front of her.

Her feet dangled several inches above the floor while feelings she had never before experienced coursed through her body. She felt safe in this man's arms despite the stirrings that she did not wish to examine too closely. He had saved her from certain injury and possible death. Why, he was a knight-errant.

She raised her face, giving him a no-doubt-stunned smile. "Thank you."

His expression registered no emotion. "As I said, women do not belong in a warehouse."

It took all of two seconds for his words to register. *The snake.* Actually, he had said "a lady," and it occurred to her that she should let go of him before he decided beyond doubt that she wasn't one. She unlocked her hands from behind his neck and pushed against his chest.

He lowered her to the ground, allowing her body to slide in a most indecent manner along his. He held her for a timeless moment, her body still pressed to his, her hands against his chest. She waited, the air locked in her chest, not knowing what to expect. This man, this situation, was completely out of her experience. Were all Englishmen this compelling?

He released her and she stumbled backward, beset with conflicting emotions. She wanted to run from the danger she sensed in him, but she also wanted to jump back into his arms and experience that delicious sensation just once more. Before she could do either, Philippe caught her attention.

"Mademoiselle Thea, *comment ça va?* That this should happen in my warehouse. It is an abomination!" Philippe grabbed her hand, going off in a torrent of French.

He turned to the Englishman without letting go of her hand. "Mr. Drake, we owe you a great debt for saving our Mademoiselle Thea. Mr. Merewether will be most grateful."

"Good." Drake's glance flicked briefly to Philippe. "Perhaps he will be inclined to grant me what I need."

Thea stared at Drake's profile and wondered at his words. He exuded an aura of self-sufficiency. That he should need something from the owner of a shipping firm on a small island like theirs seemed incongruous.

DRAKE FOLLOWED THE GENTLE SWAY OF THEA'S HIPS AS she led the way into Merewether's office. His body twitched at the sight. He frowned. Who was she? In his experience, ladies did not frequent warehouses. In fact, most would have heart palpitations at the thought of coming within a hundred feet of the rough men who worked in them. Could she be Merewether's lightskirt?

Drake's mind and body rebelled at the idea. What was the matter with him? It shouldn't make any difference to him if she sold her tantalizing body on the docks to sailors when they came to port—but it did. Her dress, a vibrant blue muslin, was too well made for a dock whore. It clung to her back in a small damp patch, and he felt an urge to reach out and run his finger along the soft fabric.

He could still feel the aftereffects of the jolt he had experienced when he first saw her. The heart-shaped face, framed by chestnut curls piled high on her head, had been set in an expression of perfect bliss. Her dress had been lifted well above her ankles, and he could not miss the fact that the chit wore no stockings. Or that she had perfectly formed ankles and calves. The kind of legs a man ached to have wrapped around his body.

Suddenly, the object of his musings turned to face him, her blue eyes reflecting apologetic regret. "It appears Mr. Merewether is not here. Why don't you sit down and I will have refreshments brought while we wait?"

He shifted his gaze around the office, looking for a place to sit. A large mahogany desk occupied one side of the room, papers strewn across its top. Kitty-corner to it reposed a table whose surface was all but covered with numerous maps and charts. Crates and barrels, partially opened, were shoved up against two walls. Yet, under the window, on the opposite side of the room from the desk, a small sofa and two armchairs were arranged in a cozy grouping around a polished tea table. His gaze flicked back to Thea. Was she responsible for the little oasis in the chaos?

It beckoned to him, but he needed to see Merewether. He could not afford the time to take refreshments. "Thank you, but I must decline. I need to speak to Merewether immediately."

She raised her brows. "I assure you if either myself or Philippe knew where he was right now, we would take you to him. The truth is, he could be just about anywhere on the island, and the best course of action would be to stay right here and wait."

Drake's hands tightened into fists at his sides. "I cannot wait. The matter I must discuss with him is of the utmost urgency."

His honor depended on it.

Her eyes widened at his adamant tone, then she nodded briskly. Turning to the warehouse manager, she spoke rapidly. "Philippe, please send someone to the house and inquire if Mr. Merewether has been there. I believe we should also send someone to inquire at the dock, in town, and if that does not flush him out, we will send runners to the local plantations."

Philippe agreed and left.

She turned back to Drake. "I will ask Whiskey Jim if he has seen Mr. Merewether. Kindly wait here; we will locate him for you as quickly as possible." She did not wait for his agreement, but turned to leave.

What a managing bit of goods. Ignoring her instructions, he followed her out of the office. He had no intention of cooling his heels waiting for her to return with Merewether.

Rarely did Drake, with his long legs, have to increase his pace to keep up with another, but Thea walked like no lady he knew. She strode ahead of him, her spine straight and her arms swinging in rhythm with her strides, putting him in mind of a military officer on parade.

He questioned his theory that she was Merewether's paramour. She could be the man's daughter. She had not called him Papa, but some children were excessively formal. However, excessive formality did not meet with a woman who exposed her legs for all and sundry. Drake shook off the musings and focused instead on his problem.

This trip had been rife with challenges, the most recent being an exploding boiler.

If he didn't reach Liverpool by the date set on his policy with Lloyd's of London, not only would he forfeit the policy premium, but he would also let down the investors whom he had convinced to share in the venture with him. He accepted that it was no longer a matter of money. He had made plenty of that. Enough to buy and sell his father many times over.

Reaching port on time had become a matter of pride.

Thea led him down aisles created by walls of crates and barrels on either side. The sound of several men's voices came from the other side of the nearest wall of barrels. Drake increased his pace until he was next to Thea.

She turned startled eyes on him. "I thought you stayed in the office."

"I'm not so easily led."

Her blue eyes narrowed. "I was not attempting to lead, sir. It was the most expedient course of action. If Mr. Merewether returns to his office, no one will be there to tell him that you need to speak to him. He might very well leave again."

She had a point. "Nevertheless, I am here. I believe I have made myself clear regarding my view of a woman alone in a warehouse."

She straightened her spine and tilted her head, giving him a look that would have done royalty proud. "I am a lady accustomed to being alone in a warehouse, and I can assure you nothing is likely to befall me in this one."

"Do you call nearly being killed by a stack of barrels toppling *nothing*?"

She hesitated and bit her lip, an expression coming into her clear blue eyes that was not easy to decipher. "That was unfortunate; however, it is unlikely to happen again. Philippe is most particular about his warehouse."

"I was under the impression the warehouse belongs to Merewether."

"It belongs to Merewether Shipping."

"As I said."

She shook her head. "Not quite. Regardless, Philippe is very possessive. He has worked for Merewether Shipping for over a decade, and he prides himself on the smooth operation of the warehouse."

Drake wondered if Philippe was a slave. Most black men in the West Indies were. Although the slave trade had been abolished for over a decade, the institution of slavery still existed. Drake supported those who lobbied in the House of Lords to abolish it.

"Slaves aren't generally given such positions of power," he said casually.

She looked at him, her blue gaze intense. "No, they are not. Merewether Shipping does not employ slaves. We employ people, free people. Men and women who can choose whether or not they wish to work for us. Most do. The pay is good and Merewether Shipping is loyal to its employees."

She had a fair bit of possessiveness herself. Most light-skirts did not speak of their protector's business as their own. She must be very sure of Merewether, or perhaps she really was his daughter. "Shall we find Mr. Merewether?"

She nodded and broke eye contact. They walked around the wall of goods and came upon a hive of activity. Sailors loaded wagons, keeping up a steady stream of curses that would make most gentlemen of Drake's acquaintance wince. Thea appeared completely unperturbed.

She headed toward the most disreputable looking of the lot, an old man with a patch over one eye and a bottle of whiskey in his left hand. "That's Whiskey Jim. He's the ship's captain."

The captain noticed their approach and let out a piercing whistle. Silence reigned, but the sailors didn't stop their work. They did greet Thea with smiles and waves, and some even pulled on their forelocks while nodding their heads. Thea returned each greeting with a smile and a nod.

"I see you haven't let down any sail, Miss Thea."

Thea smiled and shook her head. "No time. Have you seen Mr. Merewether, Captain?"

"Aye. He went to the house. Promised Miz Ruth he'd have tea with her today, he said."

"Thank you. Mr. Drake needs to talk to him about a matter of some import."

Thea turned to Drake. "Mr. Drake, may I introduce you to the most impressive captain to sail the Atlantic, Whiskey Jim?"

Drake put out his hand toward the old sailor. Thea beamed at him with unmistakable approval. "Captain, this is Mr. Drake."

"Pleasure. Captain."

"Call me Whiskey Jim. It's a fairly earned name and I'm proud to bear it."

Drake looked pointedly at the bottle in the man's hand. "So I see."

The old man laughed. "It's a better man than one that's sailed on my ships that can stand against a taste of *my* bottle."

"The captain has a reputation for smashing bottles of whiskey over the heads of unruly sailors," Thea explained.

"That wouldn't bother the lads so much, but I deduct it from their daily ration of spirits."

"I can see the captains of my ships could learn a thing or two from you."

Whiskey Jim winked at him. "That they could, my boy. That they could."

THEA POURED DRAKE TEA WHILE WAITING FOR UNCLE Ashby to return to the office. Drake's nearness unnerved her, and the hand holding the teacup shook slightly. When they had entered the office, Thea sat down on the settee expecting Drake to take one of the available chairs. He had surprised her by folding his large body onto the sofa beside her.

Worse, he sat in complete silence, watching her movements with impassive brown eyes as someone might watch a butterfly caught in a jar. Well, she was no green girl to be intimidated by a silent stranger.

She handed him his tea. "Do you have a ship in the harbor, Mr. Drake?"

He took the china cup and saucer, making the action appear elegant yet wholly masculine. "Yes. The *Golden Dragon*."

Thea shifted so that her legs were not so near Drake's. "I see. You need something for your ship from Mr. Merewether?"

She wondered if Drake would rebuff her interest as he had earlier.

"Yes."

Stifling an irritated sigh, Thea tried again. "Mr. Drake, perhaps if you told me what it is you need, I could procure it for you. You did say the matter was of the utmost urgency."

If it were indeed urgent, he would overcome his obvious reluctance to do business with a woman.

Drake leveled a look at her that made her insides melt in the most peculiar way. "Miss Merewether, urgent as my business is, it will wait until your father arrives to handle the matter."

Her father? "You are mistaken. Mr. Merewether is my associate, not my parent."

Drake's dark angel countenance became coolly dismissive. "Nevertheless, I prefer to deal with your *associate*."

The cold rejection did nothing for her rapidly deteriorating mood. His behavior had bordered on the offensive since the moment of their meeting, and though she recognized that her own actions had earned her a share of the blame, she had no desire to remain in his company.

She had her own matters of import to look into. Not least of which was the possibility that the *accident* in the warehouse had been anything but.

Thea carefully set her tea down. "As you have no interest in discussing your business with me, I'm sure you will understand if I leave you to wait for my partner while I attend to other matters."

She was being rude and perhaps even a trifle unprofessional. Both Aunt Ruth and Uncle Ashby would scold her if they knew, but Thea was past caring. Like her mother before her, Thea had as much to do with the success of Merewether Shipping as Uncle Ashby, perhaps more. That this man refused to even discuss his needs with her infuriated Thea.

She wasn't sure why. She had learned long ago to dismiss the ignorance of men. Too many could not believe a woman was capable of applying her mind to more than household management and filling the nursery, particularly men from her home country, England.

For some unknown reason, Drake's dismissal was different.

Thea could not make herself ignore his refusal to discuss business with her, nor could she stand to sit next to his intensely masculine body for one more second.

She stood. "Good day, sir."

Drake met her eyes, and his brown gaze held her in place despite her intention to leave. "Your *partner* may be used to allowing his paramour to conduct his business, but I deal only with principles."

He could not mean what she thought he meant. It was impossible. She had known arrogant men to jump to conclusions about her intelligence, but never her morals.

"Did you just call me Uncle Ashby's *paramour*?" In her

anger, she slipped into the more familiar address. It was not professional to call one's business partner *uncle*.

Drake's expression registered confusion. "He is your uncle?"

Thea did not relax her furious stance one bit. "He is my *business partner*."

Drake stood and took a firm grip on her upper arms all in one fluid motion. His glare singed her. "Is he your *uncle*?"

What difference could it possibly make to this man? She tipped her head back to return his frown and refused to answer. She would not be intimidated by his height or his anger, or influenced by his mesmerizing looks and manner.

"Ah, you must be Mr. Drake. Why are you holding Thea like that? Does she have something in her eye?"

She turned her head toward the door at the sound of her uncle's concerned voice. "No, Uncle Ashby. I was just explaining to Mr. Drake that you are not my *protector*. I believe he may be applying for the job."

Two

Lady Upworth arranged for me to see Jared. Although she is Langley's aunt, she remains kind to me. She is furious with her nephew for taking my son. Jared is so beautiful. The visit was too short, much too short. Letting him go ripped open the wound that will never heal in my heart. It is a pain I will gladly bear in order to see my precious baby, to kiss his soft cheeks and tell him I love him. Thank God for Thea's sweet presence to dull the pain of all I have lost.

April 16, 1798
Journal of Anna Selwyn, Countess of Langley

THREE THINGS MADE THEMSELVES KNOWN to Drake at once. The first was that Ashby Merewether had a keen resemblance to a fish when surprised. The second, Thea's beauty only intensified when anger sparked in her eyes. The third was a feeling of intense relief that she was no man's lightskirt.

Her outrage was still palpable, but he could see that it was now tempered with mortification. He watched in fascination

as she closed her eyes briefly, much as she had in the warehouse earlier. She muttered something. He thought it could
have been *ten barrels,* but that made no sense.

She opened her eyes again, her blue gaze filled with
mute appeal. "Please release me."

He did so, but with reluctance. Her warm skin felt silky
to the touch, and he had to force his fingers to uncurl from
around her arms. He turned to Merewether, who had managed to close his mouth, but still had the look of a startled
trout.

Drake bowed and said his name.

Merewether automatically began to return the courtesy
when he abruptly pulled himself upright. His face took on
a fierce expression that only served to illustrate how rarely
the man must frown. He did not do it at all well.

Drake smiled.

"Don't smile at me, young man. Have you been making
improper advances toward Miss Selwyn? I warn you, she is
a gentle lady and I will not allow her feelings or person to
be trifled with."

Thea rushed forward and took the older gentleman's
arm. "Do not fret yourself, Uncle Ashby. You know the
doctor has said that you must avoid undue excitement."
She turned her head and glowered at Drake as if he had
been the one to make the incendiary comment. "Mr. Drake
did not make any untoward advances. I assure you."

"Yes, but my dear, you said—"

She cut him off. "It was a simple misunderstanding.
Isn't that right, Mr. Drake?"

Her voice and posture dared him to disagree with her.

Drake didn't. "Absolutely. I assure you that when a man
hits a certain number of years like I have, he no longer
considers illicit liaisons when first meeting a lovely young
woman like Miss Selwyn. He must begin thinking of setting up his nursery—or so my mother continues to insist."

Thea's eyes widened, but she said nothing. Probably shocked speechless, Drake decided smugly.

Merewether shook his head as if in lament. "No use you looking to our Thea in that regard. She's firmly against marriage, and if my dear wife Ruth cannot change her mind, no mere gentleman has a chance of doing so."

Drake disagreed. He would think that a man would have much more success in convincing Thea regarding the merits of wedded bliss than a woman, no matter how formidable the creature. Some things could not be believed until they were experienced. Something else his mother insisted on, particularly when it came to love.

"Uncle Ashby, Mr. Drake is only teasing. He did not come here looking for a wife."

Merewether sighed. "Pity."

Thea stepped away from him, puffing out an obviously irritated breath. "He is here on business and he prefers to work with principles."

The mockery with which she said the final words was lost on Merewether, but not so on Drake.

The startled trout became a confused trout. "But, Thea, you are a principle. Didn't you explain to Mr. Drake that we are partners in Merewether Shipping?"

Thea's bland expression belied the mockery Drake saw in her eyes. "I did try."

Drake frowned. "I did not understand the nature of the partnership. I cannot say that even now I do. It is most unusual for a lady to be an acting principle in business."

Merewether chuckled. "Yes, well, Miss Selwyn is a most unusual woman—just like her mother before her."

"Nevertheless, Mr. Drake has made it quite clear he prefers not to discuss business with a mere female, so I will go about my other dealings." She turned and left.

Drake almost called out to the saucy baggage and demanded that she stay, but he controlled the inexplicable urge. He had allowed himself to be sidetracked from his objective for long enough. He turned to Merewether, only to find the other man looking at him with appraisal.

"Find her fascinatin', I'll be bound. Most gentlemen do. She's oblivious, of course. Thinks love is for weak-minded women, and marriage is an institution just this side of prison. Shame, that." The older man shook his head.

"I'm sure you are right. However, as Miss Selwyn told you, I am here for business purposes." Providence alone knew why he had made the comment about marriage.

Drake certainly didn't—unless it was for the satisfaction of watching Thea's reaction.

Merewether bobbed his head up and down. "Yes. Yes. What can we do for you?"

"I need the use of a skilled blacksmith."

Merewether stood silent as if he expected Drake to say more. When he didn't, the older man cleared his throat. "Well. Yes. Well. That is certainly possible. We don't actually have a blacksmith working for us, but I can find you one. Yes, indeed. I'll arrange for him to help you first thing in the morning."

Merewether beamed at Drake as if he had come up with an altogether pleasing solution, not a death knell on Drake's schedule and a blight to his honor.

Drake's insides tightened. "That is not acceptable. I need his services now."

"Yes. Well. You see, he is busy right now on a project for Thea, er . . . Miss Selwyn. Perhaps if you had asked her . . ." Merewether let his voice trail off.

Drake took in the now cold tea Thea had served him, the muddled chaos surrounding him, Merewether's expectant features, and the words the other man had just spoken.

Bloody hell. "She has engaged the services of the black-smith privately?"

"Not privately, m'boy. For the company. She's got him

building something to improve safety or efficiency. She's a proponent of both, I don't mind telling you."

Ah, so that was it. Drake felt on firmer ground since he had first laid eyes on the indomitable Thea. "I will compensate both Merewether Shipping and the blacksmith for the time spent away from his project here."

"As to that, no such thing—but I don't know if Thea will easily let the man go."

"Surely you are not going to tell me that Miss Selwyn's project cannot wait."

"Not for me to say, m'boy. Not for me to say."

Drake felt the small store of patience he had entered the office with slip away completely. "Couldn't you *ask* her?"

"Well. Yes. She's not here now, of course. Off supervising her project, I'm bound." Merewether's expression left no doubt in Drake's mind as to whom the older man blamed for her departure.

"Where might that be?"

"Why, in the blacksmith's shop, of course."

Drake felt a certain affinity for teeth pullers. "And where is the blacksmith's shop?"

"In town. I'll have someone show you if you like."

"The sooner the better."

Merewether disappeared through the door of the office, his head still bobbing in agreement.

He returned moments later with the warehouse manager. "Philippe has agreed to take you to Miss Selwyn. He'll find her for you if she's not with the blacksmith."

Drake said nothing, but if Thea was not with the blacksmith, he had every intention of convincing the man to take on his engine repair immediately, even if he had to pay him in bloody diamonds to do it.

PHILIPPE'S LARGE BULK MOVED WITH A FLUIDITY THAT surprised Drake as he followed the other man down the main street of the tiny village Merewether had referred to as town. White buildings with red tile roofs reminded Drake of a Mediterranean seaport. He impatiently scanned the structures for any sign of a blacksmith or stable but saw nothing.

As he was on the verge of asking the warehouse manager where exactly they were going, his thoughts were interrupted by Philippe's voice. "You are a fast-thinking and fast-acting man, Mr. Drake. This morning we would have lost our Mademoiselle Thea had you not been there. *Sacré bleu,* it was a good wind that blew you to our island."

"Did you find out the cause of the accident?" Perhaps Thea had a penchant for safety because others in the shipping company did not.

"That was a strange thing, *oui*?"

Drake made a noncommittal sound. He didn't know if it was strange or not.

"The cargo, it is all stacked the same way. Mademoiselle Thea insists on it to protect the warehouse employees. She is very conscientious."

"Then how did it fall?"

"This I do not know. It would have taken the arm of a very strong man, but that is impossible."

"There is no one on the island who would wish Miss Selwyn harm, is there?"

As irritating as Drake found her personally, he did not think her take-charge attitude enough motivation for someone to try to hurt her.

"No. No. Even the plantation owners would not do her injury."

Drake's interest was peaked. "What do you mean, *even* the plantation owners?"

Philippe smiled, his white teeth glistening against the dark tones of his skin. "Mademoiselle Thea, she speaks out against the slavery. It is not a popular position here on the island, *vous comprenez.*"

That would be an understatement. The surrounding plantations relied on slave labor to function. It was only a matter of time before they would lose their conscripted labor force, and there was considerable speculation regarding the feasibility of paying wages high enough to encourage the backbreaking labor required on a sugar plantation.

"She is not foolish enough to be vocal about her abolitionist beliefs in a climate such as this?"

Even as he spoke the question, Drake guessed at the answer.

"She does not know caution, that one. She does not consider it a political issue either, but a moral outrage, and she refuses to be silent about it," Philippe confided.

If that were true, Drake marveled that today was her first brush with danger. Perhaps it wasn't. When he voiced his thoughts to the other man, Philippe grew pensive.

"*Non. Non.* Today, it is the first time she has come so close to real harm. Mademoiselle Thea, she helps all the landowners with the shipping company. They do not like her beliefs, but they like the money she brings. Monsieur Merewether, he is a kind gentleman, but the business side of the shipping venture falls to Mademoiselle Thea, as it did to her mother before her. The plantation owners know this. *Non.* It was a very strange accident, but an accident all the same."

Drake stopped himself from arguing with the man. Thea's safety was not his concern.

Thea watched Jacob's bulging black arms operate the blacksmith's bellows. While her thoughts should be centered on her business plans, or even the new winch, they kept drifting back to her meeting with Drake. He had infuriated her, and yet she found him strangely fascinating.

Mortification at what she had said in her fit of temper still tormented her conscience. To have implied to Uncle Ashby, of all people, that Drake was trying to proposition her had been foolishness itself. Uncle Ashby's heart could not stand great shocks and she well knew it. Drake deserved a proper set-down, but as usual, her tongue had gotten away with her and she had said entirely too much. She sighed.

The man had his own purchase on mockery, should she take his remark about marriage into consideration. Undoubtedly he had said it only to discompose her. He could not be in earnest. Regardless, she would never consider such a move. Unmarried women had few enough rights. Married women had none. Olympe de Gouge had lost her life, accused of treason, for revealing the disparity between the rights of men and women in France.

Thea could not ignore the reality of the plight of her sex. If she ever married, it would not be to a hard man like Drake. Her mother had been careful to educate her regarding the pitfalls of marriage, particularly to a man of inflexible nature.

Somewhere in England, a man born the same day as Thea lived and breathed. Her brother. She had never met him, had never even seen him because of their father, a man who would tear a babe from its mother's arms to punish his wife for a wrong she did not commit—simply because he could.

"This be a mighty good winch, yes'm."

Jacob's words brought Thea back from her woolgathering.

She leaned forward to examine the tackle attached to the pulley. The spool-shaped wheel looked sturdy enough to handle the heaviest storage barrels. "You've done a marvelous job, Jacob. I believe that is exactly what we need."

"Good. Then you will have no objection to him accompanying me to the *Golden Dragon* to make repairs to its steam engine."

Thea's body tensed at the sound of that voice.

Drake. What was he doing here?

She spun around to face him and her skirts brushed against the forge, picking up soot along the hem. Intense heat from the fire licked at her arms as she came too near in her surprise.

Drake swore and, taking a giant step forward, grasped her arms to pull her from proximity to the fire. "Trouble follows you like a friend, Miss Selwyn."

She wanted to respond with a curt comment, but found the intensity of his eyes hotter than the fires in the smithy. "I do not know what you mean, sir."

He let go of her arms, although he remained indecently close. "I wonder how you avoid harm when I am not here to pull you to safety."

She stepped away from him. "I manage quite nicely. Perhaps it is your presence that accounts for my mishaps today. What think you of that?"

He laughed. The rich sound and unexpected softening of the hard angles of Drake's face entranced her.

She smiled with him. "Perhaps I am too harsh. I am truly grateful for your quick action earlier."

He cocked his brow. "And now?"

Chagrined, she forced herself to answer. "And now. Thank you for pulling me away from the forge. I lost my bearings for a moment."

He nodded. "I am glad I was here."

She almost answered that had he not been, she would never have lost her bearings, but she had allowed her unruly tongue enough license for one day. "Why *are* you here?"

"As I said, I would like to hire the services of the blacksmith for work on my steam engine."

"Your ship is a steam vessel?" She didn't understand. He was English. The only steam vessels she knew of were American, and only one had been built for ocean going, the SS *Savannah*.

"Not entirely. It is a combination sailing and steam vessel."

Ah, like the SS *Savannah*. When he didn't elaborate, she crossed her arms and tapped her foot. "And?"

He smiled. The controlled amusement in the brown depths of his eyes surprised her.

A school of dolphins took up frolicking in her insides. This tall, dark man was entirely too appealing.

"And . . . my ship's engine boiler has burst. I need the services of your blacksmith. I am willing to pay both Merewether Shipping and him for the use of his time."

"There would be no reason to pay my company for the use of an independent man's time. I believe I mentioned that we do not practice slavery." She barely restrained herself from saying more on the subject. Drake was not here to listen to a lecture on the merits of abolition.

His eyes narrowed. "I merely intended to compensate your company for the loss of the man's time on your project while he takes care of my engine."

She shrugged. "The winch can wait. It is almost finished anyway."

"Good. Then we can proceed." He turned to Jacob. "Mr. . . ."

Jacob set the winch down and pulled off the heavy gloves that protected his hands from the heat of the fire in the forge. "I'm called Jacob."

Drake put out his hand. "Jacob it is then. I'm in desperate need of your services."

The action surprised and pleased her. It apparently surprised Jacob as well.

He stared for a moment at Drake's hand, as if not sure what to do with it. Finally he wiped his own hand on the leg of his breaches before shaking hands with the other man. "You want that I fix the boiler, sir?"

"Yes. As quickly as possible."

"Where is it then?"

Drake's look of confusion would have been funny, but Thea feared it would turn to anger when he discovered Jacob's little idiosyncrasy. "On the ship, of course."

"I'll no be going to any ship, sir."

"But the boiler is on the ship."

Jacob shrugged his massive shoulders. "Best to be bringing it here if you want that I fix it."

Drake turned to her, his face a study in frustration. "Could you explain what I am missing?"

"If you want Jacob to fix your boiler, you will have to disassemble it and bring it here."

"There is no time." His frustration was a palpable force.

She felt sorry for him, but there was nothing she could do. Jacob had an uncompromising fear of the ocean and there was no way Drake was going to get him onto the *Golden Dragon*. "Jacob will not go near the ocean."

"That's ridiculous. He lives on an island. How can he be afraid of water?"

The black man drew himself up, his brows drawn together in a severe frown. "I'm no afraid o' de water."

Drake smiled. "Good. Then we can proceed to my ship."

Jacob's frown did not lessen. "You be wantin' that I fix your boiler, sir. You be bringing it here."

"I told you, *there is no time*."

"You be bringing it here," Jacob insisted stubbornly.

Drake went still. "How much?"

Jacob shrugged. "Don't know till I see it, sir."

"I mean how much to get you to come to my ship?"

"I no be going to your ship."

Drake swore and spun on his heel to face Philippe, who had remained silent since arriving. "Are there any other blacksmiths on the island?"

"No, sir," Philippe replied.

The controlled anger she saw in Drake's expression made Thea shiver. "Bloody hell." He turned back to Jacob. "I'll have the boiler here as soon as can be arranged."

Jacob picked up the winch. "I be finishing this then."

Thea smiled at Jacob. "Thank you. I'll see Mr. Drake to the wharf. Philippe, please tell Mr. Merewether that I will be with Mr. Drake."

Drake turned to her. "I can find my own way to the ship and back, Miss Selwyn."

"I'm quite sure that you can, but it will be faster if I drive you. My carriage is waiting outside as I had intended to go far island on some business. You did say that time was of the essence?"

She watched the muscle in his jaw work.

"You're a bossy bit of goods, Miss Selwyn."

"You are welcome, Mr. Drake."

HOT CARIBBEAN AIR PRESSED AGAINST DRAKE AS HE and some crew members from the *Golden Dragon* loaded the boiler into the back of a wagon Thea had commandeered.

"It's much bigger than I expected." Thea walked around him and peered intently at the boiler. "No wonder you balked at bringing it to Jacob."

Drake grunted.

She laughed. "It wouldn't have made any difference to Jacob. He spent two days on a raft surrounded by hungry sharks during an attempt to escape his life as a slave. He won't go anywhere near the ocean, not even to return to his homeland."

Drake tied a final knot in the lashing against the boiler.

"How did he end up as your town blacksmith? I thought runaway slaves were punished, not freed."

"They are." The fierce expression in Thea's eyes softened. "My mother purchased his freedom. She offered to send him back to his family in Africa, but he wouldn't go. He worked for our company until he had made enough money to open his smithy. He's married to the sweetest woman and they have six children now. The oldest just got orders to sail on one of our ships."

Drake marveled at the genuine feeling he heard in her voice. She cared, really cared about this freedman and his family. The difference between her viewpoint and that of a typical London beauty seared him. Would she care about the circumstances of his birth, or would her acceptance stop short of that?

He had no intention of finding out. He would not be revealing any secrets, of his birth or otherwise, in the short time his ship was moored in the waters of her island's bay.

He moved toward the front of the wagon to take his seat in the driver's box, only to come up short when she did the same thing. He pulled back. "Miss Selwyn, perhaps you will allow me to drive?"

She put her hand over her eyes, squinting up at him. "Why? I can assure you that I am perfectly capable of driving."

He had no doubt that she was capable of doing just about anything she set her mind to, but it was his boiler and his responsibility. He would drive. "Thank you for the offer, but it isn't necessary."

She drew herself up. "That's silly. I know the roads better than you. After all, I live here. I will drive you and your boiler to Jacob."

He had wasted all the time he could afford to. She let out a surprised shriek when he picked her up and tossed her onto the passenger side of the bench.

Before she had time to right her clothes, much less herself, he jumped up next to her and grabbed the reins. "As there is only one road between here and the smithy, I do not think it will require your lifetime of living here to navigate it."

She sputtered something about insufferable, bossy men before situating herself on the bench. Her stiff posture left no question that she was annoyed and he almost smiled. When she finally did marry, she would lead her husband a merry chase.

"Why is it so important for you to fix your boiler now?" she asked in a tone that said her curiosity had gotten the better of her anger.

Knowing it would tweak her temper, he replied, "It's broken."

She drew in a long breath that put her gentle curves in prominence, and he found himself looking at her in a way no gentleman should ogle a lady.

"I realize that." She shifted as she was facing him on the seat, and he forced his own gaze forward before she noted its direction and became offended. "But why now? Why won't tomorrow or the next day do?"

His shoulders tensed, any humor he had found in baiting her disappearing.

Three

Langley has discovered that his aunt has been allowing me to see my son. Langley is furious. He told her that if it continues, she will never see Jared again. She told me that he has plans to take the babe back to Langley Hall. Ensconced in this crackerbox of a house on the outskirts of London that my husband has seen fit to banish me to, how can I see my son? I ache for him. What can he learn of love from a man whose heart is no more than stone?

June 5, 1798
Journal of Anna Selwyn, Countess of Langley

"I TOOK OUT A POLICY ON THE RETURN DATE of my ship with Lloyd's of London."

She smoothed her skirt, reminding him of the altogether pleasing legs beneath the thin muslin. Merewether had said she was oblivious, but could any woman be that ignorant of her feminine appeal?

"So if you don't return by a certain date, you'll lose your money?" she asked.

"Yes."

"It must be a very large policy."

He flicked the reins, encouraging the horses to pick up their pace. "Not that large, but . . ." He let his voice trail off. Did he want to explain the other? Would she, a woman, even understand?

"But what?"

Blue eyes blazing with intelligence and curiosity compelled him to speak.

"I convinced several friends to invest their money in the venture."

"I don't understand. If you return a day or two late with the cargo, it will still fetch the same price in the market, will it not?"

Her understanding of business still discomposed him. "My friends did not only invest in the cargo, but they invested in the journey. They have each taken out policies as well."

She sniffed. "It sounds like a wager to me."

He smiled at her disapproving tone. "There are plenty of those, too. Many people did not believe that we could meet with any more success than the SS *Savannah*."

"But the *Savannah*'s journey was a success."

"She used her sails for the voyage almost exclusively. We wanted to use the engine to increase the pace of the journey."

"Have you?"

"Yes."

The seam connecting the boiler to the pipe for the escape valve had blown when he had insisted the captain push on with the engine through an abnormally long becalm at sea. The weakened seam was explained when they discovered that some idiot seaman had used salt rather than fresh water to refill the boiler. It had taken precious time and fresh water to rectify that part of the mess. However, without the uses of a competent blacksmith, the engine would be dead weight for the rest of the voyage.

"Then you have succeeded even if you do not return by the specified date."

He turned toward her, wondering at the certainty in her voice. "You think so?"

Her eyes shone with certainty and he had to quickly tamp down the urge to cover her soft lips, parted in exclamation, with his own.

"Oh, *yes*. Just think, you've done what no one else has been able to do. The SS *Savannah* didn't pick up cargo. She just carried passengers. But you've done both. You'll be returning to England covered in glory."

He shook his head at her naïveté. More likely he'd be returning with his honor in shreds if the *Golden Dragon*'s captain could not make up for the time lost.

THEA LAID THE FOUNTAIN PEN DOWN ON THE LEDGER and sighed. Rolling her shoulders, she tried to ease some of the tension from her body. Her office on the second floor of the warehouse was quiet, almost too quiet, leaving her alone with her thoughts.

After leaving Drake and his boiler with Jacob, she had returned to the warehouse to check the latest set of ledgers that had arrived on Whiskey Jim's ship. She looked back at the neat columns of numbers and entries.

She had not been mistaken. The discrepancies were well hidden, but they *were* there. It had not been a onetime mistake as she had hoped. The pilfering was consistent and unmistakable.

If only she knew who was responsible. She cringed at the thought that Uncle Ashby's nephew in the London office had been stealing from the company.

She could not ignore the fact that he hadn't yet responded

to her letter inquiring into the discrepancies. Could the letter have been misdirected? Cold invaded her insides at the thought that the letter had made it into the hands of the culprit, that the near-fatal accident in the warehouse earlier was linked in some way.

Drake's was not the only ship in port. Even Whiskey Jim's could have brought an accomplice to the thief down to her island. Ship captains were forced to pick up new sailors in almost every port. It was a rough life, and jumping ship at port of call was all too common. Because of that, a strange sailor found lurking around the warehouse would cause little interest and no concern.

If her near accident had been engineered, that was all the more reason for her to make the trip to England. Uncle Ashby and Aunt Ruth had to be protected, just as her mother had protected her by coming to the West Indies.

Thea looked down at the ledger again, noting the subtlety of the entries.

Did someone besides Uncle Ashby's nephew have enough knowledge and access to the accounts to perpetrate the scheme? She had to find out, and before her partner began to suspect that all was not well. If his nephew *were* the culprit, Ashby Merewether would be devastated. His already weak heart might give out entirely. She could not face that possibility.

She *must* do something.

Her eyes strayed to the letter lying beside the ledger on the polished wood of the desk. Lady Upworth had invited her to attend the Season, just as she had every year since Thea's seventeenth birthday. It would be the perfect excuse for a sudden trip to England. Aunt Ruth and Uncle Ashby had been urging her to take her place in Society for years. Even more so since Uncle Ashby's health had deteriorated.

She picked up the letter and smoothed its folds. The Merewethers had good intentions, as did her great-aunt, but she wondered if they realized how adamantly opposed to establishing a relationship with the Earl of Langley she was. She would never embrace the harsh man who had fathered her, and would not take her place in Society if acknowledging him was required to do so.

However, she *would* go to London. She wanted to meet her great-aunt, Lady Upworth. Thea knew the older woman through letters and the many sketches she sent of Jared and London life, but had never met her.

Lifting the letter, she gazed at the sketch underneath. She let her finger trail along the scar on Jared's face. He had gotten it saving the life of their half sister, Irisa, when he was fourteen. She could still remember the day it happened. She'd had a terrible nightmare that night and dreamed a beast had attacked her with its claws. The following month she had gotten a letter from Lady Upworth telling her of Jared's heroic deed and the mark left on his face.

She wanted to meet her brother. She knew so much about him and yet nothing at all. The longing to meet the flesh of her flesh grew every year. She knew what he liked, what he did, how he behaved, and what he looked like through Lady Upworth's letters, but Thea had no idea how her twin brother *felt* about anything. Lady Upworth said that he was a very private gentleman, not given to expressing his emotion.

Would he be like their father? She had to believe that he would be a better man, a kinder man. Some of her own emotions and cares must be reflected in him. They were, after all, twins.

And Irisa, would she be as mischievous as she looked in Lady Upworth's sketches? Longing to know both her brother and half sister welled up in Thea.

Her gaze went of its own accord to the window of her office. The sight of the still blue water of the harbor had been a source of comfort since the death of her mother. The island represented safety, and the sea, and adventure. As a child, she had vowed to experience that adventure someday. Evidently, the time had come.

Her eyes strayed to Drake's ship, the *Golden Dragon.* She smiled. It had sailed into their harbor at the most opportune time.

Drake's insistence that he arrive in England by the date specified on his Lloyd's of London policy would certainly be in her favor. The sooner she got to London, the better were her chances of unmasking the thief before Uncle Ashby even realized something was wrong, or before another so-called accident took place.

She simply had to convince Drake to let her sail on his ship. Remembering the conversation of the morning, she thought she just knew what it would take.

She felt a certain amount of trepidation at the thought of a five-week-long voyage in close quarters with Drake. She felt things around the shipowner that had never plagued her before. Womanly desires and inexplicable excitations. She could not seem to resist staring at him, and a mortifying urge to *touch* him plagued her.

She would simply have to find a way to avoid him aboard ship. She could not afford to be sidetracked from her goal by a gentleman, nor did she particularly wish to be beset by further odd and compelling feelings.

She took a piece of foolscap and copied down the pertinent entries. Closing the ledger, she hid it with the others that showed discrepancies. She rather doubted Uncle Ashby would get curious and go looking for them. The numbers side of business was not the dear man's forte.

"No." Although, he was not known for tact, Drake found himself being even blunter with Thea than he was with others. She was clearly used to getting her own way, but he could not accommodate her latest whim. "It is out of the question for us to remain in port while you ready for the journey."

He felt a certain amount of regret. The thought of her stimulating company on the remainder of the voyage held appeal, but he could not spare the time a lady needed to prepare for such a journey.

"Surely such a short delay would not compromise your schedule."

Disappointment warred with irritation. He did not like feminine manipulation. He had thought after their discussion earlier that she understood that he was honor bound to reach England within five weeks.

"No." He turned back to watch Jacob work, hoping she was intelligent enough to recognize the dismissal.

"How much?"

The words struck him raw, and the tether he had on his patience slipped a notch. "My honor is not for sale."

Jacob ceased his movement on the bellows and stepped away from the forge. Crossing his arms over the massive barrel of his chest, he fixed Drake with a glare. "Miz Thea, she be wanting to sail on your ship, sir."

Drake's hands curled into fists at his side as he tried to maintain what little was left of his patience. "I am aware of that, Jacob, but it is impossible. I am already losing too much time to this repair."

They would be hours ahead had the blacksmith been willing to come aboard the *Golden Dragon*.

Jacob did not look in the least repentant. He turned his gaze on Thea. "Miz Thea, you be wanting to go on Mr. Drake's ship?"

Thea nodded her head. "Yes, Jacob. Very much. I have my own schedule to keep and none of our ships will be sailing for England for at least a month."

Jacob turned back to Drake. "You take de passengers, yes?"

Drake gave a reluctant nod. "Yes, but I cannot delay long enough for Miss Selwyn to get ready."

How many times would he have to say it before both the stubborn woman and blacksmith would accept that he would not risk his honor for Thea's desire to attend the Season?

"Miz Thea, you be delaying Mr. Drake?"

Thea shook her head vehemently. "No. I can be ready to sail in two hours."

Drake laughed. He could not help it. No lady of his acquaintance could prepare for an evening at the opera in that amount of time much less an ocean voyage. Most women took months to prepare for such a journey. Even two weeks would seem short. Two hours was absurd.

"I'm afraid Miss Selwyn is not being realistic."

Thea glared at him.

He returned her glare with an easy smile. "The *Golden Dragon* will be weeks out of the harbor by the time you are packed and ready to go. You have more chance being ready for one of your own ships sailing in the month."

"You be going without your boiler, sir?"

Dread snaked up Drake's spine and, along with it, fury. "No." If he had to do the damn repair himself, he'd have the boiler and be sailing out of the harbor before nightfall.

Jacob nodded as if Drake had confirmed his belief. "It won't be ready for . . ." He let his words trail off and turned to Thea for guidance.

"Two hours," she said firmly.

"Two hours," repeated the big blacksmith.

Drake knew when to fight and when to allow his opponent to believe he, or in this case, *she* had won.

He fixed Thea with his gaze. "The *Golden Dragon* will sail in two hours *with her boiler*. If you wish to sail on her, you and your luggage will be aboard."

He would have reiterated that she would be left behind otherwise, but in a swirl of bright muslin, she was gone.

Jacob grinned at Drake. "She be aboard, sir. You can be counting on it."

Drake shrugged as if his heart had not increased its rhythm at the very thought of Thea sailing on his ship. Not to mention that other parts of his anatomy sat up and took notice as well. "If she wants to sail, she will be."

"I be finishing the boiler now, sir."

"Excellent."

THEA'S BEDROOM LOOKED LIKE A BLUE NORTHERNER had blown through it. Clothes lay strewn across the counterpane of her bed. A nearly full trunk and valise reposed on the floor near the wardrobe.

"I don't understand this unseemly haste, dear. Surely you could have waited to sail on one of our ships after taking proper time to prepare for the voyage."

Thea gritted her teeth as she answered the complaint from her adopted aunt for what felt like the tenth time in less than an hour. "You always said that if I were to attend the Season, I would have to buy a whole new wardrobe in London. Therefore, it would be silly to take the time to prepare and pack gowns that I will not wear."

Aunt Ruth sighed. "Yes. There is that. But, dear, I could wish that you would make a better impression on your great-aunt than to show up with a meager trunk and valise. Are you *sure* Mr. Drake won't wait just one more day?"

Thea almost laughed. "Quite sure, Aunt Ruth. In fact, if we don't hurry, I'll be left behind as it is."

Aunt Ruth resumed her packing. "If you say so, dear."

She muttered something about Ashby and his plans that made no sense to Thea, but she did not have time to puzzle out the older woman's meaning.

Thea handed her maid, Melly, the stack of her mother's journals. "Please pack these in the trunk with utmost care, Melly."

The older woman took the journals with reverent hands. "You can be assured of that, miss."

Thea smiled at her maid. Melly had insisted on traveling with her mother to the West Indies. She had served Anna loyally, choosing to remain and care for Thea after Anna's death. Thea had wanted to give Melly her own cottage and an allowance in thanks for her loyalty, but the maid would not hear of it. A lady's maid she was and a lady's maid she would remain, she insisted.

"Melly, are you sure you don't mind traveling with me on such little advance warning like this? I could make the journey alone."

Aunt Ruth gasped. "No such thing. You are a lady, Thea, for all your business dealings. Your mother would turn in her grave were you to even contemplate such a journey alone."

Melly agreed. "That she would. Miss, I don't mind returning to England, no matter what the hurry to catch the ship. I look that forward to it. I do."

Thea smiled. "I'm glad."

"I don't look forward to sailing, though. I was that sick the entire journey here. Your mother had her sainted hands full caring for you and me both."

Laying her hand on Melly's arm, Thea smiled. "I'll take just as good care of you. And perhaps you won't get so sick this time. It's been many years."

Melly crossed herself. "I can pray, miss."

DRAKE AND HIS MEN FINISHED HAULING THE BOILER over the side of the ship. They would set sail and reattach the boiler enroute. Turning back to the rail, he scanned the bay. No managing female in a small dingy anywhere in sight. She had not made it after all. He chided himself for believing she would.

Thea was intriguing. She was unique. She enticed him

as no other woman had, but she had proven that she was not that different from other ladies of his acquaintance. Even if she was more stubborn. In the end, she had needed more time than he could spare to prepare herself.

The captain gave orders to raise anchor. Drake stifled the urge to ask him to wait as he scanned the bay one more time for any sign of the determined female. He resolutely turned from the bay and stopped in shock at the sight that met him. Thea stood conversing with his sailors while examining the boiler. She had changed her dress and now wore a bright yellow gown of India cotton. The matching parasol tilted at a negligent angle that he was certain did little to protect her skin from the sun.

The sailor speaking to her wore a look of besotted enchantment and a smile that would make most ladies cringe. What teeth he had left were as yellow as her dress and his whiskers were stained with tobacco juice.

Thea did not appear adversely affected. The hand not holding the parasol moved with animation as she spoke. "It's so large. The engine must be huge. Could I see it, do you suppose?"

"Passengers are not allowed in the engine room." He knew even as he spoke the words that she would attempt to find some way around them.

She raised her gaze to meet his. "Hello, Mr. Drake. Isn't there any way you could make one small exception? After all, the first mate allowed a group from shore to see the engine."

He would ask the captain to talk to the first mate later. He didn't like the thought of strangers poking about the engine when it was in a state of disrepair. That engine had to help carry them back to England in record time.

Thea went on in a persuasive tone, "I should so like to see it, and the machinery attached to the paddles. Do your paddles collapse for swifter sailing like the *Savannah*'s?"

"Yes."

Her eyes lit with interest. "How does the engine work? Do you keep the boiler stoked at all times? What caused it to blow? What type of wood are the paddles made from?"

She stopped speaking when the sailors laughed, her skin going pink.

Drake moved forward and took her arm. "I would be pleased to answer your questions over dinner this evening, but right now I must see to the engine repair."

She bit her lip, her hesitation unmistakable. "Are we to have dinner together then?"

How long had she been aboard? Long enough to hear the story of his background and determine not to be seen in his company? With her voracious curiosity, it was possible. Ruthlessly forcing down his disappointment, he said, "If you would prefer not to, of course I understand." He turned to resume the move of the boiler, but her words arrested him.

"It's not that. My maid, Melly, gets seasick and I don't want to abandon her if she needs me."

He nodded, unwilling to acknowledge his strong sense of relief. He could not allow this woman to become important to him. He needed to focus on his goal of reaching Liverpool in five short weeks—a nearly impossible task, one that would be even more difficult if he allowed himself to get sidetracked by an intriguing female.

"A place will be set for you at the captain's table. If you are not there, we will understand why." As the owner of the ship, he shared the captain's table for all formal meals. It was expected of him and he enjoyed the man's company.

"That isn't necessary, truly."

Why did she insist on arguing with him over every little thing? She should be grateful. Passengers vied for a place at the captain's table. Not only was it prestigious to be chosen to dine with the captain, but fond mamas with unmarried daughters also vied for the opportunity to bring their offspring to Drake's attention. "I will instruct the steward to seat you beside me."

She did not look grateful. She looked irritated.

Pulling her arm from his grasp, she swung her body and parasol around to face him squarely. "Mr. Drake, I appreciate your offer, but I must decline. I should feel very badly leaving an empty place at the captain's table."

"I will send someone to sit with your maid should the need arise so that you will not concern yourself about leaving a vacant seat." He didn't know why he was being so insistent, but the thought of her sitting at another table sharing conversation with the male passengers gnawed at him.

She blew out a breath in exasperation. "Thank you."

He almost smiled as he realized manners had forced her to acquiesce when she clearly did not wish to.

"I believe I will retire to my cabin and check on Melly."

Good idea. What she was doing on the deck in the first place without her maid, he did not know, but someone needed to take the strong-minded female in hand. "In the future, bring your maid with you when you walk the deck."

"*Oh.*" If her spine got any straighter, the first mate could use her as a line for his navigation. "I am years past needing a nursemaid, I can assure you."

"I did not suggest you seek one out. It is a lady's maid you seem to have forgotten on this particular stroll, Miss Selwyn."

Her expression turned arctic. "I do not need you or anyone else to dictate my behavior. If I choose to walk about on deck unescorted by my maid, then I will do so."

She punctuated her words with shakes to her parasol. Twice it came perilously close to hitting him in the face. Snapping his fingers around the handle, he held it in place.

Meeting her glare for glare, he said, "No, you will not."
She yanked on her parasol. "Excuse me."

He let go just as she yanked again. Her momentum carried her back against one of the sailors, who took obvious delight in catching her. One look from Drake and the sailor let her go without a single ribald comment.

She made a show of smoothing her gown and adjusting her parasol. "If you are finished issuing superfluous orders, I will leave you to your boiler problems."

Drake was conscious of the amusement of the sailors witnessing this exchange. He abandoned his stance near the boiler and walked toward Thea, pleased when she began to back up. He did not stop until her back was pressed against the ship rail and he was mere inches from her body.

He leaned down until his face was so close she would be certain not to miss his words. "I own this ship. The only man aboard who would dare to refuse my order is the captain, and even he would consider it carefully before doing so. I suggest you follow his good example."

Wide eyes stared back at him as her breathing grew rapid. "What if my maid is sick the entire voyage? You cannot expect me to stay in my cabin for six to eight weeks."

A soft curl of chestnut escaped the confines of her pins. He wanted to wrap it around his fingers and pull her face the remaining distance until their lips met. Suppressing the urge with a supreme act of will, he forced his mind to assimilate her statement.

"Five weeks."

Her eyes were fixed on his lips. "What?"

"Five weeks. We will be in Liverpool in five weeks."

Her head snapped back. "But that's impossible. None of our ships have ever made the voyage in less than six weeks. You cannot possibly believe you will make it in five."

He gave in to the urge and touched the strand of hair. It felt like the silk thread his mother used to do needlepoint. "We will make it in five weeks."

"Not if we don't get this boiler back on the engine."

The sailor's voice jolted Drake back to reality. He dropped Thea's hair and stepped away. Without saying anything else to her, he turned back to the boiler. Her blue eyes and soft little body tempted him, but he would not forget his duty.

Four

Langley arrived unexpectedly to berate me for sneaking in my attempts to see my son. Had he arrived but five minutes earlier, he would have caught me rocking Thea to sleep for her afternoon nap. He had the gall to accuse me of being without integrity. I do not know what to do. I cannot see my son and if I stay here, I may very well lose my daughter.

June 12, 1798
Journal of Anna Selwyn, Countess of Langley

MELLY'S PRAYERS APPEARED TO HAVE GONE awry because they weren't two hours out of port and she was already intimately acquainted with the chamber pot. "Oh, miss, this rocking is sending my stomach into my toes."

Thea thought the ship's rocking rather mild, but elected not to mention it. The sound of her maid being ill was having its own effect on Thea.

She breathed deeply, regretting the action almost

immediately. "Melly, I believe I'll just open the door and let some air in."

"Yes, miss, that's a good idea."

Thea opened the door and was startled by the presence of a young seaman on the other side.

The sailor's arms were full of bundles, which he thrust toward Thea. "Compliments of Mr. Drake."

She stared down at the bundles wrapped in rough cotton that rubbed against her skin. The odor of ginger and cinnamon was unmistakable in the small confines of the cabin.

"What are they?" She didn't understand. Why had Drake sent her spices?

"Ginger tea, miss, and soda crackers. There's some salt beef and biscuits too."

"Salt beef?" Did her voice sound as confused as she felt?

The sailor nodded, his mouth split wide in a grin. "Nothing better aboard ship for settling a stomach. Most passengers won't eat it. Think it's fit only for the crew. Be a lot less green around the gills if they did, miss."

Drake had sent seasickness remedies for Melly.

"I'll try it. I'll try anything," vowed the maid as she attempted to sit up on the bunk.

"Yes'm. I'll be back with some hot water for the tea."

Thea collected her wits about her. "Thank you. That is very kind. Please thank Mr. Drake as well."

"Yes'm. I'll go for the water now."

She let him go without further protest. Drake had shown concern for Melly's comfort. Thea did not generally associate overbearing arrogance with consideration. Surely he was too busy with the repairs to his ship's engine to be bothered.

However, the inescapable fact was that he *had* bothered.

"Mr. Drake is a thoughtful gentleman."

"He's shown us consideration," Thea agreed.

Remembering the way he had held her in the warehouse that morning, Thea doubted his gentlemanly instincts were overpoweringly strong, however.

"I know your sainted mother warned you against giving your heart unwisely, but I'm sure she didn't mean you to mistrust every man you meet."

"I don't. I trust some men."

Melly snorted. "Who, if you don't mind me asking?"

"I trust Uncle Ashby. I trust Jacob and Philippe."

In fact, she'd trusted Philippe enough to tell him a little of her plan and ask him to watch over Uncle Ashby while she was gone. Surprisingly, he'd agreed without a huge argument about her stated intentions to investigate the ledger discrepancies.

"That's three men you've known most of your life and all of them old enough to be your father or grandfather. You don't fool me, miss. You don't trust young gentlemen and that's a fact."

Thea finished depositing the bundles on top of the small table that made up part of the meager furnishings of her cabin. "I see no reason to trust a man just because he calls himself a gentleman. My mother trusted my father, and look where that got her."

Melly gripped her stomach and moaned.

Thea rushed to her side and pressed a biscuit into her hand. "Try to eat this. The sailor said it would help, and he ought to know."

The maid took a small bite and chewed it slowly. Her mobcap had gone askew and her black bombazine dress was rumpled. Thea had often wondered how the maid could stand the heavy folds of fabric she insisted were proper to a woman of her station.

"Your mother had you, and she never regretted it."

"Yes, but she lost my brother, and she never got over that."

"I often wondered if we'd gone back to England, if your father would have relented. His anger had to spend itself eventually."

Thea looked askance at Melly. "You were there the day he took Jared away. You must know he would never have relented. He is much too hard a man, vicious in his proud certainty that he could never be wrong." Not to mention that, eventually, there had been no choice.

Anna Langley could not have returned to England had she wanted to, not and take up her rightful place as Countess of Langley.

Melly took another nibble of the biscuit and chewed in silence. When she spoke again, Thea was surprised.

"I was there the day your mother told him she never wanted to see him again, too. The look on his face when he left . . . If you ask me, he finally realized he'd lost her."

"He didn't want her. He was, and no doubt still is, a monster."

Melly shook her head. "You never saw him with her in the beginning. He treated her like she was glass. It was only after that blackguard told Lord Langley that his wife had been unfaithful that he changed."

Frowning, Thea unwrapped the salt beef and sliced a piece off with the knife provided. "I never saw him at all. He should have believed Mama, not some rake with a terrible reputation with women."

"Aye, but jealousy does funny things to a gentleman. Anyway, you'll be seeing him now, won't you?"

Not if she could help it. Thea had no desire to meet the man who had treated her mother so cruelly.

Thea moaned and turned in the small bunk, trying to find a comfortable position. After drinking the ginger tea, Melly had lain down and gone to sleep. Thea wished she could find the oblivion of slumber. Her stomach felt as if someone had tied it in loop knots and was drawing the string tight.

The steward had come to escort her to dinner, and she'd sent him away with a message for Drake that she was indisposed. He would probably believe she was defying him on purpose. She didn't care. She just wanted to be left alone. Her stomach hurt, her head felt as if fish were swimming in it, and her mouth tasted like sea brine.

She moaned again, trying to do it quietly so as not to wake her maid. She needn't have worried. Melly snored and flung one arm over her face. Thea wondered if there wasn't something besides ginger in the tea. The maid's sleep was terribly deep. Lucky woman.

A peremptory knock sounded at the door. She ignored it. Probably that blasted steward again, come to insist she join Drake for dinner.

The knock sounded again and Melly stirred in her sleep. Thea gritted her teeth, but knew she had to get up. It wouldn't be fair to wake the maid to experience more of this misery. She cautiously slid her legs over the side of the bed as the pounding resumed on the door. Someone was shouting something on the other side, but she couldn't understand him. The roaring in her ears blocked out the noise.

She hobbled to the door, furious with whoever was on the other side. If she didn't feel so bloody awful, she would give him a speaking-to he wouldn't soon forget. She pulled on the latch of the door, opening it a crack, and shivered at the gust of air that pressed into the airless cabin. Surely they were not so far from her island that the weather had turned cold?

"What?" She meant to snap out the question to whomever dared to force her from the relative comfort of her berth, but her voice came out raspy.

"Miss Selwyn? Are you all right?"

Her gaze traveled up the perfectly tailored breeches to

Drake's well-fitting coat. It finally made it to his face. He was frowning.

"I will not be able to join you for dinner this evening." She never wanted to eat again.

Drake pushed the door to her cabin completely open. She would have protested, but couldn't summon the energy for the effort. He took hold of her arms as if he thought she might fall. His skin was so much warmer than hers. It would no doubt shock him beyond measure if she pressed her body against his to soak up some of his warmth.

"Why didn't you tell the steward you were sick? Where are the things I sent earlier?"

"Melly ate them. She's feeling much better. Thank you."

There. She'd done her polite duty. Now if he would just let her lie back in her bed to die in peace.

"You aren't going to die."

Mortified, Thea realized she'd spoken aloud. "How do you know? You've probably never had a day of seasickness in your life." She sounded pitiful and she didn't care.

He grinned. "I've seen enough of it to know it isn't lethal."

She frowned at his apparent good humor. "So you say."

"So I know." He moved a hand around her shoulder.

She would have scolded him for taking such liberties, but suddenly his other hand slipped behind her knees and then she was suspended in air. He walked over to her bunk and laid her on it. "Stay put. I'll be right back."

It seemed like hours before she heard Drake's voice again. "Help her into her nightrail. Her corset is undoubtedly just making it worse."

Thea spoke over the mumbled words of the woman Drake had brought with him. "I don't wear a corset. They aren't healthy. Several forward-thinking physicians have already denounced them in America. It is just a matter of time before English women realize their peril."

"Bloody hell. I should have guessed you'd be too damn independent to even dress like other women."

"Don't swear at me. It makes my head pound."

He swore again and then grimaced. "I'm sorry." He pressed a wet cloth to her forehead. "This will help your head."

The other woman said, "Changing into her nightrail will undoubtedly make her more comfortable, corsets or not. Her petticoats can't be comfortable in this heat."

Heat? What was the woman blathering about? It was cold as anything in her cabin. Maybe if she were wearing the petticoats the other woman thought she was, Thea would be warmer. She wasn't about to have a stranger undress her and discover the concessions she made to the Caribbean heat. Aunt Ruth would have apoplexy if she knew.

"*No.*"

Drake soothed her with a hand on her hair. "Shh. It's quite all right. Mrs. Coombs is a companion to one of the passengers on board. She will help you change."

"I don't want a stranger to undress me."

He sighed, his expression both concerned and chagrined. "This is no time to be argumentative, Miss Selwyn. You are in no condition to dress yourself."

She felt tears in her eyes and blinked at them. It must be the seasickness. She never cried. "Please."

He brushed at the wetness on her cheek. "Very well. Mrs. Coombs and I will leave you alone for a few minutes while you change into less confining clothes."

He stood up and she had an insane urge to beg him to stay. He couldn't, of course. It was unthinkable. But his presence comforted her.

She heard the door of her cabin close. Removing the cloth from her eyes, she verified that the room was empty except for her and the sleeping Melly. She forced herself to stand. She opened the trunk, breathing shallowly lest she bring on another bout of the sickness. She pulled out her nightrail and wrapper. Undoing the tapes on her gown, she let it fall to the floor and pulled the other garments on. Mrs. Coombs had been right. They were more comfortable.

She left her dress in a heap on the floor and slowly made her way back to the bed just as a soft knock sounded on the door.

"Miss Selwyn, are you finished?"

"Yes."

He opened the door and she saw that he was alone.

"Where is Mrs. Coombs?"

"I sent her back to her dinner."

He moved to sit next to her on the bed.

"This is not at all proper."

Picking up the damp cloth, he shrugged. "Nonsense. Your maid is here."

Laughter surprised her. She didn't know she was still capable of mirth. "Melly is sleeping like she took a hefty dose of laudanum."

"The tea sometimes has that effect."

She looked sideways at him. "It must have something more than ginger in it."

He shrugged again. "A few things."

"May I have some?"

He smiled. "Want to sleep, do you?"

She eyed her maid, who snored softly. "She looks much more comfortable than I feel."

"First you need to eat some beef and biscuits."

She looked at the salted beef in Drake's hand and shook her head. "I can't eat anything."

"Your maid did."

"She wasn't as sick as I am."

"You want to feel better, don't you?"

"Yes."

"Then eat." He offered her the beef.

She ate. It tasted surprisingly palatable. Not good, but not terrible either. It's saltiness made her thirsty, however. Drake must have read her mind because he offered her the spiced ginger tea.

She took a couple sips and then he pulled the tea from her. "You need to eat some biscuit, too."

"I know I said I didn't need a nursemaid, but you make a surprisingly good one."

He didn't smile. He just met her eyes and what she saw in his made her take a hasty bite of the biscuit.

"I don't feel like a nursemaid when I'm with you, Thea."

"You don't?" Her voice squeaked.

"No."

"What . . ." She cleared her throat. The biscuit was too dry. "What do you feel like?"

His mouth came to within a breath of hers. "A man."

"May I have some more tea, please?"

He laughed and moved back. "Yes you may, little coward."

She would have argued, but for once she could not deny his words. He was right. She was a coward. The look in his eyes and the way it affected her terrified her. She took several more sips of the tea.

"This is really quite good. Whose recipe is it?"

He stood and began to pull her wrapper from her. She was too tired to protest the liberty.

"My mother's."

"She must be a very wise woman."

"About most things, yes."

"What isn't she wise about?"

"My father."

Thea yawned and did not resist when Drake tipped her sideways so that her head rested on the pillow and then lifted her feet onto the bed. "That's interesting. My mother wasn't wise about my father either. I guess we have something in common."

Drake drew the light coverlet to her chin. "We have more than that in common."

She could barely keep her eyes open. "How else are we alike?"

He tucked the blanket around her. "I want you." He gently smoothed her hair away from her face, the touch sending shivers down her spine. "You want me, too."

DRAKE SPENT A PORTION OF EACH DAY CHECKING ON Thea and forcing her to take sustenance. Even in her weakened condition, he found her more alluring than any other woman he had ever known. Both vulnerable and independent, she fascinated him.

Looking out over the ship's rail at the rapidly passing water, he felt satisfaction course through him. If they kept up their current pace, they would make port with time to spare. He turned and walked to Thea's cabin.

The maid had thanked him profusely for his help, saying that without it, she would not have gotten her mistress to eat anything. He didn't doubt the maid's words. Thea made a terrible patient, too stubborn for her own good.

His suspicion that she wore no petticoats had been confirmed the first evening when he returned to her cabin and found her dress in a pile on the floor. He had picked up the garment and folded it. There had been nothing else to put away. He should have been scandalized by her wantonness or at the very least convinced that she was no better than she should be. He was neither. He'd made that mistake once already.

Thea's innocence screamed from her clear, blue eyes when they widened at his teasing. She let him touch her, to feed her and care for her, but when he caressed her arm or touched her lips, she turned skittish. And every day he spent in her company increased his desire for her.

As oblivious to her own appeal as her uncle had claimed,

she peppered him with questions about his ship and how the steam engine worked. She wanted every last detail and he found unexpected pleasure in sharing them with her.

He knocked on her door, surprised when it opened immediately. Thea stood on the other side. Dressed. Her Capucine gown hung loosely under a shawl of light cotton.

"What the bloody hell are you doing out of bed?" He followed his question with a glare meant to make her see sense, but she responded with a blinding smile.

"Isn't it lovely? I finally feel well enough to get up." She looked ready to fall over. "I'm going for a walk. I want to see the ship I've been sailing on for weeks."

"I'll take you to a chair on the passenger deck."

Her face fell. "But I wanted to tour the ship."

"You need to work up your strength. Perhaps tomorrow."

Her mouth set in a mutinous line, she shook her head. "I don't want to lie on a deck chair like an invalid."

"Where is Melly? I can't believe she has agreed to accompany you on your little jaunt."

Thea's pale skin gained a little color. "She didn't. She's gone to visit friends she's made on board."

The knowledge surprised him. Not that the maid had friends. Thea insisted that Melly leave the cabin each day for meals and a "bracing walk," as she called it. To his knowledge, the maid never walked farther than the passenger parlor. What surprised him was that the maid would leave Thea, knowing he was due to visit soon. He came at nearly the same time every day.

"She'll be back soon, I'm sure."

"I've told her to spend the afternoon as she wishes."

"You were planning to go alone?" Unexpected anger seared him. "What if you had gotten ill? Who would look after you?"

"I had intended to walk with you." She smiled charmingly at him. "You are not too busy, are you?"

He had no doubt that if he refused, she *would* go alone.

"I would like nothing better than to escort you to a chair on deck."

"I want to go for a walk."

"Let's see how you feel when we get outside, shall we?"

She looked ready to argue, but then she nodded. "Fine."

When they stepped onto the deck and into the sun, Thea stopped and tossed her head back, her eyes closed. She breathed in deeply. "Fresh air. It's a luxury I no longer take for granted."

He couldn't resist running his finger down her cheek. Her head snapped up and her eyes opened. She stared at him in silence. He dropped his hand. "Come along before I forget that my mother tried to teach me to be a gentleman."

"Your father didn't teach you?"

"No."

They continued along the deck in a surprisingly companionable silence until she sighed. "I don't remember walking being this exhausting."

He looked down at her face and frowned at her wan expression. "Ready to sit down?"

Her eyes narrowed. "You just love being right, don't you?"

He wanted to laugh at her aggrieved expression, but he restrained himself. "Well?"

"Yes." She gripped his arm tightly with both hands as he led her up a set of steps that opened onto the passenger deck.

"Do you want me to leave you in peace once you are settled in your chair?"

"Don't you dare." She glared at him. "You have a responsibility to entertain me while I'm on deck. After all, you escorted me here. It is the gentlemanly thing to do."

The little baggage. She had insisted on coming on deck and now she tried to make it sound as if the whole enterprise had been his idea.

"I said my mother tried to teach me to be a gentleman. I did not say that she succeeded."

"Nevertheless, you would not wish me to make a poor report to her when we reach England."

"You plan on speaking to my mother?"

"I imagine I will meet her at one entertainment or another. From what Aunt Ruth said, that's about all ladies of quality do during the Season. Float from one soirée to the next."

She sounded disgruntled by the notion, which made little sense considering the Season was her chief reason for insisting on passage aboard his ship.

"You are so certain my mother is a lady of quality?"

"Do not try to gammon me, Drake. You have a lamentable sense of humor, to be sure. You could not be who you are and your mother a common woman who sells meat pasties for a living."

He stopped her and forced her to meet his gaze by placing a hand on her chin and lifting her face. "Who am I, Thea?"

"You are a man of honor and integrity."

He felt warmed by her faith in him. "A common man cannot have these qualities?"

She pulled her chin from his grasp, but didn't break eye contact. "Of course he can. That's not what I meant. You speak like a gentleman, you carry yourself with enough arrogance for a duke, though I doubt you are that or your crew would not call you mister. You are probably a second son, who by rights of personality and bearing should have been firstborn."

Her assessment hit much too close to reality for his comfort. It was time to change the subject. "Here are the chairs."

She turned to look where he pointed. Several of the elderly passengers occupied the chairs. However, the one closest to them was empty.

"You said you would stay and visit me, but there is only one chair."

He had not actually agreed, but he didn't belabor the point. "I'll sit on the deck."

She sighed. He didn't know if it was with relief or resignation. He pulled the chair away from the other passengers. He did not want to share Thea with anyone.

Once she was settled, he covered her legs with a small quilt he'd taken from her cabin. "Warm enough?"

"Yes." She looked up at him, her expression quizzical. "You take very good care of me, Drake. Why?"

"You're a passenger on my ship. I'm responsible."

Disappointment showed on her face. "Oh."

He stifled a laugh.

She smoothed the quilt across her knees. "It's a good thing not too many passengers get seasick like I did."

"Yes, it is."

She raised her gaze, her eyes filled with mischief. "You would never have a moment to yourself."

Five

I am growing stronger, for yesterday when Langley came calling again, I told him that although I wished to see my son, I never wanted to see Langley again. I could not bear it, when every meeting reminds me of his cruelty. He was so angry, I thought he might strike me. I stood and dared him to. Actually dared him. He stared at me as if I had transformed into some remarkable sea creature. He stormed from the room without saying another word. I am still shaking from my own temerity.

June 13, 1798
Journal of Anna Selwyn, Countess of Langley

ADJUSTING HER LEGS FOR COMFORT, THEA turned her face toward the sun again. She hated feeling like an invalid. What must he think of her whiling her days away in a deck chair like one of the elderly passengers? The thought that she cared entirely too much for Drake's opinion unsettled her. Drat the man. He should have maintained his overbearing arrogance and all would have been well.

Instead, he had cared for her like a treasured friend. *Or something more.*

She had not dreamed his assertion that he wanted her that first night, or had she? He had said nothing since.

"Have you worked it all out in your mind?"

His voice startled her from her reverie. "What do you mean? Worked what out?"

"Whatever has put that look of anxiety on your face and kept you silent for the past five minutes." He shifted his legs, crossing one over the other as he leaned against the rail opposite her chair. "You did say you wanted my company, but thus far you have ignored me."

"Five minutes of silence does not constitute ignoring you." She frowned up at him. "You must be accustomed to being fawned over in London. Are you very rich, Drake?"

He shrugged. "Rich enough."

"I thought so. For it certainly can't be your sunny disposition that has gotten you so accustomed to a lady's undivided attention."

The wary expression he wore turned to laughter. "You think my money is all that recommends me to women?"

"Well, you are very attractive as well." She must be honest.

"You find me attractive?"

He moved to stand very close to her chair. The sea air mixed with his uniquely masculine scent and she wanted to touch him, feel the hardened muscles of his body under her hands. Oh, she was wanton. She felt a blush crawl up her skin.

Nevertheless, she did not like the complacent air about him. "In a general sort of way, yes."

"What does that mean?"

She looked away from his too intent gaze. "It means that your overall appearance would be quite pleasing to ladies."

Looking sideways at the elderly woman nearest to them, she sighed in relief when she realized that the other woman was asleep. What an embarrassing topic to be overheard discussing.

He laughed again. "So, there is nothing particular about me that you find appealing?"

Was he mocking her? She couldn't tell.

Regardless, she had no intention of listing off the man's altogether too pleasing attributes. "Mr. Drake, that is hardly an appropriate thing to discuss."

"Little coward."

It *had not* been a dream. That is exactly what he had called her the first night on ship. She smiled. He must find something quite pleasing about her as well. Remembering her current state, her smile changed to a frown. Perhaps he had found her desirable before, but surely he could not desire her now.

"There is that look of worry again. You are biting your lip, Thea. Tell me what troubles you."

She affected a yawn. "You were right, Drake. I'm very tired. I think I'll take a little nap here in the sun."

His amused look vanished. "Are you all right? Are you sure you don't want me to carry you back to your cabin?"

She could just imagine what the other passengers would think of such a display. "No, thank you. I am content to rest here for the time being."

"Very well. I will send Melly to you."

"No." She felt like groaning at his look of implacability. "I am going to be resting. What possible harm can come to me?"

He frowned. "With you, that is a question that leaves me shuddering with the possibilities."

"That's not funny."

"I was not jesting." He pulled the quilt from her legs. "Stand up."

He was going to make her walk back to her cabin. She could not stand the thought of spending the rest of the day alone in the airless room. "Drake, I—"

He pulled her to her feet, effectively cutting off her protest. He then moved the chair back to a position near the dozing elderly woman. "Sit down."

Confused, she did as he commanded and watched in bemusement while he tucked the quilt around her again. Then he astonished her by laying his hand on the shoulder of the dozing woman.

She opened her eyes. "Eh, what is it? Oh it's you, Pierson."

"May I present Miss Selwyn? Thea, this is Lady Boyle."

Thea murmured, "It's a pleasure to meet you."

What was Drake doing?

"I'm leaving Miss Selwyn in your care."

Thea fumed. He made her sound like a piece of baggage that needed tending. "I don't need anyone to watch me nap, Mr. Drake."

He ignored her protest. "I will return later this afternoon to escort you back to your cabin."

She crossed her arms over her chest. She could return to her cabin on her own when she wanted.

He must have read her mind because he turned to Lady Boyle and said, "Do not let her out of your sight until I return."

Lady Boyle looked down her nose at Drake. "I've chaperoned six daughters through the Season and assorted granddaughters as well. Your young woman is safe in my care."

"I am not Mr. Drake's young woman. I am just a passenger on his ship." She fixed him with a gaze that dared him to disagree with her. "Isn't that right, Mr. Drake?"

He didn't agree or disagree. He merely raised one brow, bid his good-byes, and left. The sailor's curse that went through her mind was a very potent one.

Thea turned to face the older woman and forced a smile. "Thank you for keeping me company. However, you needn't interrupt your nap on my account. Contrary to what Mr. Drake believes, I do not need a keeper."

"Who are you accusing of napping? I never nap."

Thea hid a smile. "Well, I do. I'm not completely recuperated from this awful seasickness and find myself dozing in the afternoon."

"The young have no stamina."

Thea didn't know what to say to that, so she said nothing. Lady Boyle pulled knitting needles and yarn from a bag in her lap. Soon the clickety clack of her needles added to the sound of wind and sail surrounding Thea.

"Pierson is a nice young man. You could do worse."

"I don't know what you mean."

"He comes to your cabin daily to visit, my dear. His intentions are obvious."

"How did you know he came to see me each day?"

Lady Boyle snorted with amusement. "Come, young woman, surely you realize that gossip aboard ship is worse than in a small village. I would venture to guess that every person down to the potboy knows of his visits."

Heat stole up Thea's cheeks. "I know how it must appear to you all, but he only comes to see me because he's concerned about my health as I'm a passenger on his ship."

"Don't be ridiculous, gel. A man such as Pierson does not visit a young woman unless he wishes to."

Thea had begun to suspect that very thing, but she doubted Lady Boyle was correct in Drake's motives. The man had at first believed her to be a lightskirt.

"I'm sure you are mistaken. He is quite wealthy. He told me so himself. He can look much higher than a woman of moderate means and few connections, like myself."

The older woman gave her a measuring glance. "I see you don't know about his background. He ain't exactly above reproach."

Thea did not want to hear anything derogatory and said repressively, "I'm sure I don't know what you mean."

Lady Boyle nodded and gave Thea a measuring glance. "Just as I thought. He should have told you himself. Now, it's left to an old woman to break your heart. The young have no sensitivity to their elders."

Thea was torn between wanting to know more about the enigmatic Drake and refusing to hear anything uncomplimentary said about him. Her curiosity won out. "I assure you, my heart is quite safe."

Snorting again, Lady Boyle shook her head. She clearly did not believe Thea's avowal. "He's the natural child of a nobleman who has never even tacitly acknowledged him."

What did she mean? Of course Drake was natural. Did Lady Boyle think that he should be unnatural in some way? Then something she had overheard Aunt Ruth discussing with the wife of a local plantation owner tickled at Thea's memory. *Natural child* was the polite way of referring to a nobleman's bastard.

"His father has never acknowledged him?" That would be horrible for a man of Drake's proud temperament.

"No. Such a shame, too. Pierson's done well for himself and is accepted by most of polite society."

Thea had to agree. "His father is a fool." She could not imagine a father not wanting to acknowledge the dynamic man she had come to know. "If he's a natural child, how is he accepted so readily by Society?"

From what her mother had always said, Society was unforgiving about things of that nature. In fact, on occasion, Thea had received a less than warm reception even on their small island. No one knew who her father was, and not everyone believed the story her mother had concocted about early widowhood.

"His mother is the daughter of a duke. She never married, but her father would not allow her to be ostracized. In fact, he showed favor to Pierson in every way. No one who wants the duke's friendship dares ignore his daughter or grandson."

"The duke allowed Drake's father to refuse to marry his

mother?" It occurred to Thea that Drake had left her with someone who knew him quite well.

"His mother was a sweet child. Too beautiful for her own good. Pierson's father dallied with her before announcing his engagement to another woman. She didn't tell the duke she was with child until her erstwhile lover had married the other woman."

"I don't understand. Wouldn't a duke's daughter make a more advantageous match than someone else?"

Lady Boyle nodded. "In the normal way, yes. But Lady Noreen is the duke's youngest daughter. When he married the others off, it became common knowledge that he had tied up their portions in ironclad marriage settlements. Pierson's father needed cash to repair his fortune. He married a very wealthy young lady who had control of her own fortune. Upon their marriage, that control passed to him."

Thea could not believe what she was hearing. Were all Englishman without honor, or was it merely her and Drake's fathers? "That is terrible."

"Yes."

"Are you a very close friend of Drake's family?"

"He's my great-nevvy."

The blush started in her toes. How could she have asked such common questions of Drake's own aunt?

Lady Boyle laughed. "You didn't think he'd leave you with just anyone, did you, my dear? Pierson has shown more than average care for you this journey. I wouldn't be surprised if the announcement for your betrothal was made before the end of the Season."

"But I don't want to get married," Thea blurted out.

"That explains your age." The other woman's assessing glance made Thea squirm. "You're too lovely to be a spinster for lack of offers. Though living on a heathen island like you did might explain it as well. For all that you lived with Ashby and Ruth Merewether."

The old lady knew a great deal about her as well. Gossip *was* rife aboard ship.

"I cannot believe that you would be content with a spinster raised on a *heathen island* as the wife of your nephew."

Lady Boyle put her knitting away and settled back to view the scenery. "It has always been my experience that Pierson gets what he wants, and he obviously wants you. No use his family putting up a ruckus about it."

Perhaps he did *want* her, but Thea doubted very much it was for any position so permanent as that of his wife.

"Aunt Josephine, it appears you have worn Miss Selwyn out with your chatter."

Thea's head listed to one side, her eyes closed in sleep. The softened features of her face enhanced the aura of vulnerability that she tried so hard to hide. She wanted him to believe that she needed no one and could take care of herself. He knew better.

He was not convinced that her near miss the first day they had met had been an accident. The facts spoke for themselves. For barrels that size to topple would have required a very strong man pushing them. That made it a purposeful act of aggression against Thea. Considering her vocal views against slavery, it was not a far-fetched scenario.

He did not scrutinize his feelings of relief that she had insisted on sailing with him. He knew only that he was glad she was safely away.

"She dozed off a quarter of an hour ago." Lady Boyle stood and shook out her skirts. "I'm returning to my cabin for tea and a game of cribbage with Mrs. Coombs."

"Thank you for staying with her."

His great-aunt nodded acceptance of his thanks. "She's a delightful gel. Not at all put off by your birth, you know."

Drake's hand that rested on the top of Thea's chair tightened. "You told her?"

"Of course. You've already compromised her beyond redemption. She has no choice but to marry you. The gel at least had the right to know what she was getting into."

Drake wanted to hit something. Anything. "I have not compromised her."

"How do you think your visits to her cabin look to the passengers on board, nevvy?"

"I don't bloody well care."

"Perhaps not. But it's likely Miss Selwyn will, particularly when they refuse her admittance to their houses or word of this gets back and she is not extended vouchers to Almack's."

Had he done that to her? "But her maid has always been present on my visits. I behave as chaste as a bloody eunuch when I'm with her."

"Are you telling me you don't want to marry the gel?"

His aunt had a way of focusing on the important and dismissing the trivial.

"I don't know."

"Well, you had best decide soon." With that the older woman turned and walked away, her skirts swishing her disapproval with every step.

Marry Thea? He had always planned to marry a lady high in the *ton*. A woman above reproach who would prove to his father and everyone else in the *ton* that Drake was not beyond the pale. That he was worthy of recognition.

True, the one serious relationship he had carried out with a woman of quality had ended badly. He had a much more cynical view of women and marriage in the polite world now. It was a business arrangement between two interested parties. That was how he intended to handle his own marriage. After this trip, he would have enough money to buy and sell most of his peers. Although the *ton* made a pretense of turning its nose up at blunt, Drake knew that his ready cash would buy him a more than respectable wife. It would buy him a bloody paragon.

He didn't want a paragon, though. He wanted Thea—and her virginal innocence dictated he possess her only within the bounds of matrimony.

The wind picked up and Thea shivered in her sleep. He bent down and lifted her, quilt and all, into his arms. Though her eyes were closed, her face wore a small frown. She must be dreaming about something unpleasant.

THEA PACED HER CABIN WHILE MELLY SLEPT LIKE THE dead in her narrow bed. It was late, but she could not sleep.

Drake was avoiding her.

The only time she had seen him the past three days had been at dinner. He had been polite to her, but that was all. He did not offer to walk her about on deck, nor did he speak much to her after his initial inquiry about her health.

Had his aunt's words destroyed their friendship? Thea wanted to tell him she did not care a fig for Society's scrutiny, but did not know how to without admitting she had been feigning sleep during that incredibly embarrassing conversation between him and his aunt.

Not that she had had an opportunity to speak to him alone.

There was no opportunity to do *anything* alone aboard ship. She felt she would have a bout of sickness again, this very minute, if she did not get out of the cabin. She was desperate to get out under the stars. Drake had told her not to walk on deck alone, but surely it could not matter at night when no one was there to see her.

She hastily pulled on a gown of dark gray wool. Aunt Ruth had insisted Thea pack it, saying she had no clothes suitable for England's climate. From what Lady Upworth said in her letters, Thea's muslin and India Cotton gowns were all the rage right now. She had not wanted to hurt Aunt Ruth's feelings, however. So she brought the gown. It was two sizes too large and years out of fashion, but it would serve its purpose.

Carrying her shoes, she stealthily let herself out of the cabin and closed the door behind her. She tiptoed down the corridor, not wanting anyone in the neighboring cabins to know what she was about. When she reached the door to the deck, she slipped on her shoes and made her way outside.

The fresh air and freedom felt wonderful. She hugged herself and took a deep breath of the salty air. Moonlight reflected off the water, giving an enchanting feel to the night. The sea stretched on and on, making the ship that had appeared quite large in her harbor feel minuscule.

Skirting the stairway that led to the passenger deck, she walked toward the part of the ship most of the passengers ignored. Passing the entrance to the engine rooms, she wondered if she would ever get the chance to see the steam engine in motion. The door to the sailors' quarters was ajar, and loud snoring rumbled through the opening. She skirted by.

Neat coils of rope rested at the base of the main mast, and a bar used for lifting the hatches lay next it. Someone would be in trouble for leaving it out. She ran her hand along the smooth surface of the mast, amazed that such a tall pole would stand securely. Stopping to look up, she soaked in the sight of huge white squares billowing against the night sky.

No wonder Whiskey Jim had said that there was nothing so easy on the eyes as the look of a sailing ship at night.

She also liked the quiet and relative privacy night offered. The skeleton crew that made up the night watch were barely visible in their positions around the ship.

She was preparing to move on when the strong odor that often accompanied sailors alerted her to the fact that she was no longer alone. Turning to greet the sailor and ask how quickly the ship was traveling, she was caught completely unawares when he grabbed her arms from behind.

Reacting instinctively, she twisted her body. She freed
one arm and elbowed her attacker. Since she was still weak
from her seasickness, however, her blow had little effect on
the large man. He grunted, but didn't loosen his hold. He
yanked her toward him, trying to secure her free arm, and
she screamed.

"Help! I'm being attacked! Somebody, please help—"

Her shouts were cut short when a dirty hand slammed
over her mouth and nose. Frantic, she fought his hold. She
needed air. She bit him. Hard.

He yanked his hand away from her face and she sucked
in a desperately needed breath.

"You'll pay for that, you bleedin' tart." He squeezed her
and she felt as if her ribs were cracking.

She kicked her legs back, satisfied when her heel connected with his shin and his hold loosened infinitesimally.
She kicked again with all her might and tried to squirm
from his grasp while she attempted to pull enough air into
her lungs to shout for help again.

He started dragging her toward the side of the ship.
"We'll see if you like fightin' with the sharks more'n you
like fightin' with me."

He was going to throw her overboard.

Terror lent her strength and she managed to break his
hold on her arm. She swung her fist upward and connected
with the underside of his jaw. He swore and staggered. Kick-
ing his kneecap, she twisted violently once again. This time,
she broke from his arms. She dropped to the deck and rolled
toward the main mast.

"Help me." Even to her own ears, her voice sounded
weak and breathless. She could not rely on being rescued.

Her fingers closed around the iron bar she had seen earlier. *Thank you, God.*

Her attacker grabbed her feet and started dragging her
toward the side of the ship again. Taking a firm grip on the
bar, she swung with all the strength she could muster. The

bar came around in a perfect arc and connected with the villain's shoulder. He howled in pain and dropped her legs.

The sound of running feet told her that help was on its way. Her attacker must have heard as well, because he took off in the direction opposite from the running feet.

She lay on the deck, panting. Her entire body ached from the confrontation. She blessed the negligent sailor who had left the iron bar out, and Whiskey Jim for teaching her how to handle drunken seamen.

THE SIGHT OF THEA SPRAWLED ON THE DECK, HER HAND gripping a latch bar, momentarily paralyzed Drake. *What the bloody hell had been going on?*

He dropped next to her. "Thea?"

She didn't respond. Her eyes stared past him as if searching for someone else.

He shook her slightly. "Thea. What happened?"

She blinked. "Drake?"

"Yes." She was starting to scare him. Had she fallen and done injury to her head?

He wrapped his arms tightly around her and pulled her closer. "Tell me what happened."

The latch bar fell from her hand, clanging against the deck. "Did you trip on the bar?" He would find the man responsible for leaving it out and deal with him personally.

"Trip? No, I didn't trip." She tipped her head back and looked at him. "Thank the sailor for me."

"Thank him for what? You aren't making any sense." And his patience was getting thinner by the minute.

"For leaving the bar there, of course." Then she fainted.

Her head slumped against his shoulder. Picking up her limp body, he turned to the first mate. The seaman had been walking the deck with Drake when they had heard a loud curse. Not certain why he had felt instant dread at the sound—it was, after all, common enough to hear cursing aboard ship—Drake had taken off at a run. The first mate had followed him.

They had come upon Thea lying alone on deck, and for a few minutes Drake had forgotten the curse. It had not been Thea's voice he had heard. Not unless she made a practice of imitating the gruff timbre of a man.

"I think she was attacked. Alert the captain and search the ship."

The seaman nodded. "Whoever the bloody bastard is, he's probably made it back to his cabin by now, Mr. Drake."

"Search anyway."

"Aye, sir."

Drake turned and headed toward the cabin Thea shared with her maid. What had she been doing on deck at night? Even Thea had to realize how dangerous it would be for a woman alone, the darkness a cover for perverse deeds.

He stopped in front of her door and Thea's eyes opened. They filled with terror and she stiffened in his arms.

He tightened his hold on her. "It's me, Thea. No one is going to hurt you."

"Drake?"

He said, "Yes," again for the second time in ten minutes. She relaxed against him. *"Thank God."*

He waited for her to produce the key for her door. She didn't move. She just lay in his arms, her breathing much too shallow. Perhaps she had not locked the door. He tried the handle, but it did not move.

She roused a bit from her stupor. "The door is locked."

"I see that."

"I wanted Melly to be safe."

Lucky Melly. "Do you have the key?"

"Oh. Yes."

She fished around in the pocket of the voluminous gown she was wearing. When she found the key, rather than letting him release her, she leaned down and unlocked the door. He carried her inside the cabin and she shut the door behind them.

He set her on the bed and then lit the lamp. "I'll wake your maid."

"No."

"Damn it. This is not the time to worry about her rest."

She gave him a small smile. "It will do no good. With that ginger tea of yours, she could sleep through a black squall."

That answered how she had managed to leave her cabin undetected. Melly was much too protective to have allowed it under normal circumstances. He turned his back.

"Put on your nightrail."

"Perhaps you should go first."

"I'm not going anywhere."

She sighed. "I was afraid of that."

He heard sounds of rustling fabric. Then the bed creaked. "You may turn around now."

He did so and was struck by both the beauty and the defenselessness of the woman sitting under the covers. She was afraid of nothing, but she was so small compared to a man. What had she been about, traipsing on deck alone at night?

"Start."

She frowned at him. "Start what?"

"Your explanations. You can begin with what the bloody hell you thought you were doing walking on deck alone."

Six

I have taken Lady Upworth into my confidence about Thea. She has promised to help me leave England. It was a risk, but so is staying here. She thinks that I should wait until Thea is a little older to travel. I think she believes that Langley will relent. She does not say so, but she has a soft spot for her nephew. I cannot blame her. There was a time when I loved him, too. No longer. I cannot bear to be in the same room with him. My son is now a year old and I have not seen him since last spring.

September 24, 1798
Journal of Anna Selwyn, Countess of Langley

 "SURELY, THAT IS NOT THE MOST IMPORTANT issue at the moment."

Drake glared at her. "Don't bet on it."

"What about my attacker? Shouldn't you be trying to find him? Your other passengers could be at risk."

His expression turned more forbidding, if that were possible. "My other passengers know better than to walk on deck alone at night." He sat down on the edge of her bed and loomed over her. "*Bloody hell.* Even your stubborn, independent little self had to realize that it would not be safe."

She scooted back toward the wall, pulling the covers up to her chin. "Lady Boyle said that life aboard ship was like being in a small village."

"She referred, I'm sure, to the spread of gossip. Not the friendliness or honesty of the people. We've picked up passengers in every port. For all you know, every man jack of them is a rake and rogue."

"It wasn't a passenger."

"What?"

"It was a sailor."

"You saw him? Why didn't you say so? You can point him out." The smile on his face was anything but friendly. "Then I'll deal with him."

She shivered at the implied threat in his voice. "I didn't see him."

"Then how can you be sure it was a seaman?"

"The smell."

"The smell?"

"Yes." She shifted under the blanket, trying to find a more comfortable position. Her entire body felt bruised. "Sailors have their own unique odor, and unless you have passengers who go similar lengths of time without bathing and spend the majority of that time in the salty air, it was a sailor."

He didn't believe her. She could see it in his eyes.

"I know sailors. I've been around them all my life."

He still looked unconvinced. "Was he drunk?"

Remembering the man's brute strength and steadiness on his feet, she shivered and shook her head. "No. I don't think so."

"I guess you could tell that by his smell, too?"

She glared at Drake. "As a matter of fact, his breath was

too awful to have recently been cleansed with any sort of spirits."

He shook his head. "It doesn't make sense. Thea, every seaman on this ship knows that it's worth his life to attack a female passenger. Even drunk, most of them would never think of it, much less act on the impulse."

"Why isn't it worth his life to attack a man?"

Drake looked at her as if she had lost her mind. "He would have no reason to attack a man."

"Well, I didn't think he had any reason to attack me either." She moved again. There was simply no comfortable position. "Imagine wanting to throw a passenger overboard. He must be mad."

Drake grabbed her shoulders in a painful grip. "He tried to throw you overboard?"

"I have enough bruises from tonight's adventure. You needn't add to them."

He immediately loosened his hold, but he didn't release her. "Explain."

She nodded and began with the villain accosting her from behind, continuing until she had told Drake everything.

"He said something about fighting with the sharks and dragged me toward the side of the ship." She didn't realize she was crying until she tasted the salt of tears on her lips.

Drake brushed her cheeks with gentle fingers. "I don't understand."

"I don't either."

Although now that she had gone over the events again, she couldn't help wondering if this incident and the accident at Merewether Shipping were related. She could not afford to dismiss it as coincidence. Since writing the letter to the London office regarding the discrepancies in the ledgers, she'd had two nearly fatal experiences. Her instincts were screaming that the incidents had something to do with her investigation.

"You know something." His grip tightened. "Bloody hell. What is it?"

She winced and his fingers loosened again. This time he caressed her arms. "Sore?"

"Yes. I feel as if I've been tossed about in a runaway carriage."

"You have experience being knocked around in runaway carriages?" A quizzical smile tilted the corner of his lips.

"Well, yes, actually. When I was fourteen. One of Jacob's sons decided to play a trick on me and put a thorn under the harness of the horse when I was learning to take the leads."

"What happened to Jacob's son?"

"I couldn't say for certain, but he didn't sit in my presence for several days."

Drake's dark eyes glinted with amusement and she leaned into him, relaxing in the strength of his embrace. She felt safe.

"Don't you think it strange that you've had two near misses so recently?" His words, echoing her own thoughts, startled her. "Tell me what you know about what happened tonight."

She wasn't sure how to say what needed to be told, so she stalled while trying to marshal her thoughts. "I'm sure the villain who attacked me tonight was nowhere near the warehouse when that barrel fell down."

Drake remained silent, his hand making a circular motion on her back. His silence wasn't the relaxed, accepting kind, however. She felt that with every rhythmic caress on her back, he was commanding her to tell him the entire story. She didn't want to. He already thought she needed a keeper and she had no intention of allowing him to hinder her investigation. He had no right to, of course, but she wasn't a fool enough to think that would stop him.

"I already know about your abolitionist activities."

How could he? No one knew that she helped runaway slaves escape the island on Merewether ships. Not even Uncle Ashby.

"What do you mean?"

"Jacob told me how vocal you are with your beliefs on the subject."

Oh, that.

She smiled against his shoulder, breathing in the spicy scent of him. "That's neither here nor there. Of course, I'm vocal about it. Slavery is an abomination that England should never have had any part in and should abolish now. Passing laws to outlaw the slave trade is not enough."

He surprised her with his ready agreement. "You're right. However, that is a fight you must leave to the lawmakers."

She pulled away from his arms. "No, it isn't. Every citizen of our Great Nation should take up the cause until the powerful few who have made their fortunes on the deaths and forced labor of their fellow man are made to stop."

"Your opinion is not a popular one in England and even less so on the Islands."

"It's not my opinion. It's the truth. Right is right and slavery is wrong."

"Bloody hell. No wonder someone tried to throw you overboard."

She was incensed. "I thought you agreed with me."

"That doesn't mean I agree that you should risk your neck spouting off about the subject to everyone you meet."

She knew it. If he thought her discussing her beliefs on the moral cowardice of slavery was risky, he would go wild if he discovered she was conducting an investigation into thievery.

"I don't lecture everyone I meet." When he raised his brows in disbelief, she shrugged. "Just everyone who needs it."

"Who have you lectured on the ship?"

He thought she had offended someone on board enough

for them to try to kill her? "I've been sick in my cabin most of the time. I've hardly talked to anyone."

His tense muscles relaxed a bit.

"I probably said something to Lady Boyle on the subject, but she's your aunt and not likely to do me harm."

"Naturally."

She smiled at his sardonic tone. "Well, then there was the steward. He made a comment regarding Africans I had to set him straight on."

"What comment?"

"It's not important."

He frowned. "Who else is hardly anyone?"

"I may have mentioned abolition at dinner last evening."

He looked confused for a minute.

"After you left. And then there was that nasty gentleman in the passenger parlor. He's a plantation owner and went on about intelligence differences and one race serving another. I argued most vehemently with him, but I don't think he was convinced. He left the parlor in a huff."

Drake admired the fact that she could route a man, but didn't like the pattern she had set. The woman was a menace to herself and didn't realize it. "Who was the man?"

"Why?"

"I want to talk to him."

"I told you that my attacker was a sailor."

She had and she'd made a good case for it, even if he had acted disbelieving at the time. "There is a greater motivator than whiskey for villainous behavior. Money."

Her eyes widened. "Oh."

"Now, tell me the plantation owner's name."

"I don't know it. Lady Boyle would know, though. She appeared to be somewhat acquainted with him. He plays whist."

Drake nodded. His aunt was an avid card player, and if the man did indeed indulge in the occasional hand of whist, she would know him.

"I'll ask her." He stood up to leave.

He wanted to ask the first mate if he'd had any luck finding the attacker. Drake had his doubts, but he wanted to know anyway. Turning the lamp down to a faint glow, he then headed toward the door.

"Where are you going?"

He turned back toward her. "To ask the first mate what he found."

Frowning, she said, "I'm sure the villain got away."

He studied her. "You need your rest. I'll let you know my progress tomorrow."

"Do you need to leave now? I'm not at all tired and we should discuss strategy."

He saw the lie in her expressive blue eyes. She had barely stifled a yawn a moment ago and her eyelids drooped with weariness.

"Would you feel better if I posted a guard outside your door?"

She looked horrified. "No."

"Why not?"

Dealing with the female of his species was often confusing, but Thea was incomprehensible.

"It would be embarrassing. Besides, Melly would want to know why he was there."

"Then you would tell her."

She shook her head. "No."

"No?"

"You must see that if we tell her about my little adventure tonight, she would be upset. She would probably stop drinking your ginger tea to prevent me from going out again while she slept. Then her seasickness would come back. We mustn't breathe a word to her."

"Are you going to go on any more walks alone at night?"

She shuddered and he knew that whatever else had happened tonight, Thea's encounter with her attacker had scared her deeply. *"No."*

"Then I won't tell her. But don't you think she'll notice the bruises when she dresses you?"

"I started dressing myself a long time ago."

He shook his head. In many ways, Thea acted like any other English lady he had ever met, but she wasn't. She was unique. His mother required a maid to help her dress, shop, and do all sorts of things Thea was accustomed to doing for herself.

"Very well. I will swear the first mate and captain to secrecy. That will help in the investigation as well. We needn't tip our hand to the villain."

Her head bobbed up and down in agreement. "Just so. Let him think he is safe from detection. Perhaps then he'll try again, and next time I'll be ready for him."

Bloody hell. "He isn't going to try again because you aren't going to be alone again."

"Not at night, no, but during the daytime it would be just the thing. We will lure him out of hiding and nab him."

Is this what she meant by discussing strategy? Setting herself up as bait?

He stalked over to the bed and leaned over her with one thought on his mind, to put a stop to her nonsensical notion. *"No."*

Her lips parted, but she didn't argue as he had expected.

Instead, her brilliant blue gaze became fixed on his lips as if mesmerized. Her eyes glazed over with desire, and all thought of the argument fled his mind. He wanted her lips and he took them, the desire that had been building in him since he first met her exploding in a sudden conflagration of need.

THEA LOCKED HER ARMS BEHIND HIS NECK, AND RE-turned Drake's voracious kiss with all the enthusiasm at her disposal. Thrilled at the feel of his mouth on her own, she savored each sensation. His mouth tasted incredible, unlike anything she had ever experienced, and she wanted to go on tasting it forever.

She tunneled her fingers into his dark hair and relished the feel of the silky strands against her fingers. She could not remember touching another person's hair, could not remember a time when she had wanted to, but this intimacy with Drake felt so right and so very, very good. His tongue probed her mouth with expert thrusts that sent shivering awareness below her waist. She could no more help rocking against him than she could stifle the involuntary moans emanating from her.

He groaned, the sound coming from deep in his throat. Suddenly her nightgown ripped and she felt the night air against her breast. She shivered with both longing and cold, but the chill did not last long as he cupped her breast in one hot hand.

Moaning, she pushed herself against his palm. It felt wonderful.

He tore his lips from hers. "You like that, don't you?" He tugged on her nipple between his thumb and forefinger.

"It's heavenly. Don't you dare stop!"

He laughed, the sound strained. "*Bloody hell,* Thea, you aren't like any other woman I have ever known."

Cold fingers of dread snuffed her rising desire. What did he mean? "Do I disgust you with my forwardness?"

He pulled away from her until their eyes met. Gripping her chin, he forced her to maintain eye contact. "You delight me."

"But you have ignored me for *days*."

A harsh laugh escaped him. "I have tried to save you from myself."

"You're worried about my reputation, aren't you?" *She knew it*.

"Aren't you?"

She shrugged. "Not really. But it occurs to me that you may feel that you have compromised me one way and an-other."

He looked down at her exposed breast and the dark, masculine fingers resting against it and then back up at her face. She felt her cheeks heat.

"It may have escaped your notice, but I *have* compro-mised you."

She shook her head as far as his restraining hand would allow. "Oh no, you haven't. No one need know about this."

"I know about it."

"Well, yes, but no one else need be the wiser."

"Everyone on the bloody ship already thinks I'm shar-ing your bed."

"This is about that conversation I overheard between you and Lady Boyle isn't it?"

"What conversation?"

"The one where she told you that you had to marry me to save my reputation."

He frowned at her. "I thought you were asleep."

She met his gaze defiantly. "Well, I wasn't. The thing is, Drake, I don't care about my reputation, so you don't need to worry about ruining it."

"You cannot attend the Season if no one will receive you." He spoke as if to a dull-witted child.

"I know that."

"Then your reputation is of utmost importance."

She was finished discussing the paltry subject. If he was determined not to understand, she wasn't going to force the issue. She wanted to experience more of what he made her feel.

Running her fingers down his neck, she tried to look al-luring. "Kiss me again."

It must have worked because he groaned and did just that. He also moved his hand on her breast, squeezing her in the most delicious way, and she sighed with pleasure. She wanted this more than she wanted a Season, more than she had ever wanted anything in her life.

He made her feel things, and not just physical things. When she was with him, she did not feel alone as she had since her mother's death. When he touched her, she felt connected to him in a way that, in her secret heart, she had always longed for.

Drake made her feel like a woman without making her feel weak. He made her feel beautiful and desirable. How could she not want his touch?

She started unbuttoning his shirt and noticed for the first time that he wore no neckcloth. She got his shirt open and skimmed her fingers over his bare chest, noticing a sprinkling of dark hair across his chest. It felt courser than the hair on his head and she skimmed lower to explore this new discovery.

He made an inarticulate sound and grabbed her wrist. "No."

"I want to touch you."

Rather than argue, he flipped her on her back and came down on top of her. Locking his lower body against hers, he effectively prevented her questing fingers from going lower. She would have protested, but the delicious sensations she experienced as the hardness of his body rocked against her most intimate place swamped her senses. She arched her back to increase the sensations, and he plunged his tongue more deeply into her mouth.

He matched the rocking motions of his hips with thrusts from his tongue. Feelings spiraled within her. She rubbed her bared breasts against the hair on his chest and nearly fainted from the sensation it evoked. How had she lived three and twenty years without ever feeling remotely like this?

The tension inside her grew and grew, while the pleasure

increased to unbearable proportions as everything coalesced inside her. Her body seemed to contract and expand all at once, with something like explosions going off inside her.

She may have screamed. She could not tell with his mouth devouring hers. Her entire body went stiff down to her pinky toes as the ecstasy gripped her. Then her muscles all relaxed at once and she went completely limp beneath him. He slowed the rhythm of his rocking hips until he was eventually still. His mouth withdrew from hers and rained kisses along her cheek, jawline, and down her neck.

"I am surprised that wives ever allow their husbands to leave the bedroom, as this is undoubtedly one of the few benefits of marriage," she whispered, incapable of speaking in a normal tone after what she had just been through.

He shouted with laughter and Melly snored loudly, mumbling something in her sleep. They turned to look at the sleeping maid then back at each other.

"I forgot she was there." Drake's voice held astonishment.

"I did, too."

He jumped off her as if burned, leaving her more bereft than she thought possible. "We could have . . . I almost . . ."

She cocked her head to one side. "What?"

His glare was at complete odds with the passion they had so recently shared. "Damn it, woman. I almost made love to you in the same room as your sleeping maid."

She was confused. "Wasn't that making love?"

He stared at her, his brown gaze disbelieving. "How can you be so bloody innocent?"

She felt as if he'd insulted her, but wasn't certain how. Surely innocence was not a fault. "I assure you, had I met a man like you before, I wouldn't be."

"Well, it's a good thing you didn't."

"Why?"

"I would have been obliged to kill him."

He spoke with too much conviction to be jesting. Something inside her warmed at the thought that he wanted no one else to touch her. Close behind the warmth came fear. Is this how her father had been with her mother? Possessive?

Yet even now there was a marked difference. Drake did not say he would kill her, or even hate her. He said that he would kill the man.

She sighed. It was all very confusing. Much more so than contracts and ledgers, even ledgers that did not balance.

He walked over to the chest and pulled out a nightrail, his big, very male body unlike any Thea had ever seen. Returning to her, he laid it on the bed and then started tugging at the ripped gown she wore.

She slapped his hand away. "What are you doing?"

"Unless you want your maid to know exactly how you spent the night, you had better put on a new sleeping gown."

"I can dress myself."

His roguish smile surprised her. "I know, but I will like helping."

"Oh." This passion business had much more to it than she had originally thought. "Very well."

She put her arms out, to make it easier for him to pull the gown off. He laughed.

She frowned up at him, feeling at a disadvantage. "What?"

"You look like a small child about to be dressed."

She was about to be dressed. How was she supposed to look?

He pulled her gown off and stilled. She looked up and sucked in her breath at the heat in his eyes.

"Perhaps you should finish the task," he rasped, stepping away from the bed with the white lawn of her ripped gown foaming over his muscular forearm.

She shrugged into the new gown and wiggled until it decently covered her and then turned her gaze back to Drake.

He looked pained and out of sorts.

Perhaps she hadn't pleased him as much as he had pleased her. How was a lady supposed to find such a thing out? Sucking her bottom lip between her teeth, she thought how best to phrase her inquiry. Bluntness usually worked admirably.

"Um, Drake—"

"Surely after the intimacy we have just shared, you could call me by my first name," he said, interrupting her.

What difference did it make what she called him? She had more pressing things on her mind. "You may be right, but that's not important right now."

"And what is important?" he asked, his tone sardonic.

"Did I please you?" She bit her lower lip, waiting for this answer.

His dark molasses eyes warmed. "Ah, Thea . . ." He reached out and touched her cheek. "You pleased me more than I can say, but if you are asking whether or not I found completion, the answer is no."

"Oh." How was she supposed to interpret that response? She drew her knees up to her chest. "I'd like to complete you." She wanted him to feel the same overwhelming sense of rightness she did at that moment.

"I want that very much, too, but now is not the time." He leaned down and kissed her softly, first on her forehead, and then tilting her face up with his forefinger under her chin, he pressed a gentle salute to her mouth. "Good night, Thea."

"Good night."

She watched him walk out of the room, her body still pulsing from what he had made her feel. "You won't ignore me again, will you?"

He spoke without turning around. "No."

She smiled. "Good."

He left, closing the door behind him. It wasn't until she heard the key turning in the lock that she realized he had taken it with him. She jumped up and ran to the door. She shook it.

She put her mouth near the doorjamb. "Pierson?" she whispered. Then more loudly, "Drake, *come back here.*"

The only answer was the sound of receding footfalls.

Sacré bleu. The dratted man had locked her in.

Seven

*Lady Upworth has friends traveling to the West Indies:
Mr. and Mrs. Merewether. He has to leave England for
his health and has decided to open a shipping office in
the Islands. Lady Upworth has made arrangements for
Thea and me to travel with them. Melly, that paragon
among maids, has agreed to accompany us. I have put
off the inevitable long enough. I tried to wait one more
Season with the hope of seeing my son when Langley
brought him to Town, but Lady Upworth has informed
me that Jared is to be left at Langley Hall this Season.
His nurse thinks it is best.*

April 3, 1799
Journal of Anna Selwyn, Countess of Langley

DRAKE SMILED AS HE REMEMBERED THE SOUND
of Thea's furious voice calling to him through the
locked door.

He'd returned in the morning and unlocked it before her
maid had woken. No one would be the wiser about their activities the night before . . . except him. He hadn't liked

locking her in her cabin, but short of standing outside the door all night long, he hadn't known how else to ensure her safety.

She was too reckless by half. She didn't even know enough to avoid the passion that sizzled between them whenever they touched.

She was such an innocent—although after last night, not quite so. Memories of how she had shivered in his arms made his body grow taut and hard. They were only three days from port. He could keep a rein on his need until then. Once they were in London, he would make arrangements for a wedding by special license. He would not use her and discard her as his father had done to his mother.

Thea would undoubtedly argue at first, but after the events of the previous evening, even she had to realize they must be married. He knew she liked her independence, but she would grow accustomed to marriage. After all, as she herself had pointed out, it did have some benefits.

He reached Thea's door and knocked, expecting Melly to answer. Instead, Thea opened the door. She looked beautiful in a bright yellow gown. Her hair was dressed loosely and he had the impression that a few well-placed tugs and it would all come tumbling down in one silken mass.

"Don't look at me like that," she snapped.

"Like what?"

"Like you want to touch me."

"Why not?"

"I'm angry with you. Do not tell me you did not expect such a reaction."

He sighed. "About last night."

"Yes."

"I will apologize if you wish it." She had been so free the night before, but some womanly self-preservation must have finally asserted itself.

He would prefer to have this conversation in private. He edged into the room, and surprisingly, she did not object.

She turned to face him, shutting the door behind her. "Indeed, I do. I'll have your promise it will not happen again."

"I cannot make that promise."

She glared at him. "I must insist."

His frustration finally erupted over his desire to be patient and understanding with the clearly skittish female. "Bloody hell, Thea, do you truly believe after what happened last night that I can promise not to touch you again? I'm flint to your tinder and vice versa. It would be a promise I couldn't keep and I cannot, in honor, make it."

She stared at him as if he'd gone mad. "What are you talking about? I did not ask for your promise not to touch me again. In fact, I clearly remember you promising not to ignore me in future."

She would drive him daft. "What the hell are you prattling about? I thought you wanted me to apologize for last night."

"I do." She crossed her arms under her chest and shot blue fire at him from narrowed eyes. "I will not be locked in my room like a naughty child, and I do not care if you are the owner of this ship."

He started to laugh. He couldn't help it. She never said or did what he expected.

Her frown turned deadly. "Do not laugh at me, sir."

He pulled her toward him and kissed her soundly on the mouth before setting her away again. "I will try not to, but Thea, you do please me. I will also strike a bargain with you. I won't lock you in if you give me your word of honor that you will not attempt to lure your attacker and will not leave your cabin unless you are escorted."

"Are you saying that if I don't make this agreement, you will imprison me in my cabin?" She sounded outraged.

He shrugged and let her draw her own conclusions.

"Oh, very well." She wasn't happy about giving in. "It *was* a sound plan."

"It was not. Do I have your word of honor?"

She looked at him quizzically. "You would trust it?"

He didn't hesitate. "Yes."

"Then you have it. Now, regarding the other matter."

Wariness filled him. "Yes?"

"What did you learn from the first mate?"

Relieved that she was discussing her misfortune and not their passionate interlude, he relaxed. "Not a bloody thing."

"If we don't lure out the villain, we may never find him."

"No."

She bit her lip, her agitation palpable. "But Drake—"

"You gave your word."

"And I will keep it, but there must be something we can do."

"The first mate is asking if anyone saw a seaman leave quarters last night around the time you were attacked."

"Good, but is that enough?"

"It will have to do for now." He would not allow her to be put at risk.

She looked at him with those startlingly blue eyes and he wondered what she was thinking. No doubt she was frustrated he could not do more to find her attacker.

"I should like very much to learn how to give you the wonderful feelings you evoked in me last night."

The effect of her words on his body was instantaneous. He wanted to toss her on the neatly made bunk and muss both her and the covers. However, he wouldn't, *couldn't* do it to a woman who spoke like a mistress, but blushed like a virgin.

He extended his arm to her. "Although I find your interest in that area most gratifying, it will have to wait, my dear. My aunt is expecting us for a game of cards."

Her face fell. "Not whist. I'm terrible at that game. And your aunt is a shark."

"I'm afraid so."

"Very well, but do not think you can fob me off so easily regarding the other matter. You have given me your word, and your honor demands that you keep it." She put her hand through the crook of his arm.

He wanted to laugh at the bossy bit of goods, demanding that he teach her more of passion. He managed to maintain a straight face, however. He had never had the urge to smile, much less laugh, so much in his entire thirty years as he did in one hour of Thea's company.

He laid his hand over hers and squeezed. "My honor is very important to me."

She nodded. "Just so."

THE WIND WHIPPED THEA'S HAIR AS SHE STOOD AGAINST the rail, looking out over the gray waters of the Atlantic Ocean. Shielding her eyes from the wind, she lifted her gaze to the sky and watched a lone seagull dip and soar in its flight.

"Are we really that close to port?"

Drake, who stood beside her at the rail, nodded. "We'll reach Liverpool two days ahead of the contract."

She smiled at the satisfaction in his voice. She turned away from the soaring bird and focused on Drake. "Have you had any luck in identifying the blackhearted sailor who tried to toss me into the ocean?"

The satisfaction faded from his expression.

She shouldn't have said anything. He would have told her if he had, and now she had ruined this perfectly marvelous moment alone with him. They got precious few of them. The closer the *Golden Dragon* got to port, the busier he became with ship business.

Thea could not blame him for the lack of opportunity to explore their attraction. He simply did not have the time. She sighed. It was not a comforting thought. Soon, they would go their separate ways and the likelihood of her seeing him again was very small. Drake had his business to run, and she had her thief to find.

The thought of their imminent separation swept through her like the chilly wind until her heart was as cold as the skin of her arms had been before Drake insisted she wear his coat. She pulled the blue superfine closer about her and covertly sniffed his fragrance. She wanted a memory to take with her when she left, more than a stolen moment of passion with her maid sleeping in the next bed. Something to warm her heart in the future when loneliness and her work were all that she had to cling to.

She had made arrangements. She just hoped he would not think her too bold.

She realized that while she had been woolgathering, he had been speaking and she'd missed all of what he had said. "I'm sorry. My mind was elsewhere. What did you say?"

His brows drew together in an expression of irritation that she had begun to find quite endearing. "What could be more important than finding the man who tried to harm you?"

Plotting to be with the man whom she feared she was coming to love. Terrified at the very thought, she refused to entertain it. Love weakened women. It made them vulnerable to men who would hurt them and treat them with scorn as her father had done to her mother.

"What is the matter? You've gone green around the gills again. Do you need some ginger tea?"

She warmed under Drake's concern. He was a stubborn man. Perhaps more like her father than she wanted to believe, but he had a tender heart under his unbending pride and honor.

"Nothing. Please repeat what you said."

"I said that we haven't had one bloody lead that has gone anywhere. None of the sailors on watch or in quarters saw anything peculiar."

"I suppose the men in quarters were sleeping rather soundly." The combination of their daily rum rations and hard labor undoubtedly provided for very sound sleep indeed.

"Yes." His voice was clipped.

She trailed her hand down his arm. "Don't be angry. Soon we'll be in port and the danger will be past."

"That's not what my instincts are telling me."

Wary, she pulled her hand away from him and turned, grasping the rail with cold fingers. "Do not let your imagination run away with you."

"My instincts are not fantasy. What's more, you know something that you aren't telling me."

She gripped the rail more tightly, tempted to tell him everything. He would insist on taking over the investigation, or helping her at the very least. The prospect of seeing more of him, even at the cost of some of her independence, tantalized her. But it would not be fair to Drake. She could not trade upon his chivalrous nature.

Feigning a lightness she did not feel, she pointed to the gull, now a tiny speck in the sky. "It's amazing to me that although the ocean looks as vast as it ever did, we are close enough to land for birds to fly above us."

Strong fingers closed over her wrist and pulled so that she found herself against his hard chest. "Tell me."

His eyes were almost black in their intensity. She blinked, trying to regain her equilibrium.

"You must let me go. Think of my reputation." He was usually so worried about how things looked.

"I'll deal with your reputation. Tell me what you know."

"I don't know who tried to push me overboard."

"But you do know something. You must tell me. Once we reach port, the blackguard will get away."

She didn't want to talk about her attacker. She wanted to kiss Drake. She wanted to feel the lips set in such a hard line soften and open for her exploring tongue. She tried to blink away her wanton thoughts, but they persisted. Now was not the time. She would not allow Drake to get into any more trouble with Lady Boyle. Spending time in the older lady's company had convinced Thea that although Drake seemed to care little for the opinions of outsiders, his family meant a great deal to him.

"Drake?"

"What?"

"Why is it so important for you to reach port in time?"

"I told you."

"Yes, but I don't understand. You don't care what others think, and yet you are obsessed with not disappointing your investors." Wind blew against her, pressing the thin muslin of her gown against her legs. She shivered. "It makes no sense."

He slid his hand around to her back and began to rub it, warming her. She ached to return the caress, and so much more. Yet she doubted he even realized he was touching her. He looked as if his mind was somewhere far off.

"Some of the investors are my friends."

"Yes." There was that, and he'd mentioned it before, but his insistence went deeper. "There's more to it, though. Isn't there?"

Almost reluctantly, he nodded. "Yes."

"Tell me." She turned his words back on him.

"It's my father."

She felt shocked by his answer. "I don't understand. Lady Boyle said your father has never recognized you. Are you telling me he has invested in this shipping venture?"

His arms tightened around her. "My aunt is a gossip."

"Yes, but that is neither here nor there." She patted his chest to soothe him. "What does your father have to do with this shipping venture?"

"He gave my mother a substantial settlement for me when I reached my majority."

"But wouldn't he have to acknowledge you as his son to have done that?"

Drake's laugh was tinged with bitterness. "No. Things can be done in very civilized ways in the *ton*, without ever acknowledging one's mistakes."

"I don't understand."

"He made it an anonymous gift through a third party. I used it to buy my first ship."

"Oh." She was still confused.

"When I had made enough money to repay the entire amount, I did so."

"That must have made your father angry." She still didn't understand what that had to do with the shipping venture.

Drake shrugged. "I have no idea. We have never spoken."

"You have never even spoken to your father? But surely you must attend some of the same functions."

"Yes. We even belong to the same club. My grandfather is also a member." He rested his chin on top of her head. "I want my father to see my success and regret his refusal to acknowledge my existence."

She slipped her arms around his waist and squeezed him. She wanted to make the pain in his voice disappear. This was a side of Drake that she had never seen, a vulnerability that she had not imagined existed. It frightened her. The knowledge that his honor and pride hid this deep need for approval battered against her already shaky defenses. Each moment she spent with him enmeshed her more firmly in feelings she did not want.

"I've never spoken to my father either." She could not believe she'd said the words.

Her secret had been locked inside for so long that she never even spoke of her father or brother to the Merewethers. The only person who mentioned them was Lady Upworth in her letters. Even now, she wasn't prepared to tell everything, but an urge so deep she couldn't deny it prompted her to tell Drake about her father.

He pulled back until their eyes met. "I thought your parents were dead."

"My mother died when I was thirteen. I've never met my father."

Drake stared at her. "You're a natural child as well?"

She shook her head. "My parents were married, but my father behaved so despicably toward my mother that she ran away with me when I was a baby."

"He never found her?"

"He never looked."

"How can you know?"

"A mutual friend wrote often."

Drake felt as if he had taken a blow from Gentleman Jackson himself. Thea's admission staggered him. He wanted to hear more and he wanted to be alone to do it. He pulled away, took her hand in his, and led her toward his cabin.

"Where are we going?"

"Someplace we can talk without the fear of interruption."

He scanned the deck when they reached his cabin and he was relieved to see that it was empty. Taking an unattached female into his room would not go over well with his aunt, or any of the other dowagers on board.

He unlocked his door and pulled Thea inside. Once he had shut the door, he motioned for her to take a seat. She didn't have many options. His cabin was sparse compared to hers. There was one small bunk, a chair, and a very small table bolted to the floor. She chose to sit on the edge of the bunk. Light filtered in through the portal and played across the too serious features of her beautiful face, highlighting the chestnut silkiness of her hair.

Her bright skirts pooled around her feet and she gripped the mattress with both hands. She bent her head as if she found something on the floor of particular interest. "I suppose you want the full story."

Hell yes. He lifted her chin with his hand and met her eyes. "Only if you want to tell it."

She sucked in a breath and then softly let it out. "When my mother was in her fourth month of pregnancy, my father insisted she accompany him to a ball. She wanted to go into confinement in the country, but appearances were important to him and some very influential members of the *ton* were throwing the ball. Mama loved him, so she went. She became overheated after dancing a Scottish reel and she went out into the gardens. A man who had courted her along with my father followed her out of the ballroom."

When Thea stopped talking, Drake sat down next to her and pulled her hand into his. Her fingers were like ice. "You don't have to tell me any more."

"No. I want to tell you." She looked up at him and her eyes had the depth of the sea they sailed upon.

"The man who followed Mama was a rake. He forced his attentions on her, holding her against her will and kissing her. My father came upon them. He was furious. He reviled my mother and challenged the rake to a duel." She tightened her fingers in his. "They never fought the duel. The other man came to my father and promised on his word as a gentleman that my mother had approached him. He apologized to my father and the matter was settled."

She sighed. "At least between the two men. My father never forgave my mother and refused to believe her version of the events. He is a very hard, unbending man."

Drake thought his father and hers had something in common.

"He sent my mother to live in the country until she gave birth. He stormed into the room and tore her baby from her arms and left, promising she would never see her child again."

"So she kidnapped you and ran away."

A strange expression entered her eyes at his statement,

but she didn't deny it. Perhaps she did not like to think of what her mother had done as kidnapping.

"Is that why you have never returned to England?"

"Yes."

"Are you going to see your father?"

"No. I never want to see my father or have anything to do with him. He destroyed our family with his mistrust and harshness. He has no place in my heart."

Drake lowered his mouth until it was almost touching hers. "What about me? Do I have a place in your heart?"

He didn't understand the look of fear that came into her eyes. "Please, let us talk no more of this."

He wanted her to admit that she was coming to care for him, but the desperation in her voice swayed him. "Very well. There are more interesting things to do with our lips than to talk."

The kiss consumed them both. One moment they were sitting side by side on the edge of his narrow bed and the next he had her beneath him, his tongue deep in her mouth. She moaned.

He fisted his hands in her hair, and kissed her with all the uncontrollable desire that overtook him every time they touched.

She locked her arms around his back, pulling him closer until he wondered how she could breathe with his weight covering the length of her.

She tasted sweet. Like the ginger candy his grandfather's cook used to make at Christmastime. He begged the cook for more and she always warned him he'd get sick of it, but he never did. Thea was the same. He wanted her constantly, and the few stolen moments when he could actually touch and taste her only whetted his appetite for more.

The bells rang for the second watch.

He groaned and pulled his lips from hers. "Thea, we must stop. My aunt is expecting you for tea."

"I sent Melly to your aunt with my apologies. I told her I needed to prepare for arrival in port."

Since she had taken less than two hours to prepare for the entire journey, he knew her excuse was a ruse.

She smiled up at him, her eyes full of feminine mystery. "Melly is spending the next few hours with friends she has made aboard ship. Please, Drake, make love to me."

He had meant to wait until after they were wed to teach her more of passion, but all of his good intentions went up in the bonfire he saw in Thea's eyes. She was as unpredictable as the wind and he found the desire to sail her course irresistible.

Eight

The Merewethers are the kindest people. They insist that Thea and I make our home with them. Ruth adores children and has always been disappointed that she never conceived. Ashby has asked me to stay as a favor to his wife, both because Thea brings her so much joy and because he feels badly that Ruth has left all of her English friends behind to travel to this tiny island with him.

September 7, 1799
Journal of Anna Selwyn, Countess of Langley

DRAKE STOOD UP AND THEA'S HEART CRACKED with desolation. He was going to say no. Averting her gaze, she fought to hide her feelings of mortification at his rejection from him.

The sound of fabric sliding against fabric drew her attention. He was in the act of removing his cravat. He had begun unbuttoning his waistcoat before she realized the significance of his actions.

He was going to make love to her.

She wanted to say something, anything to break the

expectant silence now filling the room. She opened her mouth to speak, but nothing would come out. Her throat felt locked in rigidity as she watched the two sections of his waistcoat separate to reveal the fine lawn of his shirt.

She should be doing something. Not just sitting there like a child watching a puppet show. She pushed herself off the bed and started to undo the tapes of her gown.

"Don't."

She stopped moving at the harsh sound of his voice. She stared at him. Had she misunderstood?

He pulled her to him, an undecipherable emotion in his eyes. "I want to undress you."

"All right." She was trembling so much, she doubted she could finish the task herself anyway.

She waited while he removed everything but his smalls. They tented away from his body where he bulged in arousal, and she felt her first tremor of trepidation. Perhaps the snug fabric overaccentuated his endowment.

He brushed her cheek. She shifted her gaze to his face. The corner of his mouth tipped slightly, and she blushed as she realized that he had noticed her preoccupation with him.

"We are different, but you have nothing to fear."

She expelled the breath she hadn't realized she was holding. "Yes." Very different. Thinking of their previous encounter, she said, "This difference intrigues me."

His expression blossomed into a full-blown smile. "It intrigues me as well."

The smile faded from his face, and his eyes took on an intensity that sent her pulse jumping. He stepped forward and slowly, oh so slowly, removed the pins from her hair. She felt the weight of it as the heavy mass fell around her shoulders and settled against her back.

He touched it, his expression reverent. "Your hair is so beautiful. I have dreamed of seeing you with it hanging loose about your tempting, naked body."

Her breath hitched in her throat. "You dreamed about me?"

"A great deal."

"Oh." Fascinating. "What else have you dreamed?"

He smiled. "I'll show you."

She shivered, but not from cold. She wanted him to show her. She also wanted to touch him. She extended her hand and trailed her fingers down his chest.

He caught her hand.

"I want you. I need to touch you."

"Not yet." He pulled her toward him until their bodies were pressed together.

She slid her hands around to caress the muscled planes of his back. The feel of his naked skin, warm under her touch, sent a tremor through her.

He leaned down and nuzzled her neck through her hair. "You smell so good, Thea. It's as if you carry your island fragrance with you." She felt his hands at work on the tapes of her gown. They came loose and his fingers slipped inside to caress her through the soft material of her shift. "You are my very own tropical temptation."

She laughed at the notion that a twenty-three-year-old spinster could be something so exotic to a man like Pierson Drake.

He pulled back slightly to meet her gaze. "It's true. You've mesmerized me with your mystery since the moment we met."

"I am quite ordinary." Unlike him. "There is nothing mysterious about me."

He shook his head and his smile beguiled her. "On the contrary. Nothing about you is ordinary. You dress like a proper English lady, but leave off your stockings and corsets."

"It's too hot in the islands to wear stockings, and corsets are bad for a woman's respiration."

He stepped back and pulled her gown down by the sleeves until she stood in her shift before him. His already lambent gaze turned hot as the steam escaping through the fissures of a volcano.

"You speak with the diction and vocabulary of a lady, yet the things that come out of your mouth are far from the typical drivel that passes for a lady's conversation."

"I merely say what is in my mind."

"Precisely." His approval warmed her to her toes. "Since you have not yet been to England, you cannot know how different you are from the typical lady of the *ton*."

All the while they spoke, his hot gaze devoured her and she began to shake in reaction. His hand gently cupped her breast, and she felt as if an effervescent spring had come to life in her most feminine place. Her thighs pressed together of their own volition, and her nipples stung as they hardened against the thin fabric of her shift.

He tugged it down, and she felt her skin heating all over where his gaze touched it. She should have been embarrassed to have him see her like this, but she wasn't. The soft lawn fell in a pool at her feet and she could not move.

His gaze pinned her in place. "You are glorious."

She wanted to tell him that she found his taut hardness very appealing as well, but could not make the words come out as once again her throat refused to work. Everywhere his eyes touched, she felt as if his fingers followed, and yet he had moved to stand a little distance away from her.

"You are all that I could wish for, Thea."

She stared at him, and something in her shifted. He wanted her as desperately as she wanted him—that was obvious—but there was something more. He made himself vulnerable by telling her things she could not make her mouth utter. He did not have to tell her she was glorious, but he had. She sighed. All her life, gentlemen had ignored her and she had been content for them to do so. Yet here stood the handsomest and most fascinating man she had ever met and he claimed that he wanted her.

It was a heady thought, an enticing one.

She threw herself against him. He let out a startled breath and then locked his arms around her. He kissed her until her knees grew weak with it. His hard arousal moved against her belly and she shivered with desire.

"Make love to me, Drake."

He could no more resist the need in her voice than he could stop the tide, but he wondered if she planned to call him Drake when he was buried deep inside her. Or would she finally deign to use his first name?

He swung Thea into his arms and carried her to the small bunk. What he was about to do would be irrevocable. It would change the course of her life, and his, forever. He laid her on the bed and stood above her.

"You must be certain, Thea. We can still turn back."

She met his gaze, hers unflinching. "I do not want to stop. Please, Drake."

That final plea decided him. "I don't either."

He lay down next to her on the narrow bunk. There was barely room for him, and their entire bodies touched from where the side of her breast pressed against his chest to her legs that moved restlessly against his own.

He forced himself into complete stillness. He wanted to savor the feel of her naked body against his. She belonged to him, and when they finally came together, she would know it.

She said his name in impatient demand.

He smiled. "Yes?"

He thought to tease her a little, to heighten the tension. She forestalled him by pulling his head down for a passionate kiss. He gave in to the emotion pulsing through him and

kissed her back with all his pent-up desire made huge by
wanting. Thea moved her hands over him with reckless
abandon. She touched him everywhere, and everywhere
she touched felt like it was on fire. Her body moved restlessly against his.

He cupped her breast, delighting in the weight of the
soft flesh against his palm. He squeezed. He pushed and
pulled, almost drunk with the feel of her under his hand.
She moaned, arching her back in a silent plea for more. He
knew what she needed even if she did not. Bending his
head, he opened his mouth over her already distended nipple.

She nearly came off the bed. *"Drake."*

He stopped suckling and looked up. Her eyes were wide
and dark with need in her flushed face.

"Pierson."

"What?" Her head tossed from side to side in frantic
movement.

"We are making love, Thea. Call me Pierson."

"Pierson," she gasped, grabbing his head with frantic
fingers and pressing his face into her breast. "Don't stop."

He smiled against the generous flesh. "Aye, aye, Little
Captain."

She started to say something, but it turned into another
long-drawn-out moan when he closed his mouth over her
nipple once again. She rocked her hips and he could not resist sliding his hand down her rib cage, over the smooth
skin of her belly, and into the nest of curls at her most feminine place.

She arched toward his hand even as she protested,
"Surely you aren't supposed to touch me there."

He nearly strangled on a laugh. "Surely, I am."

"But, I thought . . ." Whatever she thought went unsaid
as he dipped his fingers into the tight, wet passage.

She groaned. He slid his finger out and back in, loving

the feel of her moist channel. This with Thea was some-thing so unlike matings he had experienced before. Never had he felt this desire to please, this sense of oneness with a woman. He ached to bury himself inside her, but it had to be right. He would make this first time perfect for her, and then she would understand that she belonged to him.

"I didn't know it would be like this."

He smiled at the wonder in her voice. Exploring with his thumb, he found the small button he sought and rubbed it experimentally as he continued the movement of his fin-ger sliding in and out of her rapidly swelling flesh.

Unbelievable pleasure spiraled through Thea as Drake's hand and mouth inflicted exquisite torture upon her body. She rocked her hips in a mindless attempt to assuage the burning ache he stoked with each thrust of his finger. "Please. Don't. Stop."

"Never."

He increased his tempo until she felt her entire body straining toward release. Remembering her other experi-ences in his arms, she could not credit how much more in-tense the sensation when his fingers touched her body skin to skin.

Suddenly her thoughts fragmented until only one re-mained. She wanted to feel him inside her. *"Pierson."*

"What, love?"

"You must finish it. I cannot stand this torment."

He kissed her breast and then stood. She watched in wonder as he pulled off his smalls to reveal his swollen manhood. If his finger had filled her so completely, how was he ever going to fit? She licked her lips. "Um, do you think perhaps there is a small problem with the disparity in our sizes?"

He rejoined her on the bed, this time kneeling between her legs, pushing them apart. She felt at once vulnerable and powerful because she knew that she and she alone was responsible for the look of naked need on his face.

"We will fit, but it will hurt at first, Thea. I know of no way to avoid the pain."

The genuine concern in his voice assuaged her fears as nothing else could have. "Tell me what to do."

He leaned down and she felt his hardness brush against her as his lips covered her own. He kissed her softly and then with increasing passion until she could not help straining against him.

"Yes, that's right, Thea, show me how much you want me."

He fit himself against the entrance to her and pressed forward. It *did* hurt. She bit her lip to keep from crying out.

He stopped. Sweat beaded on his forehead, and his breathing was labored. "Are you okay?"

She nodded, feeling anything but, although she found herself comforted by the genuine care in his tone.

He took a deep breath and expelled it before brushing her cheek with his hand. "It will get better."

Leaning up until he was almost sitting, he tucked his thumb into her nest of curls and gently rubbed her just above where their bodies joined. She relaxed as pleasure overtook the pain once again. He slipped inside some more and stopped when he met the barrier.

He continued his ministrations with his thumb as his other hand again found her breast. He played with her nipple, rolling it between his thumb and forefinger until she thought she would go mad with the wanting.

"Pierson," she panted his name desperately. "I can't stand this. It is *too much*."

She felt the precipice and knew that this time she would not be alone in going over.

Her body tensed as she arched up toward him, pressing him farther into her passage. She felt the pain, but could not give it proper notice as the pleasure threatened to swamp all her senses. She gripped his thighs, needing to feel the solid strength of his muscles beneath her fingers as her mind splintered into a thousand fragmented sensations.

She convulsed and he thrust into her fully. The pain was instantly swallowed up in pleasure as he withdrew and thrust again. As he filled her completely, she fell over the precipice, knowing that when she came to land, he would be there to catch her. She wanted to scream her pleasure, but he leaned forward and locked his lips on hers, thrusting his tongue into the interior of her mouth.

One, two, three more thrusts and then she felt the incredible sensation of him spilling his seed into her. His body went completely rigid as he found his release. His life had just joined with her own. *She could never be whole without him again.* She pushed the thought away, even as it formed in her mind. He thrust twice more, groaning against her mouth as he shuddered each time.

Finally, he collapsed on top of her and they lay like that, panting together as their heartbeats slowed.

He lifted his head and kissed her temple. "Did I hurt you?"

"Yes, a little."

He touched her face, his finger gently following the line of her jaw. "I'm sorry."

She smiled. "I'm not. I had never imagined that there could be such beauty between a man and a woman."

Or that it could alter her so completely. She still feared marriage, but could not help wishing her life could be as linked with his as her spirit was in the joining of their bodies. She wanted more than this stolen time with him. But it was impossible. She did not even know if he planned to go to London from Liverpool. Perhaps she would never see him again. The thought brought unaccustomed tears to her eyes.

He looked at her with grave concern. "What is it?"

She did not know if she could put it into words. She started to cry in earnest. "I was just thinking that once we are in port, I may never see you again." Her words came out stuttered between sobs.

He smiled. The insensitive lout. "That would be most inconvenient. I believe that in the general course of things, husbands are required to see their wives, at least upon occasion."

Her heart nearly stopped at his words. "What do you mean?"

He rolled off her and pulled her into a sitting position on the edge of the bunk. She let out an involuntary gasp. She felt very tender between her legs. He kneeled before her and took her hand. "Thea, will you do me the great honor of becoming my wife?"

Panic overwhelmed her. Marriage? An image of her mother, wasted from fever and dying, swam before Thea's vision. The words Anna had spoken echoed in Thea's mind even as her body still pulsed from Drake's possession.

She spoke as if to the image in her mind. "I can't."

"No?" He shook his head, trying to clear his thoughts. Surely he had misheard.

She looked shocked, almost haunted. "Thank you for the offer, but I am not interested in marriage." The words came out in a toneless whisper.

"Why the bloody hell not?"

She recoiled away from him. "Do not swear at me. I do not feel that I have misrepresented myself in any way. I never once promised marriage."

He stared at her, his anger building as quickly as his passion had. He didn't want to believe that he could have been such a fool. He had been used.

Again.

He had not seen it coming this time any more than the first. Damn it to hell. He would have thought that in ten years, he would have learned something about women. Hadn't she told him her reason for traveling to England was to participate in the Season? A Season meant marriage, preferably to someone both titled and wealthy. Not the bastard son of a father who had not even acknowledged his existence.

He had not been good enough for Deirdre; why had he believed he would be good enough for Thea? Deirdre had also been interested in Drake only as a paramour. Gullible youth that he had been, he had believed she loved him. And he had loved her back with all the wild, uncontrolled emotion of youth. Still, he'd been less of a fool at twenty than he was at thirty. At least then, he'd had the foresight to ask for Deirdre's hand before taking her to his bed. She had made it clear that she expected much more from a husband than a bastard with neither title nor fortune.

Three weeks after turning him down, she had announced her engagement to an aging peer. Drake had felt no satisfaction rejecting her less than subtle hints at a liaison. Nor when she had made it clear that she regretted her choice after he made his fortune. He had merely felt sickened at the lack of honor in a woman he had once believed he loved.

Grabbing Thea's clothes from the floor, he swallowed the bile rising in his throat. He hated how successfully she had manipulated him. He threw her gown and chemise at her. "Get dressed."

She let out a startled yelp and batted the cloth away from her face. She stared at him, her face suddenly colorless. "You're very angry with me."

"I'm angrier with myself." And he was. He chafed against the fact that he had been so easily duped by her innocent sensuality.

She made no move to get dressed, just sat there crushing the bright yellow muslin against her. "Why?"

"I let you use me."

Her eyes widened. "What do you mean?"

"Don't play the naïve gentlewoman with me. You bloody well know what I mean." Deirdre's betrayal had wounded his pride, but Thea's had shattered something deep inside him. He had to get out of the cabin before he disgraced himself and begged her to reconsider. He yanked his clothes on, trying not to notice that he still carried her scent. A few hours on deck would take care of that. Perhaps hard labor would also dull the ache inside. He reached for the door.

"Where are you going?"

Even in a blind rage, he still reacted to the panic in her voice. He turned back, trying to mask his pain with a façade of anger.

"On deck."

"But . . . I thought . . ."

"You thought what? That we'd have time for another tumble before you returned to your cabin and your preparations for leaving? Sorry to disappoint you, but I have things to do."

She flinched and her eyes filled with tears.

Before he gave in to the insane urge to take her in his arms and comfort her, he turned and stalked out of the cabin.

THEA STARED AT THE RECENTLY SLAMMED DOOR OF Drake's stateroom. What had just happened? She had experienced the most beautiful experience of her life and then been dismissed like the contents of a day-old chamber pot. Just because she had said *no* to his marriage proposal. Surely he must realize that after what happened to her mother, Thea was not eager to repeat the same mistake.

Two tears burned their way down her cheeks. Drake was just as hard and autocratic as her father. She had refused to fall in with his plans and so he had rejected her and all that they shared. *Sacré bleu*. Was she an idiot?

She stood up and winced at the pain between her legs and the sticky wetness. She must do something about that, or Melly would know all. She went over to Drake's washstand and made what repairs she could to her person. She dressed and then brushed her hair with Drake's brush.

She stopped midstroke and brought the brush to her nose. Inhaling the scent that had so recently filled her senses, she felt more tears cascade down her cheeks. Resolutely, she pulled the brush through her hair until she had rid herself of most of the tangles. She then pulled it into a tight bun at the nape of her neck. Securing it with pins, she surveyed her image in Drake's shaving mirror.

She looked not a whit different than she had before. But inside, she felt different. She ached, but she rejoiced, too. All of Drake's anger and rejection could not erase the joy she had experienced in his arms. Nor would she ever forget the picture of him kneeling naked before her and asking for her hand in marriage. Not if she lived to be ancient.

She had been tempted. So very tempted to say yes, but his subsequent behavior had proven her caution well founded. Or had it? She knew so little of men and what motivated their hearts. Her father's example overwhelmed all other experiences. She never forgot the pain of her mother's grief, nor watching Anna die of a fever she would not have contracted had she not been forced to flee England.

What would happen if Thea did marry Drake and then disagreed with something he wanted? Would he turn cold and hard as he had after their lovemaking? Worse, would

he one day revile her as her father had done to her
mother?

But even if she did not marry him, she would never be
completely separate from him again. She wondered how
mistresses did it—this sharing of their bodies with first one
man and then another. Thea felt as if part of her would
never be hers again, as if it now belonged to Drake. Perhaps women who sold their bodies lost so much of themselves that it ceased to matter any longer.

Shaking off the depressing thought, she opened Drake's
cabin door a small crack and peeked through it. The deck
appeared empty, so she opened the door completely and
stepped out. She was not ready to return to her cabin, but
she had promised Drake not to go anywhere unescorted
and he had trusted her to keep that promise. Regardless of
what had transpired between them, she would do so.

She had made it to the corridor outside of her room
when she heard footfalls behind her. She turned, expecting
to see the steward, and caught a whiff of the horrible body
odor she had smelled the night of her attack. Without further thought, she screamed long and loud. The sailor coming toward her stopped in midstride. He stared at her as if
she'd gone mad, but she didn't care. She would know that
foul odor anywhere.

She kept screaming and a stateroom door to her left
flew open. A wizened visage peered out. "Eh, what's going
on out here? What's all that racket?"

The sailor turned and ran toward the other end of the
corridor. The old woman muttered something about the
thoughtlessness of the young and slammed her door. Thea
had started toward the open door, but changed her tactic
and ran after the sailor. He mustn't get away.

She rushed out of the corridor and ran straight into a
solid male form. It took Thea only a second to realize that
the man holding her arms and glaring at her was Drake.

"The sailor, he's getting away. I saw him." For a moment, her relief at putting a face to her attacker made her forget her anger at Drake and she grinned. "*I saw him.* It *was* a sailor, too."

"What are you babbling about, Thea?" His harsh voice made it clear that his anger still simmered just below the surface.

She sobered at the realization. "He followed me into the corridor, but I heard someone behind me. When I turned, I smelled him." She tried to pull her arms from Drake's grip. She looked past him, but saw no one. Where had the man gone? "He's getting away. We've got to go after him."

His grip on her tightened. "A sailor was in the corridor with you? Did he try to harm you?"

"No. *No.* He was just there. But it was *him,* Drake. I know it was him. He ran away when the old lady opened her door after I screamed."

"You screamed?"

"Yes. *Sacré bleu.* Do something. Do not just stand there." She tried to shake him, but he was an immovable object.

"I didn't see anyone on deck when I came up."

She frowned over that statement. "I can't explain it. He must have run very quickly. I didn't follow him at first. I tried to go to the lady in the cabin, but she shut her door and I decided to follow him. He had a short head start."

She couldn't seem to control her mouth as words tumbled out willy-nilly.

Finally Drake moved. It was to turn her toward the staterooms. He pushed her through the door, into the corridor. "Go to your cabin. Lock yourself in. Open the door to no one. I will get the captain."

She craned her neck around to see his face. "Don't be ridiculous. How will you know who to look for without me?"

He continued to propel her toward the cabin. "You can describe him to the captain and myself."

She stopped and strained against his hold. "I want to go with you to search. I must ask him some questions." She had to find out who he worked for in order to protect Uncle Ashby.

Drake grabbed her arm and started pulling her toward her cabin again. "You aren't going with me."

His tone of voice suggested she shouldn't argue.

She tried to yank her arm from his. "I *am* going with you. I have a bigger stake in this than you do. We are talking about my safety."

"Aboard my ship, you will obey me."

He stopped in front of her room and pulled a key from his pocket. The arrogant man had gotten one for himself. She wondered what his aunt would think about that. He shoved her through the door quite rudely and turned to go.

She felt fury rise in her. "Is this what marriage to you would be like? You would demand my obedience like a well-trained dog, and when I disagreed, you would man-handle me?"

He stopped and turned to face her. He looked haunted. She felt instant contrition at her words. Which was foolish, indeed. She should be angry with him, but she could not stand the hurt she saw in his eyes.

"We'll never know, will we?"

She shook her head, unable to speak under his pain-filled scrutiny. She extended her hand to touch him and he jerked away as if burned. She sighed.

"I'm sorry. I didn't mean to hurt you."

His face became an emotionless mask. "I will get the captain. He knows every sailor on this ship as well as he knows the rigging."

His cold demeanor unnerved her. How could he talk of her attacker with such calm detachment? Flicking her a glance empty of feeling, he turned again to go.

"*Pierson,* wait. Please."

He stopped, but did not face her.

She didn't know what to say, but she could not leave things as they were. "I need to explain."

He turned slowly and she saw that his mask had slipped. His face wore a savage scowl. "On the contrary. Your actions speak for themselves. A bastard is good enough for a lover, but not good enough for a husband. Unfortunately, it is not a new idea for me. You will pardon me if I do not wish you luck in your hunt for a more suitable *partí* this Season."

She stared at him. "That is what you think? That I would take you to bed, take you into my body, and then search for another gentleman to marry?"

He glared at her. "What would you have me believe? You refused my offer of marriage."

"But not because I believe that I can do better." She twisted her hands together. "It is essential that you believe that."

He grabbed her by the upper arms and pulled her to within inches of his body. She felt his heat emanate toward her, and she longed to burrow against him, to recapture a small measure of the intimacy they had experienced earlier.

"Then. Tell. Me. Why."

She might have been able to refuse if he had not sounded so tortured.

She would not allow him to believe that his father's actions colored her view of him. "I don't want to marry, Drake. Not ever. After what happened to my mother, I will not allow a man to have the power to hurt me like that."

"I would never treat you as your father did your mother."

"How can you be sure? You're used to getting your own way." She pointedly looked around the cabin where he had dragged her.

He glared. "You cannot compare my concern for your safety with your father's baseless suspicions."

She sighed. "You don't understand. You never knew my mother, but losing my . . . me and then my father tore her apart. She grieved always. It was in her eyes, a sadness that tinged every smile. I won't risk losing part of myself that way."

"Not all marriages end like your parents'."

She knew that; she had lived with Uncle Ashby and Aunt Ruth all her life, after all. "Marriage gives men too much power over women. Even so-called good marriages. Aunt Ruth is happy in her own way, but she left all that she knew for Uncle Ashby's sake. The worst part is that he expected her to. She never had a choice. I won't put myself in that position."

"Does she complain about living on the island?"

Thea frowned. "No, but that's not the point."

"Do you think she regrets letting her husband take her from England? Does she want to move back?"

"No, but you are ignoring the real issue here."

"If her happiness is not the issue, what is?"

Confused frustration welled up in Thea. "You're twisting things."

He laid his hand on her cheek. "I'm trying to make you see reason. Marriage is not bondage. I'm sure Merewether would have willingly made the same sacrifice for his wife."

"Society would never expect it."

"Who cares? Society's expectations have nothing to do with marriage between us."

She wished she could believe him, but even if society's expectations did not rule them, the laws of England would. And once she became his wife, he could treat her almost any way he wished with impunity.

Her mind felt muddled with the events of the afternoon and his reasoning.

"We do not have time to discuss this now. My attacker could be getting away as we speak."

Leaning forward, he kissed her firmly on the lips. Then

he stepped back. "You're right. The closer we get to port, the more chance he will jump ship and swim for safety rather than risk being caught."

She gave in to the inevitable. "I'll wait here."

He nodded and then stopped at the door and turned. "We will discuss it, though. I will not let you go."

Nine

There are more English on the island than I expected, both businessmen and plantation owners. However, Ruth and I find the latter unpleasant. We cannot reconcile ourselves to the institution of slavery and I regret that perhaps I have become too vocal in my disapproval. Ashby warns me for my own sake not to go too far, but has never asked me to be quiet for the sake of him and Ruth. So, I am not.

December 3, 1799
Journal of Anna Selwyn, Countess of Langley

THE CAPTAIN LOOKED MORE LIKE LADY UP-worth's description of a dandy than a ship's officer. He wore a carnelian waistcoat, the bright red fabric embroidered with multicolored parrots, and his shirt was an immaculate white lawn topped by a collar much too tall to be comfortable for a man in his position. Even his golden windswept hair looked purposefully casual, rather than unkempt.

He smiled in a most charming manner when Drake

introduced him to Thea, and she could not help smiling
back. "Miss Selwyn, are you certain the man you saw in
your corridor was the same man who attacked you?"

"Absolutely certain." She nodded for emphasis.

"She recognized his smell." Drake moved to stand between her and the ship's officer when he made the comment.

The man gave his charming smile again. "Unfortunately
many of my crew do not avail themselves of the opportunity to bathe, miss. I find it hard to believe you could dis-
tinguish one from the other based on such a consideration."

Thea moved to sit on the edge of her bed, suddenly tired
by the events of the day and the thought that a man had
truly tried to kill her. She didn't have the energy to argue
her certainty that the man she had seen was indeed her attacker. Drake followed her to the bed and sat next to her.
She looked up at him and frowned. Surely he should not
behave so familiarly in front of the other man. Word was
bound to get back to his aunt.

He winked at her and took her hand. He squeezed it and
she felt strength return.

She turned her gaze to the captain. "I have no doubt that
the man I saw in the corridor was the villain who tried to
throw me overboard."

"Besides, what excuse would a seaman have for being
in the passenger stateroom corridor? And why would he
run when Thea screamed if he were not guilty?" Drake
posed the questions and she warmed at the knowledge that
he obviously believed her.

The captain shrugged. "As to that, I couldn't say. I would
like to think that my crew are not such a simple lot that the
mere sight of a screaming woman would send them running."

He tugged at the edges of his waistcoat. "Would you
mind describing him to me?"

"No, of course not, but first please take a seat." Having
him hover above her made Thea nervous, and she involuntarily tightened her grip on Drake's hand.

He rubbed his thumb along her palm and she felt comforted.

The captain pulled the single chair away from the small table and sat down. Thea hid a smile at his correct posture. He was unlike any other captain she had ever met.

However, as she began describing her attacker, she realized that the captain was intelligent and no doubt did know his crew as well as Drake had stated. He asked very pointed questions until she had described the villain with more detail than she thought she had remembered.

"Did he have a tattoo or anything of that nature?"

She tried hard to remember if that had been the case. She had seen the man for such a short time. "He had a gold earring, I think. Oh, and when he turned to run away, I noticed that his pants were ripped on the backside." She felt her face heat. "I don't think he was wearing any smalls."

A spark of recognition gleamed in the captain's eyes.

Thea leaned forward expectantly. "Who is it, sir?"

"A bloody bounder who should have been tossed off the ship before now for slacking. Hartford P. Fox."

Drake tensed next to Thea. "Who?"

"The lazy good-for-nothing got caught sleeping on watch and was demoted from his position as second mate. I made him a regular sailor and sent him back to live in quarters again. It appears he's as disloyal as he is lazy."

Relief washed over Thea. "Then he will be easy to find, won't he?"

"Yes," said the captain.

She turned to Drake. "You will allow me to question him, won't you? It's very important that I discover who hired him."

"You aren't coming within ten feet of the man. Have you forgotten that he tried to throw you overboard?"

She ignored Drake's glare and the officer's grunted agreement. "And I stopped him. There will be no danger.

After all, you will be there and he will be bound, I am certain."

She looked to the captain for confirmation.

"He'll be put in chains the minute I get my hands on his worthless carcass," he assured her.

She turned back to Drake. "There, you see."

"No."

"I must insist."

"You may insist until your voice grows hoarse with it, but I won't allow you to be in danger."

She tried to yank her hand from his, but he held tight. "You are not my lord and master, Mr. Drake, and I will not have you dictating my actions. I will speak to this villain, whether you like it or not."

She probably should not have spoken so forcefully because Drake's manner became acutely intimidating. He leaned over her until she had to arch her neck to maintain eye contact. She could feel the angry heat of him, he was so close. "While you are on my ship, I am responsible for you."

She swallowed. He certainly had an overweening sense of accountability.

"Is that clear?"

She nodded. He had made his stance perfectly clear, but that didn't mean she had to like it or submit. However, she didn't think that right now was the time to tell him so.

"We'll find Fox and take him belowdeck for holding," the captain said. "I'll send word when we have him in custody."

Drake acknowledged the captain's words without breaking eye contact with Thea. "Thank you, Captain."

Thea heard the man get up and cross to the door and then leave, shutting it behind him. Still, Drake kept his gaze fixed on hers. "Explain to me why you are so determined to talk to the man yourself."

She could no longer keep her secret. She had to have Drake's cooperation in questioning the villain, and he wouldn't give it as long as he still believed she'd offended one of the passengers aboard ship with her abolitionist rhetoric enough to incite revenge.

"It began about six months ago, although it's possible that it has been going on longer. I did not become aware of the problem until recently and I've only had time to review the last six months of ledgers."

As she spoke, Drake's gaze turned from angry intimidation to uncomprehending surprise. "Someone has been trying to kill you for six months?"

She frowned. "Do not be melodramatic, Pierson. That is not what I am saying at all."

"What the bloody hell are you saying then?"

She opened her mouth to answer his question and the stateroom door opened.

"*Mr. Drake.* What *are* you doing here with Miss Thea alone? It's not at all proper."

Thea squeezed her eyes shut. "Melly, you are returned from your visit."

"Yes, and it looks like I've arrived just in time, too. What your sainted mother would say if she saw you right now, I cannot tell."

Drake stood and pulled Thea to her feet with the hand he kept locked firmly in his own. "She would undoubtedly wish us happy."

Thea's gasp of outrage was drowned out by her maid's exclamation of delight. "I knew you were a man of honor, sir. I told myself, Melly, Mr. Drake wouldn't come visiting and wreaking havoc with the young miss's reputation without he had courting on his mind."

This time Thea succeeded in removing her hand from Drake's. "Stop right now. Melly, I am not engaged to Mr. Drake."

"Of course you are. He said so, didn't he?"

"No, he didn't. He made a comment about my mother wishing us happy, which given the nature of the implication, she was not likely to have done." Thea glared at both Drake and Melly. "Mama did not believe that there was anything resembling bliss in the wedded state."

Melly snorted. "The poor thing had her own reasons for feeling as she did, but it's every mother's dream to see her daughter wed to the right gentleman."

"It wasn't my mother's dream and I cannot believe that you have deluded yourself into believing it was."

Melly looked undaunted. There were definite disadvantages to having a maid who was more family than servant. "Deluded I may be, but I'm that happy you're going to marry Mr. Drake. I am."

Thea very nearly gave in to the urge to scream. She crossed her arms over her chest and fixed both her maid and the irritating Drake with a look that said she meant to be listened to. *"I am not going to marry Mr. Drake."*

When Melly opened her mouth to speak, Thea put up her hand to forestall her. "I mean it. *I will not marry.*"

Drake still looked entirely too pleased with himself to be convinced, but Melly's sullen expression said that she'd finally accepted Thea's statement.

She sat back down on her bunk. "There is a perfectly good reason why Mr. Drake is here."

They were close enough to port that Thea no longer saw the need for subterfuge. If she told Melly the truth, or at least the truth about the attack, her maid would cease hounding her about marrying Drake and the propriety of them being caught in a room together.

Drake watched the emotions flitting across Thea's face. After what had transpired between them in his stateroom, how could she deny that she belonged to him?

He put the thought aside for later because what he wanted now was the continuation of the explanation she had begun when her maid entered the stateroom. He sensed that he was going to get just that. So he waited.

Thea bit her lip, a sure sign she was thinking. It occurred

to Drake that she might not tell the whole story to her maid. He bit back his frustration.

"The other night I couldn't sleep. So I decided to take a short walk on deck and explore the ship a little more."

Melly's eye's widened. "Don't tell me you went on deck alone at night. Why, it isn't decent. What would your sainted mother have said?"

Drake didn't have a clue, but he wished the woman, sainted or not, had not said quite so much on the subject of marriage to her daughter.

Thea waved her hand, dismissing Melly's comment. "The thing is . . ." She let her voice trail off, and then taking a deep breath, she plunged on. "When I was on deck, someone attacked me and tried to throw me overboard."

Melly's face turned ashen and she collapsed on to the side of her bed as if her knees had given way. "Someone tried to throw you overboard?" She glared at Drake. "How could you let something like this happen? A respectable woman should be safe walking the decks of your ship. I've a good mind to, to . . ."

She clearly didn't know what she had a good mind to do, and Drake had no intention of giving her time to figure it out. The maid acted more like a mother hen than a servant. "Your mistress had no business on deck alone, particularly at night."

"As if that had anything to do with it. Miss Thea has a mind of her own, and that's a fact. It's no excuse for some blackguard to come along and try to do her harm."

"I didn't mean to imply that it was."

Thea drew his attention with a long-drawn-out sigh. "Listen, you two. Arguing about it isn't going to solve anything. It is imperative that I have the chance to interrogate the villain before he jumps ship and disappears altogether."

Melly shivered. "It seems to me if the blackguard disappeared, we'd all sleep safer in our beds."

"Not necessarily," Drake put in. "We have to assume the

man attacked Thea on purpose. Until he's caught, she won't be safe."

"But no one would want to hurt Miss Thea! There's no reason to believe the rogue wouldn't have attacked any un-attended lady he came across. There are wicked men in this world, Mr. Drake, that care nothing for a woman's virtue."

The look she gave him implied she just might consider him one of those wicked men. He glared at both her and Thea. "Your mistress is the one refusing to do the honor-able thing, not me," he felt compelled to say.

"Nonsense." Thea bounded off the bed and stormed over to him. "Both my honor and yours are untarnished. I won't have you implying otherwise to my maid."

He met Thea's gaze with a knowing look and she had the grace to blush. She turned away and paced to the other side of the stateroom. "Let us not get off subject. We are here to discuss apprehending the villain, not my unmarried state."

"Actually, I'm here to see that you are dressed properly for dinner. We're dining at the captain's table tonight, and I thought you'd want time to prepare yourself. All this stuff about an attacker is news to me."

Thea gripped her hands together and seemed to be pray-ing for patience. "Be that as it may, Melly, we are dis-cussing the unfortunate incident on deck now and I would appreciate your cooperation."

"I wasn't there," Melly said, looking confused. "I don't know what I could add."

"You were there the day we came aboard. Did you no-tice any of the people from home talking to the ship's crew when they came aboard to see the steam engine?"

"You think someone from the island stole aboard the ship and attacked you?"

"*Sacré bleu.* Melly, just answer my question."

"I don't remember. Everything was in such a whirl with you wanting to sail so quick like."

Thea nodded. She rubbed her temples. "Thank you. I'm sorry I was short with you. It's been a trying time."

"Do you need a headache powder, Miss Thea, or some of Mr. Drake's ginger tea?"

Thea grimaced at the mention of the ginger tea. "No, thank you, Melly."

Drake walked up behind Thea and placed his hands on her shoulders. "It's going to be all right. I won't let anyone hurt you, Thea."

"Can you stop them from hurting Uncle Ashby?"

She whispered the comment, but he still heard. He hated the broken fear in her voice. Thea was not afraid for herself, but for the man she called uncle.

He turned her to face him, ignoring Melly's sounds of protest about appropriate behavior when two people were not engaged. Locking his arms behind her back, he pulled her close. "Let me help you, Thea."

She nuzzled into his neck and just held on for a long moment. Finally, she pulled back a little. "Yes. Please, help me, Drake. I don't want Uncle Ashby hurt."

Melly stood up and walked to the door, her face the color of boiled lobster. "It's no good being a chaperone when your presence doesn't hinder such familiar behavior."

She went out, shutting the door loudly.

He swung Thea into his arms and carried her to the chair. It was safer than the bed. He sat down and settled her on his lap.

She sighed. "She's disappointed in me."

He knew she referred to her maid. "Does that bother you?"

"Yes. Melly has always been there, and though she insists on referring to herself as a maid, she's so much more."

He understood. Thea had a tender heart toward those she loved, and she loved the woman who had helped her mother raise her. "Why is she disappointed?"

"Because I won't act like a proper lady and marry you."

"Well, there is one way you can make her happy."

She frowned. "I don't think I can do that at the cost of my own happiness, not even for Melly."

"Are you so sure I would make you unhappy?" The thought wounded him in a way that he didn't even understand.

Her eyes filled with uncertainty. "No."

That was a start.

"Tell me about Merewether."

She bit her bottom lip.

"Everything," he demanded, when he realized she was in all probability trying to decide how much to say.

"Someone is pilfering from the shipping office in London. I can't tell by the books if they are actually stealing cargo or just money. I noticed the discrepancies and sent a letter to Uncle Ashby's nephew asking about them. He oversees the offices in London."

When Drake nodded his understanding, she went on.

"I never received an answer, but nevertheless went back through previous months' accounts. Once I knew what I was looking for, it was not hard to find."

"Is that why you are going to England?"

It certainly made sense. Thea was not the type of female to be tempted by the frivolous delights of the Season. She was, however, the type to take charge and go searching for the thief on her own.

"Yes. You've got to understand, Drake. Uncle Ashby's health cannot stand the cold climate of England, much less the voyage. He was in bed a month when he and Aunt Ruth returned from their last visit."

"Why didn't you hire Bow Street to investigate?"

"What if it's his nephew? How will Uncle Ashby's heart take the blow?"

Drake frowned. "He's a man, Thea. His heart will survive the blow."

"I don't mean his feelings, I mean his heart. The doctors

say it is weak. If he were to discover his nephew was stealing from us, he might have an apoplectic fit and die. He has
quite a temper and it *would* hurt him, even though he is a
man."

"So, if it is the nephew, what are you going to do?"

"I don't know. Make him resign from his position, I
suppose, and hire someone more trustworthy."

"Are you saying you aren't going to tell Merewether
about this at all?"

She stiffened in his arms. "Don't make it sound like I'm
betraying him. I'm trying to protect him, like he protected
my mother and me when we came to the island."

He couldn't help but admire her loyalty, even while wanting to curse at her independence. "If it is the nephew, your
letter alerted him to the danger, and it looks like he's decided to deal with matters by getting rid of you."

"Yes, but I'm not sure it is Uncle's nephew. Someone else
could have read my letter. Someone else could be the thief."

Not likely, but he didn't see the need to argue the point.
"You know what this means, don't you?"

She nodded. "The thief is in league with someone from
home. At first, I thought it could have been a sailor taken
on board Whiskey Jim's latest voyage from England, but
you didn't pick up any more sailors in port, or passengers
besides me. The man who tried to throw me overboard had
to have been paid by someone."

"The same person responsible for engineering the accident in the warehouse."

"Exactly, and when that didn't work, they came aboard
ship pretending an interest in your marvelous engine and
hired that disreputable sailor to hurt me."

"He tried to kill you."

She didn't deny it.

"That's why you want to question him, isn't it?"

"Yes, I need to protect Uncle Ashby from whoever is in
association with the thief."

"How are you going to do that without alerting Merewether to the existence of the thief?"

She fiddled with the top button on his shirt. In his haste to leave his room earlier, he had left off his cravat and now he could feel the delicate softness of her fingers against his throat. His body reacted instantly.

She looked up at him with a startled expression. "Really, Pierson, this is not the time to be thinking of such things."

He smiled at the prissy words spoken in a breathless voice. "You're right, but I have difficulty concentrating on anything else when you are near."

She stilled her fingers and gazed into his eyes. "Really?"

"Yes." How could she doubt it?

"That's nice," she said.

He bent his head and gently touched her lips with his own. She returned the pressure, allowing her arms to slide around his neck.

He pulled his lips away a fraction of an inch from her mouth. "You taste so good, I'm always hungry for more."

"I would not wish to be accused of being stingy." She kissed him this time, loving the feeling of freedom in doing so.

This was what she had missed after their time together in his room. The warmth. The intimacy. She felt safe in his arms—as if thieves, their cohorts, even the specter of marriage, could not harm her.

He teased at her lips with his tongue and she opened her mouth. The kiss grew passionate and soon they were both breathing rapidly.

He pulled away and pressed his forehead against hers. "We have to stop, Thea, or Melly will walk in on a much more compromising scene than she did earlier."

She knew he was right, but that did not make it any easier to acquiesce. "Very well," she said, aware that it came out a bit sulky.

He lifted her from his lap and set her on the bed before taking a seat on the chair once again. "Finish telling me about your thief."

"There is nothing more to tell."

"What do you plan to do when we reach London?"

She should question his assumption about accompanying her to London from Liverpool, but knew it would be no use. She had made her decision when she told him about the thief. She had his help now, for good or ill. However, it would be foolish to pretend she didn't want it, when she so desperately did.

"First I must make myself known to Lady Upworth."

"Your friend that has been writing you?"

"Yes."

"She's a crony of my aunt's. What are you going to do after that?"

For some reason knowing that Drake had a connection to Lady Upworth made Thea feel better. "I'm going to begin my investigation at the shipping office."

He frowned. "How?"

She chewed on her lower lip. "I had thought to simply make myself known, express my concerns, and enlist the help of Uncle Ashby's nephew. Now, I'm not so certain."

"Bloody hell. You could be walking into a nest of vipers."

Rather than annoying her, his anger made her feel safe. It felt good to lean on someone. She had not done so since her mother's death. "You are right, but I do not know a better way to approach it."

"I have an idea."

Her heart leapt with hope. "Yes?"

"I will pretend an interest in a partnership with Merewether Shipping. You will need to show me the books, and we will conduct the investigation together."

Ten

*Thea is growing so quickly, I barely recognize her any-
more. She runs everywhere and her diction is marvelous
for a child still in leading strings. Are all mothers so
very proud of their young? Perhaps Langley has done
for me one small service. In stealing my son, he has
given me appreciation for my daughter. She is my own
precious joy and I will be worthy of her.*

March 24, 1800
Journal of Anna Selwyn, Countess of Langley

"WHAT ABOUT THE LETTER? SOMEONE IN THE
London office already knows I've discovered
discrepancies in the ledgers."

He had seen the look of hope leap into her eyes. She
wanted to rely on him.

He would show her that she could trust him. "We will
allay their concerns by pretending to think the other discrepancies were anomalies."

"Won't the thief feel threatened that we are going

through the books now, and do something to try and stop us? He has already proved himself quite ruthless."

"I hope so."

Understanding dawned in her expression. "We are laying a trap and hoping the thief will try again." Her eyes dimmed. "Isn't that rather dangerous for you?"

"No more so than for you."

"But it is my problem."

"Now it is mine. You belong to me, Thea, even if you are too stubborn to admit it. That makes your problems mine." He waited for her to deny his words with her customary independent stubbornness, but her worried look only intensified.

"I don't want you to feel responsible for me."

"You have no choice." Did she think he could walk away from her now that he knew she was in danger?

"What if you are hurt?" she asked as if that was all that concerned her.

"I know how to take care of myself." He wanted to touch her and wipe the anxious expression from her face, but knew that he couldn't risk the close contact. Once he started touching her again, he wouldn't stop until he was buried inside her. "There is one matter we will have to attend to, however."

"Yes?"

"Where you will live."

"I'm staying with Lady Upworth. She's invited me numerous times. She will not mind me arriving unexpectedly." Thea sighed. "I think."

"Perhaps not, but she would definitely mind me moving in. She's set in her ways, just like my aunt."

"What do you mean, you moving in?"

"I'm staying by your side until the thief has been dealt with. He has proven himself too willing to harm you."

"I will be perfectly safe with Lady Upworth." And she sounded like she truly believed it.

"No."

She bristled, drawing herself erect, her heart-shaped face set in irritated lines. "I will accept your help, but you can forget dictating to me in this fashion."

"You like my aunt," he reminded her.

She eyed him warily. "Yes."

"She won't mind me staying as well," he explained.

She chewed on her bottom lip. "Won't the rest of the *ton* find it odd that I'm staying with your aunt?"

He shrugged. "It doesn't matter."

"Yes, it does. I'm not going to have you blaming me for damaging your reputation."

The accusation was so ludicrous, he laughed.

She glared at him. "Do not laugh at me, sir. I have every reason to be concerned. You believed that after making love, you were honor bound to propose and got angry when I said no. I won't have you saying that I misled you in this matter as well."

She was serious.

"I did not propose because of my honor."

"I heard your aunt, Drake. She believes your honor is at stake if you don't marry me just because you visited my room. I had not thought ahead when I seduced you. I did not realize that you would feel compelled to marry me afterward. I should have, but I was overcome with emotion." She looked away from him. "I'm not usually like that— emotional, I mean."

He didn't believe it for a minute. Everything she did was motivated by emotion and a fierce sense of loyalty that matched his own. Unable to withstand it any longer, he stood and went to her.

Cupping her shoulders, he forced her to meet his gaze. "I did not propose out of a sense of honor. I had already decided to marry you before we ever made love."

She stared at him, disbelief etched in every feature, her blue eyes filled with it.

He squeezed her shoulders. "I mean it, Thea."

"Why?"

The stark word hung between them and he was unsure how to answer. The why of it was something he had not considered. It had simply become inevitable and he had accepted it as such.

"You will make me an admirable wife."

Her soft pink lips twisted with derision. "*Admirable?* I cannot imagine how." Then her eyes widened and she looked at him with dawning wonder. "Are you saying that you *love* me?"

He released her shoulders and stepped back so quickly, he almost lost his balance.

Love? He had seen so-called love matches turn into screaming matches after the newness wore off. His father had promised undying love to his mother before getting her with child and abandoning her. Cicisbeos and rakes vowed their *love* for other men's wives. The *ton* was full of posturing dandies who spouted poetry about love while flitting from one lady to the next, their feelings as temporary as the beauty of the flowers they sent along with their vows of undying affection.

The only experience he had ever had with the emotion had been with Deirdre. She had said she loved him, but married someone richer and more suitable. He thought he had loved her, but had finally admitted that his pride was more bruised than his heart.

Did he love Thea?

He didn't know. He needed her, and in his mind that was bad enough.

When Drake didn't answer, Thea assumed she had made him uneasy with the question. Of course he didn't love her. She was a twenty-three-year-old spinster, too vocal in her opinions and unremarkable in appearance, for all that others said she looked exceedingly like her mother.

"I'm sorry. I didn't mean to make you uncomfortable."

He opened his mouth to speak, but she forestalled him by raising her hand. "It is better that you don't. Love me, that is."

"Why?" He looked perplexed, his dark brown eyes narrowed.

"Because I cannot marry you."

"Yes, you can. What is more, you will." He looked so certain of himself she wanted to scream.

"How many times must I tell you? *I will not marry.* Besides, I would make you a terrible wife. Surely you must realize that."

"I disagree. You are all I could desire in a wife." She wanted to argue, but he went on, seemingly determined to convince her. "First, there is the passion between us. I have no wish to wed a woman who will shut me from her room once she has given me the required heir and a spare."

She chewed on her bottom lip. "There is that." She did want him, even now, but those feelings would fade with time.

They had to.

"There is also the fact that you care nothing for Society's opinion," he continued.

"So?"

"My wife will face a certain amount of ostracism."

She wrinkled her forehead. "Lady Boyle said your grandfather refused to allow you to be ignored by Society."

He turned away, his gaze fixed on the view of the sea out her portal window. "It is true that anyone who wishes to claim his acquaintance knows better than to neglect the social niceties toward my mother and myself, but that is all surface. The *ton* is very good at making its disapproval known without actually cutting someone."

Her heart constricted at the thought of what he had endured. "That's terrible."

"But true. Any female seen in my company is censured. It's not exactly *tonnish* behavior to be courted by a bastard, even if he is the grandson of a duke."

"Have you courted many women?" She hated the notion that Drake had wanted to marry someone else.

He turned to face her, his expression unreadable. "One."

Her stomach did a funny flip-flop. "Was she afraid of Society's disapproval if she married you?"

He shrugged. "She could not see herself married to a penniless bastard."

"You are illegitimate, not a bastard, and you aren't poor."

"I was then. I was only twenty at the time and my prospects were not promising."

"Did you love her?"

"I thought I did."

His anger earlier made sudden sense. "She's the one, isn't she?"

His dark gaze narrowed warily. "The one what?"

"The one who believed you were good enough to be her lover, but not her husband." She knew she was right when he broke eye contact and turned away again. She jumped up and went to him. Reaching up to lay her hand on his shoulder, she tugged at him. "What happened?"

"I may be a bastard, but I'm not a gossip. If you want the story, you'll have to ask my aunt."

She hastily stepped back, stung by the harsh rebuke in his voice. "I wasn't trying to gossip."

He turned to face her. "None of it matters now. I want to marry you."

"Because you want me in your bed and you think it doesn't matter to me what the *ton* will say if I marry you."

"Does it?"

She frowned. "Of course not."

"Then marry me."

Longing so strong it nearly knocked her over lanced through her. *"I can't."*

"Why not?"

"I've already told you."

"You aren't afraid of anything else, why are you such a coward about this?"

She felt like he'd slapped her. She wasn't a coward. She wasn't. She was just realistic. Marriage entailed too many sacrifices for a woman and not enough benefits. Besides, she had made a promise to her mother. A promise she must keep.

"You don't understand."

"Then make me understand." He pulled her into his arms, and she wanted desperately to stay there for the rest of her life.

Pushing the impossible thought away, she struggled to get free. "Let me go."

"Explain why you won't marry me."

"I promised her. She was dying and she only wanted two things from me." Her heartbeat was loud in her own ears. "Don't you understand? I couldn't refuse."

He went completely still and she stopped her struggles.

"Your mother made you promise never to marry?"

"Not exactly." She owed him the entire truth, although it hurt to say it out loud. "I promised her I would never marry a man like my father."

Suddenly she was free—and she wanted nothing more than his protective arms around her once more.

But from the look on his face, he'd never hold her again. "You believe I'm like your father?"

"I don't believe you are cruel, but you are a hard man, certain of your own opinion and intent on having your own way."

Much like herself, she could admit, but marriage would give him the power to win against her strength of will. The law and society were both heavily weighted in a man's favor.

"You want to marry some spineless creature to ensure he can never hurt you like your father hurt your mother?"

The incredulous tone in his voice left her in no doubt how ridiculous he found that possibility.

"I don't want to marry anyone," she assured him.

His brows tipped in mockery. "What about this afternoon?"

"It was wonderful."

"I know you liked it, but have you considered the consequences?"

Wasn't she dealing with them right now?

"What consequences exactly are you talking about?" In his current frame of mind, she wasn't making assumptions about anything.

"A child. A bastard baby that will suffer all that I have and more if you refuse to give it my name."

The words slammed into her like a gale force wind. "A baby?" She stumbled backward until she sat on the chair. "I hadn't thought."

"Obviously." His expression chilled her to the very marrow of her bones.

She laid her hand against her stomach, wondering if new life had been created there in their coupling on the narrow bunk in Drake's stateroom. "Surely just the one time cannot create life."

His laugh was harsh and entirely without humor. "My mother gave herself to my father only once."

Her gaze flew to his.

Anger welled up inside her at the look of condemnation she saw on his face. "Why didn't you think of it? If we did make a baby, which I doubt, it required your full cooperation."

"Yes, it did." He walked to the door and placed his hand on the latch. "You were right when you said I am a hard man, Thea. No child of mine will ever be labeled bastard. *If you are pregnant, you will marry me.*"

He made the promise sound like a threat as he slammed out the door. She shivered. *What had she done?*

* * *

"WHAT THE BLOODY HELL DO YOU MEAN, A DINGHY IS *missing?*"

Drake's roar of fury did nothing to release the anger that had simmered below the surface since his argument with Thea two days ago. Damnation. The little minx had refused to marry him, accusing him of being like her father. Then Fox had gone to ground and an entire crew of seamen had been unable to find him. Drake hadn't slept since Fox's disappearance, and his temper was on a very short leash.

He grabbed the young sailor by the front of his striped cotton shirt and lifted until the man's feet no longer touched the deck. "Didn't the captain give strict instructions to have all the dinghies guarded until Fox was found?"

He was no longer yelling, but that didn't stop the sailor from wincing as if he were.

The sailor nodded, his face turning red. "Yes, sir, he did, but this one was under repair," he wheezed, "not seaworthy. Didn't think he could use it."

"*Drake.*"

Damnation. Thea. He didn't want to deal with telling her that he had lost Fox and their only link to the spy in the island's shipping office. *Bloody hell.* His promise to her that he would find Fox rose up to mock him. Some job he was doing of protecting her. He couldn't even find the blackguard who had attacked her on his own bloody ship. He turned toward her voice, still holding the sailor.

She came toward him with the same uninhibited stride that had caught his attention on their first meeting.

Her eyes were wide in question. "What are you doing?" She pointed to the sailor. "His face is turning purple. Put him down before he passes out."

He obeyed the bossy bit of goods with a flick of his

wrist. The sailor fell against the deck, making a large thud on impact.

Drake looked past Thea and saw no sign of Melly or anyone else, and the fury he had been trying to rein in spiraled out of control.

Ignoring the sailor, who was crawling away with crablike movements, he glared at Thea. "Where's your maid?"

Didn't she know better than to leave Thea alone with her attacker still loose? Didn't anyone but him realize the risks Thea faced?

She made a dismissive gesture with her hand. "I needed some time to think. I decided to take a walk. Melly was with me until I saw you. I sent her to the passenger parlor."

She looked as if she needed rest, not time to think.

"Fox is gone."

Her luminescent blue eyes filled with confusion. "How? We're on a ship. Won't he drown if he jumped overboard?"

"A dinghy under repair has disappeared."

"Is that why you were shaking that poor sailor?"

"He was in charge of guarding the dinghies. He's lucky I didn't throw him overboard."

"But you said it was under repair. Surely Fox would not risk it on the open sea."

"We're closer to land than you think. Besides, he's better off risking the sea than what would happen to him if he gets caught."

Her hands clenched at her sides. "When?"

"Probably last night." Damn, he hated that look of disappointment on her face. "He used darkness to cover his escape. There was no moon."

She nodded. "I know."

So she had been unable to sleep, too.

"That's it then. I'll just have to proceed with my investigation as planned and hope that nothing happens to Uncle Ashby in the meantime." She tried to sound confident, but he saw the fear in her eyes.

He couldn't resist touching her. Placing his hands on her arms, he pulled her toward him. She didn't resist, which surprised him. When he had her snug against him, she shuddered and wrapped her arms around his back.

"I missed you." Her words came out in a broken whisper.

Bloody hell. She needed to make up her mind. Either he was a cruel-hearted monster she couldn't marry or someone she couldn't live without. He couldn't be both. Didn't she realize that?

Apparently not.

He rubbed her back, trying to infuse her with his strength. "It's going to be all right, sweetheart. We'll find the thief and he'll tell me who his cohort is on the island. Nothing is going to happen to you or Merewether."

He'd do a better job of keeping this promise than he had the one to find her attacker. He had to.

"You're still going to help me?"

Caught in his own determined need to keep her safe, he didn't at first understand her hesitant question.

When he did, he had a good mind to shake her. "What the hell kind of question is that?"

She pulled away from him. "Don't shout at me."

"Do you know me so little, Thea? First you accuse me of being a cruel bastard like your father and then you imply that I will leave you to fend for yourself once we reach England. Next, you'll accuse me of seducing your maid."

She laughed and the sound cut through his anger as nothing else could have.

Her smile was like the sun coming from behind the clouds on a storm-ridden day. "I can assure you, I will *never* accuse you of seducing Melly."

He released Thea completely and stepped away from her, but felt an answering smile tug at the corners of his mouth. "I am relieved to hear that."

Her amusement dimmed. "I did not mean to insult you. But I realized that since I have refused to marry you,

you might not wish to help me pursue my investigation."

Just like that, the anger was back. "Damnation. Let us get a few things straight."

She nodded, wisely remaining silent.

"One. I am going to help you find your thief."

"Thank you."

"Two. You will be staying with my aunt while we are in London so I can keep an eye on you." When she looked ready to protest, he glared her into silence. "Think of it as insurance for your maid's safety. You must realize that if you are in danger, so are the people close to you."

Her eyes rounded in understanding and he knew he'd made his point when she bit her bottom lip. "All right."

"Three." He stopped and took her chin into his hand. He wanted her full attention for this one.

She met his gaze with her own, her eyes dark blue in their intensity.

"Three," he repeated. "You are going to marry me be-cause although I may be hard, I am not heartless—and though I may be strong, I am not cruel."

"Oh, Pierson." She said nothing else, but he took her lack of argument as a definite step in the right direction.

Eleven

Lady Upworth has sent me sketches of Jared. He is a beautiful child, perfect in every way. Sometimes my arms ache to hold him, and Thea will toddle into the room as if she knows. She climbs into my lap and sits quietly, so unlike my daughter, allowing me to rock her and sing songs I long to sing to my son as well. Lady Upworth does not mention Langley in her last letter. I think she is surprised and disappointed that my disappearance has not caused him to have a change of heart. I am neither. He has no heart and his own pride will prevent him from ever acknowledging his error.

November 11, 1800
Journal of Anna Selwyn, Countess of Langley

LADY BOYLE'S COACH LURCHED FOR WHAT seemed like the hundredth time as it hit a dip in the road from Liverpool to London. Thea grabbed the strap hanging from the ceiling and held on, refusing to land on her backside on the carriage floor again. Once was enough.

She could still feel the bruise on her hip she'd received the one time she had allowed herself to nod off.

The ride smoothed out and she let go of the strap, settling more comfortably onto the leather carriage seat. The rest of the occupants of the carriage dozed. Lady Boyle and her companion, Mrs. Coombs, sat opposite Thea and Melly. Melly snorted in her sleep, and Thea marveled at how she and the other women managed to keep their balance. No one but Thea had so much as tipped forward, regardless of how much the coach bounced along the uneven road.

Scooting toward the door, she peered out the window. The scenery was unlike anything she had ever seen. The lush green hills in no way resembled the tropical paradise of her island, and yet there was such beauty in them that looking at them gave her a physical ache. She wondered what London would be like.

Her first sight of Liverpool had made her feel faint. The busy docks and crowds of people were so unlike her island that she had wanted to stay onboard ship and sail right back to the Caribbean. Drake seemed to understand how overwhelming it all was because he had tucked her protectively against his side and kept her there throughout the making of plans for her journey to London.

He had settled her at an inn and left her playing cards with his aunt, Mrs. Coombs, and Melly before going to attend to the business associated with bringing his ship into port on time. Later, he arranged for her to travel in his aunt's coach to London.

So far, he had declined to join them, preferring to ride his horse alongside the carriage. Looking around the crowded interior of the carriage, she did not blame him. Where would he sit—on the floor? At least it wasn't raining. But the air was so cold that she shivered under the lap rug tucked around her. Drake must be cold indeed, but he hadn't complained.

Gratitude for the crowded conditions made her feel guilty. She needed time to think about all the feelings he brought out in her. He made her wish for things she had planned to live her life without. Husband. Children. She touched her flat stomach. The thought of having Drake's child should have horrified her. Instead it filled her with unmistakable longing.

Could she possibly be carrying his baby? She did not doubt he would make good his threat to marry her then. After a lifetime of paying the price for his own parents' mistake, Drake was not about to foist that sort of pain on his own child.

You are going to marry me.

His words haunted her. Did the man think he could order her to marry him? She supposed he did. Just as he tried to control so many other things. The fact that she didn't seem to mind scared her witless. Was she in danger of breaking the promise she had made to her mother?

Although I may be hard, I am not heartless—and though I may be strong, I am not cruel. His words played in her mind like the beat of the drums that echoed from the slaves quarters at night, back on her island. They had the same disturbing quality.

Was it possible to be hard without slipping into cruelty? She did not know. Her mind rejected the possibility, but her heart longed for the words to be true.

Forcing herself to push thoughts of her personal relationship with Drake aside, she tried to concentrate on the investigation. She searched for holes in Drake's plan to pose as an interested investor and couldn't find any. She had to admit that the idea would work nicely, allowing her access to the ledgers and an excuse to spend time in the London office. It would also keep her in Drake's constant company.

The knowledge both alarmed and enthralled her.

* * *

THEA TRIED TO SEE THROUGH THE BROWN FOG THAT clung to the pavement outside Lady Boyle's town house. She shook her head at the useless exercise. Between the lace curtains that Lady Boyle insisted must not be moved and the fog, Thea could not see a thing.

"He'll not get here any faster no matter how many times you look out that window, child."

She sighed and nodded in agreement with Lady Boyle's comment. "I know." She jumped up and began pacing the room. "I cannot wait to hear how it went at Lloyd's of London. He brought the *Golden Dragon* in to port on time and they will be forced to pay his policy."

"It was a very near thing." Lady Boyle's knitting needles clicked in a steady rhythm, uninterrupted by their discussion.

Thea swung to face the older woman. "Yes, it was. Imagine coming into port with only two days to spare. Drake must feel very accomplished."

She wondered if that was true. He had played down his achievement and treated his visit to the insurance company as just a routine business call.

"It was closer than that, my dear."

"What do you mean?" How could it have gotten any closer?

"He planned to have the captain give the order to drop anchor and search the ship until they found that nasty man who accosted you."

Although Drake had not taken his aunt into his complete confidence, he had told her enough for her to be infuriated that anything so unacceptable had occurred on one of his ships.

Thea could not believe her ears. "But that would have put the entire voyage in jeopardy."

"Nonsense." Lady Boyle lifted the garment she was knitting and examined it closely before setting it back on her lap and resuming activity with her needles. "Merely his policy with Lloyd's."

"I'm sure you are mistaken. Drake would never have jeopardized that policy on purpose. He told me coming into port on time was a matter of his honor."

"Apparently catching your attacker was of more import."

Of more import to Drake than his honor? She took leave to doubt it. Lady Boyle must be mistaken. She would ask Drake about it as soon as possible.

The sound of the outer door opening drove all questions from her mind.

He had returned.

She rushed out the door, ignoring Lady Boyle's instruction that a lady should never rush to a gentleman and should never run, period. She descended the stairs more quickly than might be ladylike. By the time she reached the bottom, Drake was handing his hat and coat to Lady Boyle's very correct butler.

She skidded to a halt a foot or so from Drake.

He turned toward her and he cocked his brow in question. "Is something the matter?"

She realized she was slightly out of breath. "Of course not."

"Then why the mad dash down the stairs?"

"I could not wait another moment to hear how your meeting at Lloyd's went."

He shrugged. "Much as one would expect it to go."

She wanted to throttle him. "Since I have never been to London, have never done personal business with a company so large, and have no idea what collecting a policy entails, you will just have to tell me."

Taking her arm, he led her back up the stairs at a much more sedate pace than she had used to descend them. "It was not terribly exciting. I brought paperwork from Liverpool showing the date of my arrival. They gave me a bank draft for the amount of my policy and that was that."

"What about your investors? Did they collect as well?"

"They will. Most are gentlemen of the *ton* and will send their men of affairs around to collect their bank drafts."

"But they will miss all the satisfaction for themselves."

He laughed. "I assure you, they will enjoy all the satisfaction of spending the money they made on this trip."

She wrinkled her nose. "I suppose."

They reached the top of the stairs.

She held back, not ready to reenter the drawing room. "Drake?"

He stopped and looked down at her questioningly. "Yes?"

"Your aunt said something that I was sure she was mistaken about, but I wanted to ask you anyway."

Dark eyes gazed into her own. "You're rambling again, Thea. That's a sure sign that something has you excited or upset. Which is it?"

"Neither."

He looked unconvinced.

Thea cleared her throat. "Your aunt said that you were preparing to drop anchor so the ship could be searched for Fox."

His expression showed no emotion. "Yes, but he escaped on the dinghy before I could do so."

"I don't understand."

"The closer we got to harbor, the more chance that he would jump ship to escape. I thought to drop anchor while we were still far enough out that he would not do so."

"But the search could have taken days." She stared at him, not comprehending. "Even if you had found him immediately, we would have lost the momentum we were running under."

"It doesn't matter now." He frowned, his eyes filled with frustrated anger. "He escaped before we had the chance."

"Surely that is best. If he had not escaped, you would have disappointed your investors and yourself."

He turned her into his arms, the warmth of his big body surrounding her.

She should pull away. What if the servants saw them? He would undoubtedly say that she had been compromised. However, she could not resist the intensity in his eyes.

"Your safety is more important to me than disappointing my investors."

His aunt had been right. There *were* weightier matters than his honor. It was her last coherent thought before Drake's mouth rocked over hers. Her body turned to liquid at the first touch of his lips. He had not kissed her since the fateful afternoon aboard ship when they had made love. Although she had tried to tell herself that was exactly what she wanted, she knew now that she had been lying. She wanted this—Drake's mouth covering her own intimately and with purpose.

"Pierson."

Lady Boyle's strident tones broke the hazy passion swirling around Thea. Drake released her slowly and then turned to face his aunt.

"Aunt Josephine. I did not realize you were there."

"Apparently." She pointed one of her ever-present knitting needles at him. "You also apparently did not notice that you were taking unacceptable liberties with Thea in plain view of anyone who happened by. You might very well have been seen by one of the *servants*."

Drake bowed toward his aunt. "I am terribly sorry, Aunt Josephine. I will remember to keep my libertine ways with Thea private in future."

Lady Boyle's mouth opened and shut, but nothing came out.

Thea glared at Drake. "Stop it. You will not upset your

aunt this way." She turned to Lady Boyle. "What he means to say is that he won't be taking any liberties in the future."

Lady Boyle harrumphed. "I very much doubt that."

It was Thea's turn to be speechless.

Drake popped her mouth shut by pressing her chin up with his finger. "My aunt appears to know me better than you do."

Thea batted his hand away.

Irritated beyond caution, she replied, "I sincerely doubt that is the case, unless you have a most unnatural relationship."

She immediately covered her mouth with her hand, but it was too late. The words were already out. She turned a guarded glance toward Lady Boyle, wondering if she had given the older woman a complete disgust of her.

Surprisingly, the dowager allowed her laughter to mingle with Drake's bark of amusement. "Come along, you two. You must plan your visit to Lady Upworth. She will be in alt to find out that Thea has come to Town. I am specifically waiting to take Thea shopping for her London wardrobe until Lady Upworth has been apprised of her presence. She will want to take part in the shopping, I'm sure."

DRAKE PULLED HIS CURRICLE TO A STOP IN FRONT OF the old-fashioned town house. Its exterior looked quite different from that of Lady Boyle's. Thea marveled at the brickwork, so unlike anything back home. She marveled at something else as well. Lady Upworth's home was not mired in layers of coal dust like so many buildings in London. She wondered how her aunt had managed it.

She broke the silence she had kept since leaving Lady Boyle's. "Do you think she will like me?"

"You told me that you two have corresponded since you learned to write."

She relaxed a little, thinking of the hundreds of letters she had exchanged with her aunt over her lifetime. "Yes."

"Then she no doubt already loves you."

The words warmed her and she turned a grateful smile to Drake. "Thank you."

He nodded before getting down to help her from the curricle. He put out his gloved hand and she rested her fingers in his, allowing him to guide her to the cobbled pavement. Tucking her hand into the crook of his arm, he led her to the door. It opened almost immediately after Drake had banged the large brass knocker against the door.

"Yes?"

The butler's stooped appearance and gray hair did not detract from his air of proper authority.

"We are here to see Lady Upworth."

The elderly servant stepped back to usher Drake and Thea into the hall. "Whom shall I tell Milady is calling?"

Thea's throat closed. To be so close to her aunt, the one member of her family still living that knew of Thea's existence. The opulence of the house, the foreignness of things that should be familiar because she'd heard about them her entire life, overwhelmed her, and she could not make any words get past the thickness in her throat. She threw a desperate glance at Drake, and he answered the servant.

"Please inform her that Miss Selwyn and Mr. Drake are awaiting her convenience."

She had no time to collect herself before the butler returned. "Milady will see you in her private parlor."

He led them on a ponderous procession up a flight of stairs. Opening a heavy ornate door to the left, the butler indicated they should enter. Thea could not seem to make her feet move. Drake took her arm and gently pulled her into a lady's sitting room.

The furnishings were exactly as Lady Upworth had sketched them. Matching chairs with needlepoint cushions sat opposite a fainting couch near the fireplace. The smell of furniture wax and dried flowers permeated the room. The escritoire her aunt had been so thrilled to find at a shop on the Pall Mall resided near the window. It looked exactly like the sketch she had sent, except it shone in a way that a charcoal sketch could not catch.

And next to the small desk sat an elderly woman dressed in the first stare of fashion. Her aunt.

"Is it really you?" Lady Upworth's voice came out in a choked whisper.

Gripping the edge of the escritoire, she stood and the skirts of her black gown fell in graceful folds toward the floor. The sound of rustling silk accompanied her movement across the floor.

She appeared so fragile, her step halting. Thea had not realized. Letters did not show age or infirmity. Her aunt's obvious weak condition hit her like a blow. Had she waited one more year to make her trip to England, would it have been too late?

Taking Thea's arms in a grip astonishingly strong for such a frail-looking woman, Lady Upworth pulled her into a tight embrace. Thea stood unmoving, unable to respond for all of ten seconds, then her arms lifted of their own volition and wrapped around her aunt. This was her flesh and blood. Family. She was no longer alone in the world. She hugged her aunt fiercely. They stayed that way for long moments, Thea's heart full at the thought of being part of a family again.

Finally, Lady Upworth pulled away. "Let me look at you."

Then she did just that. Eyes the same blue as Thea's own stared at her, seeming to soak in her every feature.

"You are the twin of your mother." A shadow crossed the older woman's face. "I will always regret sending her to the West Indies."

Thea shook her head. "Had you not, she would have lost me."

The older woman's eyes filled with pain. "One never knows what would have been, but she died out there. She never saw Jared again and your father . . ." Lady Upworth's voice trailed off.

Thea knew what her aunt meant to say, and didn't want her to. Not in front of Drake. She did not want him to know the full truth of her father's wickedness. It shamed her. She cast him a sidelong glance. Had he noticed the reference to her brother?

"Do not think of that now," she said to her aunt.

Lady Upworth nodded, but tears sparkled in her eyes. "You are right. That is water under the bridge. You are here now. I truthfully did not think I would live to see the day."

Guilt flayed Thea as her aunt's words confirmed her initial fears upon seeing the older woman. She was ill.

Drake offered his handkerchief to Lady Upworth.

She took it and dabbed at her eyes, inhaling a deep breath. "Thank you—Mr. Drake, is it?"

Remembering her manners, Thea made the introductions.

Lady Upworth looked thoughtful for a moment. "You're a relation of Lady Boyle, aren't you?"

"Yes. She's my great-aunt."

Sudden understanding illuminated her aunt's eyes.

Sizing Drake up, as if he were a horse about to be auctioned, Lady Upworth asked, "You're Lady Noreen's son, aren't you?"

Thea felt her insides tighten. She shot Drake a quick look, trying to gauge his reaction to her aunt's statement.

Drake didn't flinch under the older woman's regard. "Yes."

"I see." The words held a wealth of meaning and meant nothing at all. "Thea sailed on your ship to England."

Drake, still as a becalmed sea, simply nodded.

She turned to Thea. "Why did you not sail on one of Merewether's ships?"

Thea was not sure how to answer. She didn't want to

share her concerns with her aunt, and yet, she hesitated to lie. That clear-eyed blue gaze was entirely too discerning.

She had so many secrets, they began to weigh on her like coal dust, making her feel gritty and unclean. "If I had waited for one of our ships, it would have been another month. I would have missed part of the Season."

"I see." There was that comment again. "You're here now. That is what matters, however it was managed."

Lady Upworth moved to one of the chairs near the fireplace and sat down. She indicated with an elegant wave of her hand that Thea and Drake should do the same. Thea sat on the fainting couch and Drake sat next to her.

Lady Upworth raised her eyebrows, but said nothing.

"Lady Boyle thought you might want to join her and Thea shopping for her wardrobe for the Season."

Her aunt's eyes lit up even as Thea tried to stifle a groan. She didn't want to waste time shopping while she could be investigating the thefts from her company.

"Of course I will. We'll move Thea here first thing tomorrow and I'll make appointments with the modiste, the hairdresser—"

Drake cut her off. "Thea will be staying with my aunt."

His tone did not invite comment, but her aunt was no more intimidated by it than Thea had ever been.

Lady Upworth drew herself up until her spine was stiff. "Nonsense. She will stay with her family."

Drake's gaze snagged Thea's. "You said she was a friend of the family."

Chewing on her lip, Thea tried to look away from the inquiry in his eyes, but found she could not. "I . . ."

"It was a necessary deception to protect her from her father. Neither she nor her mother could ever acknowledge the connection for fear he would discover their hiding place."

Drake did not reply to her aunt.

Instead he pinned Thea with unrelenting eyes. "You could have told me."

She wanted to deny it, say he had no more right to know her secrets than anyone else, but the words would not come.

Instead she nodded her head. "Yes, I should have told you, but it did not seem important and then we were arguing."

She willed him to understand something she did not fully comprehend herself. She only knew that she hadn't felt completely safe admitting her connection to Lady Upworth until they had met.

"So you two have been arguing." Her aunt's smile was knowing. "From your letters, I gained the impression that you have more than the average amount of spirit for a young lady."

Thea felt her cheeks heat. "I assure you, the arguments are not all of my making."

Lady Upworth laughed softly, the sound melodious. "Most ladies would not admit to having started any arguments."

Thinking of her panicked refusal to Drake's offer of marriage, Thea knew she was responsible for at least one of their disagreements. She could have handled things so much differently. Beginning by not throwing herself at the poor man.

She shrugged. "I may as well admit that though Mama tried to raise me to be a lady, I fall short in many areas."

Suddenly, Lady Upworth's gaze shifted to Drake. "What do you think? Does my niece fall short in any way?"

Thea tensed and slid a sidelong glance at Drake's impassive profile. She wished her aunt had not put him on the spot like this.

"She ignores the conventions, talks with sailors like they are gentlemen, harangues most everyone she meets about the issue of abolition, puts herself at risk without the least thought, is stubborn enough for five women, argues over every trifle, and has far too much consideration for her maid to be a typical English lady."

Thea gasped. She hadn't expected him to sing her praises, but he certainly didn't need to list her every flaw aloud to her aunt. She tried to unobtrusively scoot away from him by shifting slightly toward the arm of the fainting couch. He moved with her until she was pinned between him and the arm.

She glared at him and hissed, "There doesn't seem to be enough room on here for both of us. Perhaps you should move to the chair."

He shrugged. "I'm comfortable."

"Well, I'm not." She made to rise.

His hot gaze pinned her in place. "Yes, you are."

How dare he argue with her? She knew if she were comfortable or not. "I assure you, I am not."

He turned to her aunt. "You see? She is difficult."

Thea made a garbled sound and tried discreetly to shove him off the fainting couch. He didn't budge and that only seemed to infuriate her more. Her spine was so rigid, no one would ever know she wasn't wearing a corset.

He couldn't resist pushing her just a bit farther. "She doesn't act like a proper lady on most occasions."

"I see." Lady Upworth's smile and voice told Drake that she found her niece's reaction to his comments amusing.

He was glad. He'd pushed Thea into responding with her usual open emotion immediately, wanting to see her aunt's reaction. If Lady Upworth had responded with disapproval, Drake would have protected Thea from her.

He also wanted Lady Upworth to know what she was up against in presenting her niece to Society. Thea would not be a shy maiden, easily assimilated into the *ton*. She was an Original and needed to be respected as such.

He smiled at the obvious approval in the older woman's eyes when she looked at Thea. "I believe you do see."

Lady Upworth nodded. "Yes, indeed. It will be a pleasure introducing you to Society, my dear."

Thea's shocked gaze flew to her aunt. "You can't be

serious. Didn't you hear what Drake said?" She sighed and shifted her gaze to her clenched fists in her lap. "It's true, you know. I'm not a very proper sort of person at all. In fact, by some standards, I'm a little outrageous."

Lady Upworth laughed again. "Nonsense. You are a delight. I do believe you have found quite the champion in Mr. Drake as well."

Thea's hands fisted more tightly in her lap. "Now I know you are jesting. He didn't champion me, he pilloried me with his low opinion."

He took her hand and squeezed it. "I hold you in the highest regard."

She narrowed her eyes at him. "That is why you listed all my faults for my aunt like a hawker selling his wares?"

He rubbed her palm with his thumb, feeling pleasure at the slight touch. "I was warning her."

"Warning her?" Thea's voice rose until she was almost shouting. "I am not the plague that you need to warn my aunt about me."

"Nay, you are a headstrong female who will find her place amongst the *ton* if you are protected and presented in the right fashion."

"I don't care about my bloody place in the *ton*."

"Your aunt does." He indicated the woman now watching them with avid fascination. "Ask her if it is important to her if you are accepted in all the best drawing rooms."

Thea turned her stormy gaze to her aunt. "Is it important to you?"

Lady Upworth smiled reassuringly. "Yes, it is. You needn't worry. With the help of Drake's family, you will be launched with absolute success, I'm sure of it."

Thea's hand had turned in his and now clung tightly. "I'm not a ship."

"No, dear. You are my precious niece and you will cause quite a stir in the *ton*."

"Perhaps we shouldn't worry about introducing me. After

all, I won't be in England long and it seems like it will be quite a bit of work for you. I really don't want any new clothes and I'm sure no one will even notice I am here."

Drake couldn't help it—he laughed.

She gave him a disgruntled look. "Are you laughing at me again, sir?" She turned to her aunt. "I'm sure gentlemen do not laugh at ladies, but Drake forgets that fact regularly."

"Thea, you couldn't go through the Season unnoticed if you tried. You are far too opinionated and fearless to spend much time in London without making yourself known," Drake said.

Lady Upworth added, "I thought you came for the Season."

Drake wondered if Thea noticed the calculated gaze her aunt gave her when making the statement.

"I did." Thea squirmed under her aunt's steady regard. "I mean, that is, I came to spend the Season with you."

"My dear, I would have great pleasure in launching you into Society. You have spent far too long away from your rightful place. It is time you enjoyed the many privileges to which you were born."

"It's just all so different here. Back home, I was just me. Miss Thea. Here, I suppose they will want to call me Lady Thea and expect me to wear corsets even though they are bad for a lady's respiration." Her grip on his hand tightened. "Well, I won't do it. I won't. If I am to become a member of the *ton,* they will have to take me as I am. I am too old to fit the mold of biddable debutante."

He realized that Thea had experienced enough emotion for the time being. She was beginning to sound slightly hysterical and her aunt looked exhausted, but happy.

"We can discuss your debut later," he said.

"But—" Thea tried to interrupt.

"No one will force you to wear corsets," he promised and stood. "Come. Your aunt is tired."

Lady Upworth sighed and nodded. "My constitution is

not what it used to be. Will you come again tomorrow? I should like to spend more time talking." She fixed her niece with a discerning stare. "There are still many things to discuss."

He wanted to know what those things were, but there would be time enough later to grill Thea about the things she had not yet told him. He sensed there were still important pieces of her life he did not understand.

"Yes." Thea leaned down and kissed her aunt's cheek. "I will come tomorrow. Rest now."

Drake ushered her toward the door.

When they got there, he stopped her and turned back to Lady Upworth. "You should be aware that I intend to marry Thea."

Lady Upworth snorted. "I may be old, young man, but I'm not blind."

Twelve

I must find something to occupy my mind and time. Thea is wonderful, but she is not enough. Not when I lie in bed at night wishing for my son and longing for a husband who is both friend and love. How foolish I am to even think of such a thing. Men see marriage very differently from women.

The yellow fever is coming. The islanders say that it comes every year and many die because of it. Oh, God, do not let me die. Make me strong for my daughter.

January 18, 1801
Journal of Anna Selwyn, Countess of Langley

THEA WANTED TO SHAKE DRAKE.

Skewering him with her gaze, she sat ramrod straight in the curricle seat beside him. "How could you have said that?"

He flicked the horses' reins, and the vehicle picked up speed. "It's the truth."

She let her breath out in a hiss. "Your truth, but what about the fact that I have refused you?"

"I will convince you."

His complacent assurance made her want to scream. "*Sacré bleu.* Your arrogance knows no bounds, sir."

His shrug nearly pushed her over the edge of her control. "My arrogance is well matched by your stubbornness."

"It isn't stubbornness. I made a promise and I intend to keep it."

"I would never expect you to do otherwise."

Unaccountably, his easy agreement disappointed her. "Then I cannot marry you."

"Yes, you can. I'm not your father and one day you will accept that fact." He turned his head to briefly catch her gaze. "Your mother would have liked me."

"My mother would have thought you were overbearing beyond belief."

"Perhaps. But she would have liked me."

"How can you be so sure? You never even knew her."

"Because I am a man of honor. It wasn't your father's strength that destroyed your family. It was his lack of integrity."

She shot Drake a penetrating look. Could he know the full truth? The horror of her father's final betrayal? No, surely not. "What do you mean?"

"Only a man lacking honor would be so certain his wife had none."

She couldn't fault his reasoning. If he were right and her father's baseness was the true source of trouble in her parents' marriage, then what did that say for her promise to her mother? No one could accuse Drake of being without honor. To her way of thinking, he had more than his share of that commodity. It was all so confusing. Life had been so much simpler before she discovered a thief in the company, before she had met Drake and sailed on his ship.

That blasted embezzler had an awful lot to answer for.

She went for a different tack in her argument with

Drake. "Well, if you have no thought for my feelings on the matter, consider what an upset you have probably given my aunt."

He went stiff beside her, his hands tightening on the horse's reins. "Are you worried she will not approve your marriage to a bastard? Are you ashamed of our association, Thea?"

The hot fury that welled up in her made her earlier irritation pale into insignificance.

"Don't ever call yourself that again," she growled.

He drew the carriage up in front of his aunt's town house, halting the horses. He turned to her, his face an impassive mask. "That's what I am, Thea. You might as well accept it now."

"You are *not* a bastard." She gripped her parasol so tightly that she thought the handle might break. Better that than Drake's neck. "You are the illegitimate son of a woman who by all accounts is both a lady and a wonderful mother. Your father is just plain too stupid to acknowledge you, but that doesn't make you a bastard. Do not ever call yourself that name in my hearing again."

She did not realize that her fervent speech had been overheard until a servant cleared his throat. He had come from the house to care for the horses.

Thea ignored him. "Well?"

Drake's expression did not alter, but the heat in his eyes burned her. "If that is your wish."

She nodded. "It is."

Finally, he smiled. "Very well. Can we leave the curricle now? We are starting to draw a crowd."

She looked around them and realized that he spoke the truth. They were the object of interest not only for Lady Boyle's footman, but also for a well-dressed couple in a passing carriage and a nanny with her charge. Had she embarrassed Drake with her outburst? If she had, he had only himself to blame. After all, she would not have been pushed past the point of reason had he not called himself such an atrocious name.

She made no move to leave the carriage. "I thought we were going to the London office of Merewether Shipping when we finished at Lady Upworth's."

"You need some rest." His eyes were softened with compassionate understanding. "It's been an eventful afternoon."

Emotion she did not wish to name filled her chest. She could not afford to weaken toward Drake now.

"I'm not so fainthearted." Besides, she didn't have time to waste. Uncle Ashby was at risk until they unmasked the thief. "Proceed to the office."

His eyes widened at her peremptory tone.

She sighed. "Please."

"Whatever my lady wishes." He followed his sarcastic comment with immediate action, waving the footman back from the curricle. "Inform my aunt that we will be out this afternoon. We will return in time for tea."

The footman nodded his understanding and stepped back as Drake set the horses in motion.

SOMETHING INSIDE DRAKE HAD SHIFTED AND SETTLED when Thea snarled at him like an angry tigress for calling himself a bastard. She didn't deny the circumstances of his birth, but she wouldn't allow him to belittle himself because of them. The reason, he knew, was because those circumstances did not diminish his value in her sight. He looked at her out of the corner of his eye. She sat perfectly erect, as if she were still irritated by his comment.

She could not possibly know what her ready acceptance meant to him. The only people who had ever accepted him at face value his entire life had been his grandfather and his mother. Even the rest of his family defined him by his status as a bastard. His own aunt had felt compelled to warn Thea just what she was getting when she became entangled with him.

He wanted to kiss the stubborn, delicious woman beside him until she melted against him and forgot what she was angry about. He needed to show her how much her belief in him mattered. He had given up on tender feelings after the debacle of his courtship of Deirdre, but he didn't think lust alone described his current emotions.

Although it was certainly an element of what he felt. Images of her smooth naked body stretched out on the narrow bed in his stateroom filled his head, and he realized that he wanted to do much more than kiss her. He wanted to bury himself so deep inside her she wouldn't know where she ended and he began. He wanted the right to sleep in her bed every night and rejoiced at the thought of planting a child in her womb.

Hard arousal pressed against the buttons of his fly. *Bloody hell.* She'd better change her mind about marrying him soon. Not that she showed any signs of doing so. Intractable wench.

As his body responded to his thoughts, he began to wonder if waiting to make love to her again until they were married was the best course of action. It had seemed the most honorable line to take on the ship. Her refusal to consider marriage had convinced him to stay away from her, first out of anger because the thought that she considered him in the same league as her father still rankled, then in the hopes that she would miss what they had experienced and want it enough to risk marriage.

Although sound reasoning, it didn't appear to be working. She acted as if she didn't remember the way her body responded to his. He could think of numerous ways to remind her, ways that would give them both satisfaction. How better to convince her that marriage to him was the right choice? He would show her that the afternoon in his cabin was just the beginning of what they could experience together as man and wife.

She would be forced to realize that she belonged to him.

Thea's voice pulled him from his thoughts. "Do not think that your lamentable tendency to refer to yourself in such inappropriate terms has made me forget your words to my aunt."

"She deserved to know my intentions."

"That's ridiculous. Your intentions are neither here nor there as far as my aunt is concerned."

She truly was naïve about the ways of the *ton*. "Do you remember my aunt's reaction to me visiting you aboard ship?"

"Yes, but that was a temporary aberration. Look at how calmly she reacted to finding us kissing in the hall."

His aunt's so-called calm reaction was the result of him telling her he had every intention of marrying Thea before the *Golden Dragon* had ever sailed into port. She knew once he made up his mind, he let nothing stand in his way. Not even headstrong women with independent natures and not enough sense.

"The gossip that will undoubtedly start to circulate once she begins to introduce you to Society will cause a reaction in your aunt similar to the one mine had on the ship. In other words, she won't take it calmly at all. I didn't want her to worry, so I told her my intentions were honorable."

After all, Lady Upworth had reason to doubt it. He was his father's son. As much as he would like to forget that fact, Society never would.

Thea stirred next to him and placed her hand on his arm.

She gave it a gentle squeeze. "That's very thoughtful of you, but don't you think she'll be disappointed when we don't marry?"

He had no intention of disappointing her aunt or himself. "Don't worry. She's more likely to be relieved in the meantime."

A huge breath of air escaped from between Thea's lips. "I wish everyone would give up this idea of introducing me to Society. It's just complicating everything and is bound to take time away from my investigation. Can you imagine the hours I'll have to waste shopping for new clothes?"

Thea made shopping for clothes sound like a fate worse than death. "Come, don't you think you will enjoy the time with your aunt? Besides, I have yet to meet a lady who wasn't interested in her wardrobe."

He watched her take her lower lip between her teeth and wanted to stop the carriage and cover that little lip with his own. Then he would trail kisses down her neck. She would make sexy little noises in the back of her throat. He would touch her breasts, first through the fabric of her gown, and then peeling the fabric away, he'd put his hands on her naked skin.

His already hard body began to ache. He almost missed her answer to his statement.

"I suppose I will enjoy the time with my aunt. I like Lady Boyle as well, but I'm not particularly interested in gowns and fripperies and I am not at all interested in being presented to the *ton*."

"You heard your aunt. It's important to *her*."

"She wants me to take my rightful place in Society, but that won't work."

"Why not?"

"Because I haven't been raised to it, for one thing. The girl I might have been does not exist in the woman I am."

"You do not have to be anything different than you are to charm Society. Look how well you have charmed me."

She did not smile as he had expected.

Instead, her face took on a very serious expression. "I have not charmed you. I seduced you. There's a difference."

Following upon his earlier thoughts, her comment caused no small reaction in him. His body tightened while his mind grappled with the problem of a willful female who actually believed *she* had seduced *him*. It wouldn't be a problem if she didn't sound so chagrined by the fact.

"You didn't seduce me."

"Of course I did. You did not want to make love to me, but I begged you."

The last place he wanted to engage in a discussion of this nature was sitting in an open curricle, his hands firmly engaged with the ribbons. "Perhaps we could discuss that afternoon another time."

She tapped the parasol his aunt had insisted she bring against her boot. She had argued that England didn't have enough sun for a woman to have to worry about her complexion. Understandably, the argument had gone nowhere with his aunt.

"We don't need to discuss it at all. I was merely pointing out that I didn't charm you per se and that I'm unlikely to charm the *ton*."

"Nevertheless, you will allow my aunt and Lady Upworth to present you."

"I don't want to." She sounded like a small child defying her parent.

But Thea was a mature and intelligent woman. There had to be more to this than her concern for Merewether or her fear of not fitting in with society. From what he could tell, Thea wasn't truly afraid of anything. "Why?"

She fidgeted with her parasol handle. "I don't want to meet my father. I don't want to claim him, but I will not spend my time in England lying to protect him either."

"Don't you think it may be time to meet him? To make your peace with him?"

"How can you ask that after what he did to my mother? To me?"

The outrage in her voice washed over him and he hesitated to argue the point further, but his wife would have to have her place in Society. It would be important to his mother and grandfather, and therefore to him.

"Well, didn't your mother do something similar? After all, she took you from your father and never allowed him the pleasure of seeing his daughter grow into womanhood. Perhaps you will find that he is not such a monster after all."

It wasn't that he thought her father justified in his actions, but perhaps the man was not as horrible as Thea's mother had painted him.

She gasped. "You are defending him. I thought you understood. You said yourself he lacked integrity."

"People are imperfect, Thea. Your father has his flaws, but that doesn't mean he does not love you."

And if the man didn't love his daughter, Drake would make sure they spent little or no time in one another's company. He wanted her to be happy. He wasn't convinced that her insistence on never meeting or acknowledging her father was the course that would bring her the most joy.

"What about your father? Don't you think him settling money on you when you reached your majority was his way of showing his love?"

It was not the same thing at all. His father had not wanted him, had never acknowledged his existence. Thea knew her father wanted her, at least as a child, even if he had no longer wanted her mother.

"You don't know what you are talking about."

"That is convenient." She snapped her parasol open and used it like a shield between them. She spoke from the other side of the umbrella membrane. "When you wish to harangue me about my family, you are omniscient, but when I point out a fairly obvious conclusion, I am completely ignorant. I thought you were different from those gentlemen who believe a woman cannot have a brain in her head."

Her criticism irritated him. He knew she was intelligent, but that didn't mean she was right. His father had given him money because that was the way things were done in the *ton.* It said nothing of any tender feelings the man had toward his son.

They arrived at Merewether Shipping at that moment and Drake was saved from having to answer her accusation.

AS HE DREW THE CURRICLE IN FRONT OF A LARGE BRICK building with a modest sign that proclaimed it to be MEREWETHER SHIPPING, their argument ceased to exist for Thea. Each passing mile had eaten away at her confident assumption that she could unmask the thief. London was a vast city, entirely different from her small island home.

Even Merewether Shipping looked too large, too impressive, to be her little company. Until now, the size of her company had been limited to ledgers and bank drafts. Now that she was faced with the prospect of entering the huge brick building, finding the person responsible for the attacks on her life as well as the thefts seemed impossible.

She lowered her parasol and shifted her gaze to Drake. Gratitude for his solid presence beside her overwhelmed Thea.

"Thank you."

His eyes widened a small fraction. "Why?"

"For helping me."

Drake tossed a coin to a boy and told him to hold the horses, then turned to face her.

He placed his hands on either side of her cheeks. "We will find the culprit."

She put her hands over his, drawing on his assurance and his strength. "We must. Uncle Ashby's safety depends on it."

"So does yours."

"That's not as important."

He leaned his head down until their lips were almost touching. "It is to me."

Then he kissed her, just once and very softly, but Thea

felt it right down to her toes. How could she even think of living her life without this man?

Ignorant of the shattering realization his small kiss had precipitated, Drake jumped blithely down from the carriage. He came around to help her down. She placed her hand in his, allowing the feeling of safety that always accompanied his touch to wash over her.

He kept her firmly tucked into his side as they walked toward the building. They stopped in front of the shipping office to get their bearings, as if by mutual consent, though neither said anything.

"I grow weak in the knees at the thought of you attempting this investigation alone."

She smiled at the image of Drake weak in the knees. Still, she understood his concern. The docks were teeming with tough-looking sailors and dirty children hawking everything from meat pies to penny press papers. Bawds dressed in garments that did not completely cover their rouged nipples leaned against the walls of warehouses on either side of Merewether Shipping. One woman's petticoats were dampened to show off the curves below her waist. Thea shivered in sympathy for her.

England's cold had not come as a complete surprise, but the way it seeped into her very bones did. And the smell. Thea wrinkled her nose at the odor emanating from the Thames. Garbage floated on the surface in places, but for all that, the river and docks were an impressive sight. Feelings of inadequacy and ignorance of the City's ways pressed in on her.

She shivered again, but this time at the thought of her own naïveté in believing she could have conducted the investigation alone. Uncle Ashby's life would be better served in someone else's more capable hands, but she was all he had.

Then she smiled. And Drake. Uncle Ashby had Drake on his side as well, though he didn't know it.

She pulled toward the building. "Let's go inside."

Drake gently restrained her. "What's the matter?"

She looked up into the brown depths of his eyes, and they glowed with concern.

"It's just that I realized how foolish I was to believe that someone raised on a small island, like me, could accomplish such a heavy task in this place." She waved her hand toward the brick building and the busy docks. "I had not realized the immensity of it all. Without your help I . . . I'm not sure what I would have done. It's just all so overwhelming."

"I have no doubt that you could do all that you set out to do."

She stared at him. "Truly?"

He nodded. "You are a resourceful and intelligent woman, Thea."

"Thank you." His confidence warmed her.

They entered the shipping office through a large and heavy door. As it closed behind them, the sights and sounds of the busy docks were cut off. The hallway in which they stood felt a world away from the busy activity outside. It was lined with doors, all of them closed. Not even a stray voice filtered out to lessen the feeling of isolation.

A young man, wearing a coat and pantaloons cut in the latest fashion, came out of one of the offices. His blond hair curled around his collar. He looked up from a sheaf of papers in his hands and made a small noise as if startled. "May I help you?"

"We are looking for Emerson Merewether." Thea pulled off her gloves as she spoke and tucked them into her reticule. She raised her gaze to the young man. "Would you please show us to his office?"

The man nodded. "Certainly."

He turned and headed back the way he had come, stopping at the first office on his right. He opened the door and leaned in. "Mr. Merewether, some people here to see you."

Drake led Thea into the room and she could not help smiling. It looked very much like Uncle Ashby's office back home, only it was missing the little haven of tea table and chairs. Every available surface was covered with papers or shipping crates. The man sitting behind the desk looked up to greet them. She felt as if she were seeing a young version of Uncle Ashby. Emerson had the same rounded build and jovial expression on his face.

She stepped forward and put out her hand. "Hello. I am Thea Selwyn and this is Mr. Drake."

Emerson Merewether took her hand and shook it. "Miss Selwyn? My uncle's partner?"

She nodded, extracting her hand from his grasp. "Yes. It's a pleasure to finally meet you, Mr. Merewether."

"I had no idea you were planning a trip to England?" He asked it as a question, clearly expecting a response from the man behind her.

"It's a surprise to me as well, Mr. Merewether."

"Thea's decision to travel to England was rather spur-of-the-moment. None of us had much notice of her intentions," Drake said.

He made it sound as if they had known each other a long time. As if he would have been aware of her plans. What was he about?

"I'm sorry. Mr. Drake, is it? Would you and Miss Selwyn care to take a seat?" Emerson had certainly adjusted quickly to the unexpected arrival of one of his employers.

Drake looked around him and undoubtedly saw just what she did. There was no available surface to sit on. The blond man rushed into the room and began moving papers. Soon two wooden chairs facing Emerson's desk were free. Drake escorted her to one before taking the other.

Emerson looked up at the blond man. "Barton, see about having some refreshments brought, would you?"

Laying her reticule and parasol across her knees, she

said, "That won't be necessary. We are here for a short business meeting."

Barton stopped at the door. "Would you like me to stay then, Mr. Merewether?"

Emerson shook his head. "That won't be necessary. I'll call you should I need anything." He turned his attention to her and Drake. "Barton is my assistant."

Thea nodded her understanding. "As you said, his presence should not be required for now."

Barton left and the room went silent for a moment. How was she to introduce the topic of searching the current ledgers? Drake took care of it for her.

"Mr. Merewether, I am considering expanding my shipping company by going into partnership with your uncle and Thea."

Emerson's face registered much more shock at this statement than at her arrival. "I just received a letter from Uncle Ashby and nothing was said. Had I known Uncle was looking for another business partner, I should have purchased my way into the company myself."

Oh dear. The hurt in Emerson's voice was unmistakable. Thea rushed to soothe him. "I assure you, Mr. Merewether, we had no intention of excluding you."

"I need to write Uncle Ashby. This is a most shocking development."

Thea felt their plan unraveling before her. She did not want Emerson writing his uncle.

Drake's laughter shocked her. She turned her head to see his face.

His smile was directed at Emerson. "You misunderstood the nature of our partnership. Thea and I are engaged, and as part of the marriage settlements, her portion of Merewether Shipping will come under my control."

She swallowed her gasp of surprise. She would take Drake to task later for his lie. Right now, she would go along because at least it would discourage Emerson from writing his uncle.

Emerson's smile returned. A smile so like Uncle Ashby's that feelings of longing for her life back on the island overwhelmed her. "I did not realize you meant that sort of association. May I offer you my deepest felicitations?"

Thea summoned a weak smile. "Thank you."

Drake inclined his head to acknowledge the sentiments. "In order to prepare for the marriage settlements, I would like to spend some time looking over your books."

Emerson drew himself up. "That is quite impossible. Those ledgers are confidential, sir."

Thea cleared her throat delicately and Emerson shifted his affronted gaze to her. "As acting partner, I will of course oversee Drake's perusal of our books, Mr. Merewether."

She stressed the words "acting partner" and "our" to remind Emerson just who was ultimately in charge in this situation.

He had the grace to blush. "Yes, of course. I'm sorry if I offended you, Miss Selwyn. I have come to think of the company as a family venture, you see. I am very protective of your and Uncle Ashby's interests."

She smiled her understanding. He really seemed like a dear man.

"I should like to take the books with me today. We will return them in the next week or so after I have extracted the information I need for our marriage settlements from them," Drake said.

Emerson frowned. "Surely whatever information you need could be procured here in the offices. We need our ledgers for reference. In fact"—Emerson's frown turned to a smile—"Barton could compile whatever numbers you require and deliver the papers to your town house."

She understood Emerson's unwillingness to let the ledgers from his sight.

It was really quite natural, but rather annoying. "I'm afraid Drake is a rather independent and obstinate sort of person. He will not trust the numbers compiled by anyone but himself."

"Thea is correct. I prefer to do my own accounting. My man of business finds my ways quite tiresome as I insist on double-checking all financial transactions for my company."

Emerson's face started to show signs of Uncle Ashby's temper. "I assure you, Barton is above reproach. Any numbers he supplies you with will be accurate to the pence."

Drake smiled and her heart did a small flip at the charm oozing from him. "Nevertheless, as Thea so sweetly put it, I'm rather independent and obstinate. I should like the ledgers."

"Couldn't you at least do your checking here?"

Really, it was a reasonable request and Thea was about to agree when Drake shook his head. All charm had vanished and his face took on that impassive expression she had come to think of as rather dangerous. Standing, he extended his arm to her. She took it without thinking.

Leading her out the door, he spoke over his shoulder. "Have the ledgers brought out to my curricle immediately. Miss Selwyn and I have promised Lady Boyle we will be in attendance for tea."

Thirteen

*I have discovered an aptitude for business. Ashby wanted
to let me invest in the shipping venture, but my funds are
limited. I offered to keep his books. At first, he refused,
believing such a position would be beyond a lady. I
proved him wrong. Now, I keep track of all inventories
and accounts, and yesterday I negotiated my first shipload
of cargo. It was a most amazing experience—one I look
forward to repeating in the future.*

*July 15, 1801
Journal of Anna Selwyn, Countess of Langley*

"REALLY, DRAKE. YOU DID NOT NEED TO BE SO
abrupt with poor Mr. Merewether. I think you offended his dignity."

He flicked the reins, setting the horses in motion. Thea
grabbed the side of the curricle as it lurched forward rather
quickly. The ledgers, stacked between her and Drake, shifted
and she put a restraining hand on them.

"To hell with his dignity. He is your employee and had
no business arguing with your fiancé."

"Well, as to that. Do you think it was a good idea to tell him we are engaged? Word is bound to get out."

"Word will get out anyway. Once the *ton* learns of our close association aboard the *Golden Dragon,* you will have no choice but to become engaged to me. Like it or not, you have been compromised."

She didn't like the implacable tone of his voice. "That is silly. A few visits to my stateroom surely cannot require marriage."

"We did a lot more than just visit, or had you forgotten?"

Her cheeks heated in embarrassment, but she could not deny the truth. "I remember. The moments I spent with you were the most wonderful of my life. I am not likely to forget them."

He swore savagely. "Then why refuse to marry me? No. Don't answer that. I know why. You think I'll turn into a cruel monster like your father. Has it ever occurred to you that perhaps he wasn't such a monster? That your mother's view of events was skewed by her own feelings and perceptions?"

"You don't understand."

He flicked the reins until the horses were going much faster than the rest of traffic. "No, I don't. If your sainted mother, as Melly is so fond of calling her, were alive, I would have a few things to say to her."

His sudden anger confused her. "You don't mean that. You're angry for some reason, but don't take it out on my mother. She lost more than you could possibly know, and my father is the cause. He deserves my disgust, not your championship."

Drake came within inches of another carriage. She should say something about his neck or nothing driving, but one look at his set features changed her mind.

"How do you know?" he demanded. "Don't you think he at least has the right to tell you his side of the story?

Maybe you don't want to hear that your perfect mother might not have been so perfect after all."

Moisture burned Thea's eyes. "You don't know what you are saying."

Drake was forced to slow the horses as they entered the thicker traffic of London proper. "Thea, you have an entire family here in England. People who would love you if you gave them the chance. Are you content to deny them all for the sake of your mother's memory?"

He knew his arguments had as much to do with convincing her to stay in England with him as they did with believing she should reconcile with her family. He would use any means to convince Thea that she belonged in England, *with him.*

"I don't have to deny them all, just my father."

He sighed at her insistence on that particular point. If she were going to make her permanent residence in England, she had to come to some sort of understanding with her father.

"Don't you think that will make life a trifle awkward for them and for you? What are you going to do? Have Lady Upworth introduce you as her niece, but refuse to tell anyone who your father is? They'll figure it out, you know. I doubt that many of her nephews had their wives abandon them."

"My mother didn't abandon my father. He abandoned her." Thea's outrage fueled his frustration.

There was no doubt that her father had misused her mother, but that didn't mean that the man was a complete ogre. For all she knew, he had mellowed with age—stranger things had happened. He didn't like to see Thea's generous heart torn in pieces by bitterness toward a father she'd never met.

He tried reason one more time. "She took you to the West Indies and hid from him. What do you call that?"

"Survival."

The one word said a great deal. Dread snaked in his gut. Had the man been violent? If so, he certainly understood Thea's certainty that her father was a monster. Drake would not allow her father to threaten her. He would protect her from everything and everyone—excepting himself, of course.

"Thea, was your mother afraid for her life?"

"No." Thea swiped at her eyes and he felt helpless in the face of her distress. "She was afraid he would discover me and take me away. Then she would be left with nothing."

"What do you mean, *discover* you? You said that she spirited you away after he threatened never to let her see you again."

"No, I said she took me away after he threatened to never let her see her child again."

He wished for the second time that day that they weren't publicly exposed in a carriage. She had more secrets than the War Department.

"Tell me what you mean."

He didn't expect her to acquiesce to his demand, but then when had she ever done what he expected?

"Very well." She sucked on her bottom lip, and he could almost see her mind working on the problem of how much to tell him.

Finally, her words came out in a rush like steam escaping through the safety valve on the *Golden Dragon*'s boiler.

"My brother was born first. Father stormed into the room and took him away right after my mother gave birth. She pleaded with him, but he ignored her. He didn't care how much he hurt her. I was born a few minutes after he and the wet nurse left Langley Hall. The midwife and Melly agreed to help my mother hide me. She was desperate to keep at least one of her children."

"If she loved your brother so much, how could she leave

England and never see him again?" He hated asking the question after everything else he had already said, but he had to know the whole.

"She didn't at first. She tried to see him. Lady Upworth would have my brother to visit and then Mama would come over, but Father discovered what they were doing and put a stop to it. Mama's journal says that he came by one day unexpectedly to harangue her for seeing her son. He almost found me in Mama's arms. That's when she decided that to keep me, she would have to leave England. It was a hard decision and she regretted it many times. But according to Lady Upworth, Father never softened toward Mama and would not have allowed her to see her son."

He took time digesting what she had told him. Thea had a brother, a twin brother. According to her account, she had never even met him. That must be very difficult for someone with her open heart.

"I understand you not wanting to see your father, but what of your brother? Now that you are of age, there is no risk in making yourself known and meeting him."

He had learned to live with the fact that he had half brothers and sisters who knew nothing about him. But he was a man, not a tenderhearted female like Thea.

"I'm not ready."

A memory tugged at his consciousness. "You said your mother made you promise two things. What was the other one?"

She sighed and wiped her cheeks with her gloved fingers. "To give my brother her journals. She wanted him to know that she never stopped loving him or thinking about him."

He was beginning to understand Thea's certainty that her father was beyond redemption. Not only had he torn their family apart, but he had withheld her brother from Thea and hurt her in the process.

"In effect, your mother made you promise to meet your brother."

She must have worried that Thea would never have made the trip to England otherwise. She must have *wanted* her daughter to return to their homeland.

"I plan to keep my promise, truly. Just not immediately. Everything has been happening so fast, and the most important thing right now is to find the thief and protect Uncle Ashby. But it's true—eventually I will have no choice but to meet my brother."

"You have no choice about becoming engaged, either." Didn't she understand?

The same honor that required her to keep her promise to her mother required him to marry her.

She scowled, her expression no longer one of pain, but of anger. "Of course I have a choice."

"Not if you wish to take your place in Society."

"How many times do I have to tell you that it doesn't matter to me?" Her exasperation with his reasoning was clear in her voice.

"Does your aunt's acceptance among the *ton* matter to you?"

She took a deep breath and let it out again slowly before asking, "What do you mean?"

He glanced at her. "If she continues to acknowledge you, as you know she will insist on doing, the damage to your reputation will also affect hers."

"That is ridiculous. Our friendship aboard your ship cannot affect my aunt's standing in the *ton*."

"I realize that you know little of the ways of the *ton*, but you must accept my greater experience in this matter. I am intimately acquainted with scandal. Your aunt's life will be made very difficult by our association if we are not engaged."

"That's so unfair. I don't even want to be introduced to the *ton*, and yet if I don't, my aunt will be hurt. If I do and

I refuse to become engaged with you, she will suffer. It isn't right." She pulled her lower lip between her teeth and his tolerance snapped.

"Stop that. Every time you take your lip between your teeth, I am reminded how good those lips taste and how much I want to kiss you." And he was bloody tired of driving in an uncomfortable state of arousal.

She immediately let go of her lip. "I . . . it's an old habit. I'm sorry it disturbs you."

He sighed. "Everything about you disturbs me, Thea."

She cast him a sidelong glance. "I suppose we could pretend to be engaged as long as I am in England. If it will make things better for Lady Upworth, that is."

Drake felt a slow burn of satisfaction. It would not be a pretend engagement, but he wouldn't argue that point now. "Good."

"Still, you should have told me before you said something to Mr. Merewether. I could have ruined our story by denying it in my surprise."

"You are too intelligent to be so easily tripped up. Besides, I had to think on my feet. If I hadn't said that, he would have written a very upsetting letter to his uncle."

She started to bite her lip and then stopped, giving him another sideways glance. "I guess so. I'm surprised he accepted your story, regardless."

"Why is that?" He thought he'd done an excellent job of being convincing.

The truth was like that.

"I can't believe that he accepted the faradiddle about you controlling my share of the company once we were married. Mr. Merewether and I are not totally unknown to each other, though we have never met. We have been corresponding since he took over the London office. He must realize that I would never give up my role in Merewether Shipping—even if I were foolish enough to marry."

Drake disliked the comment about being foolish enough

to marry, but understood her other concern. Anyone who knew Thea at all would realize she was not the type to give her company over to her husband's care.

"He believed it because that is what most women of his acquaintance would do."

"Is that what you would expect from your wife?"

Drake sensed the deeper meaning behind her words and hesitated before answering. "I would not expect you to give up all interest in your shipping company, but you must realize that as my wife and the mother of our children, you could not spend your days at Merewether Shipping."

"I could do a great deal of business from our home." She cleared her throat. "I mean to say, your wife could."

"Yes, you could. It pleases my family for me to conduct most of my business that way as well."

"It would not be the usual sort of marriage."

Drawing the horses to a stop in front of his aunt's town house for the second time that day, he formulated his response in his mind. Once he'd secured the reins, he took her chin in his hand and turned her face toward him. "We are not the usual gentleman and lady. We are both different, made that way by the circumstances of our births and upbringing. I don't want to marry a lady who has no interest in her business. I want to marry you. I would only ask that for the sake of our families and children, you be circumspect in your business dealings. There is nothing like the hint of trade to tarnish your standing among the *ton*."

Her brow furrowed. "Don't you think one must spend an inordinate amount of time worrying about what is and is not acceptable to Society when one lives in England? I can assure you that back on my island I did not worry overmuch about what others would think of my actions."

He grinned. "I have no doubt."

The footman came out to take charge of the curricle. Drake swung down and went around to collect Thea.

Once he had her on the ground, he tucked her arm into

his and gave instructions for the ledgers to be delivered to his aunt's library. "Shall we tell my aunt our happy news?"

"I suppose." She did not look overjoyed at the prospect. "Will she be very angry with you when you tell her it was all a sham?"

"I won't tell her."

"Oh." She stopped to think. "We could fabricate an argument and add a pretend crying off to our pretend engagement."

He gripped her arm more tightly, wanting to anchor her to himself. "Let's not plan that far into the future."

If he had anything to say about it, their very real engagement would be followed by an even realer marriage. An unconventional one, perhaps, but real nonetheless.

THEA FOLLOWED DRAKE INTO HIS AUNT'S DRAWING room, still uncertain about the false engagement deception he was set on perpetrating.

She wasn't such a fool that she didn't realize he'd prefer it to be a real one, but she was at a loss as to how to convince him that his honor would not be tarnished by not marrying her. She understood his concern for her aunt, but surely Thea's actions would not have such an impact on her aunt's standing among the *ton*. Back home on her island, one would never be ostracized simply for being related to an unsavory character.

Not that she was unsavory, but she did seem to have a difficult time adhering to the ways of the Polite World every moment of every day.

"Mama, this is a pleasing surprise."

Thea's thoughts scattered to the four winds at Drake's words. His mother had come to London? She was sure Lady Boyle had told her that Lady Noreen was not expected in Town for the Season. Thea had been disappointed, for she had wanted to meet a lady of the *ton* with the courage to bear an illegitimate child and raise him as her own.

But now the thought of meeting more of Drake's family gave Thea heart palpitations. What would Lady Noreen do when she heard of the supposed engagement?

She was a duke's daughter; she would want more for her son.

Thea's gaze flew with trepidation to the beautiful, petite woman Drake had spoken to. Lady Noreen shared Drake's dark hair and brown eyes, as well as a feminine version of his perfectly formed features, but she was tiny beside her tall son.

"Pierson." Smiling, Lady Noreen reached her hands out toward him.

He crossed the room with rapid strides and took her hands in his, leaning his big body down so he could kiss her cheek. "It is good to see you."

"I have missed you, darling."

Thea knew that such open affection between members of the *ton* was not the usual way of things, and she took an instant liking to this woman who had given Drake birth, and had taught him that there were more important things in life than mere societal strictures.

He stood up, his smile enigmatic. "Ah, so that explains your presence in Town when I distinctly remember you saying you had no plans to attend the Season."

"Do not be silly, Pierson." Lady Noreen's soft, melodious voice was tinged with censure. "You know very well I've come to meet the woman you plan to marry."

His muttered imprecation barely registered as the small woman waved her hand toward Thea. "Come here, my dear. I have been waiting these past five years or more for my son to choose a bride. I wish to wait not one moment longer to meet you."

Thea felt inexorably drawn across the room by the woman's warmth and genuine desire to meet her.

She stopped in front of the other woman and remembered at the last second to curtsy as her mother had taught her. "It is an honor to meet you, my lady."

Lady Boyle nodded her approval. "Nicely done, Miss Selwyn."

Amusement lurked on the edges of Thea's lips as she curtsied toward the old woman. "Thank you."

"Ah, she has a sense of humor and impeccable manners. I like that."

Thea's amusement vanished and she cast a worried frown toward Drake, but he was not looking at her. His attention was fixed on his mother as if he was trying to interpret her reaction to Thea.

It was left to her to tell the elegant Lady the truth. "I'm sorry to say my manners are sporadic. Mama and Aunt Ruth tried their best, but social rules on my island were not so strict as London. I'm afraid I have some terrible habits."

"Nonsense, gel. You are a sweet young lady, and so I've told my niece." Lady Boyle's championship was as pleasant as it was unexpected.

Surely the old woman was not blind to Thea's faults.

Even more shocking were Drake's words. "She is perfect, Mama. Do not let her convince you otherwise."

Thea spun to face him, her hands on her hips. "That is not what you told my aunt. You listed my shortcomings for her like a man intent on his last confession before going to meet his Maker. Does your own mother not deserve the same honesty?"

"But I have told her the truth, sweeting. You are perfect for me."

His words warmed her clear to her toes, and she had to clasp her hands to stop them from reaching out to touch him. "Oh, Drake . . ."

His eyes spoke a message she feared to translate as they stood in silent communication for several seconds.

Finally, he broke his gaze from hers and smiled at his

mother over Thea's shoulder. "You will love her, Mama."

Blushing, Thea turned back to face his mother to find the dark brown eyes so like her son's glistening with moisture.

"My lady?"

"I am very happy at this moment, Thea. May I call you Thea?"

"Yes, of course."

"And you must call me Noreen, at least until you are married to my son. Then you will call me Mama."

Tears burned Thea's own eyes. "I would be honored to do so."

But her heart was heavy. She did not wish to see this woman hurt by the disappointment of a broken engagement. And it was apparent no other outcome could be expected. Lady Noreen loved her son and wanted to see him happily settled.

The deception of the engagement was taking on a life of its own.

THEA ESCAPED TO LADY BOYLE'S LIBRARY AND FELL into the nearest chair. Slipping her shoes off, she wiggled her toes and wished she had the courage to lift her skirts and massage her feet. She didn't. Not after spending the entire day shopping in the company of her aunt, Drake's mother, and Lady Boyle. Those worthy ladies had taken it into their heads to help her prepare for the role of Drake's wife as well as to take her place in Society.

She didn't even bother to stifle a groan at the thought. How could she have allowed Drake to convince her to go along with his phony engagement scheme?

His arguments had seemed so sound in the carriage, when she was still feeling emotionally vulnerable from their discussion about her family. Now she was sure there had to be a better way to protect her aunt's reputation. She hated lying, and the deception had only just begun. Everyone she met from this point forward would believe that she was engaged to Drake.

He'd made sure of that by putting an announcement in both of the major London newspapers. She had protested the announcement as unnecessary, but he had said the damage was already done. Besides, he argued, his mother would expect it.

His mother.

Thea genuinely liked Lady Noreen. She was everything a lady of the *ton* was expected to be and yet she was also kind, loving toward her family, and fiercely protective of her son. It hadn't taken Thea any time at all to work out that Lady Noreen had remained unattached through her son's childhood so there would never be a risk of him being rejected and shunted off to live with relatives in some remote location.

She wanted only the best for Drake and had sacrificed her own pursuits to ensure he got it. Lady Noreen was in alt over his decision to wed, treating Thea just like the daughter she never had, which made the false engagement even worse, to Thea's way of thinking.

When she had brought her concerns on that score to Drake, he had dismissed them with the assurance *he* had no plans to disappoint his mother.

Was it any wonder she spent a good part of each day wanting to throttle him? Thea asked herself.

The confusing part was that she spent the rest of her time wanting to touch him. It was his close proximity. He never let her out of his sight, except when she went shopping with his mother and the others. He'd been quick enough to make himself scarce this morning when Lady Noreen announced their intentions.

Drat the man. If he was going to plague her, he should at least have the decency to stand by her during an ordeal like shopping for clothes in London. She tipped her head back on the chair and allowed her eyes to shut. She would rest for just a minute before tackling the ledgers again.

"My poor, exhausted darling."

Thea's eyes flew open at the sound of Drake's voice, but she had been half asleep and it took careful thought to reason out what he had said. When she did, she frowned up at him.

He loomed over her, looking altogether too tempting in his simple, elegant clothes. He made other men, particularly the London dandies she had seen, look foolishly ornamented.

"So, you have come out of hiding now that the torture is over."

He widened his eyes innocently. "Torture? I thought you went shopping."

She straightened in the chair and groaned loudly at the stiffness in her body. "Same thing. Have you ever been shopping with your aunt?"

He put out his hand and she took it. Pulling her to her feet, he said, "Once. For some new gloves."

The mere mention of the word *gloves* made her shudder. Lady Boyle had insisted on buying gloves to match every one of the new outfits they had ordered, and she had made Thea try them all on, as if one pair of gloves were going to fit differently than another. "Then you have some small idea of what I have been through. I thought my aunt a frail old woman, but she and Lady Boyle left me gasping for air after the third modiste."

She hobbled after him on swollen feet as he pulled her across the room to a small sofa under the window. The light played over the crimson cushions invitingly. She liked Lady Boyle's library. Its quiet simplicity soothed her. The same books she had grown up reading graced the shelves and gave her a feeling of belonging amid this all too foreign environment. She loved the smell of rich leather and paper that permeated the room as well. It was so much better than the city smells that assaulted her the moment she left Lady Boyle's town house.

"I thought all ladies liked the excitement of buying a new wardrobe." She could tell from the devilment sparkling in his eyes that he was trying to bait her.

"Our aunts and your mother certainly do. Even if it is for someone else. In fact, I'm sure that aspect enhanced their enjoyment. *They* didn't have to suffer through the fittings."

He pressed her down onto the sofa. "But you did not enjoy it."

She glared up at him. "Do I look like I've had a pleasant afternoon? I spent hours being poked and prodded by women who must have read the works of the Marquis de Sade."

He made a choking sound. "Do not tell me that you have read his work."

She was back to wanting to throttle him. "Of course not."

Drake nodded and joined her on the sofa. "So how do you know about him?"

"I was raised in the West Indies, not a convent. Sailors talk. Especially the French." How had they gotten onto such an obscure and uninteresting subject?

She wanted to tell him her complaints, not discuss sailors' gossip, but all thought of gossip and complaining went right out of her head when Drake lifted her feet into his lap.

Shifting the hem of her gown above her ankles, he exposed her feet. "You are wearing stockings."

Sometimes he said the strangest things. "Naturally. Have you not noticed how cold England is?"

His light touch made her insides put lie to her words. England, cold? Not at all.

"I was remembering the first time I saw you. You had your skirt up and were fanning your incredibly alluring ankles. Ankles covered with nothing but the hot Caribbean air."

His voice sent shivers up her spine. *Alluring ankles?*

"I didn't know you were there." Her voice, which only moments ago had been waspish, now came out breathless.

He had that effect on her.

Fourteen

Ashby and Ruth are concerned that I spend too much time at the warehouse, that the company of sailors is not good for me or my small daughter. I have found the sailors to be an honest lot, for the most part, and though their conversation is colorful, I never feel threatened around them. I have had to be more circumspect with Thea, however. This morning she asked for a bloody biscuit. Ruth nearly fainted, but I fought a desperate urge to laugh.

October 12, 1803
Journal of Anna Selwyn, Countess of Langley

HE LAUGHED SOFTLY AND BEGAN TO MASSAGE the underside of one of her feet. "That is one of my favorite memories. You looked so uninhibited and blissful."

Blissful was having your feet massaged by an incredibly handsome man like Drake. She relaxed against the cushions of the couch.

"That feels so good." If she were a cat, she would have

purred with the pleasure of it. However, she felt compelled to add, "I'm sure your aunt would have palpitations if she walked in and found you doing this."

His grin was wicked. "I locked the door."

Her gaze flew to the library door, shut firmly against intruders. "Lady Boyle will pitch a fit if she finds out."

He gave her a measuring look. "What did my aunt say that you are so concerned about her reaction?"

"She and my aunt spent the day lecturing me on the proper behavior of a woman affianced to the grandson of a duke."

"And Mama?"

"She showed considerable restraint and merely pointed out that as you move among the *ton,* I would be expected to do so as well. Do you have any idea how I dread disappointing your mother? I had to be on my best behavior every moment, and I *hate* lying to her."

"You really had a grueling day, didn't you?" The sympathy in his voice and magic of his massaging touch did a good deal to sooth her sensibilities.

"You cannot imagine how awful it was," she agreed. "I stood for hours being fitted for more gowns than I'll wear in a lifetime, much less this one short Season."

"And getting new clothes holds no appeal for you?"

She let her eyes flutter close, concentrating on the wonderful heat of his large hands on the pinched muscles of her feet. "It's just so different from my island. There, if Aunt Ruth wanted me to have a new dress, she and Melly made it. I never had to go shopping for fabrics." The prettiest textiles from all over the world came through their small port. "You would not believe how low the modiste wanted to cut the neckline on my gowns. England is much too cold to expose so much of my person to the elements."

He made a noncommittal sound and his fingers continued their ministrations.

"Doesn't it strike you as odd that I'm supposed to wear

those horrible stays, several layers of petticoats and other undergarments, but expose my bosom to all and sundry?"

He chuckled.

"It is not a bit amusing . . ." Her voice trailed into nothingness as he began to rub the other foot also and her entire body liquefied. "Oh, that is just right."

"I am sure you told the modiste what you felt regarding current fashions." He still sounded amused.

"I did, but my aunt was most insistent regarding stays. She wasn't at all impressed with the findings of the American physicians."

"Lady Upworth convinced you to wear a corset?" He didn't sound pleased by the prospect.

"No. Thankfully, Lady Boyle stood up for me on that count and said one could not expect a lady raised in the wilds to adopt every English custom. I wasn't exactly raised in the wilds, but I didn't belabor the point. Arguing with your aunt is exhausting."

He moved his strong, warm fingers up to her ankles. Did he have any idea of the effect he was having on her?

Her legs tingled in the most amazing way, and a totally inappropriate desire for his hands to move higher beset her.

"And will the gowns show a great deal of your bosom?"

"What?" How could he expect her to think when her body was on fire?

He repeated his question, the amusement conspicuously absent from his voice.

"No. I was quite firm and would not allow her to cut them any lower than my current fashion. I have no intention of contracting the ague because the English style dictates too little fabric in one's gowns."

"Good."

She didn't respond. She was too busy trying to deal with the feelings elicited by the move of his hands from her ankles to the lower portion of her legs. He alternated between caressing her with soft light strokes and kneading her muscles. It felt delicious and relaxing, but also wonderfully intimate.

How had she gone so long without his touch? She wanted, no *needed,* to feel his hands on her bare skin again. All of her.

She opened her eyes and found him looking at her. The flames in his eyes matched the firestorm blazing inside her.

"Are you by any chance trying to seduce me?" she asked with mortifying breathlessness.

His fingertips inched above her knees, sending frissons of pleasure arcing up her inner thighs to the core of her. "Do you want me to?"

"Yes." Then the reality of what she was saying intruded. "I mean *no.*"

She tried to pull her legs from his grasp, but he wouldn't let go. One hand held her legs while the other continued the incendiary caresses.

"We can't do this."

His fingertips slipped onto skin that no other man had ever touched. "Why not?"

For a minute she couldn't remember any good reasons to stop. She searched her mind frantically while his touch sent thought after thought flying to oblivion.

Oh, yes. "A baby. We might make a baby."

His hand did not still its movements. "That would be bad?"

"Yes."

"Why?"

Feverish with excitement, she tried to remember why her getting pregnant would be a bad thing. The image of her body big with Drake's child was more alluring than any ankles ever could be, and it was only with great effort that she was able to remember her objection to the idea. "Then you would insist on marriage."

He leaned toward her until his lips almost touched her own. "Thea, you are a very intelligent woman."

"Thank you," she breathed.

"But sometimes your stubbornness overcomes your insight."

She frowned. What was he trying to say?

"I will insist on marriage anyway." Then his lips were on hers, hot and demanding.

Giving up any attempt at rational thought, she fell into the kiss with all the enthusiasm at her disposal.

DRAKE EXULTED IN THEA'S WHOLEHEARTED RESPONSE as his mouth devoured hers.

She writhed against him with the same sweet abandon that she had exhibited on the ship. Did she have any idea of the effect her passion had on him? Without breaking the kiss, he slipped his hands farther under her skirts and grasped her hips to pull her astride his lap until her unprotected feminine center was pressed close to the bulge in his pants.

She rocked against him and he came within a breath of exploding right then and there.

He cupped her bottom and forced her to still her movements. She groaned against his lips, shuddering. Using the same kneading movements he had on her feet, he caressed her backside, letting his fingertips stray to the apex of her thighs sporadically, until she was straining against his hands.

She tried to move herself against him.

"Wait, sweetheart. You aren't ready yet."

Eyes, unfocused in their passion, looked back at him disbelievingly. "I was ready days ago."

So she *had* been craving his touch.

He smiled. "I want you begging."

"I did the begging bit the first time. Couldn't we just skip that part and make love?"

He laughed at her serious expression.

Suddenly it struck him how difficult it must have been for an independent and proud woman like Thea to ask him to make love to her, *to beg* as she put it. "Shall I beg this time?"

From the smile that transformed her passion to joyous delight, he assumed she liked the idea. He kissed the pink shell of her ear and nibbled on her earlobe.

She panted, pressing her breasts against him with her small, shallow breaths. "That feels good."

"Will you please allow me to make love with you?" He whispered straight into her ear, allowing his breath to caress sensitive nerve endings.

She shivered and started unbuttoning his shirt with impatient fingers. "If we do, you will think I have compromised you again."

She had that backward, but since she didn't sound as concerned as her words implied, he let it go and licked his way down her neck to her collarbone. "Please?"

She finished unbuttoning his shirt and slipped her hands inside, showing that no matter what she said, she did indeed want him. The feel of her small fingers playing across the heated skin of his chest made him swell more painfully against her.

"We aren't married, Mr. Drake. What would your aunt say?"

It finally dawned on him that the little baggage was teasing him, and he growled against her throat.

Using his teeth, he pulled the fabric of her dress away to expose one firm, round breast. Her breath hitched and then expelled in a long hiss as he took her nipple into his mouth. He suckled her for several seconds, working his tongue over the hard nub until her breast rose and fell in harsh rhythm against his mouth.

Her hands curled into fists against his chest. *"Pierson."*

He loved it when she used his first name. It implied she

was aware of him on a wholly intimate level. He was the only one who brought her to this place. The only man she had ever allowed to touch her body so familiarly.

Primitive possession and male satisfaction coursed through him. *She did belong to him.* Now and forever. He gently released her nipple from his mouth and showered her breast with tiny, biting kisses.

Squeezing her bottom, he rubbed her against his rigidity. "Do you feel me, Thea?"

"Ye-es."

"Can you feel how hard I am?"

Her answer was to give him a hot, openmouthed kiss that sent his mind reeling.

He broke his lips away from hers. "Will you give me the relief I seek?"

She met his gaze, hers serious and intent. "Is it merely relief you seek?"

He could not believe the doubt he read in her eyes. "*You* are what I seek. *I need you,* Thea. I have never felt this desperate to touch and be touched. I have been furious with you for refusing to marry me."

She sighed. "I know. You feel obligated to marry me after I seduced you aboard ship. You have been angry that I would not bow to the dictates of your honor."

His laughter startled him. How did she always manage to do this, amuse and exasperate at the same time?

"Honor has nothing to do with my anger, sweetheart. I want to be in your bed every night. Sometimes I lie awake for hours aching to hold you. Without marriage, I don't have the right."

She kissed the side of his cheek, near his ear, and whispered, "You are holding me now."

Yes, he was. Their discussion of marriage could wait until afterward. His body would not be denied another moment. Evidently hers would not be either, because she slipped her hands between them to undo the buttons on his pants. Her fingers rubbed against him as she worked the buttons and he groaned, sounding like a man in purgatory.

Which he would be until he could be ensconced in the haven of her body. "Hurry, sweetheart. I cannot wait much longer."

"I can't either."

Finally he was free. She circled him with her fingers and squeezed. He let out a feral shout and almost tumbled them both off the small sofa.

Stroking him up and down, Thea gave him a mischievous smile. "I believe you were in the process of groveling, were you not?"

He brought one hand around and slipped his finger into the dewy curls at the apex of her thighs.

Rubbing the swollen nub he found there, he said, "Please."

She arched into his hand and gave a muffled cry against his shoulder. He continued touching her while she writhed against him, her breath labored and uneven. He took her silence for acquiescence and tried to tip her back onto the sofa. She resisted, pushing against his chest to keep him in place.

Did she want him to beg some more?

But the look in her eye was not one of teasing. She looked like she was trying to work something out. He held his breath. If she were coming up with valid reasons not to make love, he was doomed.

Keeping his manhood in one hand, she slipped forward until his tip pressed against the opening to her feminine center. He could not believe what was happening. Was his innocent Thea planning to ride him?

From the look of concentration on her face, he had to assume she was.

She smiled. "It will work like this, won't it?"

He nodded, his tongue frozen in his mouth.

She let go of his shaft and he could not help surging upward and into her.

Her eyes went wide as her tight passage stretched to accommodate his hardness. "You feel bigger than I remember."

He forced himself to remain motionless. "Does it hurt?"

She shook her head. "No. It feels . . ." Her voice trailed off and she moved experimentally against him. "It feels wonderful."

Sweat trickled down his temples. "Yes, it does."

She rocked against him, increasing her rhythm and the breadth of her movements until the pleasure began to build at the base of his hard flesh. He pressed against her back so that as she came forward with each thrust, her sweetest spot rubbed against his pelvic bone.

She sucked in her breath, her eyes closing and her head falling back. *"Oh."*

He lowered his head to her breast and teased the swollen peak with his mouth. Her fingers locked in his hair, their grip frantic. He welcomed the small pain, not knowing how long he could hold out, but determined she find her completion first.

"Pierson. Oh, Pierson. Oh, *Pierson.*" She chanted his name as her rhythm increased to a frenzied level.

"That's it." He looked up from her breast, and his breath caught in his throat at the look of rapture on her face. "Yes, just like that. Let go, Thea. I want to feel you lose control."

She did, her entire body convulsing. Her feminine muscles clenched around his hard member until he felt his own release as inevitable as daybreak well up in him. He thrust against her, once, twice, a third time. She shuddered anew with each thrust, and when he shot himself inside her, tears pooled in her eyes.

"I can feel the warmth of you filling me."

"You are mine." He thrust against her again and felt

himself drained dry by her sweetness. "Do you understand? I am not just in you. I am part of you."

She collapsed against him, allowing her head to rest on his shoulder. "When we make love, I cannot tell where I leave off and you begin. It is as if our bodies are one."

She couldn't know how revealing her words were. She might not realize it, but she had as good as admitted that there was no going back for them. They were too linked, inescapably connected by the miraculous things that happened when their bodies united.

He held her for several minutes, the room silent but for their harsh breathing slowly returning to normal and the sound of the mantel clock ticking away the passing time. He let his gaze wander around the library and smiled. He would not have described this particular room as seductive, but he would never again be able to enter it without thinking of this time with Thea.

The clock chimed the hour and she stirred against him. "Your aunt will be expecting us in the drawing room for tea soon."

He carefully disentangled their bodies, gently setting her off his lap. "You are right. If we are to discuss our investigation, we must hurry."

"Is that why you came?"

He shrugged. No need for her to know how desperate he had been to touch her.

She grinned. "You got sidetracked."

"Yes. But now we must focus on the task at hand."

She stood up and brushed her skirts into smooth folds again. "So you are saying that you had no intention of seducing me when you came into the room?"

He couldn't see her face as she bent to straighten her clothes, so he could not tell if she was teasing him or not.

He sidestepped her question. "We need to discuss the thief at your shipping company."

"Oh, that must be why you locked the door. You didn't want to be disturbed or overheard discussing that sensitive subject."

His hands stilled in the process of tucking his shirt back into his pants. "Are you mocking me, Thea?"

Her head came up and the sparkle of amusement in her eyes brought an answering smile to his lips.

He stalked toward her and breathed in satisfaction at her retreat. "You tease me at your own peril, little baggage."

She tried to dart around him, but he caught her. "If we were not expected downstairs for tea, I would exact retribution."

The smile left her face.

Her blue eyes grew luminescent. "I must be shameless because even knowing that your aunt expects us, I want you to."

He caressed her cheek. "Admit you belong to me."

He hated the look of wariness that settled over her features. He bit back a stream of curses only with great effort. He kissed where his fingers had just touched.

She sighed and turned until her lips touched his.

She kissed him gently, then stepped away. "I'm afraid."

Her admission touched him. It could not be easy for a woman with her pride to admit the weakness of fear.

"What is it you fear, Thea? Do you fear me?"

He didn't even like asking the latter. The possibility that she might say yes tore at his insides. She had said once she believed him to be like her father. Did she believe that still?

She turned and moved toward the desk. Stopping, she absentmindedly turned the pages of the ledger sitting on top. He wanted to repeat his question, but forced himself to wait patiently for her answer.

"I fear marriage. I fear living in England amidst people so preoccupied with one's appearance that they cannot possibly know a person's heart. I fear for my uncle's safety, that I will not discover the thief in time. I fear my aunt will die and leave me when I have just found her." Her voice broke. "How could I have waited so long to come? She invited me often, but I waited. Because I was afraid."

The last of her words came out in a broken whisper. He strode across the room and laid his hand on her shoulder.

She turned her face until their eyes locked.

She gave a small, sad smile and shrugged. "I believe I fear myself most of all."

Her honesty humbled him.

He pulled her against him and wrapped his arms around her, holding her tightly. He didn't ask her what she meant. He understood what it was to fear oneself. Growing up, he had refused to look in a mirror for fear of seeing the resemblance to his father that others had remarked upon. He didn't want to become the kind of man who would seduce and then abandon a lady.

He had often wondered why his father had ever courted his mother. He had known from the outset that Lady Noreen's marriage portion would be tied up in legal settlements. The thought that his own father was so dishonorable that he had pursued an innocent woman for the sake of conquest alone chilled Drake to his very bones.

He had feared that same failing might reside in his own heart. Until he met Thea. Every protective instinct he possessed had come roaring to the surface when he met her. Although he had craved her touch almost from the first moment, he had never once considered making her his mistress or taking her maidenhead and then moving on. He wanted her forever.

He would do anything to protect her, including pressuring her into a marriage that she thought she didn't want.

But not right now.

Making love had softened her, broken down some of her defenses. If he pushed her, she would draw those defenses around herself in an impenetrable wall. He rubbed her back until he felt her relax against him.

He rocked her from side to side for several minutes of silence before releasing her and stepping away. "Let's talk about Merewether Shipping."

Her eyes widened as if she had expected him to pursue the earlier conversation, but he was too much the tactician to lose ground in an effort to gain it.

Their investigation was a much safer topic of conversation. "Did you find anything else in the ledgers?"

Thea frowned at his question. "I have found nothing so far, except evidence that the thieving has not stopped." She slammed the ledger on the desk shut. "There must be a clue in here somewhere as to who is responsible, but I cannot find it."

"It's fairly obvious who the culprit is, Thea."

She cocked her brows at him. "Who?"

"Emerson Merewether."

She traced the letters on the bound leather cover of the ledger. "No. I don't believe it. He's so much like Uncle Ashby. There must be another explanation."

He shook his head. "It has to be someone who has access to both the ledgers and the warehouse. Thea, who else could it be?"

"What about his assistant? That Barton fellow. He looked shifty to me."

He smiled at her description. "Shifty?"

"Yes." She nodded. "Didn't you see the way he dressed? Too stylishly for a shipping clerk. And he insisted on staying to hear our discussion."

Drake moved around to sit at the desk. He opened the ledger that Thea had shut and looked at the neat entries. "He's more than a shipping clerk. He's Emerson's assistant. His preference for dandyish clothing does not make him shifty, and he did not insist on staying. He offered and left immediately after Emerson declined that offer."

"Don't you see? He's just clever. He knew better than to insist, so he casually offered—and I don't think we can dismiss the possibility that there could be other suspects. If Emerson runs his office at all like Uncle Ashby, there are many times during any given week when the records are accessible to whoever might come by his office."

"I very much doubt that Emerson is that lax. Life in London is not like it is on the island."

She frowned. "I've discovered that, but I still think we should consider the possibility."

"And I think you are allowing your affection for Ashby Merewether to bias your feelings toward his nephew."

"Emerson as the culprit doesn't make any sense, Pierson."

He paused. "You called me Pierson."

"It is your name, after all."

"But you have only ever used it on my insistence or when we have made love."

She shrugged. "We are on somewhat intimate terms. Calling you Drake seems a bit formal."

He had thought so after their first kiss.

"Uncle Ashby has no children," she said, going back to the original topic, the telltale pink of her cheeks betraying how discussing their intimacy affected her.

"So?"

"Emerson knows that his uncle's half of Merewether Shipping will eventually go to him. He has no reason to steal from a company that will eventually belong to him."

"Unless he needs funds *now.*"

She bit at her lower lip. "I suppose."

"I'll have my man of affairs conduct some inquiries into Emerson's financial circumstances."

Her brows drew together. "What about Barton?"

"I'll have him investigated as well."

She nodded. "Good. You need to watch out for those self-effacing types."

Drake smothered a laugh.

She was really reaching, but once the investigation was complete would be soon enough to shatter her illusions about Emerson. Merewether's nephew or not, he was the likeliest candidate for the thefts. Not to mention the attempts on Thea's life. If Drake discovered that Emerson was indeed responsible, the jovial man would lose his affability . . . permanently.

THEA LEANED TOWARD HER AUNT AND WHISPERED, "Does she not realize she is singing a tragedy?"

The young debutante entertaining her parents' guests at the preseason musicale smiled charmingly as she sang of her lover dying beneath the waves of the open sea.

Lady Upworth whispered back, "She's showing off her best asset. Hopes it will make the gentlemen forget she can't sing worth a pence."

Wincing as the smiling girl hit another discordant note, Thea had to agree.

Lady Boyle, who sat on her other side, had nodded off. Thea was amazed that Drake's aunt could sleep without allowing her head to list to one side. If anyone were to look, they would assume she had closed her eyes to focus on the music. Thea knew better and she envied the older woman's oblivion to the indifferent entertainment.

The ability to escape the unpleasant must run in the family because Drake had also managed to avoid the untalented singer, having disappeared almost as soon as they arrived. It annoyed Thea. He was the one who insisted on announcing their pretend engagement to the entire world. The least he could do was to stay by her side and deal with the curious stares and pointed questions posed by the perfectly correct, but not always polite, members of the *ton*.

Lady Noreen had had the good sense to skip the entertainment altogether.

The awful song finally ended. Thea made to stand, but her aunt's hand arrested her. With dawning horror, she realized that yet another young lady had come forward to entertain them.

The blushing girl sat down next to a large harp and began to slide her fingers across the strings. Hope surged through Thea at the lovely sound until she realized that sliding her hands up and down the strings seemed to be all the young woman knew how to do. By the time the song ended, she was sure she never wanted to hear the harp again.

The harpist was followed by a pianist who played passably, a flautist who did not, and another singer who shook with nerves through her entire song. When her aunt's measured breathing indicated she, too, had fallen asleep, Thea began to feel acutely persecuted. The evening had been her aunt's idea after all. Why bother to come if she intended to sleep through the program?

A young lady with a pixie face, golden brown eyes, and blond hair, who sat on the other side of Lady Upworth, caught Thea's eye and gave her a commiserating smile. Thea returned her smile, feeling warmed by at least one friendly face among the *ton*.

They both turned to face the front again at the same time, and it was only as her gaze settled on another debutante that the message her brain was trying to give her pierced her consciousness. An image rose in her mind of a sketch she had studied many times. The girl in the sketch was smiling and had two charming dimples, just like the young lady sitting on the other side of Thea's aunt.

Thea took another surreptitious look at the young lady who had smiled at her in such understanding. It was. She was certain of it. Why had her aunt not warned her?

Perhaps because she believed you would then cry off the entertainment tonight, a small voice in her head accused.

Her heart began a swift palpitation; her palms became sweaty inside her gloves and her eyes smarted with unaccustomed tears.

The young woman seated so demurely beside her aunt was Lady Irisa Selwyn, Thea's half sister.

Fifteen

Lady Upworth has written that Estcot has returned to town. I never told her that he was the one who had caused the rift between Langley and myself. Apparently he left Town around the same time I did. He has returned, and under a cloud. He has gotten some country squire's poor daughter pregnant. She refused to marry him and even attempted to take her own life to avoid it. Once the story got out, he was completely ruined in the eyes of the ton. He has finally gotten his just deserts.

February 24, 1804
Journal of Anna Selwyn, Countess of Langley

THEA SPENT THE REST OF THE MUSICALE WITH her mind racing. She could not absorb the fact that her own flesh-and-blood sister sat not five feet away. When the hostess finally stood to thank everyone for coming and invite them to refreshments in the other room, Thea heard the words through a fog.

Miraculously, both her aunt and Lady Boyle woke immediately and put on the perfect performance of someone who had listened the entire time and enjoyed it. She would have been highly amused at their antics if she weren't in such a state of shock.

"Are you ready to go, dear?"

Thea stared at her aunt. They had come just to sit through two hours of untrained musicians?

Not to mention the fact that Lady Upworth knew perfectly well that Irisa sat beside her.

"There is a buffet in the other room," Thea said, not yet ready to deal with the other.

Lady Boyle tut-tutted. "No good. She's a skinflint, that one. Much better food at home."

If she could sit through interminable hours of entertainment that was anything but, they could suffer an indifferent buffet to assuage her hunger. "Listening to the music has increased my appetite."

"Don't know how it could have. Fairly ruined mine," said Lady Boyle.

"I believe I could use a glass of punch," Lady Upworth remarked, her gaze assessing as she looked from Thea to the young woman beside her.

Irisa was speaking to someone to her right, so was not part of the discussion, but Thea felt sure her sister would be staying as well. The question was, how did she feel about meeting the other woman for the first time? Certainly, she would not make herself known to Irisa, but even to simply speak with her when her whole life they had never even been able to share a correspondence . . .

At that moment, Lady Boyle capitulated. "Come along, then." She led the way toward the other room. "It'll please our hostess that we've decided to stay for the buffet. Most of her guests leave after the music."

Thea felt a spark of trepidation. If the buffet were worse than the entertainment, it must be awful. Still, she *was* hungry, and if she ate nothing, what would her excuse for staying be?

She saw that Lady Boyle had been right about most of the guests leaving because there was a very short line at the buffet table and only a few of the eating tables were occupied. She found punch for her aunt and saw both Lady Upworth and Lady Boyle seated before making her way to the food table.

As she surveyed the fare offered, she didn't see the reason for such a lack of enthusiasm. True, the food had none of the flare or color that she would have found at a buffet back home, but then most of England's food was bland compared to the fare she had been raised on.

As she took a lobster patty and placed it on the small china plate, she heard a soft voice to her left.

"Do you think we acquire the ability to sleep sitting up as we get older, or is it something one is born with?"

Feeling uncertainty and excitement in a volatile mixture inside her, Thea turned to Irisa. "I don't know, but I'll admit I have wished more than once for the knack."

Putting out her hand, her sister said, "I am Lady Irisa Selwyn." Turning to a lovely, willowy creature with brown ringlets cascading down her back, Irisa said, "This is my bosom beau, Cecily."

The brunette smiled charmingly. "You will have to forgive Irisa's impetuousness. She forgets herself."

Irisa laughed, the sound touching Thea's heart. Her sister's laughter. She had not been sure she would ever hear it.

"Don't mind Cecily," Irisa said. "She would wait to have our chaperones introduce us, but that seems silly to me. You are here with my aunt, after all."

Thea felt a rash of gladness at Irisa's flouting of convention. "It's nice to meet you both. My name is Thea Sel—" She could not give Irisa her real name. Not yet. She pretended to cough and then said, "Selby."

"Miss Selby, you are here with Lady Boyle and Lady Upworth, aren't you?" Cecily asked, apparently questioning Irisa's claim that Thea had arrived with her aunt.

Thea nodded.

"They're both quite well placed in the *ton*," the other girl remarked.

Thea wasn't sure how she was supposed to respond to the comment. "They are very kind ladies."

"And talented," replied Irisa with a small laugh.

Thea smiled, blinking back moisture she dared not let the others see. She and her sister shared a sense of humor. Lady Upworth had said so, but to feel the truth of it was an amazing thing.

They chatted some more as they finished filling their plates. Thea's heart was beating so rapidly, she was sure the other two had to notice, but they did not. Thea learned that Irisa was in Town with Cecily's family as her own parents were not yet arrived for the Season. Thea could not lament that fact.

She was relieved there would be no opportunity just yet to run into her father.

"I'm sure I'll see you again," said Irisa as she turned to go with Cecily.

"I look forward to it," replied Thea, more fervently than Society would dictate.

She watched Irisa walk away with an odd sense of incompletion. This girl was her sister, but her birth had been the final act in a play that had kept Thea's mother out of England until her death. Thea had never blamed Irisa, and she had desperately wanted to meet the sister she had known about since birth and never seen.

Now she had, and she was impressed not only with her sister's charming manner, but the innate family similarities.

How incredible to feel such a sense of recognition for a virtual stranger.

She returned to her aunt's table, her hands unsteady.

Drake had arrived and sat regaling her aunt with the tale of Jacob, the blacksmith, who lived on an island but was afraid of the water.

He stood as she approached and pulled a chair out for her.

She took it, still lost in her thoughts of her sister. "Thank you."

He smiled at her and filched a stuffed mushroom from her plate.

His sharp gaze swept over her face. "What's the matter?"

She could not very well share her heart's confusion where they could easily be overheard, but she wanted to tell him about meeting Irisa. But that would mean admitting she'd kept yet another secret from him, and she would have to explain the whole sordid thing—oh, it was all such a mess.

Drake picked another canapé off her plate.

"If you are hungry, get your own food," she said, still annoyed he had left her to face the torture of the musicale alone.

He laughed. "I'm doing you a favor, but if you don't appreciate my sacrifice, by all means finish your own food."

She let her gaze slide to the innocent-looking fare still on her plate. He must be teasing her. She picked up the lobster patty and took a small bite. It tasted a little different than those back home, but she attributed that to English cooking. She ate the rest of it and the remaining food on her plate to prove to Drake that she didn't for a minute believe he was helping her by eating her food.

"Are you ready to go now, dear?" asked Lady Upworth when Thea had finished.

"Yes, if we hurry, we'll be able to make an appearance at the Bickmore rout," Lady Boyle put in.

Thea's stomach sank. "Bickmore rout? I thought we were going home."

"Nonsense. The evening has just begun. You must realize that once the Season starts, you will be out until dawn most evenings."

Stay out until dawn? When would she sleep? Panic

coursed through her. Being introduced to Society was going to be a horrible inconvenience.

Drake stood and helped his aunt, then hers, and finally Thea to her feet. "I'm afraid I have some things to discuss with Thea this evening. She will have to forgo the pleasure of the Bickmore rout."

Lady Boyle's eyes narrowed. "I trust it will not require locking the library door as it did the other afternoon." She turned to Lady Upworth. "These young people have no idea how their actions appear to others. Can you imagine the disaster if a servant had happened upon the locked door instead of me?"

Thea almost groaned aloud.

She had not told her aunt about Lady Boyle catching her and Drake locked together in the library. She was still mildly irritated with him for forgetting to unlock it after they had finished making love. His aunt had rung a peal over both of them that rivaled anything her mother had ever done when she was a child.

Thankfully, Lady Upworth did not demand explanations. She merely raised her brows and said, "I'm sure their actions appeared much as they were. Speaking of which, while you are conversing with my niece this evening, I suggest you take time to discuss setting a wedding date."

"It's one of the first items on the agenda," Drake said blandly.

THEA MANAGED TO HOLD HER TONGUE UNTIL DRAKE had seen Lady Boyle and Lady Upworth to her aunt's carriage.

As he helped her into Lady Boyle's closed carriage, she chastised him. "Does nothing shame you? Our engagement is a sham. Do you think to add a false wedding date that must then be broken?"

He settled her on the carriage seat and then joined her.

The carriage lurched into motion and she fell against him, bumping her nose on his shoulder. "Ouch."

Setting her back against the squabs, he kissed her gently on the offended body part. "We will set a real date, one I have every intention of keeping."

"You are so mule-headed."

His laughter filled the small confines of the carriage. "Then we are a very good match. I've never met another woman as obstinate as you."

In the darkness, she could not tell if he was teasing her.

She frowned. "For a man who is supposedly my betrothed, you do a poor job of playing your part."

"What do you mean?"

"You abandoned me practically the moment we arrived at the musicale." Remembering her annoyance at being left to listen to the awful entertainment, her voice turned waspish. "Surely no one will believe we are engaged if we are not seen together."

"An engaged couple may attend the same functions, but no one expects them to spend all their time together."

She tried to ignore the heat emanating from his body, so close to her own. "Do not tease me."

"I assure you, I am not."

"But that is ridiculous. How can you wish to marry someone you do not want to spend your time with? Why, after the marriage, the close proximity could drive you mad."

He laughed again and she wanted to throttle him. "Marriage in the *ton* does not require close proximity. Some husbands and wives keep separate residences entirely."

A different home than Drake's? The thought appalled her. "That's terrible."

Drake shrugged, his arm rubbing against her shoulder. Even through her cloak, she found his touch exciting.

He said, "It isn't unusual."

She stiffened in her seat. "Is that what you expect of marriage? It sounds like a very lonely existence."

"I have no desire to spend my time alone, particularly my nights."

She shivered at the promise she heard in his voice.

This conversation was getting dangerous. "Nevertheless, you deserted me tonight. Why?"

"I wanted to verify some things my man of affairs has discovered regarding Emerson and Barton."

"What things?"

"Emerson appears to have very expensive tastes in mistresses, and Barton buys his clothes at the most exclusive tailors."

"I told you there was something fishy about him! But the news about Emerson must be old information. He became engaged recently."

"Yes, I know. To the daughter of a wealthy cit."

"Then you must realize that his taste in mistresses, expensive or otherwise, is no longer an issue."

"Thea, do not be naïve. Many gentlemen keep mistresses after marriage."

How dare he sound so condescending? "If I were to marry, my husband would not keep a mistress."

He reached around and pulled her chin toward him and kissed her firmly on the mouth. "No, I won't. You are the only woman I want."

She warmed at his words, but wasn't ready to let go of their earlier conversation. "What makes you think that Emerson is one of the men who will keep a mistress?"

"He already has one."

"Are you certain? Perhaps she used to be his mistress."

"That's what I tried to verify tonight. My man of affairs said that Emerson's current paramour is a widow in the *ton*. A lady with very expensive taste in jewelry. Unfortunately, the gentleman I hoped to speak to was too involved in his hand of whist to gossip. He did say that he'd heard the widow was seeing someone involved in trade."

She chewed on that thought for a moment. "Drake?"

"Hmm?"

"You are involved in trade, but no one appears to censure you because of it."

"I am very discreet."

"Oh."

"It makes my mother happy."

"I see. She would be embarrassed if you flaunted your business acumen."

He shrugged. "It's part of living among the Polite World."

"The thing is, I don't know if I can live my entire life in bondage to the rules of Society."

Would he understand her need for freedom? He had refused to accept her fear of marriage, taking it as a personal aspersion on his considerable honor.

"You are unique, Thea. I don't expect you to behave as every other English lady of the *ton*."

She bit on her lip and tried to marshal her thoughts. "You do expect me to be proper."

He slipped an arm around her waist and pulled her onto his lap. "I expect you to be you."

"But what if that is not enough? What if I embarrass you or Lady Upworth? Aunt Ruth says that I'm not at all proper in most of my thinking. On the island, that didn't seem to matter, but here every word I utter is scrutinized. I can't even wear the same gown to more than one major engagement or I'll be considered gauche. Your aunt said so. It's all so frustrating. Why do the gowns I wear matter more than who I am and what I think?"

During her tirade, he had begun to kiss a path down her jaw line.

He kissed the corner of her mouth. "You'll get used to the *ton* and they will come to adore you."

She turned her head away. "What if I don't want to get used to them? I don't like the way everyone here avoids discussing the really important things like abolition, yet will spend hours exploring the ramifications of wearing kid gloves versus silk ones with a ball gown."

He went back to kissing her, this time focusing on the nape of her neck since her face was turned away. "I'm not in the least bit interested in gloves and I'll talk abolition with you anytime you like."

"No, you won't. You don't want me to discuss important moral issues for fear I will offend someone. You said so aboard ship."

His hand slid inside her cloak, and strong, warm fingers skimmed over the exposed flesh above her bodice. "I thought someone had tried to kill you because of it."

She couldn't think when he touched her like this. "Pierson, you must stop. We cannot become intimate in your aunt's carriage."

He squeezed her breast through the thin lawn of her gown and she moaned.

"Why not? We did in her library."

She sucked in a breath as he lowered his hand to caress the juncture of her thighs through her gown. "Please stop. We will soon reach her town house and I prefer not to have the footman open the coach door and find me in a complete state of dishabille."

"I thought you did not wish to bow to the dictates of Society." He kissed the side of her neck.

Heat pooled inside her, ready to erupt in the passion that he instigated.

It took tremendous effort to continue resistance. "I want to be free to discuss important matters, not be labeled no better than I should be."

He sighed and removed his lips from her nape. "You are right, but I don't have to like it."

The bulge against her hip testified that he truly did not

wish to stop. Neither did she, and that knowledge galvanized her to action.

She scooted off his lap and moved to the opposite seat, hoping the small distance would help both of them to maintain better control. She gripped her hands tightly together to prevent herself from reaching out and touching him. She fought a desperate urge to launch herself back into his arms, and hang the consequences.

"What are we going to do about our investigation?"

"I have set a watch on the warehouse. Someone is moving cargo. Our most promising alternative is to catch them in the act."

"That is perfect. Even if the culprit is not one of our suspects, we shall catch him. I should have thought of that earlier," she said with no little chagrin.

She saw the outline of his shoulders rise and fall in a shrug in the shadow of the carriage.

"No. Truly. The idea is inspired," she insisted.

"It was the logical next step."

"For someone with a brilliant mind like yours, perhaps."

He shrugged her praise away. They sat in silence for several moments, and Thea's thoughts turned instantly to the meeting with her sister.

Drake's voice caught her by surprise. "What are you going to do about your father?"

Did he but know it, his question carried more weight than it ever had before, but she could not yet see a solution to change her course of action. "Ignore him."

"That will be difficult once the Season is officially begun, particularly if you plan to spend any significant time with Lady Upworth. According to my aunt, she is a very social creature and has her family members to call often."

"It is a problem, but not insurmountable. She will understand if I do not visit when he is expected to be present."

"What of entertainments? Your father undoubtedly attends them as well. How will you avoid seeing him?"

"The same way you avoid seeing your father," she couldn't help saying, and not with a little bit of exasperation.

Of all people, Drake should understand her desire to stay clear of her father.

"The avoidance is mutual," was his clipped response.

She sighed.

She had hurt him. "I'm sorry, Pierson. I didn't mean to bring up a sore subject, but surely you can see that I find the discussion of my estranged parent just as wearing."

"I see that your stubbornness extends even to your family, and that although you should consider reconciliation for both your aunt and your brother's sake, you won't."

Incensed, she replied, "What about my sake? I don't want to be reconciled to the man who tore my family apart. He destroyed something inside my mother. What about my loyalty to her?"

"That's what this is all about, isn't it? Your mother. You think that if you reconcile with your father, you've desecrated her memory. Well, she's gone, but others are still alive. Lady Upworth wants peace in her family. She wants you to take your place in Society. She helped your mother and you. Don't you owe her loyalty, too? And what of your brother? He deserves to know you."

He knew nothing of Irisa, but his arguments applied to the younger woman as well.

Thea felt tears prick at the back of her eyes for the second time that night. "I am loyal to my aunt." Her voice threatened to break. She took a deep breath, trying to calm herself. "I explained that I will make myself known to my brother."

And her sister, too. Someday.

Suddenly he was on the seat beside her with his hand laid gently against her cheek. "I'm sorry, sweetheart. I'm pushing you too hard."

"Why are you doing it?" she asked, unable to help herself.

He remained silent for so long, she thought he would not answer, but then he spoke. "I thought it was because I wanted you to settle into life in England, to develop ties here so you wouldn't want to leave."

When he didn't go on, she prompted him. "That's not the reason?"

"It is part of it. Understand something—I mean for you to stay."

She did not doubt he spoke the truth. He had been very clear about his intentions from the afternoon they made love on the ship. Perhaps if he loved her, it would make a difference. She was honest enough to admit that her desire to remain unwed was wavering.

But he didn't love her, and she wasn't sure passion was enough. She didn't want to dwell on those thoughts now, however.

She wanted to understand why he kept pressing her to acknowledge her father. "What's the rest of it?"

"I hated not knowing my father." His voice came out stark, full of remembered pain.

"And . . ." she prodded gently.

"Although I have long since determined he is not a man worth knowing, the desire to be acknowledged by him has never completely left me."

He would feel it a weakness to need the approval of a man who had never once acknowledged him, and Thea felt a rush of understanding.

"You're trying to force me to reconcile with my father because it's an option you wanted, but never had."

"Perhaps."

She knew the one-word admission had cost him. The pain in Drake's voice tugged at her heart.

"Did you ever tell your mother or grandfather how you felt? Perhaps they could have arranged a meeting."

His hand fell away from her cheek. "I never admitted my weakness to anyone else."

It was her turn to comfort him.

She turned toward him and took his hand in hers. "It isn't a weakness to want to know your family."

"My sisters and brothers don't even know that I exist."

She could imagine how that knowledge must have eaten away at his pride and sense of honor. "That's why you are so adamant that I meet my brother. But Lady Upworth said my brother has not yet come to Town."

"He deserves to know you."

Just as Drake deserved to know his siblings, but never would.

She couldn't leave it at that. "You don't need your father's acknowledgment or approval, Pierson. You have become the most honorable and worthy of men without it, a man others would do well to pattern themselves after."

"If that is truly how you feel, then you would not be afraid to marry me."

"You don't love me."

He pulled her shoulders around until she faced him. "You don't believe in love any more than I do. You think it weakens women. Ashby Merewether told me."

She couldn't deny his charge, so she focused on something else. "What happens when you stop wanting me?"

"I'll never stop wanting you." The words sounded suspiciously like a vow.

THEA SLID ANOTHER SURREPTITIOUS GLANCE AT DRAKE as he took notes on the ledger spread open at the library desk. His fingers holding the pencil were so strong and she remembered how much pleasure they brought her. Pleasure that had come with a price, if only he knew it. What would he say if she told him about her experience over the chamber pot this morning?

She felt perfectly well now, which was more alarming than if the nauseous feeling had persisted. If it had persisted, she could convince herself that it was due to illness, or land sickness, though that ailment was better known to occur after long sea voyages. Her time aboard the *Golden Dragon* had neither been so long in duration, nor so recent, that land sickness could be a realistic explanation for waking this morning with an overwhelming urge to cast up her accounts.

She had never heard of a flu lasting only as long as it took to void one's stomach either. And although her skin had been clammy to the touch, she had not had a fever. She had to definitely rule out illness as an excuse. That left only one alternative.

Morning sickness.

She was pregnant with Pierson Drake's child.

Sixteen

Langley must now realize that Estcot's word of honor is as reliable as Prinny's temper. Had this happened five years ago, I would have taken the first ship back to England, sure that I could finally convince Langley of my innocence. Yet, in all this time, he has never mentioned me to Lady Upworth. She despairs of raising the subject of my seeing Jared anymore because of his cold reception to the idea. It is no use. I have built a life for myself and Thea here. There is no hope of seeing my son before he reaches his majority.

March 1, 1804
Journal of Anna Selwyn, Countess of Langley

THEA HUGGED THE KNOWLEDGE OF HER PREG- nancy to herself, thrilled despite the ramifications it must bring.

The prospect of bearing Drake's child sent warmth and trepidation cascading through her all at once. Could she risk her freedom and perhaps her happiness as well by marrying him?

She chewed on her lower lip. Were she to admit the truth, she would have to acknowledge that the decision to marry him had occurred the moment she accepted his body into her own. Not because he so arrogantly assumed she would marry him, but because once they had made love, he owned a part of her that would never be wholly hers again.

It had been inevitable. No matter how desperately she had tried to protect herself from her feelings for him, they had steadily grown within her.

She feared she loved him—and it was all his fault.

With silky black hair that she longed to bury her fingers in, eyes that mesmerized her with their intensity, and a male physique that Gentleman Jackson would be proud to possess, Drake was more attractive than any gentleman had a right to be.

Added to his immense physical appeal, he had unswerving honor and diligence. Even his arrogance drew her. It went against everything she believed she would want in a husband, and yet she found that she actually had come to rely on it.

When she lacked confidence, his supreme assurance buoyed her. When she had first stepped off the ship and realized what a totally different world England was from her island, her belief in herself and her ability to find the embezzler in her company failed. Drake, on the other hand, had not wavered in his certainty that they would unmask the thief before any harm could come to Uncle Ashby.

Further, he exhausted himself making it happen. She had noticed dark rings under his eyes this morning at breakfast. When she had taxed him with it later, he admitted that he had been participating in the nightlong watch over the Merewether Shipping office.

He pushed her to make amends with her family, but only because he wanted her to have everything. A place in the *ton,* a father, a brother. If only he knew the final act of cruelty her father had committed. He would understand that though she would attempt to have a relationship with her brother, she could never give her father a place in her life.

"What?" His irritated voice startled her out of her musings. "You've been staring at me for the past ten minutes. What is it?"

She stalled for time before answering his question. "Does it bother you when I look at you?"

"It bothers me when you look through me." He pushed the ledger away. "We will find the thief. You need to stop making yourself sick with worry about it. The man I sent to watch over Merewether is tough and trustworthy. He won't let anything happen to your uncle."

There was another example of his protective concern for her. He had sent an agent to watch her uncle immediately upon reaching port even though she had told him about her confiding in Philippe.

"I'm not worried about Uncle Ashby." At least he wasn't the foremost worry on her mind.

"Then what is the matter? Is it because I pushed you last night about reconciling with your father?"

She shook her head. She knew that Drake would not force the issue, regardless of what he believed to be best. Look at the issue of their marriage. Although he made his desire to marry her clear, he had not resorted to intimidation or blackmail. He had brought up her aunt's place in Society and then protected it with their engagement. He could have used her consideration for Lady Upworth to force her hand, but he hadn't.

"I have never been good at parlor games, particularly the guessing variety." He leaned back in the chair behind the desk, tapping his pencil against his other hand. "Why don't you just tell me what has you so preoccupied?"

"I think I may be pregnant." She blurted the words out without making any attempt to soften them.

He shot up from the desk, dropped the pencil, and practically leaped over the desk to reach her.

He gripped her shoulders. "How can you tell? Have you missed your menses?"

She smiled at the urgency in his voice. "It hasn't been long enough, but this morning I woke feeling every bit as seasick as I ever did aboard ship."

He dropped his hands and stepped back. "What are you going to do?"

She cocked her head to one side and studied him. He didn't look like a man who had just heard he was going to get his own way in a very important matter. He looked wary, as if he were bracing himself for a blow.

"What do you mean?"

He curled his hands into fists. "Are you going to marry me—or go back to your island and pretend to be a widow like your mother did?"

If she had any doubt that she could trust him, it dissolved with his question. He was giving her a choice, refusing to allow her to feel trapped, although he must realize as she did that her returning to the island as a widow would be ludicrous. No one would believe it.

"I had thought to marry you."

"Why?"

She hadn't expected that question. If he thought she was going to admit tender feelings for him when he wasn't even sure he believed in love, then he was in for a disappointment.

"You made your feelings about having a child of yours grow up illegitimate very clear. I thought you would be happy with my decision."

"I am happy."

"Well, you aren't acting like it." If she sounded like she was complaining, she felt justified.

The tears came as a complete shock.

"Bloody hell." He stepped forward and pulled her against him. "Hush, sweetheart. I am happier than I can say that

you've agreed to marry me. Even if I don't completely understand why."

She sniffled against his shirt. "I should think it's obvious. I'm pregnant with your child. It is the accepted course of action."

Laughter rumbled in his chest even as he rubbed her back in a soothing motion. "You so rarely take the accepted course that I can't help being a little surprised when you choose to do so."

Honestly. She had expected a much different reaction, and her patience had worn thin waiting for it.

She struggled against his confining arms. "Let me go."

Rather than let her go, he leaned down and caught her legs under her knees and swung her up into his embrace.

"Put me down."

He ignored her protest and carried her to the infamous sofa near the window.

He sat down with her ensconced firmly in his lap. "Relax. All this struggling can't be good for the baby."

She snorted.

From what she had seen of pregnant women back home, babies could withstand a great deal. "Our baby is not so fainthearted."

"Then stop struggling, because if you don't, we are going to end up making love again and this time I didn't lock the door."

She glared at him, but stopped squirming against his lap. The growing bulge under her thigh confirmed that he meant what he said.

"If you don't want to marry me, I'm sure I can manage on my own. I am financially independent and every bit as capable as my mother of raising a child without a husband."

He gripped her chin with his hand and forced her to meet his gaze. "We are getting married. You agreed to it and I'm not about to let you renege on your word. My baby will be born with my name."

"I never said I wanted our baby to do otherwise. You are the one acting less than enthusiastic about the idea of marriage."

He frowned and the wary expression came back into his eyes. "Perhaps I had hoped that you would want to marry me for my sake, not just as penance for allowing me to make love to you."

"I didn't say it was penance."

"You did not have to."

She couldn't believe it. He felt insecure. It was there in his eyes. He thought she wanted to marry him only because of the baby. How could she convince him otherwise without sharing her innermost feelings?

Feelings she still did not trust.

"I'm not marrying you just because I'm pregnant."

"Are you saying that you decided to marry me before you got sick this morning?"

Placing her hand on his shoulder, she sighed. "No."

"Then you *are* marrying me because of the baby."

"Well, isn't that why you want to marry me?"

"I asked you to marry me after we made love the first time."

That was true. Suddenly she felt better than she had in days. He must have some tender feelings for her. She could not believe that he had proposed to every woman he had ever lain with. He'd surely be married several times over by now if that were the case.

She brushed his cheek with her fingertips. "It's true that my morning sickness precipitated my decision, but I would have come to the same one eventually, regardless."

"What of your promise to your mother?"

"Melly is right about one thing. Mama wanted me to be happy." Leaning forward, Thea caressed the skin of his jaw with her lips. "Marrying you will make me very happy."

As she said the words, she knew deep in her heart that they were true. She wanted him in her life. The thought of returning to her island without him, to spend the rest of her years alone, held no appeal. She might be independent, but she wasn't stupid. She knew a good thing when she saw it, and a life with Drake would be a very good thing indeed.

"Your happiness is necessary to my own. I will do everything in my power to see that our life together never causes you to regret your decision."

Tears stung her eyes at the promise in his voice. He might not love her, but he cared for her. Her father had claimed to love her mother, but had been the instrument of her unhappiness. Drake did not claim to love Thea, but she knew with absolute assurance that he would devote himself to making her happy.

"You are crying again."

She nodded, her throat too constricted to speak.

"Have I said something to offend you?"

She shook her head.

"I had heard that pregnant women were emotional, but I confess I am not sure how to deal with it."

She smiled. How could she put into words what she was feeling right now? She had spent her entire adult life, and most of her girlhood, convinced that marriage was a fate worse than death. Now that she faced the prospect with Drake, all she felt was anticipation and relief that she would not have to tell him good-bye.

Happy tears seemed like the appropriate response.

"WHAT DO YOU MEAN, THE WEDDING IS SCHEDULED IN *two hours?*"

Thea felt hysteria rising like a tidal wave inside her. Married? Today? She grabbed frantically at the doorjamb to her room. It felt solid enough. She hadn't dreamed the loud knocking and Drake's demand for an audience from the other side. She truly was standing in the doorway to her room wearing nothing but a nightrail and wrapper while Drake informed her that they were scheduled to marry in less than two hours.

"*You've gone mad.* We can't get married this morning. The banns haven't been read. I don't have a dress. Nothing has been planned. *It is impossible.*"

Drake smiled at her with the devil's own charm and waved a piece of white parchment in front of her face. "This is a special license. It says that we *can* marry today. You cannot tell me with the numerous new dresses you have bought, you don't have one suitable for a small wedding."

She interrupted before he could go on. "For someone else's small wedding, not my own."

"Don't whine, Thea. You are the one who told me you cared nothing for clothes."

"I didn't say nothing, or maybe I did, but I didn't mean I cared not a whit what I wore to my *wedding.*"

He had the unmitigated gall to shrug. "You will look beautiful in whatever you choose."

He refused to understand.

She ground her teeth in an effort not to scream. "What of a wedding breakfast?"

"Lady Upworth has planned a small gathering at her home."

"*You told my aunt about our wedding before you told me?*"

"You don't need to shout, sweetheart. I'm standing right here. Of course I told her, or how could she have planned the breakfast? Now stop being difficult and get ready." He pulled his watch from his waistcoat pocket, flipped it open, and looked at it. "You have an hour and forty-five minutes before we have to leave."

He sounded so bloody logical, except what he was saying made no sense. The blackguard.

"I think that if you wanted to be guaranteed of my

cooperation, you would not have waited to spring my wedding on me as a fait accompli with less than two hours to prepare."

An expression of guilt crossed his features, and then she understood. That was the whole point. Drake still wasn't certain of her and he believed this was the way to ensure she showed up at her own wedding. Give her no time to talk herself out of it. His next words confirmed her suspicions.

"What would you have had me do? Wait for the banns to be read and risk you changing your mind? Marriage makes you more skittish than a newborn foal. Once the deed is done, I'm sure your nerves will settle."

She wasn't positive that she agreed with him, but one thing was certain—he would settle down once the deed was done. He had been acting all over strange since she'd agreed to marry him three days ago. Not only did he make himself a complete nuisance wanting her to put her feet up, rest, and other such nonsense supposedly good for a woman in her delicate condition, but he had spent the last three days recounting the benefits of the wedded state. Just last night at dinner, he had informed her that married women lived longer. Just look at the evidence of his aunt and Lady Upworth. Why, they were practically in their dotage and both had been married.

She could only be grateful that her morning sickness had not come back the last two mornings. She was positive she had enough on her plate without the awful nausea.

"You should have told me about the wedding. A woman wants more than a single bloody hour to prepare for such an event. *Sacré bleu.*"

His brows drew together and she knew that his patience was slipping. "Thea, you've spent most of your life thinking you wouldn't get married. Our child will be in leading strings before you are ready."

"I'm talking about the things that go along with a wedding, not my mental preparation." She wanted to shake him, but knew from experience that he was immovable. "As for my not being ready to marry, I already agreed to do so. Do you doubt my word?"

He wrapped his fingers around hers over the doorjamb and moved forward until their lips met in a soft, lingering kiss. She closed her eyes, savoring the sensation. When it ended, he pulled his mouth away from hers, but remained close. She opened her eyes and met his watchful gaze.

"I trust your word. Knowing that you already agreed to marry me, I convinced myself that you would be pleased about a surprise wedding. It would take the advance worry out of the event for you."

She sighed. She was beaten and she knew it. She had given him her word. What's more, she actually wanted to marry the dratted man.

"I'll be ready in two hours and not one minute less. I'll be late to my wedding, but I won't get married looking like I just rolled out of bed."

His smile made her small sacrifice seem worth it.

MARRIED.

The single word continued to resound through her mind with the force of a town crier, despite the innocuous conversations she engaged in during her wedding breakfast.

She was *married*.

Thea played with the ruby ring Drake had given her during the ceremony, the large oval stone a profound weight on her finger. She had never intended to marry, had never looked to her wedding day. If she had, she could never have imagined the way this day had actually turned out.

From the moment Drake had pounded on her door announcing their wedding plans, she had been in a constant state of activity. Even now, she could not completely relax. Lady Upworth had invited every member of the *ton* who had come early to Town to the "small" wedding breakfast she had planned. Or at least that was how it appeared to Thea.

She had shaken hands and received good wishes until her fingers had grown numb. Finally, her aunt had allowed her and Drake to leave the reception line, but not together. Drake had been instructed to make his aunt comfortable and to mingle, while Lady Upworth had taken Thea in tow to introduce her to some people she had not yet met.

Impossible. She had certainly met every person in the English-speaking world by now.

Once Lady Upworth had introduced her to an elderly couple that had somehow managed to avoid the receiving line, she allowed Thea to find some food. She stood at the buffet table, considering the incredible diversity of offerings, when a familiar voice interrupted her thoughts.

"Hello, again."

Thea turned and met warm brown eyes.

Her sister had come to her wedding breakfast.

"Hello. I did not realize you would be here."

"Aunt Harriet was most insistent. She is quite fond of you."

"She has said many complimentary things about you as well, Lady Irisa."

Irisa's smile touched Thea deep in her heart. "I am glad."

Thea looked around her, feeling awkward, but unwilling to let her sister simply walk away, she said, "I'm not entirely sure how she managed to orchestrate such an impressive gathering on the little notice she received."

"Oh, everyone attends her gatherings. Her buffets are legendary." She indicated the laden table with a meaningful look.

"Besides, she's top of the trees amidst the *ton*. Everyone who is anyone angles for an invitation to her entertainments. I can tell you, Cecily and her mother were in alt to be invited to your wedding breakfast. They had not yet received an invitation from my aunt, but now Cecily and I are bosom beaus. Our plans to be fitted for our presentation dresses were dust the minute the invitation was delivered."

Thea really enjoyed her sister's chatty, open nature and ached to tell her the truth about their relationship.

She reached out impulsively and squeezed the girl's hand. "I am very glad you came. I find the press of people somewhat overwhelming and seeing a friendly face has certainly helped."

Irisa smile grew conspiratorial. "I'm sure your *husband's* face is sufficiently friendly, but I appreciate your kind words about my humble self."

Thea laughed aloud.

What a refreshing young woman her sister was. If Irisa only knew how confused Thea felt about Drake right now. She wasn't completely over her irritation that he had surprised her with a wedding, nor did she like the fact that he had not admitted any tender feelings for her.

Although she adored the look of desire that came into his eyes when he gazed at her, she was fast coming to the conclusion that a woman needed more than merely to be wanted physically by the man she had given her life to. Particularly when she had tender feelings of her own she was being forced to come to terms with.

"There you are, Irisa. Mother has been looking everywhere for you."

Cecily's voice came from behind Thea. She and Irisa turned to see the other girl.

"Hello, Cess, I'm just chatting with the guest of honor, or one of them anyway," replied Irisa.

Cecily's brows rose. "I see. Mother wants you."

Irisa's smile slipped. "I'm also getting a plate of food. It *is* a breakfast and I am hungry."

"Really, Irisa, you exhibit entirely too much appetite for a lady."

Personally, Thea thought Irisa could do much better for

a bosom beau than this rather haughty young woman, but seeing the storm clouds gather in her sister's eyes, Thea sought to smooth the waters. "Surely your mother would not mind Irisa sharing breakfast with me. I do hate to eat alone."

Cecily's polite smile cracked slightly. "How kind of you, but I'm sure Irisa does not wish to disappoint Mother. She is Irisa's chaperone until her parents come to Town."

While she had still been rather overly concerned with correct behavior, Cecily had been much warmer the other evening at the musicale. What had changed to make her treat Thea with such freezing politeness now?

"Of course." Thea turned to Irisa. "I'll see you again soon, I'm sure."

Cecily's mouth thinned. "That is unlikely."

Thea asked, "Why? Are you planning to leave?"

She caught Irisa's gaze. Her sister looked pained and her cheeks were stained with a blush.

"I thought you were in Town for the Season," she said to Irisa.

She had planned on getting to know her more thoroughly.

"I am certain we do not frequent the same entertainments as your husband, so we are unlikely to run into you." The condescending tone of Cecily's voice grated on Thea's good humor, but the implication of her words completely dispelled it.

How dare the chit imply that she was too good to attend a function with Drake?

"I notice that you are here this morning and so is my husband. How do you explain that, do you suppose?"

Cecily waved two dismissive fingers. "Lady Upworth is very high in the instep. Everyone knows that. There is no stigma in attending one of her functions."

The look she gave Thea implied she didn't know how a lady of such stature among the *ton* had lowered herself to throw a wedding breakfast for Drake and his wife.

Thea wanted to slap the supercilious expression right off the miserable creature's face.

She let her voice go dangerously soft. "Are you implying that there is a stigma attached to my husband?"

Irisa jumped in before Cecily could reply. "Of course not. Cecily is being rather silly." She gave the other girl a quelling glance from angry brown eyes. "I'm sure she doesn't want to say any more."

"Well, really. It's not as if it's a big secret. Your husband's parents weren't married. That hardly puts him as our social equal."

Thea's blood boiled over into hot temper.

She moved until her face was mere inches from the hapless Cecily's. "My husband is the grandson of a duke, a gentleman who has made it clear since my husband's birth that he will tolerate no slights of any kind to either Lady Noreen or Pierson. I must assume that you do not mind insulting a duke, but I assure you that your mother will not be nearly so complacent."

Cecily's expression changed to one of confusion. "I didn't realize, I mean to say, I just assumed that since the duke and the rest of the family did not host the breakfast, nor attend the wedding that they . . ."

"They what?" Thea prompted, feeling unholy satisfaction in the consternation that had replaced the false politeness on Cecily's features.

"I just thought . . . That is to say . . ."

Irisa sighed, drawing Thea's attention away from her rude friend. "She and her mother assumed Mr. Drake's family did not recognize him since they didn't come to Town for the wedding and Mr. Drake didn't take you to the country to be wed from one of the family estates."

Cecily gasped.

Irisa shrugged. "I heard them talking about it this morning. I tried to tell them that it shouldn't matter, but her mother *is* rather a stickler for propriety. So is mine."

Thea stepped back from Cecily.

She turned and smiled at Irisa. "You are right. It shouldn't matter. My husband is a fine, honorable man. However, the truth is that his family not only acknowledges him, they are rather protective of him. Surely the fact that we are currently staying with his aunt, Lady Boyle, would indicate that the family ties run deep.

"In addition, both that worthy lady and Pierson's mother are here at the wedding breakfast."

Cecily smiled the same warm smile she had given Thea the other evening at the musicale, the smile Thea now knew was false. "I hope you'll forgive my confusion. I wouldn't want my mistake to impact your friendship with Irisa or myself."

The girl did not want to be cut by Drake's family, but Thea didn't bother to argue. "Do not concern yourself. *Irisa's* will always be a welcome face."

Cecily blanched slightly when Thea emphasized Irisa's name, but did not comment.

"I suppose I had best go find out what your mother wants." Irisa gave a last longing glance at the buffet table.

"I'm sure Mother would not mind if you kept Mrs. Drake company during breakfast."

Irisa's eyes narrowed at Cecily's words.

But Thea smiled sweetly. "I wouldn't want your mother to be *disappointed*." She inclined her head to Irisa. "I do believe I will see you again in the future."

Irisa agreed with a wink that made Cecily's mouth tighter, and both girls walked away.

Seventeen

Thea is so bright. I am determined to see her educated in everything in which she shows an interest. My daughter will learn more than needlepoint and pianoforte. Although she will learn those things, too. She is intelligent enough to absorb it all. Her father scoffed at my desire to read books on what he considered unfeminine subjects. He thinks ladies too weak-brained for Latin and mathematics. Thea is not too weak-brained for anything.

January 15, 1805
Journal of Anna Selwyn, Countess of Langley

DRAKE STOOD ROOTED TO HIS SPOT NEAR Thea. He watched, paralyzed by the conversation he had just heard, as she filled a plate with some of the many delicacies her aunt had browbeaten her cook into preparing for this morning's festivities.

He had learned early on to ignore the raised brows and subtle rejections on his own behalf. He would never grow inured to the slights his mother endured because of his

existence. How could he have exposed Thea to this subtle
form of ostracism for the rest of her life? She deserved so
much better, and yet he had practically forced her to marry
him. Forced her to accept a lifetime of raised eyebrows and
knowing looks.

She turned from the buffet table and nearly ran into
him. Her mouth tipped at the corners in a soft smile of welcome. How could she look at him that way after what he
had made her endure, married less than a day?

"Hello, Pierson. I was beginning to think that there was
another unwritten rule in the *ton* that a bridegroom could
not converse with his bride at their wedding breakfast."

He looked down at the plate of food in her hands and
frowned. "You were supposed to let me get that."

"Oh. I suppose that's another rule. Well, I don't think I
shall be very good at keeping it. I like to eat when I'm hungry, not when you've gotten around to remembering me."

"I'm sorry. I should have come to you sooner."

Her smile faded. "What is the matter?"

He should have hidden his reaction.

Hadn't he lived thirty years without telling his mother
how much he regretted what his presence in her life had
robbed her of? Marriage, acceptance among her peers, the
things a lady longs for. Every lady except his wife. Thea
had not wanted marriage, nor had she been particularly
concerned with her place among the *ton*. She had changed
her mind about marriage. Would she change her mind
about needing the approval of her peers as well?

She set her plate down on a nearby table, and then taking his arm, she led him out of the crowded room. "Come
on. You look like I felt the other morning just before I made
nodding acquaintance with the chamber pot."

They ended up in her aunt's private sitting room.

She walked over to the desk and trailed her fingers
across the polished surface. "She sent me sketches."

He shook his head, trying to clear his thoughts. "What?"

"Of the desk. And all the rest of the furniture." Thea made a sweeping motion with her hand, indicating the entire room. "She wanted me to know what it looked like. She sent me sketches of many things. London. Her country home. My father's home. Lords and ladies dressed for balls. So many things. I felt as if I knew England so well, though I had never been here."

Thea came to stand right in front of him. "She couldn't put it all in her sketches, though, not even in her letters. For instance, she could not truly explain London fog when my whole experience had been with clean, clear mists. She could not explain the dawn chorus or the cobbled streets, the smell of the Thames or the overwhelming crush of people."

She laid her hand on his cheek and he felt her warmth seep into him. "There was something else she could not convey in her letters. Something I would not have believed had she tried."

She stood silent, her hand resting against his cheek, and he felt an overwhelming desire to know what she meant.

"What?" he asked hoarsely.

She reached up with her other hand and framed his face. "The way people here judge you by the things that do not matter. The clothes you wear. The amount of beauty God has bestowed upon your person. The circumstances of your birth."

She pulled his face down to meet hers and he felt helpless to stop her. Her words and tone mesmerized him.

She kissed him, softly, gently, with promise. "You are an honorable man. A true gentleman. A man I am proud to call my husband."

Then she kissed him again and it was anything but gentle. It was as if she were trying to imprint her certainty on his lips. She let her hands slip behind his head and she locked her arms together, forcing his mouth against hers. He groaned, wrapped his arms around her, and took control of the kiss.

He slanted his mouth over hers again and again until they were both panting from desire.

Knowing that if they didn't stop he would make love to her, he pulled away. "We should get back to the breakfast before our absence is noted."

"You would think that our disappearance would be *expected*."

He shrugged. "No."

She frowned. "Let me guess, another *tonnish* rule?"

He laughed at her disgruntled tone. "You'll learn."

She didn't look as if she believed him. "I did warn you that I did not strive to be a perfect patterncard of Society. Remember?"

"I remember."

She nodded, looking a little relieved. "Good."

How could she worry about living up to Society's standards, when no matter how hard he tried, he never would?

"Thank you," she said.

Her words took him by surprise. "For what, kissing you? I assure you, it is my pleasure."

"No. For marrying me."

Suddenly, it was too much. "How can you thank me after what you went through with those ladies by the buffet table? Marrying me has opened you to such attacks."

She nodded as if she had worked something out.

"I thought you might have overheard. You looked so strange when I saw you. Not at all your confident, some might even say arrogant, self." Earnest conviction filled her eyes. "The thing is, I do not like hypocrites. I should be very disappointed to invest time in friendship with someone only to discover that they are shallow and base. My marriage with you has the effect of illuminating such flaws quickly in those I meet. It is a benefit I had not considered."

He didn't know what to say. She couldn't possibly see marriage to him in that light. Yet she radiated sincerity with every fiber of her being. She believed she meant what she said. Yanking her into his arms, he decided to believe her as well.

They did not return to the wedding breakfast for another hour.

WHEN THEY DID, HIS AUNT IMMEDIATELY ACCOSTED them. "Where have you been, you naughty children? People have been asking for you, and I've had to pretend to have seen you here and there."

Giving a pointed look to Drake's hastily finger-combed hair, she said, "One would have thought if you could not wait until your wedding night to engage in such activity, at least you would have the foresight to straighten your appearance."

Thea smiled in glee as her thirty-year-old, shipping magnate husband blushed guiltily under his aunt's glare.

She released his arm. "Go fix yourself. You will notice that your aunt finds nothing remarkable in my appearance."

Drake obeyed and went.

Lady Boyle turned to Thea. "You're a saucy gel. I like that. Pierson did remarkably well in choosing you to wed."

Thea felt her own cheeks heat, but for a different reason entirely.

Lady Boyle's praise pleased her. "Thank you."

"Yes, well, you're a definite improvement over the other ladies he has paid attention to. Stuffed prigs, the lot of them."

Thea thought to tease the older woman. "Surely you aren't finding fault with ladies who are more amenable to the rules of the *ton* than myself."

Not after the hours Lady Boyle had spent drilling Thea on the ways of Society.

"There is knowing the rules and there is being a slave to them."

Thinking of the difference between Irisa and Cecily, Thea had to agree.

"I was sure my nevvy would up and marry one of that lot and then where would the family be? With an inconvenient connection, that's where."

Drake's family certainly was unique among the *ton* if they believed that a stickler for propriety was an inconvenient connection.

"There was no risk of that, I'm sure. Drake is a very independent sort of person. I cannot imagine him making the mistake of wedding a lady such as you describe."

Truthfully, she didn't want to envision Drake even dancing with another woman, much less courting her.

Lady Boyle shook her head sadly. "You don't know. He dangled after one miss, a pudding head if there ever was one. Thankfully, she married an aging peer and Pierson narrowly escaped making a lifetime mistake."

Thea did not want to discuss Drake's past amour. The only woman he had ever admitted to loving.

"It's all his father's fault, of course. Pierson set himself up to marry a paragon with impeccable bloodlines to prove to his idiot of a father that he is worthy."

Thea couldn't help admiring Lady Boyle's perception. She doubted that many people saw beneath Drake's confident exterior to understand his need for approval from a man who would never give it. Still, she didn't think Drake had actually planned to marry into the peerage. He wasn't so mercenary.

She said so to his aunt.

"Don't you believe it. He had it mapped out. Even convinced me to help him make a list of worthy candidates. He was going to spend this Season finding the perfect wife." Lady Boyle nodded. "I'm so very relieved that he had the sense to marry you instead."

Thea laughed, knowing Lady Boyle did not intend the words as they had come out. Her amusement was short lived, however. The news that Drake had planned to find a wife this Season disturbed her. She tried to tamp down the irrational jealousy it provoked.

Lady Boyle's eyes filled with concern. "Are you well?"

Thea pasted a smile on her face. "Yes. Why do you ask?"

"You looked for a minute as if you'd eaten the lobster patties at the musicale. I felt terrible I hadn't stopped you when I heard what a commotion they caused among the guests. But when you didn't come down sick, I thought I must have been mistaken when I thought I'd seen you eat one."

Thea tried to make sense of what the dowager was saying. "Do you mean to say that the guests got ill after eating the patties?"

Lady Boyle nodded. "Oh yes. I told you that hostess was a skinflint. The food made quite a few people ill. Cast up their accounts until their stomachs were empty is what I heard. Good thing it didn't cause anything worse. Nothing more devastating for a hostess than to have someone die from the food at one of her entertainments. Have a hard time getting guests to come after that."

That was certainly one way of looking at it.

But the musicale hostess's future social success was not Thea's immediate concern. If Lady Boyle was right, and she had come to respect the dowager's nose for gossip, then Thea had not experienced morning sickness, was probably not pregnant, and had married without the least need to do so.

How did she feel about that? She couldn't say for sure.

Lady Boyle looked at her strangely. "Are you sure you didn't eat those patties?"

"If I did, they certainly wouldn't be affecting me now," hedged Thea.

"I suppose so. Maybe you should sit down. A wedding is a lot of excitement for a young gel like yourself."

Any other time, Thea would have laughed at the older woman's concern, but right now she thought perhaps Lady Boyle was right. Maybe she should sit down.

"Ah, there you are, nevvy. Looking much more presentable, I might add. You've worn your wife out. Take her to find some food and a place to sit."

"My pleasure."

Rather than showing approval for Drake's immediate agreement, Lady Boyle frowned.

Her gaze focused on something behind Thea. "I thought he was still out of Town."

The dowager's voice came out low, as if she were whispering to herself. Thea could barely make out the words. Who could have upset Lady Boyle so? Was the duke here? Would he be furious his grandson had married a woman in trade?

Though feeling like a craven coward, Thea did not wish to turn around and face the wrath of Drake's family. Instead she stepped nearer to her husband, seeking the security of his presence. He put his hand out to steady her, and she felt her heart constrict.

He looked into her eyes, his filled with concern. "It's going to be all right, sweetheart."

Rather than reassuring her, his words filled her with dread. Why hadn't he told her his family would be unhappy? He had implied that they would be thrilled at his choice in wife. Perhaps Lady Boyle was the only unconventional one among them.

Refusing to be intimidated by an unseen menace, Thea turned to face the newcomer.

And nearly fainted.

She heard a roaring in her ears, so could not make out the words exchanged between the man and Lady Boyle. All warmth drained from her body, and she clutched the air desperately behind her, seeking the solid form of her husband. His hand grasped her own, and some warmth seeped back into her. He pulled her near until she was standing close enough to feel the heat radiate from his body. Still, she did not speak. She couldn't.

The man was rather handsome in a cold sort of way. His black hair was sprinkled with gray, and there were lines around his mouth and eyes. From frowning or laughing? His eyes held polite interest and something else, annoyance maybe, as he spoke to Lady Boyle.

"I've come to be introduced to the guests of honor." He looked around the room with slight disapproval. His gaze had not yet settled on Thea and Drake. "Lady Upworth has gone to a tremendous amount of expense and trouble for Mr. Drake and his new wife. I thought I should meet them."

Lady Boyle nodded, still looking a bit peaked in Thea's opinion. "Yes, of course."

She turned toward Thea and Drake. "May I present my nephew, Pierson Drake, and his wife, Althea Drake?"

The man's cold gray eyes settled on Drake first as he offered his hand in greeting. Then they slid to Thea and he froze. His eyes grew wide, and for a moment all coldness left his face to be replaced with disbelief.

Did he recognize her? How could he? But she would know him anywhere. Lady Upworth had sent countless sketches of him over the years. They were the only ones that Thea had never thanked her for, had never commented on.

Because she truly had no desire to know her father.

As he looked at her, his face lost all color. His eyes filled with fear and something that looked like longing.

His voice came out a croaked whisper. "Anna? Could it be you?"

"Anna Selwyn is dead." The words dropped like heavy, jagged stones from her lips.

The man, her father, blanched. "Yes, of course. She died after the birth of our son." The words came out as if memorized and uttered many times, lifeless and without meaning.

She refused to accept the lie. "On the contrary. She died several years ago from a fever that often kills Europeans in the tropics. She died with her son's name on her lips."

Her father—but she refused to think of him thus—*Langley's* knees buckled and he grasped blindly at a nearby table for support. "I . . ." His eyes burned with intensity. "You knew her?"

"Yes, I knew her."

His mouth opened again, but nothing came out.

Lady Boyle intervened. "I believe this conversation would be better conducted in a more private location." Although her eyes were filled with understanding, there was steel in her voice.

Drake placed his arm around Thea, pulling her into his side. "Perhaps later. It is time my wife and I left."

Thea did not resist as he led her from the room.

"Wait." Langley's voice was desperate. "I need to talk to you, Mrs. Drake. When can I call upon you?"

She did not turn around. She couldn't.

Drake answered for her. "If my wife wishes to speak with you, she will send word."

His voice did not invite further comment and Langley subsided. Or at least she assumed he had. He made no more attempt to prevent her and Drake from leaving.

She and Drake did not speak as he led her to the carriage and settled her against the cushions. He gave instructions to the coachman and then stepped up into the carriage and sat across from her. He must have sensed that she needed space to breathe. She felt as if her lungs could not get enough air.

The carriage had been making its slow progress through the London streets for several minutes before she spoke.

"He thought I was my mother."

"You must look like her." Drake's voice was soft, comforting.

"But my mother would have aged since he last saw her. How could he have thought I was her?"

"The shock of seeing you, looking so like her, after all these years would have done it."

"Twenty-odd years. He hasn't seen my mother since I was a baby. How strange. Although she died ten years ago, sometimes I feel as if I've seen her just yesterday. Is it the same for him, do you suppose?"

Drake didn't answer. He just looked at her as if waiting for something.

"What?"

"It must have been difficult to see him like that."

She drew her gloves off, focusing on each finger as if it mattered. "It was unexpected."

"It was a bloody disaster."

Her head came up at his harsh tone. "Why are you so upset? You've been pushing me to meet him all along."

He flinched as if her comment hurt. The truth sometimes did. She should know.

"You should have had the opportunity to meet your father for the first time in private. Your aunt should have left instructions for him not to be admitted."

"She could hardly do that to her own nephew."

"She bloody well could have."

Something triggered in her memory, and she felt herself staring at Drake as if seeing him for the first time. "You knew."

He raised his brows in inquiry. "Knew what?"

"Who he was. You knew he was my father before I said anything. You told me it would be all right."

His expression turned wary. "Yes."

"How?"

"Your aunt told me when I went to speak to her about marrying you."

He had gone to speak to her aunt?

Things started slipping into place in her mind, and although she was not morning sick, she certainly felt nauseous. "Lady Boyle said that you planned to find a wife this Season."

Although he did not smile, his eyes grew warm. "Yes, but you saved me the trouble."

"She said you wanted to marry a well-connected paragon."

He shrugged. "One's plans are not always reflective of the eventual outcome."

She nodded. "That is true. I am not a paragon." She met his gaze, her heart feeling battered. "But I am well connected."

His eyes narrowed. "What are you trying to say?"

"Simply that you got what you wanted in a wife. Your insistence that I make amends with my father is beginning to make sense. You married an earl's daughter and want the *ton,* particularly your father, to know it."

"Bloody hell. What crackbrained notion has a hold of you now?"

She looked down at her hands. Why had she taken off her gloves? She couldn't remember. Her fingers were cold, like the rest of her. She started to slide her gloves back on her hands, carefully pulling each wrinkle in the silk flat.

Her ring fell into her lap and she slid it back on, over the glove.

She raised her gaze to him. "It isn't a crackbrained notion. You want to prove to your father that you are as good as he is, even better maybe."

Drake said nothing, his mouth set.

"You built a shipping empire until you could buy and sell him several times. That wasn't enough, so you made plans to marry high in the *ton.* You believed that would prove the circumstances of your birth did not matter. That although your parents had not been married, you were still considered above reproach."

His eyes had lost their concerned softness and now burned with angry disbelief. "You think I married you to prove something to my father?"

"Why else?"

He stared at her as if she'd gone mad. "What about our child, or had you forgotten that tiny fact while creating this ludicrous scenario in your head?"

She rested her gloved hand against her abdomen and felt grief. "The lobster patties at the musicale were bad. Several people got sick from them."

He didn't look like he understood what she was saying. She spelled it out for him. "I wasn't morning sick. I'm not pregnant. I did not have to marry you."

"Morning sick or not, you could still be pregnant. The fact is, we behaved irresponsibly and marriage was our only alternative."

She wanted to refute his words, deny that marriage had been a necessity, but what would be the point? They were married now, and a small voice tormented her with the knowledge that, necessary or not, it was what she had *wanted.*

"Believe what you will. Why didn't you tell me your plan to marry well?"

His laughter was harsh. "You make it sound as if I betrayed you. It is an accepted practice for both ladies and gentlemen of the *ton* to marry well. My plans to seek such a wife this Season are certainly nothing to upset you now. I married *you.*"

"Yes, you married me. But you intended for me to take my place in Society. You tried to convince me to on enough occasions that you cannot deny it now."

He expelled a frustrated breath. "I believed that you would be happier knowing your family." He leaned forward, intensity shimmering in the air between them. "I did not marry you in order to fulfill some underhanded desire to prove to my father that I am worthy."

She couldn't maintain eye contact, so she dropped her gaze to her lap. "I didn't say it was underhanded."

He tilted her chin up with his finger and wouldn't let her look away. "You think I only want you to know your father so that you can be recognized as an earl's daughter."

"Yes, I do believe that."

He dropped his hand away from her face and sat back.

His face lost all expression. "I know my reasons for marrying you, and I thought you did, too. Apparently I was wrong."

"I suppose there is my half of Merewether Shipping. It makes a sizable dowry, does it not?" she accused, reckless in her desperation for him to deny such paltry reasons for marriage.

"Believe what you like."

He tossed her words back at her with cold precision, and she wanted to weep. She needed him to convince her that she was wrong, that he had married her for something other than a plan calculated to prove his value to the rest of the *ton*.

However, he remained broodingly silent for the remainder of the carriage ride to his town house. *Their* town house, she corrected herself. For better or worse, they *were* married.

When the carriage stopped, Drake stepped out and then turned to help her down. As soon as her feet were safely on the ground, he pulled his supporting hands away.

She wanted to protest. Where had the intimacy they had shared in her aunt's sitting room gone? She had to acknowledge that its disappearance was her fault. Drake wasn't the one accusing her of nefarious motives in marrying. She sighed and followed him into the house.

It was a new structure, built in the current architectural style. She liked the simple lines and balanced proportions very much. She turned to tell Drake so, but her words died in her throat at the coldness in his eyes.

He introduced her to her household staff, instructed the housekeeper to show her to her room, and disappeared. He did not reappear for dinner, and she discovered he had left the house. When he had not returned by midnight, she gave up waiting for him and made ready for bed.

Although the events of the day had exhausted her, she could not sleep. Too many things competed for attention in her mind.

She had met her father for the first time. He hadn't looked like a monster, but then she knew he wouldn't. The thing that surprised her, the thing she couldn't get past, was the vulnerability she had seen in his eyes when she spoke of her mother. As if he had a wound that hadn't healed.

In his concern for her, Drake had rushed her out of the town house before she'd had a chance to see if her brother had attended the breakfast with Langley. Had he been there? The thought she had been within touching distance of her brother and not known it tormented her.

But nothing like her conversation with Drake in the carriage. It kept repeating over and over again in her head. At first the constant repetitions had served only to fuel her anger at her husband. Then memories had started to intersperse with the harsh accusations she had made against Drake in her mind, and she began to feel wretched.

The fact that he had planned to marry a paragon high in the *ton* was neither here nor there. As he had said, he'd chosen *her*, Althea Selwyn, and no one could accuse her of being a paragon. Accusing him of wanting her to make peace with her father for his own ends had been a direct hit against pride that had been forced to withstand years as the illegitimate son of a man who would never acknowledge him.

She shuddered at her own needless cruelty.

Even if he did have ulterior motives for pressing her to get to know her father, Drake wasn't aware of them, and making the accusation had hurt him. Besides, he had made his intentions toward her clear aboard ship, long before finding out that she was the daughter of an earl.

She rolled over and punched her pillow, trying to vent some of her frustration and anxiety.

What if he couldn't forgive her? Had she doomed her marriage with her sharp tongue and accusations? It wouldn't be the first time that she had delivered such a strong blow to his pride. Would she ever forget the look of pain on his features as he knelt naked before her, having asked for her hand and been bluntly rejected?

Then she had kept right on refusing, not giving in to his desires or her own. Still, he had persisted. Had insisted on doing right by her and the child they may have created.

He had also helped her in her investigation just as he had promised, arranging for men to watch Uncle Ashby and the London warehouse. Not caring that the investigation took him away from his own business, he had pursued the thief as if it were a matter of his considerable personal honor.

After all that, she had to go and accuse him of marrying her for her place in society and her half of Merewether Shipping. She almost laughed aloud. Drake was wealthier than she'd ever dreamed of being, and once society learned of her father's duplicity, her connection to him would not improve her or her new husband's standing in the *ton*.

He'd certainly gotten no prize in his bride.

If he could not get past her latest attack on his honor, she did not know what she would do.

She slid her hand between the sheets along the other side of her bed. The side that he should be occupying. It was their wedding night, after all, but he wasn't there. She lay, lonely, longing for his presence, not even sure when he would return to their home.

What was the matter with her? Why had she behaved so abominably toward him?

The truth hit her like one of Whiskey Jim's bottles.

The love she was so afraid of acknowledging made her vulnerable to her own insecurities. She loved him so much she would die for him, and it terrified her that he did not love her even a little in return. That fear muddled her reasoning, and she had struck out and hurt him as surely as his lack of deeper feelings toward her had made her heart contract in pain.

Love did not always make one kind, she realized.

Her depressing thoughts were interrupted by sounds from the next room that indicated her husband had finally returned.

It was about time.

Despite her remorse for her treatment of him, indignation rose in her. Didn't he realize how inappropriate it was to desert his wife on their wedding day?

She would certainly tell him so. She would also humbly beg his pardon for casting aspersions on his honor.

She pulled on her wrapper and approached the connecting door between their rooms. Should she knock? What if it was locked? That prospect held her paralyzed for several seconds, but taking a deep breath, she put her hand on the knob and turned.

It moved easily under her fingers and the door swung inward. Drake had already doused the light, and the only illumination was a pale stream of moonlight filtering through a small crack in the heavy draperies.

Eighteen

He has remarried! Lady Jacqueline D'Annis. He stole my son for sins only imagined and yet has done far worse. His is truly the act of the depraved. I am still the Countess of Langley—and yet a woman in England lives by that title. A woman shares my husband's bed and his life, mothers my child. That is what I cannot forgive. Lady Upworth could not bear to tell me until I made plans to travel to England. She admitted that Langley has told everyone that I am dead. I will return to England and I will see my son. Langley will not dare deny me now.

March 7, 1807
Journal of Anna Selwyn, Countess of Langley

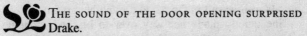 THE SOUND OF THE DOOR OPENING SURPRISED Drake.

He had expected no visit from his wife on this night.

He felt guilty for abandoning her on their wedding day, but if he had stayed, he feared his fury at her accusations would overflow and burn them both. In an attempt to focus on something besides his wife's painful lack of trust, he had gone to Merewether Shipping, not expecting to discover anything new in broad daylight.

He had been wrong on that count and found it incredibly ironic that after all the late nights he'd spent watching the warehouse, the thief had acted during the day.

He still didn't know if it was Emerson or his assistant and thought Thea's supposition it could be someone else very unlikely, but orders had been given for the transfer of a shipment from the warehouse. According to the spy Drake had planted in Merewether's warehouse, it was a shipment of goods that should have been part of the cargo brought on an investment ship from Sri Lanka, goods not yet sold.

Instead, the goods had been marked for delivery to a small warehouse located not a mile from Merewether Shipping. Drake had followed the shipment along with one of his men and waited in the shadows for Emerson or his assistant to show up. They had waited in vain. Drake had left two men watching the building, sure that it housed more goods stolen from Merewether Shipping.

They were given instructions to contact him if anyone else arrived or the goods were moved again.

The sound of Thea moving across the floor toward his bed affected him like a siren's call, and all thought of the investigation disappeared like morning mist.

He had returned expecting a cold bed on his wedding night, convinced Thea had no interest in sharing it after her unprovoked attack in the carriage.

So what was she doing tiptoeing across his floor? He bloody well wasn't in the mood for another argument.

She quietly made her way over to his bed, stopping when her wrapper brushed his counterpane. "Drake?"

He didn't respond immediately, and she put her hand on his shoulder and shook him. "Pierson. Wake up. I have something I need to say."

His hand shot out in the darkness and gripped her wrist. To hell with arguing. She would feel better, and so would he, if they made love. She squealed as he yanked her down onto the bed and rolled over to pin her to the feather ticking.

He kissed her, his mouth open and hot. He allowed all the pent-up hunger he felt for her to come out in that kiss.

She let out a startled gasp and then returned his passion with an ardor that belied her earlier anger or a current desire to argue. He had her wrapper off and was working on her nightgown when she protested.

"Don't you want to hear my apology?"

Apology?

He leaned down and kissed the breast he had just bared. "I want to hear you moan."

She did. Right then and several more times over the next hour. He made love to her until they were both limp and exhausted.

She lay cuddled against his side, her fingers splayed across his chest.

He said her name.

"What?"

"Now I'll hear your apology."

He smiled in the darkness when she laughed.

She grew silent, then leaned up and met his gaze in the shadows. "I truly am sorry I accused you of marrying me for money and position."

"I married you because I wanted to, Thea. It is as simple as that."

She smiled a little sadly. "I believe you."

Why was wanting her not enough? He remembered her words the fateful day they made love for the first time. She had asked if he loved her. Did she want him to? *Did she love him?*

More importantly, was he capable of love? He didn't know. But for the first time, he desperately wanted to be.

Her generous apology deserved an answering one. "I'm sorry I left you alone on our wedding day."

"You should never just walk away from an argument," she said, sounding quite serious and full of authority. "You must always try to work things out. It is the only way to have a strong marriage."

He did not agree. There were times his anger might cause more hurt, and when those times came, she was much better off if he left. "Our marriage will be strong because we will make it so, not because we will always do the right thing. Sometimes we will hurt each other, Thea, but I will never walk away from our marriage."

"I won't either."

He hadn't realized how much he needed the assurance until she said the words.

"Where did you go today?" she asked.

He told her and then related what he had witnessed at the warehouse.

"That's wonderful." She hugged him. "We're bound to catch the embezzler any day now. I don't know how I would have done this without you."

The admiration in her voice filled him with bone-deep satisfaction. "You aren't still thinking that Emerson is innocent, are you?"

The man was either guilty or inexcusably ignorant of his own business affairs. There was no other explanation for the discrepancies in the company's ledgers.

She squirmed closer, wrapping one of her legs over his. "I know it looks bleak for him, but he's so much like his uncle, and Ashby Merewether is an honorable man, almost as honorable as yourself."

He smiled in the dark at her compliment until he remembered one of the points they had not discussed from their argument. "Do you truly feel trapped in marriage to me?"

She rubbed her check over his shoulder. "No. It would be easier to think that I was forced to marry you, but I made the decision and I can't even pretend that the thought of carrying your child was the deciding factor."

He wondered what that factor had been, but felt like he'd pushed his luck far enough for one day. He focused instead on her first statement.

Already thinking he knew the answer, he nevertheless felt compelled to ask, "Why would it be easier?"

She played with the hair on his chest. "I don't know. The feeling of not being responsible for a decision I had convinced myself I would never make, I guess."

He let out a relieved breath. She might feel as if she had broken her promise to her mother, but she wasn't saying so, and he would take what he could get.

He leaned down to kiss the top of her head. "You aren't going to regret marrying me."

It was an ironclad promise he intended to keep.

She kissed his chest, above his right nipple. "And you aren't going to regret marrying me." She yawned. "Even if I'm not a patterncard of socially correct behavior."

Unbelievably, he felt himself stir.

He slipped his hand down her thigh, thinking that a perfect paragon would bore him to tears now that he'd met Thea. "Sweetheart?"

"Mmm?" she asked drowsily.

"You may not be pregnant now, but I think I can safely promise that you soon will be."

He drowned her surprised laughter with his lips.

THE NEXT MORNING, THEA WAS TAKING A MENTAL INventory of the changes she wanted to make to her new home when her aunt was announced. Drake had gone to check on the warehouse holding the stolen goods, and had insisted that Thea remain at home. She had protested until he reminded her that Lady Upworth intended to call that morning.

Thea gave the butler permission to show her caller into
the drawing room. She planned to start her decor changes
in this room. Drake obviously preferred stark simplicity,
but she wanted to make the large town house a home. She
could not fault the drawing room's furnishings. Well-made
sofas and chairs clustered around sturdy tables, but it was
missing the curios and pictures that made a room cozy.

She smiled at the idea of cozy being applied to the
large, elegant room, but she would give it her best effort.
Even the drapes were a solid, nondescript color. The fabric
was heavy and of the highest quality, but she did not particularly care for it. She would like patterned velvet in a warm
yellow.

The dowager entered, leaning on her ornate cane. "Good
morning, dear. Where is that handsome husband of yours?
Surely he has not abandoned you the very day after your
wedding?"

Thea smiled. "He is on an errand of business on my behalf." It was true, although not the whole truth.

Lady Upworth nodded approvingly while taking a seat
near Thea. "You will, of course, relinquish your interest in
your company now that you are married."

She would do no such thing, but Drake had shown her
that discretion with family was valuable, so Thea ignored
the comment. "Thank you for the lovely breakfast yesterday. You went to much too much trouble on our behalf."

"Nonsense, you are family."

Thea impulsively leaned forward and kissed her aunt's
wrinkled cheek. "You are a dear woman."

Lady Upworth's eyes sparkled, but she dismissed
the comment with a wave of her hand. "I'm sorry about the
shock you had yesterday. I did not expect Langley to come
so early to Town. It is not his usual manner."

"I'm quite all right. Drake took very good care of me."

"Lady Boyle said that he ushered you out of the room so
quickly, she barely realized you were leaving."

"He wanted me to have time to get used to the notion of seeing my father."

Her aunt sighed. "Yes."

"Was Jared with him?" The possibility had haunted Thea since the day before.

"No, though he did come to Town."

"Why did they come early?" She discovered she was curious about the goings-on of this family she'd never known.

"Irisa." Her aunt frowned. "Evidently they're angling for a betrothal to the Duke of Clareshire. The servants told your father Irisa could be found at my house."

"But she's only sixteen."

"And his grace is sixty if he's a day. I don't know what your father is thinking to encourage the match. All the fault of his wife, I've no doubt. She's a hopeless social climber."

"I cannot believe a mother would encourage a daughter barely out of the schoolroom to marry a man old enough to be her grandfather. It's wicked." Mama would have fought the devil himself to protect Thea from such a fate.

How could Irisa's mother be so different?

"You don't know the current countess. A duke at any age is considered quite the catch in Jacqueline's eyes. I've always felt she somehow precipitated your father's final idiocy toward your mother."

Perhaps. Thea didn't want to think about her father or Jacqueline right now. She would much rather focus on unemotional issues, such as how to catch a thief. However, her aunt was not finished with the topic.

"I spoke to Langley after you left yesterday."

Wary, Thea probed her aunt's gaze with her own. "What did you say to him?"

Had Lady Upworth told him Thea's secret?

Before answering, the dowager leaned forward and took Thea's hand and held it. "The time for truth has come, my dear. I made a mistake sending your mother to the West

Indies. Had I not done so, she would be alive and your father would not have married Jacqueline."

Although she had mentioned a similar feeling before, Thea had not credited the depth of guilt her great-aunt carried about the past events within her family. The older woman's eyes had filmed with tears, the pain and remorse in them unmistakable. Before Thea had a chance to comment or offer comfort, she continued.

"Had I told the truth to your father years ago, things would be much different." Two tears spilled over and rolled down Lady Upworth's withered cheeks. "I promised myself that if you ever came to England, I would tell my nephew the truth."

Compassion for her aunt's pain welled up in Thea, but it was tempered by a sense of betrayal. "Don't you think that was my decision to make?"

"No, my dear, I do not. Your father has made his mistakes, and he hurt your mother terribly. For that reason I supported her decision to flee with you and make a new life for herself. However, he is your father and he has a right to know that you are his daughter. His sin was not against you, and he has paid for the sin he committed against your mother by losing that which he held most dear, his wife."

Thea wanted to argue with her aunt. She wanted to tell her that if Langley had held her mother dear, he could not have done the things he did, but she was not a child any longer. Life was not made up of easily distinguished colors, but more a rainbow of shades, one melting into the other. The motivations and actions of others were not so easily judged.

"He also lost you. The daughter he never knew."

"Pierson said something to that effect to me once." Thea's voice came out softer than she had intended. She took a deep breath and attempted to speak more normally. "I didn't want to admit it, but perhaps you both have a point. I still don't know if I am capable of having any sort of relationship with him. *If I want to.*"

Lady Upworth squeezed Thea's hand. "It will be up to him to prove to you that he is worthy of your affection."

Thea's heart constricted. "Are you sure he wants to?"

The old woman looked troubled. "I know he wants to know you, but he's afraid of the scandal from his past. Of Irisa and Jared being hurt by the truth."

"If he has a right to the truth, then so do they."

Smiling, albeit mistily, her aunt agreed, "You are right, of course, and Langley will come to realize that. We are dining en famille tonight at his town house. Will you come?"

Thea felt herself tense.

The thought of sitting through dinner with virtual strangers, one of them a man who was both her father and the bogeyman of her childhood, made her wince. "I do not think I am ready for such an occasion."

Her aunt sighed, but nodded her lovely white head. "You have a point, my dear. Perhaps you will see your way clear to coming for a visit after dinner. Both your sister and your brother will be there."

Thea bit her lip, her desire to meet her twin and her trepidation at the thought of spending time with Langley at war within her. "I don't know."

She needed time to think, and there was still the embezzler to consider, Uncle Ashby's well-being to worry about. Any relationship she might develop with Langley could not overshadow the responsibility she had to the man who had helped her mother raise her.

DRAKE RETURNED HOME TO FIND HIS WIFE STARING broodingly into the unlit fireplace in the drawing room. She looked up as he entered, and some strong, unnamed emotion slammed through his chest. She was so beautiful, so courageous, more intelligent than most men and more determined, too.

She had risked the unknown, her own emotional comfort, and even her life to prevent harm to her adopted uncle. She stubbornly insisted on finding the embezzler to her company, having refused Drake's offer to continue the investigation alone. She was beyond anything he had ever imagined finding in a wife. He vowed he would be what she needed in a husband.

"What are you thinking when you look at me like that?" she asked.

"That I have an uncommon wife and I want to be worthy of her."

Her eyes widened and then misted over. Jumping up from her chair, she flew across the room to land with a thud against him. He closed his arms around her, shocked by her reaction.

She returned the embrace and spoke against his waistcoat. "How can you think that after everything?"

"Everything?" What idea had taken root in her active imagination now?

She nodded against his chest. "Yes, everything. I seduced you. Spurned you. Mistrusted you. And even now you are busy with my investigation while your business suffers."

He forced her to move away enough for him to look into her tear-drenched blue eyes. "You may not have noticed, but I was hardly an unwilling participant the first time we made love. For you to believe otherwise is not only an insult to my manhood, but absurd."

She blinked the moisture away from her eyes and stared at him in wonder.

"Furthermore, had you accepted my proposal immediately, I would not be so certain now that our marriage is what you truly desired. Yesterday was a difficult day for you and you allowed your emotions to rule your head, saying some things you did not mean, but in your heart of hearts, you did not doubt me." He said it not merely because he wanted it to be true, but because he believed it.

She trusted him far more than she realized, or she would never have married him.

She looked so vulnerable that he could not stop himself from leaning down to offer her a soft kiss of reassurance. Her lips were pliable and willing under his, and the mating of their mouths turned into something hot and out of control before he remembered that he had brought visitors back with him.

The sound of a throat clearing behind him told him that they had been shown into the drawing room.

He lifted his head from Thea's intent on making one final point. "I will have you know that I am quite capable of supervising an investigation and overseeing my business. I would not have you think that I am an inferior businessman."

Her smile was like walking from a fog-shrouded London night into a ballroom lit with hundreds of candles. "I am glad to hear that, since I hold your business acumen in such high esteem."

The way her body pressed against his belied any belief his business acumen was of primary consideration to her at the moment, but he'd learned he liked her teasing.

"Mr. Drake?"

She looked around his shoulder, her eyes widened in surprise. She had just realized they had visitors. Her gaze shifted back to him, a question in their beautiful blue depths.

"I've brought some guests."

She broke away from him, her pretty cheeks turning the color of a rose in bloom, and turned toward the two men occupying the other end of the drawing room. "So I see."

"Barton was making a mad dash for parts unknown when Hansen, the bright fellow standing next to him, convinced him to come talk to me instead."

Thea crossed the room and stood in front of Barton. "So, you've brought him here so I could question him as well?"

The blond assistant swallowed audibly, his nervousness apparent in his shaking fingers and pinched lips. "I haven't done anything wrong."

"Then why were you leaving the city?" Thea did not sound as if she believed the assistant.

Drake had his own doubts, but Merewether, not Barton, had been seen going into the warehouse storing the stolen goods. Barton's tale sealed the other man's guilt.

Knowing the news that her adopted uncle's family was to blame for recent events would upset her, Drake slipped his arm around Thea and hugged her to his side. "Tell my wife what you told me, Barton."

"Mr. Merewether came to me and said as how you suspected me of stealing from the warehouse. He offered to help me hide in the country until he found the true culprit and cleared my name. He told me you planned to have me sent to Newgate." Barton shuddered at the name of the prison. "I didn't steal anything. I noticed discrepancies in the ledgers months ago. When I went to Mr. Merewether with my concerns, he said he would look into it, but that it was probably simple calculation errors. Since he kept the books, I had no choice but to accept his word."

"You could have contacted me via letter," Thea chided.

Barton nodded, clearly miserable. "Yes, but I wasn't sure of anything, and Mr. Merewether took over all the accounts after that. He kept the ledgers locked in his office. I had no way of substantiating my claim."

"You should have tried." Drake was not as calm about it as his wife. His hold on her tightened. He could not bear the thought of losing her. "When Thea discovered the thefts, he sent someone to try to kill her."

Barton's face lost what little color had remained after being accosted while trying to flee the city. "I didn't realize."

Thea squeezed Drake's arm. "He did not succeed, my love."

Was he her love?

He could not demand an answer to that question in the middle of their investigation, but soon he would.

Thea measured Barton with a glance. "I don't suppose you would have any idea of who Mr. Merewether sent to our island?"

"You mean you don't know?" Barton asked, sounding surprised.

"No."

A little color returned to Barton's face and he pulled himself erect. "I believe I know the answer to that. I saw Mr. Merewether pay one of our previous dockworkers a substantial sum of money before sending him aboard a Merewether ship bound for the island. It could be someone else, but I doubt it."

Drake's irritation nearly spiraled out of control. "Didn't you find that behavior odd?"

Barton held himself perfectly erect now. "I do not make it a policy to question my superior's actions."

The only thing that prevented Drake from doing the prissy assistant bodily injury was the restraining hold Thea had on his arm. "Pierson, you must remain calm. We now know who the infiltrator on the island is. Mr. Barton can give us his name and description."

Barton nodded vehemently. "Yes. I can."

Drake decided to wait until the man had given them the information before he knocked Barton senseless for allowing Thea's life to be put in jeopardy.

HE WAS STILL ANNOYED TWO HOURS LATER AS HE DROVE his curricle toward Merewether Shipping's office, the assistant and Hansen following in a hansom cab. Thea had not allowed him to beat even a modicum of sense into the irritating Barton.

Thea sat silently by Drake's side as they made their way through the congested London traffic. Her voice surprised him when she decided to speak. "Lady Upworth came to call."

"She had said she would."

"Yes."

He waited, knowing that she would get around to whatever occupied her thoughts eventually.

"She told Langley the truth."

"No one can force you to see him. I won't allow it."

He saw her nod from the corner of his eye. "Thank you."

"Do you want to see him?"

"I . . ." She fell silent for almost a full minute. "I want him to tell me why he never searched. Why he married Jacqueline."

A completely unexpected thought came to him.

"If he never searched, then he did not know for certain your mother had died. He could have been committing bigamy." Then an even more disturbing thought took its place, a possibility that should have occurred to him before, but never had. "Was your mother dead when he married the current countess?"

"No."

No wonder Thea had so strongly resisted the idea of acknowledging her father. "The bloody bastard."

"You were right when you said that he lacked honor. He also lacked morality."

"Yet your aunt told him the truth about you. Why?"

"She feels responsible for my mother's death and for Langley's marriage to Jacqueline. She is convinced that had she told him the truth about my existence and Mother's flight to the West Indies, neither event would have transpired."

"That is a heavy burden to carry."

"Yes, I know. Almost as heavy as the burden a daughter might carry believing that had she not been born, her mother would never have left her son and country to live on an island that eventually killed her."

Drake understood this type of guilt, and he refused to allow his wife to torture herself with it. "You were a gift to your mother, not a curse. You must accept that, Thea, or you discount all the sacrifices she made to keep you."

He felt her gaze burning into him and slid his away from the surrounding traffic for a moment to meet it.

"It's true," he assured her.

"Then you, too, must accept that you are a gift to your mother and that her sacrifice in keeping you has not been in vain."

Drake laughed harshly. "She had no choice."

Thea shook her head. "Do not be a fool. She could have gone to the country, given birth to you, and given you away with no one the wiser. Your grandfather's connections are certainly enough to have ensured the safety of her secret."

Feelings inside of Drake shifted in a way that left him breathless. He had always defined himself by the fact that his father did not value him enough to acknowledge him, not the reality that his mother had wanted and loved him so much she had accepted a lifetime of Society's censure to keep him.

To have the right to call him son.

Unfamiliar moisture gathered in his eyes, and he blinked it away. "She is a very special woman."

"Yes, she is, and the evidence is in how well she raised you." Thea's words reached down into his soul and wrapped themselves around his heart.

Since meeting her, he had begun to care less and less about proving himself to Society and his father. In that moment, the desire to show his father he had value disappeared entirely from inside Drake. Thea had been right—his life was defined by his mother's love, not his father's rejection. And his value resided in the man he had become, not the man who had helped make him.

The freedom he experienced at Thea's words was unlike anything he had ever known. Yet another reason to give thanks to his Maker for this incredible woman who was his wife.

When they reached the warehouse, he had been so mellowed by his thoughts that he wanted only to kill Emerson, not torture him first for trying to hurt Thea.

Nineteen

The fever has caught me. I am weak and I know that it will only get worse. I have watched others die of this malady for over a decade and know what is to come. I have tried to fight it, but I feel I am getting weaker. I have only one regret—that I did not return to England to see my son sooner. So close. The journey has been planned, but now I know it cannot be made. I will never touch his face or hear his laugh. And he will never know me, never know how my love for him has grown all the years of our forced separation.

May 16, 1807
Journal of Anna Selwyn, Countess of Langley

THEA FELT SLIGHTLY SICK AS SHE AND DRAKE entered Merewether Shipping's office for the second time since she had arrived in England. The prospect of having Ashby Merewether's nephew arrested left her feeling hollow.

Had the thefts been the only consideration, she would have simply fired the man without a reference, but he had hired someone to kill her and she could not be sure that Uncle Ashby was safe even now.

The corridor leading to Emerson's office echoed with the sound of her and Drake's footsteps as well as those of Hansen, Barton, and the two Bow Street Runners who accompanied them. Drake had insisted on bringing the Runners along to take Emerson into custody.

Certain Drake would have preferred to execute his own kind of justice, she hadn't argued. Emerson faced prison and possible exportation to Australia, but if he only knew it, those options were far more lenient than other ideas Drake had expressed.

Lightly tapping on Emerson's door, she and Drake waited for an invitation to enter. When it came, her husband pushed her behind him and entered the room first.

Emerson sat at his desk, either oblivious to his predicament or a consummate actor.

He smiled when they entered. "Congratulations on your recent nuptials, Mr. and Mrs. Drake. I read the announcement in this morning's paper."

Thea could not believe this jovial man was responsible for the thefts and attempts on her life. He sounded so terribly sincere in his happiness for her, looking almost smug about it.

Then his eyes widened at the sight of the Runners as they came into the office. His smile slowly slipped away.

"I worried Uncle's plan would go awry like this, but he was sure you wouldn't call in the Runners." He looked nervously between her and Drake. "There's something I believe you need to know."

Drake removed his driving gloves. "Unfortunately for you, we've already figured it out."

"I've told them the truth, Mr. Merewether," Barton inserted.

Emerson looked at Barton as if his brains had gone to let. "The truth?"

Thea's heart filled with aching sadness. "Uncle Ashby is going to be so hurt."

Drake stood beside her, emanating anger, his glare causing Emerson to flush. Sweat beaded at the young man's brow, and he dabbed at it with a handkerchief.

"I wouldn't mind doing the old man a little harm myself right now." He looked at the Bow Street Runners. "I assure you, their presence is unnecessary."

Thea had gasped at Emerson's first statement, unable to credit such a lack of loyalty. Now she glowered. Did the man have no conscience at all?

"On the contrary. Their presence is eminently necessary. My husband might be tempted to mete out his own brand of punishment were they not here. You should be grateful I insisted on bringing them along."

Emerson frowned, dabbing at his brow again. "You mistook my meaning. Please, if you will allow me to explain, all of this can be cleared up."

"No explanation is necessary. Your behavior speaks for itself." Drake shifted beside her, and Emerson flinched as if in preparation for a blow.

"Take him into custody." Drake's tone dripped ice.

The Bow Street Runners moved forward, but Emerson jumped from his chair and backed away, his eyes widening with obvious fear.

"Please, if you would just let me explain." He looked imploringly at Thea.

She hardened her heart against the man who looked so much like her adopted uncle. "It's no use denying the charges. The evidence is not in your favor."

"There is no evidence—I mean, not really." He sidled farther away from the approaching Runners. "It was all part of Uncle's plan to get you here to England."

Thea blinked at the desperate sincerity in his voice. Emerson should write Penny Press novels, his lies were so convincing.

Thea forced aside her desire to believe Emerson. "Uncle Ashby would never condone someone trying to kill me."

Emerson's fear became a palpable thing. "Kill you? What are you talking about?"

"You damn bloody well know what she's talking about." Drake stepped to the right, cutting off any hope of escape for Emerson in that direction.

"They know about the man you hired to go to the island office and spy on Mrs. Drake." Barton's voice came from behind Thea.

Confusion showed on Emerson's rounded features. "What man? I hired no man."

"It's no use denying it, sir. I've told them everything."

"How could you have discovered Uncle Ashby's plans? Did you read my letters?" Emerson did not sound in the least bit guilty; he seemed more outraged than anything else. "I thought they appeared as if they had been read, but the wax seal was not broken."

"I won't lie for you, sir. Mr. and Mrs. Drake know the truth already. You've been stealing from the company."

"Yes, of course I've been stealing. Well, not stealing really, but temporarily storing company goods in an alternate location. Uncle's plan would not have worked otherwise."

Thea stared at him. He was mad. He belonged in Bedlam. He talked of his perfidy as if it were something Uncle Ashby would wholly approve of. Perhaps he deserved their pity, but insane or not, he had hired someone to kill her. She turned from him, not wanting to look at him any longer.

"Please. Take him away."

"No. You must listen to me. I have proof of what I claim. I assure you."

"Wait." Drake's voice rang with authority.

They stopped their cautious approach to Emerson.

"Explain this plan of your uncle's to me."

Barton shifted beside her, and she caught a look of

consternation on his face before the blond man's features went blank once again. Her attention returned to Emerson as he began to speak.

He moved back to stand behind his desk.

"Uncle Ashby wrote me several months ago asking for my help in a plan to get Miss Selwyn, I mean Mrs. Drake, to come to England. I have his letters here as proof." He knelt on the floor beside the desk and unlocked the bottom drawer. He riffled through the papers and then riffled some more. Finally, he stopped and looked up at Thea, his expression ashen. "The letters are gone."

Thea's anger broke free. "Of course they are not there. Uncle Ashby would never have condoned your actions. What a faraddidle." She turned to Drake. "Must we listen to this?"

To her surprise, her husband nodded. "Yes, I think we must." He turned to the Bow Street Runners. "Stand by the door, please."

That brought a strangled sound from behind her, and suddenly her arm was in a painful grip as cold metal pressed against the side of her neck. She registered the look of terrified rage on Drake's face at the same time as she realized the hand holding her so bruisingly belonged to Barton.

"I won't be staying around to hear the explanations, if you please. Mrs. Drake and I are going to take a little trip." He started dragging Thea backward, the barrel of the gun pressed hard into the flesh of her neck. "If anyone attempts to follow us, I'll shoot her."

Drake took a menacing step forward. "What good is she to you dead?"

"I don't have to kill her," Barton replied in a voice that made shivers of dread chase down her spine.

Her husband stopped moving.

"Everyone, over behind the desk." When Hansen didn't move fast enough to suit him, Barton barked, "Now."

Soon all the men were behind the desk, effectively putting a barrier between themselves and Thea and her captor. Breath sawed into her lungs as she tried to think of how to get out of her predicament. But the feel of the gun barrel and the stench of Barton's fear made it difficult to concentrate.

Frightened men did unpredictable things. She'd seen that often enough on her island.

"Toss your key over here," Barton ordered Emerson.

Emerson glared, but did as he was told, picking up a large key ring from his desk and tossing it toward Barton.

"Pick it up," Barton told her and pulled the gun from her neck, though he kept it trained on her.

This might be her only chance, she thought as she bent forward to grab the key ring. As she straightened, she swung her hand with the key ring in it back toward Barton, hitting him where Whiskey Jim had taught her hurt a man the most. She immediately threw herself to the left, away from the direction the gun was pointing. A howl of pain accompanied a loud crack as the pistol discharged, its ball burying itself harmlessly in the scarred wooden desk.

Then an animal roar rose above the sound of running feet, and she turned in time to see her husband pick up the already wounded Barton and toss him headfirst into the wall. The blond man hit with an audible thunk and then slid down the wall to land in a motionless pile of dandyish clothing.

The Bow Street Runners took over from Drake, dragging the unconscious man to his feet as her husband dropped on his knees beside her. "Are you all right, my darling?"

She blinked up at him, liking the sound of that word on his lips very much. "Yes, but I should like to get off the floor."

"In a moment."

"Why—?" Her words were cut off as his mouth claimed hers in a bruising kiss.

She was breathing in short gasps and pressed tightly against him when Drake eventually pulled his lips away from hers.

"You took a huge risk." Anger kindled in her husband's dark molasses gaze.

"It would have been an even bigger one to go with him."

The anger drained as quickly as it came, and Drake shuddered against her, his eyes going a bleak shade of brown. "Never again."

She kissed his chin. "Never again."

His arms tightened around her until she could not breathe, and she squeaked out a protest. He loosened his hold, but only enough to lift her to her feet.

Emerson stood in front of a barely conscious Barton. "I trusted you and you betrayed my trust."

Barton merely glared, his expression showing no remorse.

"Take him away," Drake ordered the Bow Street Runners. "We'll be along to make formal charges later." He turned to Hansen. "Go with them. I don't want there to be any chance of him escaping. Do you understand me?"

Hansen nodded, his face set in determined lines. "You can count on me, sir."

The Runners half dragged, half carried a resentfully silent Barton from the room.

Drake turned to Emerson. "Explain."

The other man grimaced. "I'm not sure I can explain everything, but I'm starting to see what happened. Why don't you and Mrs. Drake take a seat?"

Drake did as Emerson suggested, but instead of putting Thea in her own chair, he pulled her into his lap. She didn't even think of demurring. Her husband's big body was still trembling from her near miss, and she wanted to give comfort as much as she needed to receive it.

Emerson poured a whiskey for himself and Drake and a glass of sherry for her before sitting down at his desk. She sipped at the dry wine while her husband swallowed the entire glass of whiskey in one gulp.

She gasped, but he just shrugged. "I needed it. I'm overset."

She would have laughed, but he so clearly spoke the truth.

She snuggled closer and turned her attention to Emerson. "What was this plan you were telling us about?"

"Uncle Ashby and Lady Upworth both despaired of ever convincing you to journey to England. He lit on the idea of making it look like there was a thief in the shipping office here. He knew you would come to investigate yourself, rather than allow him to make a trip so dangerous to his health."

"That was very clever of Uncle Ashby." He'd been quite right; Thea had reacted exactly as he predicted.

"You say Lady Upworth knew of these plans?"

"Yes, Mr. Drake."

"But how did Mr. Barton become involved?" Thea asked.

Emerson drew a wax sealer from his desk drawer. It was identical to Uncle Ashby's.

"He must have broken the seal on the letters, read them, and then replaced it with this."

Thea nodded. "But what did he hope to gain?"

"Money."

"How?"

Emerson rolled his shoulders. "I have just this week become aware of missing inventory from the secret warehouse. Expensive inventory. I now believe Barton was stealing from that warehouse, hoping to blame me for the thefts."

"Surely he must have realized from reading the letters that Uncle Ashby would have cleared you."

"By then, he would have been far from England." Drake's voice vibrated in his chest against the hand she had placed there. "Remember, he stole the letters as well."

"You think he planned to run?"

"I'm sure of it. Hansen caught him trying to leave town, if you remember."

She did remember. "And he tried to get out of coming to confront Emerson."

He'd said he was afraid of facing his employer's temper, but Drake had insisted on his presence.

Her husband nodded. "Yes."

Emerson took another sip of his whiskey, still looking rather shaken. "I trusted him completely. I will naturally resign my position. My judgment is clearly not sound."

"Nonsense. Anyone can be taken in by an imposter." She thought of her mother's mistaken belief that Langley loved her in the beginning of their marriage and thanked God for sending a man like Drake into her own life. "In fact, I think we need to discuss the possibility of partnership. I cannot take such an active role in business now that I'm married, you know."

She had no intention of significantly curtailing her activities, but Emerson would need help now that Barton was gone, and making him a partner seemed the right thing to do after almost sending him to gaol.

Emerson's expression turned hopeful. "You cannot mean it."

"I do." She smiled. "You will be married soon. I'm sure your wife will be pleased at your change in circumstance."

He actually blushed. "She's a wonderful woman. Her family is very well off. She could have married almost anyone, but she accepted my proposal."

Thea remembered the rumors of a mistress and was absolutely certain they were no longer founded in reality. Emerson was clearly besotted with the girl he planned to marry.

"I believe we will make the partnership a wedding gift. I know Uncle Ashby will approve." She turned her face up to meet her husband's eyes. "What do you think?"

"I think any man who is partly responsible for our meeting deserves a considerable reward."

The comment sent warmth throughout her body while Emerson beamed with an astonished happiness that he made no effort to hide.

THEA CURLED INTO DRAKE'S SIDE, SATIATED FROM HIS loving. He'd brought her home after stopping to press formal charges against Barton and had taken her straight to bed.

"It's hard to believe it's all over," she murmured.

"If we had not been watching Barton along with Emerson, we would never have known he was responsible for the attack on your life." Drake's voice sounded strained.

She rubbed his chest in a soothing motion, but the knowledge the villain had hired someone to spy on her, with instructions to see she met with a fatal accident when she made arrangements to come to England, made her shiver. Apparently the spy had overheard her talking to Whiskey Jim and inquiring about his next run to England.

"He thought nothing of killing me simply to protect himself and the few thousand pounds he had stolen from the company."

"There are men who will kill for a glass of whiskey."

But her husband was not one of them. He had made his own fortune and had never stooped to nefarious means to get it.

She kissed his flat male nipple and smiled when he shivered. "I think it's time for me to keep my second promise to my mother."

Drake's hand gently cupped her shoulder. "Do you want me to send word inviting Jared to join us here?"

She leaned back and looked into the rich depths of his eyes. "No. I want to go to Langley's town house."

"Are you sure?"

She nodded. "I'm sure."

"When?"

"My aunt told me that they are going to have dinner en famille tonight. She has invited us to come afterwards. You will come with me, won't you?"

His hold on her tightened. "How can you doubt it?"

THEA DRESSED IN ONE OF HER NEW GOWNS FOR THE confrontation with her father. Its deep blue muslin brought out the blue of her eyes and contrasted nicely with her dark hair. At least that's what Melly said. The high waist accentuated her womanly curves, and Drake's eyes darkened with appreciation when he saw her.

"You look lovely, Thea."

"Thank you." He looked quite wonderful himself in his black evening clothes, and she told him so.

He helped her into her cloak and led her out to the carriage. The ride to the Langley town house was too short for her to brood much over the coming confrontation. It seemed as if one moment the carriage had started and the next they were stopped before her father's house.

The butler showed them into the drawing room without announcing them when she told him that Lady Upworth expected them. Drake put a protective arm around her waist as they entered the room, and she leaned into his body for comfort.

A woman of middle years, who had to be Jacqueline, sat on a chair by the fireplace, tatting lace.

The other occupants of the room sat around a small table playing cards. Lady Upworth faced the door, opposite a tall man with dark, almost black, hair. *Jared.* Irisa sat to her aunt's right, and Langley sat opposite his daughter.

Lady Upworth raised her gaze from her cards when they entered and gave them a warm smile of greeting. "Thea. Mr. Drake. How lovely that you decided to join us. Now we are truly *en famille.*"

Langley's head shot up and his gaze locked on Thea and Drake. Irisa also set her cards down to peer at the new arrivals. Her smile was every bit as warm as their aunt's.

Langley's eyes widened with recognition and he turned to his aunt. "You did not tell me that you had invited Mr. and Mrs. Drake to join us."

Lady Upworth shrugged, apparently unconcerned by the censure in his voice. "I wasn't sure they would come. I did not wish to set your hopes up."

Not waiting for her nephew to reply, she turned her attention to Irisa and Jared. "Children, I would like you to meet your sister. Thea Drake, née Selwyn."

Jacqueline's voice rose from her place by the fire. "Geoffrey, you mustn't allow this woman to make false claims. Have her thrown out at once," she exclaimed.

Thea wanted to throttle her aunt for her bluntness, and yet the truth was out now. She let her gaze shift to the woman who had taken her mother's place in Society. Thea felt a surge of pity for her. The future held unhappy revelations.

Langley shook his head at his wife. "We can't hide the truth any longer. My aunt is determined to expose all."

As her father's words registered, Thea realized that he had already revealed the truth to his wife. At least part of it.

Jared stood and turned around to face Thea. The scar that marked his face stood as a reminder of all the things they had missed in one another's lives. His eyes were filled with wariness. His gaze slid past her and met that of her husband.

She felt Drake stiffen beside her.

She wished she knew what Jared was thinking. She had been waiting for this moment for her entire life. Did he want to know her? Would he ever want to know her?

She lifted the books she held in her arms toward him. "These are our mother's journals. I promised her as she lay dying that I would bring them to you. She wanted you to know how much she loved you."

Jared made no move to take the leather volumes. "My mother died soon after my birth."

Thea's eyes filled with tears.

"No. She didn't. Your father"—she looked at Langley knowing the accusation she felt was in her eyes—"*our* father took you from her and told her that she would never see you again. He didn't know about me, and she feared that once he did, he would steal me away, too. She fled with me to the West Indies, where she died."

Jared's eyes narrowed and he turned to Langley. "Is she speaking the truth?"

Langley's face had turned the color of parchment. "Yes."

Thea moved forward until she stood a foot from her brother. The next words out of her mouth surprised her.

They were not what she had intended to say. "May I touch you?"

Jared's eyes widened a fraction, but other than that, his expression did not change.

"I have seen many sketches of you. I imagined you so often, what you were thinking, what you were doing. I need to know you are real." She reached out her hand and, when he did not move away, placed it over the scar on his cheek. Her fingertips tingled when they came into contact with the puckered flesh. "I had a dream. A nightmare. When this happened."

He didn't speak, and she let her hand fall away. She laid the journals on the table. "One day you will want to read them. You will want to know her. Perhaps, one day you will even want to know me."

She turned to go, her promise to Mama fulfilled.

His hand snaked out and grasped her arm. "I do know you." He pulled her back around to face him. "I've dreamt about you many times. Once I dreamt that you cried uncontrollably and I was desperate to comfort you, but you were just an image from my dreams. Not real."

A small, strangled sound emanated from her throat. She threw herself against him and proceeded to dampen his shirt with her tears. He let his arms close around her awkwardly and then patted her back.

Suddenly everyone in the room was talking at once. Jacqueline's strident tones mixed with Lady Upworth's nononsense statements. Langley's voice talked over Irisa's, and Drake overrode them all with a demand for quiet.

Jared let her go and Drake pulled her back into his side. Irisa demanded an explanation and Thea attempted to give it amid several impatient interruptions from her sister.

When she was done, Irisa turned toward her father. "Papa, why didn't you go after Thea's mother?"

Thea's heart beat a wild rhythm as she waited for the answer to a question she had longed to ask herself.

Langley moved to stand near Jacqueline and laid his hand on her shoulder. Thea could appreciate his show of support for his second wife. She couldn't be finding it easy to hear her husband's sordid past.

"Papa?" Irisa prompted.

"At first I believed she'd run off with Estcott." Thea gasped in outrage and he sighed. "She left Town at the same time. She had rejected me completely by then, and I thought she had come to the conclusion that she'd married the wrong man. We both courted her, you see. When he returned to Town, his reputation in tatters from what had happened in the country, I realized that Anna had never been with him. That I had been wrong about everything."

"Why didn't you search then?" The words were torn from Thea.

Her father met her gaze, his filled with sorrow. "I was too proud to beg. I thought if she held any affection for me or her son, she would have returned."

"She was too afraid of losing me as well."

Drake squeezed her as if to remind her of their conversation regarding her mother's joy and willing sacrifice in keeping her.

Langley nodded, seeming to age before her eyes. "I realize that now."

Irisa cocked her head and looked at her father as if he were a butterfly on a pin. "I think that if I loved someone, I would beg."

Langley said nothing.

Jacqueline put her hand out to take his. Thea wondered if perhaps true affection existed between the two. She hoped so. Or their marriage would not survive her final revelation.

Following the previous pattern she had set, Irisa precipitated the final unveiling as well. "When did your mother die?"

Thea took a deep breath and let it out. She met her aunt's gaze and saw the need for truth there. "Ten years ago."

Twenty

I received a letter from Lady Upworth today. It contained a sketch of Jared. He looks so much like a man. My heart aches to think that I might not recognize my own child should I see him face to face, but there is little chance of that. I look for him in Thea, hoping that he resembles her in her ability to love. She is so generous with her affection. I must teach her to protect her heart—she is so eager to open it to others. I worry there is little time left to do so.

November 23, 1809
Journal of Anna Selwyn, Countess of Langley

IRISA STARED AT HER, THEN SHIFTED HER GAZE to her parents, then back to Thea again. "But I'm sixteen."

Thea nodded. "Yes."

The silence in the room pressed in on her, and she turned to Drake, seeking some of his strength for the final confrontation.

He brushed her cheek with gentle fingers, his eyes full

of warm emotion. "The truth frees us, Thea, no matter how difficult to utter."

She nodded and turned back to her family. "When Mama learned of Langley's final perfidy, she was devastated. I think Lady Upworth kept it from her as long as she could, but Uncle Ashby planned a trip to London. Mama intended to accompany him. She wanted to see Jared. Lady Upworth realized the trip would be a disaster and wrote Mama with the truth."

Jared's face lost all color, and the pink flesh of his scar stood out against the pale skin of his cheek.

He turned to Langley, accusation blazing in his eyes. "You married Jacqueline while my mother was still living."

When Langley did not respond, Jared turned back to Thea. She desperately wanted to comfort him. The betrayal and pain she saw in his eyes broke her heart.

"Mama canceled her trip to England, horrified at the scandal you would be forced to endure if the truth became known. It wasn't until later that she hit upon the idea of using Langley's behavior as a source of blackmail."

"She was going to blackmail him?" Jared asked.

"She was going to force him to let her see you."

"But she never came. I never met her."

Thea bit her lip and shook her head. "No. You never saw her. She contracted the fever two weeks before our ship was to sail. Although she recovered somewhat, she never again had enough strength to make the voyage. Eventually a second bout of the fever killed her."

Now that the entire truth had been told, exhaustion overwhelmed Thea. She wanted to go home with Drake and let him hold her until she fell asleep, safe in his arms. She also wanted to reach out and comfort her brother, but she did not have the right. They were practically strangers.

Langley stared at Jared, who looked at him as if he had turned into the devil himself.

Langley erupted into speech. "You must understand.

I convinced myself that your mother truly was dead or she would have come back to me, to you. Then there was Jacqueline. She carried Irisa and I could not let my child go through life with the stigma of illegitimacy."

Jacqueline burst into noisy tears and ran from the room.

Irisa crossed her arms and tapped her foot against the carpeted floor. "Knowing Mama, she seduced you and trapped you into marriage when she got pregnant. Being a squire's daughter, she probably figured marriage to an earl was worth the risk." She sighed. "Poor Mama." Then Irisa's face cleared and a smile like the noonday sun came out. "This means I am a bastard."

Drake stiffened next to Thea.

"Irisa," Lady Upworth admonished, "you will not use such language."

Irisa apologized prettily and then turned to Thea. "I cannot thank you enough. His Grace will never marry the by-blow of an earl. *I'm free.*" She laughed with delight. "I'm truly free."

Lady Upworth smiled. "There is that, my dear, there is that. Your mother won't be quite as relieved as you, I fear."

"Serves her right. Knowing Papa, he probably told her about Thea's mother and she still chose to marry him."

Jared asked, "Did you tell her?"

Langley looked up and said, "Yes. She was willing to risk it. She, too, believed Anna must be dead." He faced Irisa. "She wanted you to carry my name."

"I'll bet."

Thea smiled at Irisa's forthright approach to life. She suspected the affection that had started on mere acquaintance would grow deep between the two of them.

"Do not be too hard on your mother. She has only done what she thought was best for you."

Irisa nodded, her expression turned serious. "She can't help caring so much about the polite world and their opinions. I don't suppose you would be willing to continue to keep your secret from Society?"

Drake spoke for the first time since the conversation had begun. "Thea is very good at keeping secrets. She wants to know you, not hurt you."

"My husband is right. There is no reason to tell the rest of the *ton* the truth."

"What about the fact that you are my daughter? Do you wish to reveal the connection?"

Thea met her father's gaze. "I want to claim my family. Aunt Harriet and Irisa are already in my heart too deeply for me to deny them."

"I prefer not to tell Society that Irisa's mother and I weren't truly married when she was born, for her sake, but I want to claim my daughter. I owe it to Anna. I owe it to you."

"It will be difficult to keep the one secret while revealing the other," Jared said expressionlessly, his voice and manner showing that the night's revelations had opened a chasm between him and their father.

"Every family has secrets. We can keep ours," replied Lady Upworth.

"Well, Thea, what do you say?" Langley asked.

"I want to be part of my family and see no reason to share a secret that is really more my sister's than my own."

Irisa threw her arms around Thea and hugged her tight. "I've always wanted a sister."

Thea allowed her father to embrace her, though she could not force herself to return the affectionate gesture. Perhaps in time. As her aunt had said, he would have to prove himself worthy of her love.

He stepped away. "Welcome home, daughter."

Jared reached out and touched her. His eyes still bore the marks of shock, but they held wonder as well. He kissed her cheek and then stepped away.

Thea went forward and hugged Lady Upworth. "I love you."

The dowager dabbed at her eyes. "I love you, too, niece. I always have."

Irisa caught all their attention when she moaned, "Does this mean I still have to marry His Grace?"

EMOTION, SO STRONG IT THREATENED TO OVERWHELM him, coursed through Drake.

Thea stood at her window, looking out into the fog-shrouded London night. She wore no wrapper over her nightrail, and the soft contours of her body pressed against the sheer fabric.

She turned her head when he entered the room, a soft smile of welcome curving her mouth. "Why is it that we have separate rooms? I suppose it is some unfathomable custom among the *ton*. It seems silly, though, to have a bed we never use. Don't you think?"

Ever since he and Thea had left Langley's town house, Drake had been struggling with a way to express how proud he felt of his wife. Her musing about the eccentricities of the *ton* sidetracked him.

He walked over to where she stood near the window and drew her against him. "Not all husbands and wives sleep together."

Her eyes filled with amusement. "Come, you cannot convince me of that faraddidle. If that were true, successions would soon die out."

He laughed and a sense of peace stole over him. He would never regret marriage to this enchanting woman. A name attached itself to the feelings that had bedeviled him since he met her. Love. He was top over tails in love with his wife.

Laughter welled up and spilled over again. He could not wait to share the words with her. Surely she would then express her own love for him. He was certain that she loved him. Nothing but love could have prompted her to take what she considered to be the considerable risk of marriage.

"You are incorrigible, wife."

She shrugged. "I'm just not as gullible as you seem to believe."

He swept her up in his arms and headed toward the bed. "I wasn't teasing you, sweetheart. Many husbands and wives meet in their bedrooms only long enough to ensure children."

Her lips nuzzled his ear, and she breathed into it when she spoke. "I must warn you now that in this I am not willing to bow to the dictates of Society."

His entire body reacted to the feel of her hot breath against his ear. What had she said? Oh, yes.

"You would mind sleeping alone now that we are married?"

"You promised me I would never be lonely at night."

He stood her next to the bed and rid her of her nightrail before shedding his dressing gown, the only garment he wore. Her eyes reflected desire as her gaze traveled down his body, stopping to linger on his rapidly swelling manhood. She shifted her gaze back to his face, and her smile turned wanton.

He wanted her so much that his body ached for the release he found when they came together, but first he wanted to talk.

No more teasing. "I'm proud of you."

She reached out and touched his chest, her fingers burning a path down to his navel. "I know. You're a very special man." She looked up and met his gaze. "My brother is different than I imagined."

"He was raised by your father, not your mother."

She nodded. "Yes. I know. I want to get to know him. I think that's what my mother wanted when she made me promise to take her journals to him."

"You are a woman of uncommon honor, Thea."

She said nothing, and he hated the feeling that tightened his chest. He was almost sure that she loved him—but did she still feel that she'd ignored her mother's last wish by marrying him? The pain of that thought hit him like a blow.

She slid her hands up and around his neck, then leaned forward and kissed one of his nipples. He needed her. Now.

"What's the matter?"

Her question barely registered as his rising passion overwhelmed him. He shook his head, not wanting to think about anything but the softness of her beautiful naked body so close to his own.

She wouldn't let it go, though. Twisting her face away to avoid his lips, she demanded he answer her.

He pressed his forehead to her temple. "I'm glad that you were able to keep at least one promise to your mother."

She gripped his face in her hands and forced him to meet her eyes.

Fierce intensity blazed at him. "I kept both promises to my mother. She didn't want me to marry a man like my father, and I didn't."

"You were afraid to marry me. Afraid I would turn cruel."

"That was foolish. No two men could be more different. You were right when you said that he allowed his pride to destroy our family. It was his weakness that hurt my mother, not his strength. You are strong, Pierson. So strong that sometimes it scares me. But not because I think you will ever hurt me. Because I fear sometimes I will fail to be the wife a man of your character deserves. You swallowed your pride, pursuing me even when I had rejected you."

Tears stood out in her eyes.

He brushed away the moisture from her bottom eyelids with his thumbs. "I had no choice. I love you, Thea. I need you."

Her head dropped. "You humble me."

He tilted her chin up and kissed her. Hard. "I love you."

He waited, almost not breathing, for her response.

"I love you, too, Pierson. I love your arrogance, though I would have thought that impossible. I love your gentleness, your strength, your stubbornness, your loyalty, your honor, but most of all, I love you for the way you make me feel."

He brushed one pink nipple with the back of his fingers. "It's a good thing I let you seduce me then."

She laughed. "I didn't mean what you make my body feel, though that is a most wondrous gift." She laid her hand over her bare breast. "I meant what you make me feel in here. You fill my heart up to overflowing."

It was his turn to feel humbled. He resolved to be worthy of the great trust she had given him, trust made more difficult to extend because of her background. He would never take her love or her trust for granted.

With a suddenness that knocked the breath right out of her lungs, Drake yanked Thea to him. She didn't even get out the smallest protest before his lips rocked over hers. Not that she would have protested. She had not been overstating the case when she told him she considered her body's reaction to him a tremendous gift.

A gift almost as priceless as his love.

She returned his kiss with unfettered passion, desperate to feel one with him after the emotional upheaval of the last few days. He ran his hands all over her body, but when they slipped between her thighs, her knees turned to water.

She collapsed against him, pressing her aching breasts against his chest. "Love me, Pierson. *Please*."

Lowering their bodies to the bed, he whispered against her lips. "Now and forever, love. Now and forever."

Epilogue

Drake Hall, England
1821

❧ THE BABY CRIED.

Her son. The beauty of the squirming infant hurt in a way she wanted never to end. She had given birth to life. Wonderful, innocent life.

She pushed herself up in the huge four-poster bed, ignoring the admonishment of both her maid and the midwife to rest. She had to see her son. Each moment with him was a gift she had never thought to have.

The heavy door of the master chamber slammed against the wall. Thea's gaze flew to the sight of her husband's towering frame outlined in its opening. His face wore the same worried expression it had so often since he had discovered she was with child. He met her eyes, and in that brief glance she knew nothing would ever be the same. They were a family. Now and forever.

"I came as quickly as I could. You are so headstrong. Trust you to go into labor two weeks early when I am away on business."

He strode over to the bed and glared down at her, but his frown did not reach his eyes. Their dark molasses depths were filled with warm approval.

He did not turn away from her, but spoke to the midwife. "Give me the babe."

"It is a son. Our son. Are you not thrilled?" Her words came out soft, supremely happy.

"*Thrilled* is a paltry word for what I feel." He took the baby from the midwife. "He is beautiful." He looked up from the tiny bundle. "My love, you have given me the greatest gift imaginable."

Turning his attention back to the child, Drake said, "I will be all that a father should be."

Her heart filled with the love that grew each day of her marriage to him. "How can you help it? You are all that a man should be in every other respect."

He turned glassy eyes to her. "How can I thank you, Thea? You have fulfilled every dream that I harbored deep in my heart."

She smiled through tears that burned a path down her cheek. "It is only fair, my love. You have brought to life dreams that I was afraid to even admit to myself that I had."

He reached out and pulled her close, their baby between them. Although she was exhausted from the birth, she felt energy surge through her at the connection with both her husband and her newborn son. Mama would be happy. She would approve of Drake, and she would have loved her grandson.

Thea intended to speak often of Mama to her son. Anna Selwyn would not be forgotten, nor would her legacy of love. She lived on through her daughter, and Thea vowed to be worthy of the sacrifices her mother had made to raise her in the light of love rather than the shadow of suspicion.

Perhaps Jared would learn to live in the light of love as well. One day he would be willing to read the journals. Until then it was enough that he and the rest of Thea's family chose to be part of her life. But even had they not, she would never complain because she had Pierson Drake.

A man who made marriage a blessing.

When she thought of the fears she had harbored about marrying him, she smiled. He had proven to her that he loved her for who she was. She still ran Merewether Shipping, discreetly of course. She gave lectures on the subject of abolition and invited influential members of Parliament to her town house to discuss it and other important issues.

Drake invariably supported her. Their marriage was not without conflict. She and Drake were both too strong willed for such a feat, but in the things that really counted, they were as one.

She leaned forward and kissed the corner of his mouth, while resting her hand on their son's head. He turned and smiled into her eyes. The promises she saw there would last a lifetime. She had no doubt.

Turn the page for a special preview of
Lucy Monroe's next novel

Tempt Me

Coming soon from Berkley Sensation!

London 1824

IRISA FACED LUCAS ACROSS THE SMALL LIBRARY. The fog-dampened night could not intrude on the warm coziness of the room.

Lucas's mouth curved in a loving smile. "You came."

She nodded, her throat too clogged with emotion to speak.

He extended his hand. "Come here, my love."

She moved forward as if in a daze, drawn by the warmth in her lover's eyes as much as by the implied command in his stance. She wanted him.

Desperately.

And he wanted her.

As soon as she was close enough to touch, he reached out and pulled her to him. The feel of his warm skin on her bare arms sent shivers down her spine. He did not stop pulling her until her body was an inch from his own.

She knew he would kiss her now. Finally. She had waited so long, but instinctively knew the wait would be worth it. Lucas's mouth settled on hers, his lips warm and

vibrant against her own. She shuddered and he pulled his
mouth a breath from hers.

"Are you all right, my love?"

"Yes. Please. Kiss me again."

He did so with alacrity while one arm moved around
her waist. His other hand settled on her shoulder, his fingers sliding under the fabric of her gown. She blushed at
the intimate touch, but did not pull away. He groaned low
in his throat and tugged the tiny cap sleeves of her gown
down until the swell of her breasts were exposed. Then
he . . . Then he . . .

Oh, fustion! Irisa's daydream came to an abrupt halt.
What *would* happen next? Authors always stopped at the
most interesting parts in the novels Irisa read. For instance,
she assumed a gentleman placed his fingers under the fabric of a lady's gown with the intention of baring her un-
mentionables, but she couldn't be *sure.*

And she certainly had no idea what said gentleman
would do once he had succeeded in pushing the bodice
down. She thought the bit about shuddering and groaning
had been well done, considering her lack of personal experience and knowledge in this area. Not that she would shun
a bit more of both, particularly if Lucas offered the instruction.

Stifling a sigh, she reluctantly brought her attention back
to the Bilkingtons' elegantly appointed supper room and her
partner's monologue on hunting hounds. Lady Bilkington
had an infatuation with green and gold, much in evidence in
the room's decor.

Irisa smiled and nodded at Mr. Wemby during a short
pause in his speech. Thus encouraged, he launched into an
enthusiastic story about one of his favorite hounds. She
went back to her pondering, assured once again that her rejection of his suit the year before had been the right choice.

Mr. Wemby was kind, but he had far more interest in his
hounds than in any person of his acquaintance. And like

the other suitors she had rejected over the past four years, he did not stir her passions . . . not like Lucas.

However, the chances of Lucas offering anything more than a polite greeting seemed slim indeed. Earl of Ashton, he was acutely aware of his responsibility to his title and was known as an absolute paragon of gentlemanly virtue. There were even those amongst the *ton* who went so far as to call him *The Saint*.

She'd heard it had something to do with his family, but she didn't know what. Because of the unkind things said about her brother's disfigurement and her sister's unconventional upbringing, Irisa abhorred and shunned gossip. Even if it meant learning less about a man as fascinating as Lucas.

What could she possibly learn from scandal mongers but half-truths and innuendo? One day, she would ask him about his nickname . . . if they were ever on intimate enough terms to allow such a liberty. Until then, she would make do with daydreams fueled by her belief that under his perfectly controlled exterior beat a heart as passionate as her own.

Others amongst the *ton* would laugh at such a conclusion, but she just *knew* she was right about him. In all the novels she had read, gentlemen very much like Lucas seethed with hidden passions regardless of their cold outward countenance. And on several occasions when he debated issues he felt strongly about, the quiet intensity in his voice had sent shivers down her spine—and to other less mentionable regions of her body.

She had great hopes of engaging those passions on a more personal basis. Since their first meeting at a house party, he had been consistent, if not effusive, in his attentions. Upon arriving in Town for the Season, he had begun to court her with all the polite restraint to be expected of a man nicknamed Saint.

One might even suspect he was on the verge of making

an offer. Much to her parents' relief. However, to *her* chagrin, he had not so much as held her hand while driving in
the park. She wanted to know what Lucas's lips tasted like.
She wanted to know what happened when a man put his
hand under a lady's bodice and she wanted him to be the
man to show her.

As much as she wanted his passion, she also craved
more of his company. She didn't want to dance with a
string of boring partners only to have the monotony relieved the prescribed two times by Lucas. Tonight, he
hadn't even ensured he got the supper dance, thus the one-
sided conversation with Mr. Wemby over the small supper
table.

It was one of Lucas's little habits, this giving up the
supper dance with her occasionally. She assumed it was his
way of not drawing unwanted attention to their association.
At least he didn't compound the frustration his conduct
caused her by asking someone else. When Lucas didn't
partner her, he made himself scarce from the ballroom during the half-hour break in music.

"Lady Irisa. Mr. Wemby." The deep tones of Lucas's
voice pulled Irisa from her thoughts.

She raised a startled gaze to see him standing by their
table as if her secret wishes had drawn him to her side. The
prospect was a pleasing one, if fanciful.

Eyes the color of blue glass were fixed on her with a
hint of amusement, his black brow raised with just a touch
of mockery. His sedately tailored black evening clothes
molded the body of a tall Corinthian.

"Hello," she replied, her voice husky from surprise.

What was he doing here? It was wholly out of character
for him. Her heart took a sudden lift at the sign that Lucas's behavior with her was not entirely predictable.

Mr. Wemby had stopped midsentence in his story and
now blinked at Lucas as if unsure how the other man had
appeared. "Good evening, Lord Ashton."

"I've just left a friend of yours in the card room, Wemby. He's looking for advice on putting a new pack of hounds together for this year's hunt."

Fairly quivering with excitement at the prospect of discussing a subject so close to his heart, Mr. Wemby stood quickly. "I'd better see if I can be of assistance then."

Lucas inclined his head. "I'll escort Lady Irisa back to her mother for you."

Mr. Wemby's head bobbed in agreement. "Kind of you. I'll return the favor sometime." He left without another word to Irisa.

She stared after his retreating back, more amused than offended. "There is no question how conversation with me rates against the prospect of advising another gentleman on the purchase of a hound."

"With Wemby perhaps, but if you will notice, I am still here." The words washed over her with unexpected intensity and she found herself once again raising her gaze to look at him.

His mouth was still tipped in that amused way he had, but his eyes burned into her with undeniable force.

With, dared she hope, passion?

She smiled, feeling her heart race in her chest. "Yes, you are still here."

He extended his hand in a manner so like her daydream that for a moment, she hesitated between reality and fantasy. Gathering her wits about her, she took the proffered hand and rose from her chair. Lucas transferred her grip to his arm and led her from the supper room.

"Are you truly going to take me back to Mama?" The dancing would not resume for fifteen minutes or more.

"Perhaps you would care to join me for a stroll around the perimeter of the ballroom?"

She'd rather retreat to the privacy of the terrace. But no doubt Lucas would consider such behavior shocking.

Stifling a sigh of regret, she forced her features to assume an expression of polite enthusiasm. After all, at least she would be with him. "With pleasure, my lord."

IRISA'S SMALL HAND GRIPPED HIS FOREARM TIGHTLY and Lucas fought back a smile at her enthusiasm to remain in his company. Her complete lack of the subterfuge so often found in ladies among the *ton* had been one of the first things that drew his admiration.

Her sweet face and golden brown eyes expressed her emotions honestly. They had made it obvious as he watched her from across the supper room that she found Wemby's company a trial. The socially polite smiles she had bestowed upon her supper partner had not fooled Lucas for a minute. Her unfocused gaze had said it all.

Not that anyone else would notice. Much to his own pleasure and surprise, he had come to realize that what was obvious to him when dealing with Irisa was not so clear to others.

So he had concocted a plan to rescue her. He realized that in doing so he might draw attention to their relationship, but he was willing to take the courtship to the next level. He planned to call on the Earl of Langley in the morning and ask for permission to pay his addresses to Irisa. Lucas had no doubt she would accept him. Even if she did not show such blatant pleasure in his company, a woman of twenty was considered practically on the shelf. She would undoubtedly be grateful for an offer of marriage.

He still found it difficult to believe she had remained unmarried. Admittedly, her tiny, curvaceous figure was not the current rage. However, combined with her honey blond hair and warm brown eyes, it made for an altogether lovely package. Remembering the erotic dream that had woken him in the middle of the previous night hard and aching, Lucas acknowledged that he found her more than lovely.

He found her bloody desirable.

"I must admit I am grateful to whichever of Mr. Wemby's friends sent you in search of him. Since making his acquaintance last Season, I have become an expert on hounds. 'Tis a pity I'm not at all interested in the hunt."

He knew Irisa did not mean to mock Wemby. She never indulged in that particular *tonnish* pastime. It was a mark of her sweet nature that she had indulged Wemby's passion for hounds in conversation. Lucas would be pleased to have her indulge *his* passions as well, only he was certain were she to do so, boredom would not come into it for either of them.

"I hesitate to admit this, but I made it up," he said, quelling his lascivious thoughts with strict control. "I'm sure Wemby will find a friend more interested in his discussion of hounds than yourself, but none actually awaits him."

The sound of her laughter affected his already overactive libido and he had no choice but to steer her toward the terrace before she, or someone else, noticed the growing state of his arousal. Not that he expected a lady of Irisa's sensibilities to let her gaze wander below his chin, but nevertheless, a gentleman's evening clothes left very little to the imagination.

As they stepped from the brightly lit ballroom into the shadowed world of the deserted terrace, Irisa's head snapped up and she stared at him, owl-eyed. "My lord?"

"It was getting a trifle warm in the ballroom. I thought you could use the air."

She nodded, sliding closer until their bodies almost touched. "Air. Yes, air would be very nice."

Her lips were parted as if about to say something, but she remained silent, gazing up at him.

She could have no idea just how delectable she looked at that very moment, how incredibly kissable. Her all too welcoming expression did nothing to aid his body in returning to less embarrassing proportions. He had to get himself under control, and quickly, or he was likely to shock the innocent right into a faint, and compromise her into the bargain.

He needed a diversion.

"I've decided to invest in your brother-in-law's most recent shipping venture." One of the things he enjoyed about Irisa was that she conversed intelligently on topics of import.

She did not pretend, as most ladies of the *ton* attempted to, that everything outside of the social sphere did not exist.

"Sh-shipping venture?"

"Yes. He told me you knew all about it. It's a sound investment."

Her hand dropped from his arm and she moved a small distance away. He breathed a silent sigh of relief. Without her nearness, he could regain control. His reaction to her innocent provocation astounded him, but he would dwell on how best to master it and himself later. He could not allow marriage, or the prospect of it, to undermine the self-discipline he had spent so many years perfecting.

"Yes. I know about it," she replied, her voice subdued all of a sudden, "I made a small outlay on the venture myself."

He would not have thought Langley the type of man to give his daughter any sort of financial independence. "Are you in the habit of investing in your brother-in-law's ventures?"

Her creamy white shoulders rose and fell in a ladylike shrug. "Actually, in the past my investments have been mostly in Thea's business dealings and the 'Change. Up until now, Drake's transactions have been too large or too risky for me to take part in them."

Lucas's ardor completely dissipated on a wave of shocked disbelief. "You invest in the 'Change?"

"Yes." She looked at him, her expression as innocent as always, except for a spark of something in her eyes he could not quite name.

If he did not know better, he would say it was defiance, but Irisa was too biddable a lady for such an emotion.

"How long has your father been allowing you to engage in such cork-brained behavior?"

She moved back another step, her posture becoming stiff.

"Papa has nothing to do with it," she replied in freezing accents, sounding for all the world as if she thought it was none of his business.

He strode two steps forward and grasped her shoulders, forcing her to face him. Even in his anger, his body registered the feel of her silken skin beneath his fingers. "Are you saying you have been investing your money without his permission?"

She lifted her head quickly, meeting his look squarely. "I spend my allowance as I see fit."

Her pin money? Either she had a very large allowance or she made very small investments. "I'm surprised you had the resources available to take part in Drake's latest venture."

To Lucas's knowledge, Drake required a minimum outlay from even his smallest investors and it would require a great deal more than pin money. Perhaps Drake had made an exception for his sister-in-law's whim.

She bit her lip and shifted her gaze to a point beyond his shoulder, for all the world as if she intended some manner of subterfuge.

His grip on her arms tightened involuntarily. "Tell me."

Ignoring his command, she turned her attention to the point where his hands gripped the soft skin of her upper arms. He forced his fingers to relax somewhat, realizing his hold might very well be uncomfortable.

"If someone came out of the ballroom and found us here, they would assume we were in a passionate embrace," she said in a curiously wistful voice.

Bloody hell. She was right. He quickly released her

arms, but did not step away. She would not distract him that easily.

"Explain to me how you were able to invest in the shipping expedition."

She adjusted first one, then the other of the white evening gloves she wore and then smoothed her skirt as if they had been engaged in an invigorating country dance rather than standing almost completely still for the past several minutes.

Snapping open her fan, she used it as a shield for the expression on her face. "You overstep yourself, sir. I do not owe you an explanation of my actions or my finances. We are not connected in any way."

Her fan might protect her face from his scrutiny, but the icy remoteness in her voice left him in no doubt as to her frame of mind.

Without another word, she stepped around him and returned to the ballroom before he could assimilate either her surprising stubbornness or the cool challenge in her voice. Didn't the chit realize she belonged to him? They were as good as engaged. Of course she owed him an explanation.

He followed her with every intention of telling her just that, but a return to the bright candle glow in the ballroom brought back his reason.

What was he doing?

For the second time that evening, he had very nearly lost control. This time he would have made a spectacle of himself in a way he had vowed long ago never to do. He was one Ashton who would not follow in his mother and younger brother's scandalous footsteps.

Watching Irisa join her current partner on the dance floor, he willed her to look at him. Their discussion was not finished. She refused to return his gaze, stubbornly keeping her head angled away from him and her focus entirely on the gentleman accompanying her.

He knew it was apurpose because she had once confided

she did not care for Lord Yardley's company. Lucas had
learned the other man had courted Irisa two Seasons ago,
but her father had denied his suit. He was certain that she
only agreed to dance with the Yardley because she knew to
refuse would cause comment, and she was a lady in every
sense. The perfect antithesis of his mother, in fact.

The image of Irisa defiantly snapping her fan open rose
before his eyes.

His lovely, biddable, beautiful, little paragon had
sprouted a willful streak.